THE

MARLOWE MURDERS

Laura Giebfried & Stanley R. Wells

FOR ANDREA –
nous vous remercions pour tout ce que vous faites

December, 1955
Exeter Island, Maine

I remember everything.

And not because I was born with a gift, or one of those eidetic memories that people claim to have because they can seemingly recall a random moment in their life perfectly. No, I trained my memory. I peeled it open and found out how it worked, and then I tightened every screw and oiled each gear to make it better and faster and more capable. I spent eleven years of my life making it faultless, to the point that I can tell you word for word every conversation I've had or overheard, and name every punctuation mark in any book I've read, and recount the pattern on a man's socks that peeked out from the hems of his trousers as he tapped his loafer next to me in a lecture hall. I can do it all. But I can't, it seems, alter my demeanor enough to be likable – and so there I was, dismissed from my doctorate program, stripped of my accomplishments, and being ferried off to an island off the coast of Maine to pay for the person I had become.

A gust of wind leaped up onto the ferry boat to pierce me with its chill, shocking me out of my moment of self pity. I yanked my swing coat tighter around me. The ferryman hadn't told me it would be this cold.

"Is it much farther?" I called to the him, my voice straining to be heard over the howling air.

The silk scarf tied around my head was threatening to come loose, and my hands were raw despite my leather gloves. I clutched my arms against my chest, wishing that I would just go numb.

Without turning around, he raised his hand and pointed up ahead at the fog. It parted a moment later to allow the slowing ferry boat through, gliding past us before sealing itself up again as though it was a gate closing on the world we had left behind, and finally Exeter Island came into view.

It was blanketed in white snow with thick black, jagged trees sticking out from it all over, and the rocks on the shore were slick with ice. The sight of it flattened as it hit my mind, sliding down to file itself away. It wasn't a very inviting image, and yet it didn't really matter: I had already told John Marlowe that I would take the job.

The ferry pulled up alongside the dock a few minutes later. I had barely stepped off of it when the ferryman unceremoniously tossed my suitcase down beside me. It clattered against the ice-covered wood and slid away from me.

I turned to look at him, my eyebrows raised in disapproval, though his attention was already back on the wheel.

"Aren't you going to walk me up to the house?" I asked him. My voice sounded unusually timid from the chattering of my teeth, and I fixed my scarf tighter around my head and chin.

"Nope." His form was mostly hidden beneath layers of thick clothing, though his hollow face and skeletal cheekbones poked out as he spoke. I wondered if the cold had all but eaten the flesh from his bones, just as it was threatening to do to mine. "I've got to pick up the groceries before closing. But it's a big place: you'll find it."

"Yes, I'm sure I will," I replied, turning away from him. "Thank you."

"You're welcome."

"I was thanking the path, actually, since it's the only thing helping me find my way."

He responded by turning the key in the ignition. The roar of the motor filled the air and the ferry shot back across the water and disappeared into the fog. I retrieved my suitcase and made my way off the dock, throwing him an annoyed look over my shoulder despite knowing he wouldn't see it.

I trekked through ankle-deep snow, following the partially covered path that wound around clusters of dormant trees. I caught glimpses of silvery-blue shingles and turrets that rose up in cones to pierce the low hanging clouds, but it wasn't until I stepped out into the clearing of the front yard that I saw the Marlowe house in its entirety.

The facade spanned nearly a hundred and fifty feet, with ornate reliefs carved above the windows, heavy wooden shutters with chipped paint, and red gingerbread trim that dripped from the roof like blood. It was a motley assortment of styles, as though the house's enormity was due to the fact that several houses had been shoved together to form one, and I felt as though I had been shrunken to the size of a doll as I stood beneath it.

"Jesus," I muttered, wondering what I had gotten myself into. Professor Marlowe hadn't said anything about the house being so large, though perhaps I ought to have assumed as much when he had informed me that it was on a private island. My mouth twitched as I looked at it, imagining myself teetering on a chair as I dusted the tops of paintings. Six months shy of finishing my doctorate degree and I was working as a maid. If it wasn't so utterly disheartening, I might have laughed at the sheer absurdity of it all.

I heaved my suitcase up the front steps to the covered porch and rang the bell. Crudely carved columns greeted me from either side. To my left, the torso of a woman with her arms raised high stared at me with wooden eyes. She looked like a mermaid who was trying desperately to escape the sea. Or perhaps, I backtracked, crossing my shivering arms as I waited, she was just trying to escape the bitter cold.

As I turned to see if the column on the right mirrored the first, the front door swung open and an old woman in a flour-covered apron answered. With her curly white hair and round face, she looked a bit like Mrs. Claus, though her narrowed eyes were dark and burned like coal.

"Hello," I began, "I'm Alexandra Durant –"

"Servants use the side door."

She had a thick, gruff Irish accent and a withering glare. I blinked.

"Alright," I said. "I'll make sure I use it next time."

I gave her the polite smile I had practiced in my residence hall mirror before I had left and waited for her to step aside to let me in. She didn't move.

"It's in the back," she said, pointing a stubby finger for me. "I left it open."

She made to close the door on me, but I stuck my foot out to stop it. If she expected me to trudge through any more snow in my stocking-covered legs, then she was sorely mistaken.

"I'll use it next time," I repeated, pushing my way into the house and dropping my suitcase onto the black-and-white tiled floors. A large chandelier covered in cobwebs hung two stories above us. It sent a crisscrossing pattern of shadows over the older woman's surly face.

"You'll do as you're *told* next time – and don't yell: the Foyer echoes," she chided, though my voice had been nowhere near loud. "What did you say your name was?"

"Alexandra Durant," I said, irritated that I needed to repeat myself. "And yours?"

I knew she wasn't Mrs. Marlowe, for John had a photograph of his parents on his desk at the university.

"To *you* I'm Mrs. Tilly," she said. She looked me up and down with suspicion in her eyes. "So: you're the new girl."

"Yes."

"How old are you?"

"Excuse me?"

"How old are you?"

"I'm twenty-nine," I said, though I didn't see what it had to do with anything. Mrs. Tilly raised her eyebrows.

"Are you married?" she asked.

"No."

"Have you ever *been* married?"

"No," I repeated, my voice more rigid than I had intended it to be.

She gave me a look of utmost disapproval.

"Well, why not?" she said. "You're a bit *old* to be single, aren't you?"

I opened my mouth and then shut it again to keep myself from saying something impolite.

"I've been in school," I said, "getting my doctorate."

"Oh, *school*," she said, dragging out the word as she went. "You must have studied quite hard to end up working as a servant."

"Well, I –" I started, nearly delving into the details of what had brought me there, but then deciding better of it. "I haven't finished yet."

"No? Then why aren't you there now? December seems like an odd time to start a new chapter in one's life ..." She waved her hand in the direction of my boots, off of which melting snow was pooling onto the floor. "You'll need to take care of that before someone slips. And go change into something proper, for goodness sake – preferably before you're seen. You'll be in the nanny's room on the third floor."

"I'm not a nanny," I said, wondering if she had been expecting someone else and that was where the confusion was coming from. "I'm the new maid – Professor Marlowe hired me."

"Of course he did," she snapped. "And you'll be in the nanny's room. That's what he told *me*."

She pointed at one of the staircases, dispelling any reprieve I had been about to grant her. I lifted my suitcase to go upstairs, leaving her and my expectations of a proper greeting behind. I could feel her eyes boring into the back of my head as I walked, and an uneasiness came over my skin as I imagined what type of woman Mrs. Marlowe would be. One who cared about her servant's age and marital status, evidently. Not that it mattered, though, I reminded myself as I reached the second floor landing and headed to the next set of stairs: I was going to do the job no matter what.

The emptiness of the house was unsettling, and the third floor – with its low ceilings and peeling wallpaper – made it more so. I wasn't sure how Mrs. Tilly expected me to find the nanny's room: the house, if possible, seemed even bigger on the inside. I weaved in and out of dusty, forgotten rooms filled with broken furniture and poorly taped boxes, twisted the knobs of locked doors, then finally found the one intended for me. A single bed was made up with white sheets and a scratchy wool blanket, and on top of it laid a black dress, white apron, and frilly mob cap. There was a door on the far wall that I assumed led to a bathroom, but upon opening it I found a dusty old metal crib with an infant's white Christening gown laying within it. The only window was boarded up from the outside, and the room was blanketed in darkness. It seemed far too forlorn to be a nursery.

Going back to my room, I lifted the maid's uniform with a scrunched nose, then put it back on the bed. I would introduce myself to Mrs. Marlowe in my traveling clothes, I resolved, taking off my coat, gloves, and scarf and tossing them down beside the uniform. She needed to understand that I was bound for a separate career, and that being her maid was just a small stop that her son had provided me with on the way to achieving it.

I returned downstairs, wandering through a labyrinth of hallways that took me past a Billiard Room, Ballroom, Study and Portrait Room. The house almost seemed as if it hadn't been lived in for a long time, though John had told me that his mother hadn't left the island in over twenty years.

I found the kitchen at the very back of the house. Mrs. Tilly was holding an envelope when I entered, but upon seeing me tossed it down to the table.

"Mr. Marlowe sent that for you," she said. "Quite a starting pay for a maid, isn't it?"

I picked it up. It had been torn open despite being addressed to me, and several crisp fifty-dollar bills were sticking out. I leafed through them to count them.

"There's only three hundred dollars here," I said.

"And?" she asked.

"And he said he'd give me five hundred."

"Did he? That's an *extremely* large sum of money for four weeks of work. Perhaps you're mistaken."

"I don't make mistakes with my memory. He said he'd give me five hundred."

"Well then, I suppose you'll have to take that up with him," she said with a note of smugness in her voice that suggested she had been the one to open – and redistribute – my wages.

"Though I'd advise against it: you wouldn't want him to think you're greedy, after all."

She pulled out a large cleaver from the knife block even though she was only chopping onions. It made a *thwacking* sound as it hit the chopping board.

"Somehow I doubt that's what he'd think," I returned, pocketing the envelope with narrowed eyes, though I knew that by the time I was back at the university and had the chance to talk to John Marlowe, there would be no way to prove that she had taken the money. "But I think I'll take it up with Mrs. Marlowe. Where is she?"

The cook paused and looked up, the cleaver still clutched in her hands. She looked me up and down with uncertainty.

"What?"

"Where's Mrs. Marlowe?" I repeated. Mrs. Tilly only stared at me blankly, seemingly more confused than frightened by my threat. "My employer."

"Your employer is Mr. Marlowe."

"No," I corrected automatically, "he said I'd be working for his mother, so *she's* my employer."

The hand holding the cleaver dropped down to Mrs. Tilly's side as she surveyed me, scraping the edge of her apron.

"Oh, he did, did he?" she said. Her face twitched, but I couldn't read her expression. She seemed to be fighting a smile. Between the horrid journey I had taken to get here and her attitude, I was beginning to lose my patience with her.

"Can you tell me where she is?" I asked. "Or should I wander the house *loudly* calling for her?"

The cook raised her eyebrows and returned to her vegetables, and even though I was staring at the back of her head, I could hear the chuckle escape her lips. Her voice was a bit too high when she answered.

"No, you shouldn't do that," she said. "You'll find her in the Augustus Suite on the second floor."

"Thank you." I turned to leave, but then another question came to my mind. "Where's the telephone?"

"Why would you need to know that? Making social calls already?"

"I just want to tell my mother that I've arrived. So she doesn't worry."

"You're still living with your mother? Well, you really are a spinster, aren't you?"

I didn't respond. Mrs. Tilly smiled unkindly at me.

"It's in the Study," she said. "But don't go talking too long. I'll be sure to tell *your employer* to take it out of your wages if you do."

I left the kitchen without another word. If the heat in the house hadn't melted some of her frostiness by now, then I doubted anything ever would.

I followed the hallway back the way that I had come, stopping when I reached the Study. A candlestick telephone sat on top of the mahogany desk. I took a seat in the leather chair and dialed the number for my aunt's apartment.

"Hello?"

"Hi, Aunt Janice. Could you put my mother on?"

There was a sigh. Not of annoyance, but perhaps pity.

"I don't think I should, Alexandra. It's not one of her good days ..."

"I'll be quick."

Static came over the line as she fumbled with the handset, and I could hear her calling for her sister. A moment later, my mother's voice sounded. It was anxious and confused.

"Hello?"

"Hi, Mom," I said. "I just wanted to tell you I made it to Maine. I'm on the –"

"Who is this?"

"It's Alexandra," I said, dropping my voice lower even though surely no one was around to overhear me. "Your – your daughter."

"Janice!" my mother called. "Janice – who is this?"

"I just wanted you to know that I got here safely," I carried on, though I knew she wasn't listening. "So you don't have to worry. And I'll – I'll come see you again as soon as I get back."

"Janice, I think they've got the wrong number ..."

There was a loud *thud* on her end. She must have dropped the phone. A moment later, my aunt came back on.

"I'm sorry, Alexandra. But you know how difficult it is for her, especially if she doesn't see you."

"Will you tell her where I am? When she asks?"

"If she asks."

She sounded bitter. I couldn't tell if it was with the situation or with me, though.

"It'll only be a few weeks," I told her. "And I'm getting paid a lot of money. We could take her to another psychologist. A specialist."

There was a long silence. For a moment I thought the line had gone dead.

"You can use the money for whatever you want, Alexandra."

"But?" I asked, because I knew there was one.

"But I think we both know it won't do her any good."

"It'll do us even less good to stop trying," I said a bit too harshly. My aunt gave another sigh.

"I just don't want you to waste your life trying to fix something that can't be fixed."

She waited for my response, but I didn't have one – though I tried to find one even so long after she hung up the phone. I stood and left the room, suddenly wishing that I was back on the ferry in the numbing cold rather than the open, defenselessness of Mrs, Marlowe's house. But everything could be fixed, and everything could be righted. I just had to discover how.

I weaved my way back to the Foyer, then slid my hand up the banister of the closest staircase, letting it guide me to the second floor to circle around the landing. None of the wall sconces were on, and the only light came from the Foyer below, which barely raised the hallway from pitch darkness. I squinted to read the golden nameplates on the doors that I passed. Baxter, Prudence, Mabel, Fletcher, Eleanora, Lillet ...

I reached the door labeled Augustus and raised my hand to knock against the wood. There was no answer. I folded my hands together as I waited, automatically filing away the assorted names of the rooms to ensure that I remembered them all for later.

Creaking came from behind me, and I half-turned to see

the door to the Lillet Room opening a crack. The movement was so slight that it might have been a breeze that had caused it, though I couldn't be sure. Then a voice – so high and childlike that it almost didn't sound human – called out from within.

"You came back."

I took a step toward it, curiosity pricking my skin.

"No," I said. "I only just arrived. I'm Alexandra Durant –"

But before I could say more, the door slammed shut. I shifted uncertainly in my spot, suddenly getting the impression that Mrs. Tilly was playing a trick on me by sending me to the wrong room. After all, Professor Marlowe had said that his mother lived alone except for the cook and ferryman. I briskly turned back to the Augustus Suite and knocked again. More silence followed.

"Mrs. Marlowe?" I said, raising my voice further so that she could hear me through the wood, but by now I was almost certain that she wasn't inside. I knocked one more time and then opened the door. A breeze rushed over my face.

"Mrs. Marlowe?"

No one answered. I stepped into the room uninvited.

Utter cold enveloped me. All of the windows were open, blowing the deep purple curtains away from the glass in streams of velvet, though the sunlight that flitted through them barely lit the room and certainly did nothing to warm it. The air that I breathed was released in puffs of white as I exhaled, obscuring my view. I walked through it to get further into the room.

The bedroom immediately struck me as a room of neglected splendor: the walls were gilded and the fireplace was golden, but it was tarnished and battered, and the silk pillows and fur blankets draped over the armchairs looked worn from years of use. Even the cushions on the window seat, which was large enough to hold an entire family comfortably, sank down in the middle beyond repair, and there was a stale odor that permeated the fabrics and made my eyes water. As I moved to cross the room, the indistinct faces of animals that had been turned into rugs glowered up at me with blank black eyes.

"Mrs. Marlowe –?" I tried one last time, but then I spotted her. She was laying on top of the covers of the bed, dressed in a long-sleeve black gown adorned with crystals. I moved closer to better see her, and as the curtains blew upwards, her form was illuminated by sunlight. Her iron-gray hair was pulled back from her face to reveal an unsightly brown birthmark that stretched over her right cheek which hadn't been visible in the photograph I had seen of her, and the frown lines on her skin were so deep that they looked like canals that had been drained of their water source.

A gasp came from the hallway, and I swung around to see a figure with a frigid white face. She looked at me for a split second before fleeing down the hall. Shivers ran up and down my skin, and as I turned back to the bed and stared down at John's mother, a surreal sense of understanding came over me. The cook had been right: I wasn't working for Mrs. Marlowe.

Mrs. Marlowe was dead.

CHAPTER ONE

There were twelve people on the island, not counting the dead body, of course, and when the doorbell rang to announce the arrival of the thirteenth, the snow had begun to fall again, and it would surely be the last time for the night that someone would be able to access the Marlowe Estate.

Abandoning my search of the kitchen cabinets, I hurried toward the front door, wiping my dusty hands on my apron as I went and wondering why none of Mrs. Marlowe's children had informed me that anyone else was coming. The hallways seemed to have narrowed in the three days since I had arrived, making the house even darker and stranger, and I weaved through the East Room and past the Ballroom and Billiard Room with the childish fear that if I went a step too slow, something might reach out to drag me into the shadows.

Or maybe I already was in the shadows, I realized.

I reached the Foyer and pulled open the front door. A gust of wind greeted me and scattered snow all over the black-and-white tiled floors. A man stood on the porch, bundled up to combat the cold, and the little bit of his face that was visible was raw and red from the harsh ocean wind. He had undoubtedly just come off the ferry, though Mr. Kneller hadn't come with him; he was probably back at the guesthouse enjoying his solitude.

The man stepped past me to come inside, snapping the door shut behind him. Shaking the snow from his head, he stripped off his overcoat and scarf and hung them up.

"Can I help you?" I asked, my arms still outstretched with the intention of taking his coat for him.

"I'm here for the wake."

He had hair and eyes the color of espresso and wore a herringbone three-piece suit with no tie. A button was missing on the left arm, quite unlike the perfectly pressed tuxedos that the men in the Parlor had on, and there was an air about him that I recognized well enough to know that he didn't belong there. I put my arms back at my sides.

"Mrs. Marlowe's wake?" I asked, as though there was any possibility that he was looking for another person's wake at another house on another island, but had just gotten off at the wrong stop.

"Yes."

"The wake was at noon. You missed it."

"I see," he said, looking only mildly concerned. He had a clipped voice: poised and proper, but distinctly American-enough to know that he wasn't part of the family.

"Well, this was when I was told to come."

"And you are ...?"

He tilted forward ever slightly.

"Isidore Lennox."

Though I was certain no one had mentioned anyone by that name, the way he was looking at me with such sureness was throwing me off. With my hands behind my back, I snapped the rubber band against my wrist to jolt my memory. Nothing came.

"I'll just ... go announce that you're here," I said.

I crossed the Foyer and knocked twice on the Parlor door before entering. The Marlowes were seated in a circle of tufted chairs and love-seats while a Nat King Cole song played on the radio from the table in the corner; his deep, calming voice was out of place amongst the bickering. I listened to it for a moment, reveling in the sound of *Chestnuts Roasting on An Open Fire*, but as my throat tightened at the memory of all the times my mother had played his records, I focused my attention back on the task at hand. I scanned the beaded evening dresses until I found the eldest of Mrs. Marlowe's children, Bernadette. She had perched herself on a chair much too small for her girth and seemed incapable of freeing herself. With her black feathery shawl and small eyes, she looked like a giant stuffed vulture.

"Mrs. Carlton?" I called to her, but my voice bounced off of the conversation I had interrupted. I ought to have been telling John Marlowe of the guest's arrival, but since he had been purposefully avoiding me since he had arrived the day before – ignoring my efforts to find out why he had hired me to work for his mother when she was, most certainly, dead – I saw no point. Not right now, anyway.

"And when I looked in, I saw it standing over her bed!" Edie was saying, her fingernails digging into either of her bony arms and her prominent teeth chattering.

"It's the wine, Edie. Some people can't handle their liquor," said Marjorie.

"That's the pot calling the kettle sloshed," Bernadette said in a carrying whisper, taking another sip of her brandy.

Marjorie glared at her.

"I can handle my liquor just fine, Birdie," she snapped, though her blotchy red cheeks disagreed.

"Oh, yes – I know," Bernadette said. "That's why you drink so *much*."

I cleared my throat.

"Mrs. Carlton?" I said, louder this time, but it didn't help.

"I'm telling you that it was a ghost!" Edie exclaimed. "Bill saw it, too!"

Edie's husband was sipping his drink and didn't seem to notice that he had been pulled into the conversation until his wife jabbed him in the side. He pushed his glasses up the bridge of his thin, crooked nose and looked around.

"Didn't you?" Edie said, giving him a look that determined his answer for him.

"I ... well, there was certainly some sort of movement ..."

"Well, that proves it," Marjorie said dryly, downing the rest of her drink. Her face had now taken on a purplish hue, clashing horribly with her bright orange hair.

"I've seen a lot of odd things since we arrived, too, Edie," Rachel said. She was dressed in a rigid black gown and had a thin, delicate silver cross hanging around her neck. Beside her was her husband, and despite the fact that he was in a wheelchair, even he was wearing a tuxedo for the occasion, though the front had been stained by the saliva dripping from his open mouth. "Shadows from the trees outside, the moonlight shifting –"

"It wasn't a shadow!" Edie cried. "It was still daylight! And the ghost – it looked like Mary –!"

"You're being ridiculous, Edie," John said, adjusting the red bow tie around his neck. "And now you're getting hysterical –"

"I am not hysterical!"

"Mrs. Carlton!" I nearly shouted, and Marjorie, at least, heard me.

"Birdie!" she snapped at Bernadette, then jabbed her finger in my direction. "Shut up for a minute and pay attention to your maid!"

"If she wants me to *hear* her, she has to speak *louder*," Bernadette replied as though I wasn't in the room. "Now, Edie, the house is very old. What you're hearing are the sounds of the wood contracting and expanding due to the temperature changes –"

"Mrs. Carlton, there's another guest who's just arrived –" I began again, but Bernadette couldn't, or was pretending not to, hear me. "– should I let him in?"

"Did you hire another servant of some sort, Birdie?" Marjorie called. "It's bad enough that you fired Tilda –"

"*I* didn't fire Tilda," Bernadette said. "John did,

though goodness knows why. She knew how to do things properly –"

"That woman was ancient: she ought to have been let go years ago," John said. "Just because she came over on the boat with Mother was no reason to pretend otherwise."

"At least Tilda knew how to iron wool," Bernadette muttered.

"I'll have another drink, when you get the chance," John said, shaking his empty glass in my direction in what was now the closest he had come to speaking to me since he had arrived. I took the glass from him and went to the bar cart to refill it, not bothering to ask what he was drinking. It was always –

"Give me the Macallan," he called, as though I could have possibly forgotten.

"Mrs. Carlton," I said as I slopped some into his glass and brought it back over to him, "there's another guest waiting out in the Foyer."

"Has Cassandra finally come down?" Rachel asked, apparently unaware that the doorbell had rung. I didn't blame her: it was difficult to hear anything other than the incessant chatter coming from all directions, let alone anything outside of the room.

"No," I said. The fifth Marlowe sister still hadn't emerged from the room where the odd, childlike voice had called to me on my first day at the house, and though I had been bringing food to her door three times a day, I had never so much as gotten a glimpse of her. "It's a man. He's just arrived, so –"

"There are no more guests, dear," Bernadette said. "I have four sisters and a brother, and they're all here with their significant others – except for Marjorie, of course."

"She doesn't care that I'm divorced, Birdie," Marjorie snapped. "Only you do."

"I don't need to know the reasons why your

husband left you," Bernadette said, holding up her hands as though surrendering despite asking the firing squad to shoot. "I was just telling young Alexa, here, that everyone who was supposed to be here came."

"Alexandra," I corrected automatically, but Bernadette hadn't heard me. She cupped her hand around her ear.

"I can't hear you if you don't speak *louder*, Alexa," she said, her own voice rising to demonstrate for me, but John had gone back to arguing about the supposed ghost sighting with Edie, and Bill was trying to start a discussion with Rachel, and it was impossible to speak louder without outright screaming.

"Leave the poor girl alone, Birdie," Marjorie said. She rolled her eyes at me. "Who's in the Foyer, Alexa?"

"It's – ah – it's a man," I said, thrown off by the seemingly permanent damage that had been done to my name. "He said his name's Isidore Lennox."

The buzzing of voices dropped, and silence apart from the low hum of the radio met me as though I had just said something vulgar. Eight pairs of eyes turned slowly toward me.

"Lennox?" Bernadette repeated, suddenly capable of hearing me quite well.

"You must be confused," Edie said. "He wouldn't show up here."

"Apparently he would," Marjorie said, "or else he wouldn't be standing in the Foyer –"

"Well, who invited him?"

"No one invited him," Marjorie replied. "No one *likes* him."

"Just because no one likes him doesn't mean no one invited him," Bernadette said.

"Does that mean it was you?" Marjorie shot.

"Certainly not. Like I said, everyone I knew to be

invited showed up at the proper time."

"Well, this is horrible," Amalia said, setting her drink down so that she could cross her arms. She looked at John as though doing so might negate what I had just told her. "It's not appropriate for him to be here – he's not family."

"Neither are you," Marjorie said in an undertone, and Amalia threw her a withering look suggesting that, since she had married the family patriarch, she was far higher up than her red-headed sister-in-law would ever be.

"Alexa, why don't you ask him to come in here?" Rachel said kindly. "Maybe he'd like a drink –"

"Maybe he'd like to *leave*," Marjorie said. "God knows there isn't enough liquor on earth to stand being in a room with him."

"Spoken like a true alcoholic," Bernadette whispered loudly.

Marjorie's mouth opened to retort, but Rachel cut her off.

"We can't just leave him out in the Foyer."

"Can't we?" Marjorie said.

"It's our house now," Amalia said, laying her hand over John's to show off the dime-sized diamond on her finger. She tossed her dark hair over her shoulders, and with her elegant gown and heavily made-up face, she gave off the impression of a woman who was still clinging desperately to what had once been her striking beauty, but now only held resentment for the way wrinkles had sneaked onto her face and weight had crept upon her figure. "I think we ought to tell him to leave. Immediately."

"But somebody obviously invited him," Rachel said. "He couldn't have just guessed when the wake would be –"

"He might have read about it in the papers and come as soon as he could," Amalia said.

"Then how did Mr. Kneller know to pick him up?"

Rachel asked.

Marjorie narrowed her eyes at her.

"Yes, Rachel," she said. "How *would* Mr. Kneller know?"

"I don't know," Rachel replied. "That's why I asked."

"Who among us regularly chats with Kneller –?" Marjorie began, but Bill quickly cut her off.

"This is ridiculous," he said. "The man's standing right outside the door. Let's just bring him in and ask him what this is all about."

"I don't think that's a good idea," Amalia said, looking again at John. "He's obviously come for the money. There's nothing in the will that gives him any right to it, is there?"

"Mother was very good about keeping it up to date," John said.

"Even so," she persisted. "He might've found a loophole, or he's planning to challenge it –"

"In that case, I'll ask him for some advice," Marjorie said. "I wouldn't mind challenging it myself."

"Alexa," Rachel said, turning to me. "Why don't you tell Lennox to make himself comfortable while he waits –?"

"He cannot!" Amalia said, looking horrified. "What if he goes through the rooms pocketing things?"

"I doubt it will come to that, Amalia," Bernadette said. "The Tiffany lamp can't fit in his breast-pocket, after all ..."

"Well, someone should keep an eye on him anyway," Marjorie said. "I already got cheated out of most of my inheritance, and I don't need help losing any more of it from him –"

"The estate was always going to John," Amalia snapped. "You didn't get cheated out of anything –"

"I got cheated out of a lifetime of favoritism and overindulgence," she returned icily, "all because I wasn't born a son –"

"Let's not start that again," Rachel said calmly. "We're all very happy for John –"

"Really? Then why were you practically on your knees begging him for money yesterday to help you out of your debt?" Marjorie asked. "I'm surprised you would bother to humiliate yourself. You ought to have known he'd say no."

Rachel's cheeks flushed as though she had been slapped in the face. She looked down at her hands, which were twisting around in her lap.

"I can't be blamed for others' financial failures," John said. "Just because you and I shared a womb doesn't mean I'll share my money. You're all acting as though you thought Mother's allowances would last forever."

Rachel's face was now the color of a cooked beet. Her mouth was clamped shut, either to stop her from retorting or vomiting. She continued to stare down at her hands, though John was paying her no mind anyhow. I had the sudden urge to say something despite knowing nothing about the situation, only because John was ignoring her in the exact way he had been doing to me since he had arrived. Just as I opened my mouth to speak, though, Rachel spoke again.

"I just thought," she said quietly, "since James' care has been so expensive ..."

As she trailed off, I looked over at her husband. He seemed older than the rest of them, with a few strands of hair that had been combed over his balding head and skin hanging down from his expressionless face. By the look of him, he had never been a handsome man: he had a narrow face and pronounced nose, with small, pale eyes that turned down in the outer corners. Or maybe spending years in a wheelchair had done it to him, I considered briefly, before realizing that I didn't want to dwell on what had happened to him.

"I told you *years* ago that it would be much cheaper to put him in an institution," John said, unmoved by Rachel's reddening eyes. "You were the one who insisted on keeping him in your home."

"If anything, you should be paying for James' care, John!" Bill said angrily, but John only raised his eyebrows.

"Why?" he asked. "I don't believe in charity: it makes people weak. Though if you do, you're welcome to give Rachel some money. Though with all the bad investments you've made, I doubt it would do much good ..."

It was Bill's turn to flush, but before he could respond, Bernadette gave a hefty sigh and turned back to me.

"Alexa, go entertain Lennox," she said. "Keep him occupied while we sort this out –"

"And keep his hands where you can see them," Marjorie added.

Lennox was staring up at the chandelier with his hands in his pockets when I stepped back into the Foyer. I wasn't sure what they were expecting me to do with him. It wasn't as though I could pull out a deck of cards and invite him to play Blackjack for the next hour: he wouldn't want to play with someone who always won.

"If you'd like to come to the Dining Room, Mr. Lennox, I can bring you some coffee."

He glanced over at me.

"No, that's alright. I'll wait here."

"It's not very comfortable," I said. "And it might be a while. They're ... discussing you."

He didn't look surprised. If anything, he seemed rather amused, though his eyes were so dark that it was hard to tell for certain what laid behind them. He scanned me thoughtfully.

"I'll be fine."

"It could be hours," I tried again, not intent on standing in the Foyer with him for an undisclosed amount of time. I had more important things to do: namely searching for the money Mrs. Tilly had stolen from me and deciding how to confront John about the false pretenses under which he had hired me.

"Have they asked you to watch me?"

I glanced up at Lennox's voice. He was surveying me carefully.

"Technically," I said. Given that the Marlowes' voices were still booming from inside the Parlor, I saw no reason to lie to him: he had undoubtedly gotten the gist of their conversation. "Are you going to steal anything if I go out for a smoke?"

"Nothing that doesn't belong to me," he said, "though I'll join you if it makes things easier."

He didn't seem to realize that I wanted to be alone. Rather than outright telling him, I gave him the would-be polite smile that had become strained in the past three days and handed him his coat before donning mine.

The air outside was as frigid as ever, but it was a welcome contrast to the stuffiness inside. The storm was picking up, and snow pelted us as we stood there. It took me several moments to light my cigarette with the wind whipping the flame from my lighter. Lennox lit his own in one flick.

"I'm not sure that I got your name," he said, leaning against the pillar of the wooden mermaid who was now covered in a shroud of white snow.

"Alexandra Durant," I said, stressing each syllable to ensure that he, too, wouldn't mispronounce it. "Not Alexandria – Alexandra. And Durant is with a 't.'"

Lennox appeared mildly amused by how emphatic I was, but made no mention of it. He flicked his cigarette toward the porch railing to rid it of ash.

"You're not from around here," I commented.

"What makes you say that?"

I took another drag of my cigarette. Though I wasn't about to tell him as much, he simply had the distinct air of being *from away,* as my mother used to say.

"Your shoes," I said.

He glanced down at his feet.

"Mainers don't wear oxfords?" he asked.

"Not in this weather, so you obviously didn't realize how much snow would be on the ground. You *are* wearing cashmere-lined gloves and a wool scarf, though, so you know how to handle the cold. So ... you're probably from New York. Maybe Philadelphia. But not originally, since you don't have the accent."

Lennox raised his eyebrows, his amusement mixing with a look that suggested he was more than a bit impressed.

"New York," he confirmed. "And you're from Maine?"

"Originally. But I go to school in Massachusetts."

"Then what brought you out here?"

"I ... just needed the money. I'll be going back to university after the holidays are over."

He gave me a look as though he knew I wasn't being entirely truthful. But I would be back in school in a few weeks: that's what John had promised me.

"What do you study?"

"Psychology," I said. "I'm getting my doctorate."

"Really?"

He looked a bit startled, but the reaction was hardly unexpected. Since I had started graduate school, six of my professors had asked me if I had mistakenly shown up in their classroom, and even after telling them that I was in the right place, more than one had commented that I would be better off seeking my M.R.S. degree. I waited impatiently for Lennox to say something similar.

"What's your dissertation about?" he asked instead.

"I won't bore you with the details," I said in a breath of gray smoke that swirled up to the porch ceiling.

"I hardly think you could: I'm a psychiatrist."

"Well, a psychiatrist and psychologist are two different things."

"Yes," he said, a small smile tugging at his lips as though he was fighting the urge to laugh, "I'm aware."

He was looking at me in a odd way, almost as though he was trying to read a text that was typed in too small a print. There was something about him that I liked, though I couldn't quite place it. Perhaps it was the genuineness in his voice that I so seldom heard, for I refused to believe that it was because he was handsome. His hair had been blown out of place by the wind, and I had the urge to reach up and fix it. Instead, I crossed one arm over my chest, holding the other one up so that I could stick the cigarette back to my mouth.

"Understanding and preserving the way information is encoded, stored, and retrieved in the adult brain," I said.

"Excuse me?"

"That's my dissertation. Understanding and preserving the way information is encoded, stored, and retrieved in the adult brain."

"Ah. Studying the memory must be interesting."

"It's important."

"Yes, I imagine it is," he said with the same smile. "What made you choose –?"

His question was cut off by the faint sound of a bell jingling from inside. I dropped my cigarette and stamped it out, then hurried inside with Lennox in tow, though not quickly enough: Bernadette had come out to the Foyer to find me, summoning bell in hand. She threw us a disapproving look as we entered.

"Bring him in now, Alexa," she said, then retreated back into the Parlor.

The Parlor was only twenty feet away, but I made a show of leading Lennox over to it and letting him inside even so. As we entered, John waved his empty scotch glass at me. I took it from him and went to refill it. Lennox stood by the door. No one invited him to sit down.

"Isidore," John said, turning halfway in his seat to look at the younger man. "How nice of you to join us."

"I was told I missed the wake," Lennox replied. His voice was even, but the words were brusque and the friendliness in it from moments ago was gone. He gave John an odd stare. "I must have gotten the time wrong."

I dropped two ice cubes into the glass and sloshed the scotch over them, then brought it back to John.

"Not to worry," John said. "If you'd like to see Mother, she certainly hasn't moved. But perhaps it should wait for the morning."

He tilted his chin down at Lennox, and whatever meaning he was trying to convey must have worked, because the doctor responded with a stiff nod of his own.

"We assume you've come for the money," Marjorie called. "We'll save you the time: you're not getting any."

"I've only come for the night," Lennox replied. "I'll leave first thing in the morning."

"You'll leave *tonight,*" Amalia said.

"I don't think I can do that. The ferryman could barely see the dock on the way over, and the storm has worsened since then."

"Kneller will do as he's told," Marjorie said.

"We can't ask him to operate the ferry in this," Rachel interjected. "It would be dangerous –"

"Even better: two birds with one stone."

"He can stay the night, surely –"

"He's not sleeping in the house!"

"It's not like he can go to a hotel," Bill commented, but Amalia gave him such a withering look that he fumbled his glass and sat back in his seat in silence.

"Maybe we could put him with Kneller," Edie suggested.

"There's no room in the guesthouse," Rachel said.

"You would know, wouldn't you?" Marjorie shot, but Rachel ignored her.

"Then we'll put him in the cellar," Amalia said. "Or better yet – outside."

"I'm sure we can find a place for him to sleep," Rachel said, throwing a glance at Lennox and giving him an apologetic smile. "He's welcome to have the Prudence Room since James and I are downstairs –"

"I'm not sleeping next door to him!" Edie exclaimed.

"Well, then I'm sure we can find a place," Rachel said. "It's not like there isn't room."

"It isn't a matter of space, though, is it?" Marjorie replied crisply.

"Well, it's my house now," Amalia started, "and I say –"

"It's not *your* house: it's John's house, as loathe as I am to say it," Marjorie said, "so no one cares what you have to say."

Amalia straightened in her seat, raising herself as high as possible without actually standing.

"My *husband* cares what I have to say," she said, looking pointedly at John, though he, in turn, was paying her no mind. His ears had perked up and he raised a hand to silence his siblings, then a small smile came over his face. He nodded toward the radio.

"Ah, listen to that," he said as a new song began. Nat King Cole's voice had been replaced by that of a female singer's, and she crooned out a sad tune. *You made me love you: I didn't want to do it, I didn't want to do it ... You made me want you, and all the time you knew it, I guess you always knew it ...*

Marjorie raised her eyebrows.

"Judy Garland. Very nice," she said briskly. "Now can we get back to –"

"*You Made Me Love You,*" John said as though she hadn't spoken. He turned his gaze to Lennox, his smile stretching wider. *You made me happy sometimes, you made me glad. But there were times, Dear, you made me feel so bad ...* "Mary loved singing this."

Lennox offered no reaction other than to shift in his spot, and though his face was the stoic expression of a man who didn't appreciate having a discussion about whether or not he was doomed to sleep outdoors interrupted for a song, his eyes didn't match. For a moment I got the feeling that he was terribly sad, but then the look in his eyes vanished and I was sure I had imagined it. I filed the name *Mary* away in my head; it was the second time it had been mentioned that night.

Gimmie, gimmie, gimmie, gimmie what I cry for. You know you've got the brand of kisses that I'd die for – the voice from the box continued, and Edie flinched. *You know you made me love you –*

"Turn that off," Rachel said suddenly, addressing no one in particular, though Bernadette was too busy swaying to the music, and Bill was humming along to the melody. Marjorie only rolled her eyes and took another sip of her drink.

You made me cry for, I didn't wanna tell you, I didn't wanna tell you. I want some love that's true –

"Turn it off!" Rachel said again, and this time her

insistence got my attention: she had leaned over to put her hand on Edie's shoulder, who appeared to be crying behind her white, shaky hands. I moved across the room and spun the little black power dial until it switched off, ignoring John's protest to keep it on. Judy Garland's voice softened and cut away.

"Thank goodness," Marjorie said. "Though at least her version is tolerable. Mary's interpretation of Al Jolson was so off-key it made my head spin –"

"Can we get back to the fact that there's an intruder in my house?" Amalia snapped. She turned to her husband. "John – *fix this!*"

John was staring at the radio, a dissatisfied look on his face as though he was a child who had just had a favorite toy taken away and was plotting how best to get it back. He downed the rest of his drink in one gulp, then shook the remaining ice around in the glass. It clinked back and forth for a moment before he responded.

"Well, I think if Lennox wants to stay ... then he should stay."

The contorted faces of his wife and sisters met him in disbelief.

"What?" Amalia said.

"Are you suffering from something, John?" Marjorie asked. "Other than narcissism?"

John ignored them. He was smiling at Lennox, a funny little smile that sat over his red bow tie, and he put his glass down and folded his hands neatly in his lap. Something about the expression made my skin crawl, and I had to rub my forearms with my hands to get the feeling to go away.

"I'm a hospitable man," he said. He nodded at the doctor. "And since I want you to feel right at home ... you can sleep in the nursery."

Lennox's arm twitched. The movement was so slight that I almost missed it, especially since his face was still void of emotion, but on second glance I could see that his eyes had darkened.

"Oh, John," Rachel said. "You can't possibly –"

"It's just a room," John said coldly. "I don't see what the problem is. I'll have the maid set up a bed for him."

"He can't sleep in there. Not after –"

"The nursery will be fine," Lennox cut in, his tone as dull as his expression.

He was looking at the other man steadily. For a moment I wondered what it was all about, but then a separate realization struck me: the nursery was the room directly connected to mine, and the only way for Lennox to go in and out of it would be to walk straight past my bed. My neck cracked as I hurried to look at John.

"Alexa, show Dr. Lennox up, will you?" he asked.

I cleared my throat.

"Well, I –"

"I told you to show Dr. Lennox upstairs, Alexa," John repeated, waving his hand at me as though he was chasing a fly from the room.

"I know you did, but –"

"Then I don't understand why you're arguing," John replied. "Show him upstairs."

"It's just that I'm not sure you remembered –"

"Show Lennox to his room."

"But –"

"Jesus, John – where did you find this girl?" Marjorie said. "It's like having an untrained dog around. Next she'll be pissing all over the carpet ..."

I bit my tongue to keep myself from retorting. John had turned his back on me. I stood rigidly in place as I stared at the back of his balding head. The complete disregard with which he had been treating me since his arrival was squeezing painfully at my chest, and it felt as though my ribs would crack from the pressure. I turned on my heel and led

Lennox from the room. A sinking dread was filling me: the type that warned me I had made a terrible mistake by accepting the job he had offered me, and try as I did to shake it off, it settled itself in my stomach and burned at my insides.

All I knew was that if John wouldn't talk to me now, then I would make sure he spoke to me later.

CHAPTER TWO

I left Lennox in the Foyer while I went to the Pantry to retrieve the nursery key. The little tag that hung from it was so worn that it was difficult to read, and the metal had corroded and rubbed off on my fingers. I pocketed it and returned to the Foyer. I had told him that I was simply going to check that the servants' door was locked for the night; I saw no reason to add that, since I had been made to sleep in such close approximation with him, I was planning to lock him into his room.

"It's this way," I told him, ushering him up the stairs to the third floor. I unlocked the door to the nanny's room and showed him across to the nursery. My eyes went to the empty crib that was just an outline in the darkness from the boarded up window. It looked even more barren now than it had when I had first seen it, and as I compared the scene with the one in my memory, I noticed the white Christening gown had disappeared.

"There are cots in the storage room," I told him. "I'll bring one in for you."

"I can get it myself."

"It's no trouble," I said.

"I really don't mind," he repeated, and there was a note of firmness in his voice. Perhaps he heard it, too, because he added in a more gracious tone, "I don't want to make more trouble for you."

He glanced backwards into the nanny's room. I could see his eyes running over my unmade bed and the clothes I had left on the radiator. I wondered if he saw the prescription bottle on the nightstand.

"Who's staying in there?" he asked.

"I am."

He raised his eyebrows.

"Is there someone in the maid's room?"

"No." I didn't have time to wonder how he knew the layout of the house. I had to get back downstairs before John went to bed. "But the previous maid who left still has her belongings in there, so they put me in here."

Lennox made an odd face. It was almost as though he thought I was lying.

"Well," he said, setting his leather case on the floor. "I'll knock if I have to come through."

I nodded and returned downstairs to the Foyer, taking a seat on the second step of the far staircase as I waited for the family to leave the Parlor. They filed out over the next two hours: Rachel and James first, then Edie and Bill, then Bernadette, then finally Marjorie until only Amalia and John remained inside. I stood and moved closer to the door. I could hear their muffled voices through the wood. Hers was tense, but his was untroubled. He sounded as confident and persuasive as he had when he had assured me that he could help me finish my doctorate.

They came out ten minutes later. John threw a glance in my direction, then whisked Amalia toward the stairs. I hurried after him.

"Professor Marlowe –?" I began, but he ignored me and started up the steps. "Professor Marlowe, I was hoping to talk to you –"

He was halfway up the steps and showed no signs of slowing. Amalia reached the landing and disappeared. A wave of irritation flooded over me.

"Professor Marlowe!" I said, my voice echoing around the large room, and the sound of it was too loud for him to ignore any longer. He turned to face me with an innocent look as though he hadn't heard me calling him.

"Yes?"

"I need to speak with you," I said.

"It'll have to wait until the morning. I'm very tired
–"

"No," I said rigidly, but as his eyebrows raised, I
evened out my tone to make it more polite. "I – I need to
speak with you. About my job."

"What about it?"

He didn't bother to come back downstairs. I
swallowed back my resentment, trying to decide where to
begin.

"You told me I'd be working for your mother," I
said.

"And?"

"And she's dead," I said. I wondered if anyone had
informed him of how I had arrived at the house three days
before and requested to see Mrs. Marlowe, only to discover
her laying in her funeral clothes upon the bed. Mrs. Tilly
had undoubtedly had a good laugh; Bernadette had been
none-too-pleased to find me, and had subsequently branded
me a moron for being unaware as to why I had really been
hired – knowledge that everyone else, apparently, was privy
to except me.

John stared at me, the hint of a smile beginning to
tug at the corners of his lips. He gave a little shake of his
head.

"Is that a problem?" he asked, and there was such
confidence in his voice that it shook my own.

"Well, I – I just don't understand what I'm doing
here –"

"You're doing the same thing you'd be doing had
my mother still been alive," he said. "It really makes no
difference."

"Then why'd you tell me I'd be working for her?"

"The situation unexpectedly changed."

I snapped the rubber band against my wrist to jog
my memory. He had specifically told me in his office at the

university that I would be working for his mother. That had been four days ago. Bernadette had told me her mother had been dead for five.

"No, it didn't. She died on the twentieth: you hired me on the twenty-first. You must have known."

The smile momentarily slipped from his face, but then it reappeared wider. He slowly made his way down the stairs toward me. I had the sudden urge to run, but shook it off and firmly planted my feet on the floor.

"I think you're making this more complicated than it needs to be," he said. "You'll work here, supervised by various family members who will report to me, and we'll see if you do well enough to come back."

"But why didn't you just tell me that in the first place?"

"Maybe I didn't feel it was necessary," he said. "Maybe I wanted to see how you'd react once you got here. Not well, in case you were wondering. No wonder everyone says you're difficult."

"I'm not difficult: you just told me something completely different, and I now don't know what you want me to do –"

"I've told you what I want you to do: several times, in fact."

"You told me you wanted me to look after your mother. You didn't tell me anything about serving dinner and drinks for her wake."

John gave a sigh.

"Alexa –"

"Alexandra," I automatically corrected.

"Alexandra," he said, somewhat disapprovingly, and I wondered if he was purposefully making mistakes just to see how I reacted. "You want to be a psychologist, correct?"

"Yes."

"Well, being a psychologist requires certain

personality traits," he said. "Patience, sensitivity, passion ... empathy."

"I have those."

John's smile tightened.

"According to your professors," he said, "you're critical, judgmental, and fault-finding to an extreme. They say in clinical situations you often jump on those who misremember things –"

"That's the whole point of my research: training the brain to remember correctly. Of course I point out if they don't do it right."

He sighed again.

"Alexa –"

"Alexandra."

" – I want to help you. I think you're highly intelligent for a young woman, evidenced by your academic record. Unfortunately, you seem to be lacking the behavioral responses that are, by society's standards and my own, necessary to form any type of working relationship. Do you understand what I'm saying?"

"No."

"You're going to be given some situations here that you're unfamiliar with, and you need to learn to react the way you think a professional psychologist would. Someone makes a mistake? Kindly ask them about it. *I see you've mentioned going for a walk on Sunday, but just to clarify, the last time we spoke it was supposed to be on Tuesday. See?*"

I shifted my jaw. He seemed neither nervous nor concerned, and yet he didn't seem wholly unfeigned, either.

"I can be polite," I said.

"Good, good. Let's try it out in the morning, shall we?"

He turned to go back upstairs.

"But –" I said, stopping him. "I still don't understand what I'm doing here. Isn't everyone leaving after the wake?"

John turned back to me, the hint of a smile still on his face.

"Birdie might stay longer to look after the house. She's under the impression that you've been hired solely as her maid, so you'll stay as long as she sees fit."

"How long will that be?"

"A week, maybe two. I doubt she'll stay past New Year's. Are you going to be bothered if the job is shorter than previously discussed?"

"Well, I –" I paused and changed my tone in an attempt to be gracious. "It's just that you said you'd pay me for the month."

"And I did. Don't worry, I won't take any back."

"But – five hundred dollars for two weeks of work?"

"Is that a problem?"

I gave him a hard stare. He knew as well as I did that it was an obscene amount to pay someone for cleaning and following orders. Mrs. Tilly had already made several comments about it, and though I still planned to retrieve what I was certain she had stolen once the family was gone, a part of me couldn't help but agree with her, especially since my real payment ought to have been getting back into my program.

John searched my face.

"You're hesitant," he said. "Perhaps the money embarrasses you? Or perhaps ..." He took one step down the stairs toward me. " ... perhaps you'd like more?"

"That's not what I was going to say."

"I didn't say it was. I said that perhaps you'd like more. How much were you hoping for? How much would you be willing to take before the uneasiness is justifiable?"

"I'm not sure what you mean, Professor Marlowe," I said. I clasped my hands together. I didn't like the way he was looking at me.

"Maybe another five hundred when you're done? Maybe ... a thousand?"

I shook my head.

"I didn't ask for more money," I said.

"I know you didn't ask. But you want more, don't you? More to pay off your college debts? More to pay for your mother's care?"

I opened my mouth and then closed it, unable to voice what I was thinking. John seemed to know regardless.

"I know all about her, Miss Durant," he said. He took another step downward. "I know all about *you*. So who will take care of her when your aunt no longer can?"

"I will."

"And how will you do that? You won't be employable without a PhD – not as a psychologist, at least. I suppose you could get work doing something, of course ... being a secretary. But the pay won't really be enough, will it? Not for her care. Especially since you don't have a husband."

A lump formed in my throat. It burned against my esophagus and threatened to choke me.

"So what are you going to do if this doesn't work out?" he continued. "What's your backup plan?"

"I – I don't have one, Professor Marlowe."

"I hear you visit her every weekend," he said. "Cambridge to Bangor must be an exhausting trip to make so often. Are you exhausted, Miss Durant?"

He was on the bottom step now. My hands were still clasped together, and sweat built up on my palms the closer that he got.

"I ..."

"Are you exhausted?"

"I don't – I don't think of it that way."

"Yes or no?"

"I – yes, I – I suppose I am, Professor Marlowe," I

said, hoping to keep him from taking another step closer. He smiled.

"I thought so. So, if you do your job well enough here, let's say there will be ... one thousand dollars when you leave: to take the stress off of you. How does that sound?"

It sounded like more money than I could hope to make in a year, but far from feeling at ease, I felt more uncertain than ever.

"I'm just not sure I understand what I'll be doing for it," I said.

John gave me an exasperated look. I nearly mirrored him: there was something he was withholding from me.

"You'll be working," he said, the hint of impatience returning to his voice. "Working as a polite, assiduous maid who will one day become a polite, assiduous psychologist."

I gave him a long stare. The top of his balding head was shining and his eyes had gone dark and beady. I had seen that look before: it was the same one he wore when he told me I would be working for his mother. He was lying to me.

He started up the stairs again, but I couldn't hold back any longer.

"What kind of situations?" I called after him, and he paused and turned back around.

"Excuse me?"

"You said I was going to be given some situations here that I'm unfamiliar with," I said hurriedly. "What kind of situations?"

"If I told you, you wouldn't be unfamiliar with them."

"Like sticking me in an adjoining room with a man I don't know?"

"Did I?" He gave a thoughtful look. "I must have forgotten: I'm not too familiar with the servants' floor."

"Does the university know about these situations?"

I went on, not caring that his lenient expression was lessening. "Or is this a solo project you're working on –?"

John descended the stairs so quickly it was as though they had turned to a slide beneath his feet. His hand closed around my wrist, pinning me in place. The sentence died within my throat.

"Let me ask you something, Miss Durant," he said dangerously, and his face was so close to mine that his unshaven cheek scratched my own. "Does this make you uncomfortable?"

"I – what?"

His fingers tightened, and the grip was so strong that it felt as though my bone would snap at any second. He gave me a shake.

"I asked if this makes you uncomfortable," he growled.

"I – I – yes –"

"How about now?"

He squeezed harder. His fingers were right over the spot where I wore the rubber band, and the raw skin on my wrist started to break open. My eyes watered and my throat went dry.

"I said, *how about now?*"

"Yes – yes – it's uncomfortable –"

"How about now?"

The pain was so intense that I could barely speak, and the urge to cry out was only halted by the instinct that if I did, he would silence me completely.

"Yes – it's uncomfortable –"

"Say *no*," he said, putting his face right into mine and choking me with the stale scent of whiskey on his breath.

"W-what?" I said, too flustered to understand.

"Say *no.*"

"I – I – *no.*"

John let go of me and I stumbled backwards, losing my footing and falling onto the black-and-white tiles. He brushed off the front of his shirt as though I might have dirtied it.

"That's better," he said, and his voice was pleasant and chipper again. "Now, you'll be thrown into certain situations while you're here, and – like a good psychologist – you need to react appropriately. No judgment. No criticism. Nothing makes you uncomfortable – understand?"

"I ..." I clutched my wrist where he had released it, willing the pain to go away, but I had no response. Something shifted out of the corner of my eye and I looked up at the banister. The dark outline of a woman was looking down on us, though I couldn't make out who it was. I stared at her, willing her to come help me, but she only retreated into the darkness.

John turned back to the stairs.

"Goodnight, Alexa," he said as he made to leave. "And since remembering is your forte, then remember this: you're asking for acceptance into a man's world. You might think you're smart enough, and you might hope you're strong enough, but I assure you that you're not. So if you want to succeed, then you need to stop thinking about what you want and start realizing that what you need is a very separate thing."

The soles of his dress shoes pattered up the stairs, though I didn't watch as he left. My eyes were fixed on the floor and my injured wrist was pressed into my stomach as I waited for the pain to pass.

He was just testing me, I told myself ten minutes later when I finally stood up and ascended the stairs. I glanced around the second floor landing, thinking that perhaps the woman who had watched us would be waiting for me, but only the darkness stared back. My steps were shaky and weak as I climbed the stairs to the third floor; it felt as though my legs would give way at any moment. I shook my head as I tried to convince myself more effectively: he was doing it because he saw something in my academic work and understood the importance of my research.

I went to the nanny's room and immediately snatched up the prescription bottle on the nightstand. Uncapping it, I tapped out four round white pills, popped them in my mouth and swallowed them dry, then yanked open the drawer and pulled out the envelope of cash I had stowed there. I held it in my hands, frightened of letting it go and yet more frightened of what it meant. For there was no mistaking the sheer cruelty in John's eyes as he had gripped me, and no chance of believing that it was just an act he had put on to illustrate a point. I could hope that he had hired me simply because he enjoyed seeing me run to and from the room as I carried plates of food, or being scolded by his sisters, or biting my tongue when someone said something incorrect – but I feared there was another reason he wanted me which would explain exactly why he was willing to pay me such a large sum of money.

Opening the topmost drawer of the bureau, I rummaged to find my extra garters, then pulled the remaining bills from the envelope and laid them flat across my thigh and strapped them into place. I checked my reflection in the dirty mirror, turning back and forth to make sure that the hiding place was undetectable. Whatever John or the rest of the household had planned for me, I was at least leaving the island with my money.

A quiet knock came on the door. I startled from my thoughts and turned around.

"Yes?" I called, my voice rigid and my hands balled into fists as I imagined John coming into the room, but it was only Lennox. He stepped over the threshold with a blanket tucked beneath his arm.

"Sorry," he said, noting my tone. "The linen closet only had sheets."

"It's fine."

I waited for him to cross into the nursery, but he stayed in his place. I could feel his eyes on me even though I wasn't looking at him.

"It's fine," I repeated.

"But are you?"

He looked at me steadily with the same intense stare that he had given me on the front porch, and I had the sudden feeling that he could see straight into my head.

"Yes." I shifted my jaw and brushed off the front of my uniform. "I just – I had a bit of a disagreement with Professor Marlowe."

"I would be more than happy to sleep in the Parlor, if that's what it was about."

"No, that wasn't it."

He waited almost as if encouraging me to go on, and though I thought I knew better than to open up to a stranger, the words tumbled out of me even so.

"He just – he seems to think that he can degrade me," I finished.

Lennox shifted the blanket to his other arm.

"I'm sorry to hear that," he said carefully. "Though – if I may be so bold – you don't seem like you'd allow him to."

"No, I wouldn't," I said, more to myself than to him. "I'd see him dead first."

I didn't realize that the words were leaving my mouth until it was too late, and I clamped my jaw shut but to no avail. The drugs were rendering me uninhibited. Lennox courteously pretended not to have heard me.

"Well," he said, giving me a tight smile, "goodnight, Alexandra Durant with a *t*. And it was nice meeting you, in the event that I leave without seeing you in the morning."

He retreated to the nursery and shut the door. The wall lamp in his room went out a few minutes later, taking with it the light that had spilled across my bedroom floor from beneath the door. The sound of the *click* jolted me to my senses. However John's words had affected me, I couldn't get angry. I couldn't get emotional. Emotions did nothing but get in the way of how I had trained my mind to work, after all, and if I let that part of me slip away, then it wouldn't matter what else happened. I stood and went to the nursery door, then slid the key into the lock and turned it as quietly as I could, sealing him inside, before retrieving my room key and tiptoeing back to the door to the hallway and locking it, as well.

I changed into my nightclothes and got back into bed. If it turned out that the fifteen hundred dollars was for something more, I decided, I wasn't worried. I wasn't about to sleep with John Marlowe, no matter what price he thought he could pay me. I tapped out a fifth pill and put it beneath my tongue to dissolve, needing an extra one to ensure that thoughts of him wouldn't keep me awake. As my mind went hazy and my breathing slowed, numbness came over me and slowed my rational thoughts to a halt, and my head filled with visions of ghostly figures in the dark corridors of the house that called me by a name which wasn't my own, tormenting me until the blackness took over and I fell into a silent sleep.

***

The alarm woke me up at quarter-past five, though it must have been ringing for over an hour: I had set it for four. I groggily sat up and held my head in my hands, relieved at the deep sleep but mournful of having to wake from it so soon. I pulled my stockings, dress and cap on, fumbled to find where I had left the keys beneath my pillow, then carefully unlocked both doors. My shoes had been scattered across the floor, though I had thought I had left them neatly at the end of the bed. I rubbed my temples again, knowing that I ought not to have taken the extra pill. They were supposed to temporarily pause my memory, not make me forget what I had done during the night.

I stooped to retrieve the shoes, feeling moist wood beneath my stockinged feet despite the heat plowing through the radiator. I quickly put the shoes on, not liking the fraught feeling that was creeping up on me, and went downstairs. Snow had built up on the windowsills all around the house and more was still coming down. With the darkness camouflaging the contents of the nearby rooms and the wind rattling the dead foliage in the trees outside, the house seemed especially grotesque, as though the arrival of Lennox had started something odd and sinister.

In the kitchen I filled the sink with soapy water and started rinsing the glasses I had neglected to wash from the night before. The moonlight was reflecting off the snow in the yard, making the view one long endless sheet of white. As I set the glasses on the drying rack, I noticed a ring of purplish flesh circling my wrist where John had grabbed me. Two large fingerprints closed it like a latch. I pulled my sleeve down further to hide it.

I pulled a pack of cigarettes from my pocket and went through the pantry to get outside. I leaned down to shield the flame with my body from the wind, and took a deep drag in as I tried to make sense of it all. I had hoped that the freezing temperature would shock my senses, but instead it sank into my skin as though making its home in my bones, and I shook as I smoked, both out of cold and fear.

A fistful of red caught my attention in the distance, out of place in the black and white scenery. I stared at where it was nestled just above the snow only thirty feet away from where I stood, watching as it waved to me as I waited longingly for a solution to my predicament to come. What did John want from me, I wondered? He wasn't going to tell me – that much I knew – at least not until it was too late for me to flee.

I finished my cigarette and threw it down to the ground. And I wouldn't flee, I told myself. I wasn't a frightened child running into her parents' arms; even if I wanted to, I couldn't. I turned to go back inside, but the dot of red in the distance gave another beckoning wave, and so instead I took a step off the porch and squinted toward it in an attempt to discern what it was.

"For Christ's sakes," I muttered, recognizing it at last and angrily starting toward it. It was John's bow tie, gently flapping in the breeze. My mind flashed back to how it had hung around his neck the night before while he held me at the base of the stairs, and I thought I could almost smell the scotch reeking off of him as I neared it. He must have gone out for a midnight walk and tossed it aside, just as I feared he was planning to toss me aside.

The snow was nearly two feet deep in the area just off the path where it sat, and cut against my ankles as I stepped into it. The tights did little to protect my skin from the cold: I ought to have gotten my boots from the Foyer. Perhaps it had blown off of his neck after all, for if John had walked out there, then the harsh winds had blown snow to fill any trace of his footsteps. I hurried closer to the tie, intent on grabbing it up just as he had grabbed me and squeezing it in my freezing hands before bringing it inside to neatly re-tie and place in his spot at the breakfast table to find. If he wanted to play a game, after all, then I could play along. I could be the polite, assiduous servant he claimed that he wanted. I could follow orders and ignore inconsistencies, and I could smile and nod along just the way he hoped I would. But if he thought that I would continue to smile and nod when I returned to the university, then he was gravely mistaken – because that wasn't who I was, nor whom I would ever be.

I leaned down and grasped the tie, my mind too focused on the thoughts zipping through my head to pay attention to my physical surroundings. It was only when I gave it a firm yank that the realization started to sink in, but not quickly enough, so I gave it another hard pull and –

A body started to rise out of the snow, heavy and frozen as I lifted it by its red noose. I jumped back, releasing it and bolting back to the house at full speed. I clambered through the servants' door, shouting to wake the household even though I knew it was to no avail: for no matter how quickly I got help, John Marlowe's frozen form could thaw but never move again.

CHAPTER THREE

The cigarette was still burning in Lennox's hand, though he appeared to have forgotten it long beforehand, and a caterpillar of ash fell from the filter and disintegrated into the snow. It was the only movement other than the snow descending from the sky in what felt like hours since most of the members of the household had emptied into the yard to surround John's body. Just his face was visible; the rest of him was buried. He looked like a infant swaddled in a blanket.

Nobody had spoken, until –

Amalia let out a terrible, guttural shriek. It got lost halfway up her throat and barely escaped into the air. Her hands clapped over her face as though trying to prevent another sound from coming out, and then she dropped to her knees beside the body, her beautiful face twisted and her dark eyes glistening. Rachel closed her eyes and bowed her head at the sight of her twin brother. Her dark hair fell like a curtain to hide her long, worn face from my view.

"Well, we should call some paramedics," Marjorie said briskly, skipping past words of grief.

"And say what?" Bernadette asked. "'Our brother's buried in the snow drift – please come and dig him out?' It's not like they can resuscitate him."

"We can't just leave him here," Rachel breathed.

"Why not? He's not going anywhere."

"Stop being morbid, Marjorie," Edie said. "John's dead!"

"How ... how did this happen?" Bill asked. He looked more startled than anything, and kept shaking his head. "How did he die?"

"I think it's safe to assume that he froze to death,

Bill," Bernadette said.

Amalia looked up, finally pulled from her reverie.

"He froze to death – *thirty feet from the house?*" she demanded. "Why was he outside at all?"

"He's your husband: shouldn't he have been in bed with you?" Marjorie said.

"He would have been! But he was restless and he – he wanted to stay up!" She looked around at the circle of mourners. "He was upset after – after – after that man showed up!"

She pointed at Lennox, who seemed to finally notice that his cigarette had burned down to just the filter. Dropping it, he took out a new one and brought it to his lips to light.

"I wasn't aware that I caused him any distress," he said, his tone diplomatic. "I'm sorry if I did."

"You certainly did!" Amalia said, clambering to her feet. She brushed the snow from her knees. "He – he – he wanted nothing to do with you –!"

"So he went outside to put distance between the both of them?" Marjorie asked, sounding anything but convinced.

"I'm sure Isidore had nothing to do with it," Rachel said. "This is just … a horrible tragedy."

"Exactly," Bernadette said. "What's done is done. Now we just have to decide how to move forward."

"We can't leave him out in the snow!" Amalia exclaimed.

"Why not? It's not like he'll be cold," Marjorie said.

"Please, Marjorie –" Edie said, "– he was our brother!"

"I'm just being practical. What would you have me do – dig him out and put him upstairs with Mother?"

"That's exactly what we should do!" Amalia said.

"Great. Get a shovel, then," Marjorie snapped.

"No one's going to dig him out," Bernadette said. "We should leave him here until the police come."

"I'm not leaving my husband out here with the – with the vermin and mice –!"

"I'm going to go inside," Rachel said, glancing back at the house. "I don't want James to worry."

"*Can* he worry?" Marjorie said in an undertone, but Rachel either didn't hear or simply ignored her.

It was strange seeing them there. They were still in their nightclothes, and Edie's hair was in rollers. With their bathrobes sticking out from beneath their coats, they looked a bit like children playing dress-up rather than the sophisticated, wealthy people I had been serving tea and scones. As a gust of wind rattled through the trees to shake the dead branches and scatter us further with snow, the sky darkened despite the sun rising on the horizon, and the gray clouds that hung over us appeared so threatening that the family members broke off to return inside until only Lennox and I remained.

I crossed my arms, still only dressed in my uniform and house shoes but not ready to leave despite how my shivering arms tried to persuade me. For despite what the Marlowe sisters seemed to think, I simply couldn't picture a man as calculating and assertive as John Marlowe drunkenly stumbling through the snow, especially mere hours after the way he had so confidently told me how the world worked. I kept my eyes fixed on the red bow tie, watching as the ribbon of fabric pulled and tugged, longing to escape the dead man's neck. A wave of nausea came over me at the sight, amplified by the extra medication that I had taken the night before. For I had spoken of this, I thought suddenly. I had told Lennox that I would see John dead before allowing him to degrade me, and now he was. It was as though an unknown advocate had fulfilled my wishes, only I had mistakenly asked for the wrong thing.

I looked at Lennox. A frown was pulling at his brow.

"When I said – what I said – last night," I told him hurriedly, "I didn't actually want it to happen."

Lennox glanced up.

"I know," he said. "This is just ... an unfortunate coincidence."

"It's a bit too odd of a chance, though, isn't it?"

"I believe that's why it's called a coincidence."

"No, not that part. I meant, it's a bit too odd that John Marlowe would let himself die like that."

Lennox gave me a look.

"I guess we don't have as much control over these types of things as we'd like to believe," he said.

"I guess not," I agreed, though my memory gave a sudden tug as though searching for the reasoning behind why I couldn't agree with the idea that his death had been accidental. I tried to follow where it was leading me, but my head was too foggy. I gave Lennox a nod and left him to return inside.

"Alexa," Bernadette said as I stepped into the Foyer minutes later. "Coffee and tea will be served in the Dining Room this morning."

"What?"

Bernadette sucked in her cheeks and her midsection swelled as she looked at me.

"Coffee and tea in the Dining Room," she repeated. "Are you daft? We certainly can't eat in the breakfast nook: John's body is right outside the window!"

I blinked, nearly moving to follow her orders when the reality of the situation sunk in. John was dead: the deal I had made with him was off. For a moment I considered that he was simply pretending to be dead in a farcical ploy to see how I reacted, but then his pale, bluish face flashed before my vision and the idea vanished.

"I understand that," I said rigidly, though admittedly the fact that she could still think of eating was rather difficult for me grasp. "I just don't understand why you think I'll be serving you."

"Excuse me?"

"Professor Marlowe hired me. He's dead."

"He hired you to work for *me.*"

"Well, I have no interest in working for *you,* so I think I'll go pack my belongings. So, if you'll excuse me ..."

I moved to go toward the stairs, but Bernadette blocked me. With her hands on her hips and her sable robe drowning her in a layer of soft black, she looked more like a vulture than ever.

"You aren't going anywhere, young lady."

I threw her a look.

"Yes, I am," I said.

"Oh you are, are you? And who gave you permission to do that?"

"I don't need permission. I don't want the job anymore."

"I don't care if you want the job: your contract isn't up."

"Then don't give me a good reference," I said irritably, trying to push past her, but I simply bounced off of her huge stomach.

"My brother paid you five hundred dollars for this little job of yours," she said, her voice dropping to a menacing whisper. "You and God only know the reason why – and I doubt He's too pleased about it. Now, I was told I'd be getting a maid for as long as I decide to stay here, and that's exactly what I intend to have. If you don't want the job, then go. But leave the money behind."

She put out her hand. I stared down into her open palm. The flattened bills beneath my garter scratched against my skin.

"It's my money," I said.

"Oh? And what have you done to earn it?" She waited for an answer that I couldn't give, then nodded in confirmation. "I thought so. Now, you will either continue your work or give me back that money."

I swallowed. I couldn't leave the island without the money, not when I was already leaving without my spot at the university. I searched Bernadette's face, willing her to understand that there was no monthly allowance or inheritance waiting for me that would allow me to continue onward without a job, but one look at her narrowed eyes stopped me from speaking. She didn't know what I had been working so hard to achieve, nor would she care.

"I can't give it back," I said. "Mrs. Tilly took two hundred from me."

"Well, you're a quick thinker, aren't you?" Bernadette replied. "Think you can pull one over on me? Blame the cook and sneak off with half the money?"

"No, I – it's true –"

Bernadette stuck a short, pudgy finger in my face.

"You either hand over the full amount, or you stay," she repeated. "Frank won't be ferrying you anywhere otherwise, and if you get any other ideas, I'll have you arrested for theft."

I bit down on the insides of my cheeks until they burned.

"I'm not a thief," I said.

"So I guess you'll be staying, then," Bernadette replied. She took a step back from me. "Now, coffee and tea in the Dining Room – immediately. And I don't want to hear another vulgar word out of your mouth."

I didn't dare call her bluff. The ferryman had no reason to take pity on me and bring me back to the mainland, and I had no desire to obtain a criminal record. I turned and marched toward the kitchen. It wasn't as though

I had anywhere to go right now, anyway.

I started a pot of coffee on the stove. Mrs. Tilly was shaking her head as she stirred the cream of wheat at the burner beside me, her round face flushed and her free hand clutching the necklace that normally hung beneath her apron.

"You come for a funeral you wind up dead ... It's not right, I tell you. It's not right," she said, tears clinging to her eyelashes. "A magpie must've come to his door and cocked its head at him. It's not right ..."

She glanced over at me, perhaps thinking that I would echo the sentiment, but I ignored her. Her twisted idea of morality would garner no sympathy from me, at least not until she admitted that she had stolen my money.

As I waited for the coffee to percolate, my fingers tightened, forming my hands into fists. The anger I had felt for John the previous day had intensified, and whereas I had been upset with him for tricking me into coming to the island, I was furious now that he had died. He was supposed to have gotten me back into my doctorate program. It was as though he had died on purpose just to spite me once again, though my rational mind knew it wasn't so.

I wordlessly transferred the coffee to a china pot and brought it to the Dining Room.

"Shall I make it the usual way, Mrs. Carlton?" I asked Bernadette, re-adopting my polite tone before adding three heaping spoons of sugar and half the pitcher of cream to her cup. She nodded in approval.

My arms were rigid as I continued around the table to serve the rest of the family. I pointedly ignored the tears clinging to Amalia's eyelashes as she waved me away from her, noting that she was apparently too distressed to eat but not so distressed that she couldn't model her sadness for her in-laws; disregarded the frightful glances that Edie threw around the room and the sour glare that had glued itself to

Marjorie's face; and turned a blind eye to Rachel's quiet expression and Bill's confused one. Perhaps they were all in shock, but none of them seemed sorrowful about John's death. Or maybe, I considered as I reached the end of the table and dutifully stood with the coffee tray in hand, I was simply projecting my own feelings of discontent and disconnect onto them, and they weren't as aloof as they appeared.

"Is there anything else I can get for you, Mrs. Carlton?" I asked.

Bernadette wiped her mouth with her napkin and set her cup back on its saucer.

"I think it would be best if you phoned the police now," she said. "Advise them that we're about to begin breakfast; I don't want them showing up before we've finished."

I blinked, not sure whether to be appalled or unsurprised that none of them had thought to call the police sooner, then set the coffee pot down and went to the Study.

I picked up the handset with no intention of actually conveying Bernadette's absurd request to the operator, but was met with silence. I tapped the receiver cradle several times to see if the dial tone would come back on, then followed the line to the wall to ensure that it was still intact. The storm must have affected it. I decided that I would wait a few minutes and try again. I was in no rush to return to the bickering voices in the Dining Room anyhow.

I opened the desk drawers and shuffled around the contents. An old stack of yellowing papers scribbled with tiny, messy writing sat next to an empty ornate golden sheath, a dip ink pen and its various tips, and a worn photograph of a young girl sitting in a clover-covered field with a small, well-groomed dog on her lap. I stared down at her with the odd sensation that I had seen her somewhere before, then willed my mind not to harass me with the unknown. I couldn't stop myself from wondering what was going to happen next, though. What was I going to do now that John was dead? Be Bernadette's maid? Return to the university and beg for another chance? They wouldn't uphold my agreement with John; I wasn't even certain that he had been planning to uphold it himself. I closed my eyes and rubbed my temples, trying to think of what I could do. I couldn't go home: not without the money and no way to take care of my mother.

I plucked one of the pen tips up and held it between my thumb and pointer finger, holding it there as I breathed and breathed in an attempt to fill myself with something other than the utter hopelessness that I felt. When no relief came, though, I pressed down on the tip until it poked through the skin and created a bubble of blood. I imagined pressing the point to my skull and creating a hole through which the solution to my predicament could escape. But the answer wasn't there, I knew, tossing the tip back down. All that I could be certain of was that, whatever John had been planning for me, this had not been it – and I didn't know whether to be relieved or not.

I wiped my finger on my skirt and picked up the handset again. There was still no dial tone. My mind shifted, returning to the image of John's body out in the snow. A dead man and no way to phone for help: what was the likelihood of that? I shook my head and pushed the concern away. My rational mind knew better than to give in to the eeriness of the bitter cold island. It was just as Marjorie and Bernadette had said: he had simply died.

I retreated to the Dining Room to inform the Marlowes about the phone line.

"What do you mean, *out?*" Bernadette said. "It can't be *out.*"

"There's no dial tone, Mrs. Carlton," I said, unsure

of how to make it any clearer. "The storm might have blown it out."

"The storm couldn't have blown it out," Bernadette said. "It's an underwater line."

"Something could have hit the junction box," Bill said, but she paid him no mind.

"Alexa, you must be mistaken."

I bit down on my tongue.

"Perhaps I misheard, Mrs. Carlton," I said.

"Someone with competence go check on it," Bernadette ordered.

No one moved. Bernadette narrowed her eyes.

"Lennox, I assume you're not an imbecile," she said. "Go call the police."

Lennox was sitting at the farthest end of the table from her, quietly drinking his coffee. He glanced over at me.

"I doubt I'm more skilled at listening for a dial tone than Alexandra," he said, and there was a hint of crispness in his voice as he warned her not to challenge him. I felt a rush of approval for him, along with a sense of satisfaction that my instinct to like him had not just been about his looks after all.

"So maybe the storm hit the junction box," Bill muttered again.

Bernadette gave a huff.

"Remind me what time you're leaving again, Lennox?" she asked irritably. "Directly after breakfast?"

"I'm not entirely sure anymore," he said. "Given the circumstances."

"Well, this is just wonderful," Amalia said scathingly. She tossed her long hair over her shoulders and shook her head. "We should have never come to this house in the winter!"

"I'm so sorry that my mother didn't die at a convenient time of year for you," Marjorie said with the least amount of pity I had ever heard in a voice. "I guess we Marlowes just don't think of others when we decide to kick the bucket."

"My husband is dead!" Amalia said.

"Yes, and you seem simply *devastated* about it."

"More devastated than all of you," she snapped. "Maybe you're hoping that your mother's estate will be divided up between just the five of you now – is that it?"

"There's an idea: maybe John *purposefully* froze to death just to spite you so that you wouldn't get any of the money that you've been banking on getting ever since you laid eyes on him!"

"I don't – I'm not – I don't care about that!" Amalia said indignantly. "And if anything, you all probably conspired to kill him because you're upset that he got the island!"

"Now that's just absurd, Amalia," Rachel said.

"Is it? Is it more absurd than him wandering outside for no reason, then freezing to death instead of just coming in?"

"He was obviously too drunk to make it back," Bill said.

"Alcohol consumption increases the risk of hypothermia," Bernadette said. "Blood flow to the skin and extremities increased, making him feel warm, while actually his body got colder."

"He had three scotches! Four at the most – that's barely what he drinks at a dinner party!"

"Maybe he had more," Marjorie said. "He might've been down here drinking after we'd all gone to bed."

"Speaking from experience?" Bernadette asked in her carrying whisper.

Marjorie ignored her.

"Listen, he had a few extra drinks, fell in the snow and died," she said. "It's not that difficult to believe,

Amalia."

"Yes, it is!" she screamed. "And the way you're all acting is – is proof! You did this! I know you did this!"

"You really think that we murdered our own brother, Amalia?" Marjorie said. "Maybe you and Lennox should go sit in the other room for a little while – I'm sure he can sort you out –"

Amalia stood up so quickly that her legs bashed into the table, sending coffee splattering over the sides of everyone's cups. I stepped forward to mop up the mess.

"You're the crazy ones," she spat between clenched teeth, looking at each of John's siblings in turn. "I'll find out which one of you did this, and I'll take you for everything you have!"

"You've already inherited everything we might have had," Marjorie said blandly, wiping the bottom of her coffee cup as she lifted it to take another sip.

Amalia stormed from the room. As the door slammed shut, a lingering unease filled the space she had left behind. I kept my eyes trained on the coffee soaking my cloth, watching the fabric turn from white to brown. Something was tugging at my memory, but I couldn't separate my thoughts clearly enough to get to it.

"That couldn't be true, could it?" Edie said at last. "Someone – someone murdered John?"

"Of course not. When the police show up, they'll confirm what we already know," said Bernadette. "It was an accident."

No one else seemed quite so certain. Bill was glancing around nervously, his tall, thin frame quivering; Edie's face had paled to a shade whiter than white; Marjorie's jaw was locked. Rachel was simply staring down at her coffee, seemingly numb.

"I think I should go tell Cassandra," she said after a moment, standing up. She tucked her curly hair behind her ears. "She needs to know."

"There's nothing stopping her from coming down," Marjorie said, but Rachel had already hurried from the room. Marjorie rolled her eyes. "Well, she's feeling guilty, isn't she?"

"She had nothing to do with this," Bernadette said.

"Of course not," Marjorie replied. "But that doesn't change the fact that she wanted him dead."

The Marlowes turned to look at James, who was struggling to bring his coffee cup up to his mouth in a slow, arduous movement, and an uncomfortable silence rose up around them that wasn't broken until Rachel returned several minutes later.

"Cassandra's not taking it well," she said as she took her seat. "She'd like her breakfast brought up, if you could let Mrs. Tilly know, Alexa."

I left to do so. When I returned, the sisters were still arguing.

"But I never saw John too drunk to know what he was doing," Edie was saying. "He could drink half a bottle of whiskey and still walk straight!"

"And maybe he did walk straight," Marjorie said. "Straight outside."

"But –"

"Maybe Mr. Kneller saw something," Rachel cut in.

"I'm sure Mr. Kneller *has* seen something," Bernadette said in that same carrying whisper, and Rachel's face flushed.

"Why don't you ask him to come over?" Rachel said, turning to me as she pointedly ignored her eldest sister.

"Oh," I said. "Well – sure."

Mr. Kneller lived just an acre away in the guesthouse, a little stone cottage which was only the size of a double garage. It was situated on the edge of the yard against a backdrop of forest trees and soundless air. I climbed up his front steps and rang the bell just as the sun had risen above the trees. He answered a minute later.

"Am I late?" he asked. "Usually they don't need the path cleared until ten or so."

I had only caught glimpses of Kneller in the days that had passed since he had ferried me over to the island, but now that I saw him close up, his skeletal features had softened somewhat, though his skin was still as pale as bone. He was in his seventies, perhaps, with tufts of hair that stuck out wildly all over his head as though he so often pulled his hat from his head that he never bothered to smooth it, and he wore a wide, toothy grin as though he found everything about the world endlessly amusing, including me. I was rather surprised that Bernadette hadn't ordered him to adopt a more solemn expression by now.

"No," I said. "I'm supposed to tell you – Professor Marlowe died."

Kneller frowned.

"John's dead?" He pulled a face, not of remorse, but of concerned interest. "You want a cup of coffee?"

"I –" I began, thrown off guard by his response, "I'm supposed to bring you back to the main house."

"I'm not going over there until I've had my coffee. You want to wait or go ahead?"

I followed him into the kitchen. It was small and cramped, and his table was mostly taken up by a large book that had been propped open.

He poured some coffee into a mug and handed it to me before taking a seat. He indicated the chair across from him.

"How'd John die? Heart attack?"

"We don't know," I said tonelessly. "I just found him out in the snow."

"You say that with such sorrow," Kneller returned, clearly not meaning the words.

I shifted my jaw, debating whether to blame my apathy on numbness, but then decided against it. It wasn't as though Kneller seemed particularly upset, either.

"I'm just telling you what happened," I said.

"Was there some sort of accident?"

"That's what they want to ask you: if you saw anything."

"If I saw a man die outside my window, I like to think I'd walk over and inform his next of kin," Kneller said, his toothy grin returning. "I wouldn't just wait around for them to send the maid over to question me."

"Well, they're going to want to ask you themselves anyway, so you'd better come over."

"Ah, yes, all the Marlowe women together in one room, cross-examining me – it's my lucky day." He gave a gleeful laugh. "*In the room the women come and go, talking of Michelangelo ...*"

I stared at him blankly, though he didn't seem to notice.

"I'm actually a bit excited," he said. "It's not every day I'm invited up to the main house."

"You were just up there a few days ago," I said. "You brought the groceries into the kitchen – remember?"

"That doesn't count: I was ordered, not invited."

"I'm fairly certain you're being ordered now, too," I said, taking a sip of my coffee. "It's not like they're having you over for crumpets and tea."

Kneller waved off my sardonic tone.

"No, those days are over," he mused. "Sylvia used to have me over for tea every Tuesday to help her open the mail – four o'clock sharp. Granted it was because she'd gone completely blind, but I take what I can get."

"So are you coming over?" I asked.

"I will, I will. I'm in no rush, though. I'd rather hear your version before they try and sell me theirs."

"I don't know what you mean," I said, even though I had an inkling that I did. It wasn't as though there was nothing odd about the Marlowe family, with their put-on airs and carefully coined diction, not to mention the lifestyle that was better suited for the 1920s than the 1950s. "I just found him dead outside, and now his family's trying to figure out what happened."

"Have they called the police yet?"

"No. The phone's out."

"Is it? They must not be happy about that."

"Mrs. Carlton is: it's giving her time to eat breakfast," I said without thinking, but before I could worry that I had spoken out of line, Kneller laughed.

"Ah – *there will be time, there will be time,*" he said, raising his cup to me, *"to prepare a face to meet the faces that you meet; there will be time to murder and create, and time for all the works and days of hands that lift and drop a question on your plate; time for you and time for me, and time yet for a hundred indecisions, and for a hundred visions and revisions, before the taking of a toast and tea."*

"Excuse me?"

"T.S. Eliot," he said, tapping the book that lay on the table between us. "He often ruminates about time."

"Oh."

"Oh?" Mr. Kneller echoed, his tone turning incredulous. "'Oh' is all you have to say about the greatest poet of the century?"

I shrugged.

"I don't really like poetry."

"You can't dislike poetry. That's like saying you dislike food just because you have an aversion to green beans."

"Well, I don't like any poem that I've ever read," I said, not grateful for the way he was deciding my feelings for me. If he had been like me, he wouldn't care for poetry, either. "But whatever you say."

I lifted my mug to take another sip of coffee before deciding against it. The lines he had recited were settling into my memory, and though I hated the way they took up space there, I hated the alternative more: forgetting. As the words *time to murder and create* circled back through my thoughts, my mind returned to Amalia's accusation that her husband's siblings had plotted to kill him. The idea sounded like a crazed conspiracy from her mouth, and yet it had just occurred to me what was bothering me about John's death: both the servants' door and the front door in the main house had been locked when I had gone out that morning. If the house had been in its original state then the information wouldn't have meant anything, but I knew for certain that the other four external doors in the house – which I had found in the Sun Room, the Ballroom, the Lounge, and the Cellar when I had first toured the house to memorize its layout – had all been boarded up.

"Something wrong?" Kneller asked, eyeing me over the rim of his mug.

I set my coffee down and leaned toward him.

"Do you think Professor Marlowe could have been murdered?" I asked. My voice carried no emotion. Kneller raised an eyebrow.

"Why would you think that?"

"The doors in the house were all locked. He couldn't have gone out and locked them behind him: not with the deadbolts, at least."

Kneller's eyebrows raised further, and for the first time he genuinely looked surprised.

"Well, that's rather interesting," he hummed. "Is that what the family's saying?"

"No, that's what I'm saying. I haven't told them yet."

"You plan to?" Though his head was bare, he made

a motion as though tipping his hat at me. "You're a brave girl."

"I just think they should know. So do you think it's possible?"

He gave a coarse laugh.

"Do I think it's possible that a man like John could have been murdered in his own house after inheriting millions of dollars that his siblings wished they had?" He drained the rest of his coffee from his mug and stood up. "Why, yes, Alexandra – I do."

He grabbed his coat to put on, then ushered me toward the door, a smile pulling at his face.

"Now let's get over there, or else the murderer might be after us next."

They sat Kneller down and grilled him, then sent him out to shovel the path upon determining that he had seen nothing. It was unclear why the path had to be cleared at all, seeing as the weather was rendering it impossible for him to operate the ferry, but he was out there even so, walking back and forth and back and forth as he scraped the heavy snow from the frozen gravel while more continued to pelt down, clearly much stronger than he looked. I watched him from the window of the Eleanora Room while I was supposed to be cleaning, wondering how and when to relay my thoughts about John's death to the family.

I decided to tell them while they were eating lunch. The Marlowe women had arranged themselves at the table, along with a nervous Bill and disgruntled Amalia, and I had just finished bringing the tray of creamed chicken pasties around the table. While everyone's mouths were occupied chewing rather than speaking, I cleared my throat.

"Mrs. Carlton?"

Bernadette had her eyes fixed on her fork, seemingly counting how many peas were in the bite of food she was about to consume. She ignored me.

"Mrs. Carlton, I wondered if I could bring up –"

"Are we not having wine?" Marjorie asked loudly, cutting me off as she looked around the table.

"It's barely noon," Bill said.

"Tell that to the woman who takes her morning coffee with liqueur," Bernadette informed him.

"I think we should be having wine," Marjorie continued firmly, "given the circumstances."

"The circumstances of your alcoholism?"

"The circumstances of our brother's death, Birdie," Marjorie snapped. She turned to me and flicked her fingers. "Alexa, go get a bottle. Something fortified."

"A fortified wine is hardly appropriate to drink halfway through a luncheon –" Bernadette said, "though I suppose, given your drinking habits, something that strong is akin to soda pop to you ..."

I put my tray down and stepped from the room, leaving them to continue their tiff while I fetched the wine. As I made my way down to the Cellar, though, it occurred to me that I had no idea what a fortified wine was. I grabbed a Riesling and a Madeira and hoped that one of them fit her description, then hurried back upstairs and down the hall to get to the Dining Room before I missed my chance to speak. Just as I neared the door, Lennox stepped out from the opposite hallway toward it, too, causing me to crash into him.

"Sorry," I said, barely managing to stoop and catch the wine bottles before they fell to the floor. I straightened back up and swept back a long coppery strand of hair that had fallen from beneath my cap. Lennox's eyes followed it as I tucked it behind my ear, his brow furrowing.

"Are you going in?" I asked, indicating the door.

His eyes snapped back to my face.

"Yes," he said quickly, but instead he took a step back. "After you."

"Thank you," I said stiffly, wondering why I suddenly felt so awkward. I moved to the door then changed my mind. Turning back to him, I showed him the bottles of wine. "Do you know if either of these are fortified?"

"Madeira is."

"Great," I said in thanks, slipping the Riesling into my apron pocket to stow for later. Lennox raised his eyebrows.

"You want to serve them the fortified one?"

"Mrs. Pickering asked for it."

"Ah."

"You don't think it's a good idea?"

He pulled a face and shrugged.

"I think, given the amount of alcohol they're likely to consume ..." he said carefully, "I'd be inclined to give them the Riesling. Or better yet, a sparkling cider."

"And I'm inclined to agree with you," I said, then added in jest, "– but only if you tell Mrs. Pickering it was your idea."

I turned and pushed into the room with Lennox behind me. As I went to the bar cart and uncorked the Madeira, Marjorie's voice barked over the clinking of silverware.

"What do you think you're doing?"

I halted and looked over at her, but she was talking to Lennox. He paused on his way to an empty chair and put his hands into his pockets.

"I was going to have lunch," he said simply.

"Not with us, you aren't," Marjorie said. "You can go beg Mrs. Tilly for scraps if you're hungry."

"I invited Isidore to join us," Rachel said quickly, glancing between her sister and Lennox. "He's our guest."

"'Guest' implies that one of us invited him," Bernadette said. She nodded to me as I filled Marjorie's wine glass to indicate that she wanted some, too. "He's more of an intruder than anything."

"Well, I invited him for lunch, so he's a guest," Rachel said. "Please sit down, Isidore. Alexa will get you a plate."

"Well, *fine,*" Marjorie said angrily.

"It's probably for the best anyhow, dear," Bernadette told her calmly. "We wouldn't want him roaming the bedrooms while we're all down here ..."

I left the room and circled to the kitchen at the back of the house. Mrs. Tilly was just sitting down to eat when I came in.

"I need another pasty," I said, stopping her before her fork could pierce the one on her plate.

She looked up in annoyance.

"Did you drop one?" she asked.

"No."

"You did, didn't you? I told you to be careful carrying the tray –"

"I didn't drop anything: I just need another one."

"Well, I don't have another one: I made the right amount, and if you did something to one of them, it's on your head."

"You made enough for the family," I corrected, "but I need one for Dr. Lennox."

Mrs. Tilly's expression soured further.

"Oh." She picked her fork back up. "I'm not cooking for that man."

"He needs some food. He's waiting."

"Then share your lunch with him," she said, nodding to the sandwich she had left for me on the counter. It was nothing more than two slices of bread with the rinds of leftover cheese in it. "Better yet, give him the whole thing: you could stand to lose a couple of pounds if you're hoping to ever find a husband, especially at your age."

It was a rich comment coming from her, given that she was as old and stout as the seventy year old case of Guinness in the basement, and yet it still stung me. I crossed my arms.

"Mrs. Langston told me to get him a pasty," I said firmly. "Now, you can either give me yours or I'll go tell her – in your own words – why he's not getting one. It's your choice."

Mrs. Tilly sneered at me, but shoved the untouched plate of food into my hands. I smiled at her before returning to the Dining Room and placing it in front of Lennox. As he thanked me, I straightened and once again tried to get the family's attention.

"Mrs. Carlton," I began again, "I –"

"Is this the only course?" Bernadette asked, staring down at the wilted garnish on her plate, which was all that remained of her lunch.

"I –" I stammered, "I think so. But I was trying to tell you before that –"

"It just doesn't seem like a proper meal," she went on, ignoring me.

I had half a mind to bring her into the kitchen and show her my lunch, but I gave a stiff nod instead.

"That's all that Mrs. Tilly made," I said in a would-be apologetic voice.

"You really can't blame her, Birdie," Rachel said. "It's quite a shock for her, too, I'm sure ..."

"Why should it be a shock for her?" Amalia snapped. "She's just a cook! It's a shock for me!"

"Speaking of which," I hurriedly cut in, "I wanted to tell you that I noticed something about Professor Marlowe's death that I –"

"Servants are to be spoken *to* and not *from,* Alexa," Bernadette chided. "You evidently need more practice in the latter."

I bit my tongue and attempted to silently count to ten, but only made it halfway before trying again.

"It's just that I noticed something concerning Professor Marlowe –"

"I don't want to talk about John right now," Edie said. "Not while we're eating."

"And drinking," Marjorie said, lifting her flute glass and shaking it to inform me that she needed a refill.

I grabbed the bottle and poured her another generous serving, then turned back to Bernadette.

"It's just that I realized when I went out this morning –" I started, but Bernadette waved her hand at me to stop.

"I told you to be quiet, Alexa," she said angrily. "How many times must I tell you before you understand?"

I clamped my mouth shut. If the family had no interest in their brother's death, then I would simply tell the police when they arrived. Just as I stepped back to take my place by the wall, though, Lennox spoke from the far end of the table.

"I'm interested to hear what you have to say," he said, ignoring the Marlowes and looking at me. "You noticed something when you went out, you said?"

"Just because we're letting you eat with us doesn't mean you're allowed to speak, Lennox –" Marjorie began, but Rachel cut her off.

"I'd like to hear what the maid has to say, too," she said, then nodded for me to go on.

I folded my hands behind my back, readying to snap the rubber band around my wrist if I needed to.

"When I went out this morning," I said, almost in awe that I finally had their attention, "I unlocked both the servants' door and the front door."

It didn't garner the reaction I had been intending. Edie and Bernadette glanced at one another while Marjorie and Rachel simply blinked. Only Lennox seemed perturbed by the statement: he shifted in his seat, sitting up a little straighter as he looked at me.

"What does that have to do with my husband?" Amalia snapped.

"Both doors have deadbolts on them," I said, hurrying to explain myself. "If Professor Marlowe went outside and – you know – never came back in, then shouldn't one of the doors have been unlocked?"

The family glanced around the table, each seemingly looking to the others for an explanation as to how it could be possible. From my left, I saw Bill throw an intent look at Lennox as though trying to convey something, but the other man avoided his eyes. I frowned.

"Well, that doesn't mean anything," Marjorie said.

"Yes it does," Amalia said slowly, setting her silverware down. "It means that someone murdered my husband!"

"What?" Edie said, frantically looking around. "Why does it mean that? It's just a locked door –"

"She's saying that if the doors were locked, it means that someone else locked John out there," Marjorie said. Her voice was clipped. "Though I seriously doubt –"

"Why would the door need to be locked at all?" Amalia said. "We're on an island: it's not as though a passerby might come in!"

"My mother always insisted upon it," Bernadette said. "It made her feel safe."

"And I'm sure she feels very safe now," Marjorie said wryly.

"This is proof!" Amalia screeched. "Someone killed my husband!"

"It proves nothing," Bernadette returned. She threw me an irritated look. "The maid's just confused."

"I'm not confused," I said rigidly, but Bernadette

paid me no mind.

"I remember seeing Alexa unlock the front door," Bill said. "So she's telling the truth about that."

"Then she must be confused about the servants' door," Bernadette argued.

"John wouldn't go out the *servants'* door!" Amalia said, looking horrified.

"It's closer to where he was found," Marjorie said.

"He wouldn't go out the servants' door!"

"How do we even know Alexa's telling the truth?" Edie asked. "Maybe she locked the doors before we came down –"

"Why would she lock the doors?" Marjorie asked witheringly. "To make us *think* that John was murdered?"

"Maybe," Edie said. "Maybe she thinks it would be – be funny –"

"Oh, for Christ's sake – it wasn't the maid!" Marjorie said, inadvertently coming to my defense. "It wasn't anybody, probably! John was just drunk!"

"Then why were the doors locked?" Amalia challenged.

Bernadette made an impatient sound and turned to me.

"This is ridiculous," she said. "Alexa's obviously mistaken."

I looked at her steadily. I didn't make mistakes with my memory.

"I'm positive," I said. "The doors were locked."

"Meaning that someone purposefully locked him out there to kill him –!" Amalia said.

"John must have gone out without any of us realizing it," Rachel said, cutting in to moderate the argument in her kind voice, "and then someone locked the door, not realizing he was out there."

There was a halfhearted murmur of agreement.

"So," Rachel persisted, "who locked the door last night?"

No one spoke. Marjorie looked around haughtily, waiting for someone to speak up. Bill was wringing his napkin between his hands, unsure of what to do. Edie still looked terrified. The silence stretched on for several minutes, with everyone appearing to not want to be the first to speak, until –

"If John was locked out," Lennox said quietly, "why didn't he just ring the bell?"

Amalia opened her mouth to shoot off a scathing response, but then seemed to realize she didn't have one and shut it again. Marjorie threw her hands in the air.

"Because he was drunk!" she said. "How many times do I need to say it?"

"Then why were the doors locked?" Amalia and Edie asked in unison.

Before anyone could answer, the Dining Room doors opened and Mr. Kneller popped in. He pulled his hat off as he entered.

"Paths are all done, Mrs. Carlton," he said.

Bernadette's head snapped up, looking startled that Kneller would dare walk inside, let alone without taking his boots off. Her eyes narrowed at the snow dripping on to the floor.

"What about the back patio?" she said. "You're sure it's clear? I want to be able to see the stones."

"Completely," he replied. "Just let me know if you'll be needing anything else today."

"We'll need you to check on the phone – for some reason it's not working. And – " she added as Kneller turned to leave, " – and I think it would be best if you dig John out."

Everyone stared at her.

"Dig him out?" Kneller repeated. He seemed to be

suppressing the urge to make a joke. "And put him ...?"

"With Mother in the Augustus Suite," Bernadette said.

"You can't dig him out!" Amalia said. "If he was murdered, then we should keep him where he is until the police come!"

"At the rate the snow's falling, the police won't be able to find him until May if we leave him be," Bernadette replied. "And if they can't get here before nightfall, then the animals will have him before morning."

Rachel made an odd sound as though she was choking. She stared at her sister.

"Maybe we ought to discuss this first, Birdie," she said. "I don't think it's wise to do anything rash."

"What do you propose? We take a vote?" She rolled her eyes. "All in favor of leaving him be, say 'aye' ... "

No one responded, though I wasn't sure if it was because they disagreed or were too shocked to speak.

"Moving him inside could be problematic," Lennox said. "His body's frozen right now, and if it's not restored to temperature at a proper rate, it could seriously affect the autopsy results."

"The Augustus Suite is plenty cold enough: Mother's body has been keeping well."

"Not for long, though," Marjorie said. "She was supposed to be buried this afternoon."

"Is that not happening?" Edie asked, looking wildly around.

"Of course it's not happening!" Marjorie barked. "Are you completely daft?"

"Thawing a body is a very delicate operation," Lennox said, cutting into their spat. "If he begins to warm up, his outer body will begin to decompose while his organs remain frozen –"

"Well," Marjorie cut in, "if Lennox thinks we

should keep the body outside, then I'm in favor of bringing him in."

"I think Isidore has a good point," Rachel said.

"And what about my point?" Bernadette asked. "An autopsy won't do any good if the body's been ripped apart by rodents –"

Kneller gave a slight bow and took a step back toward the door.

"I'll let you discuss this a bit more," he said. "Just let me know –"

"*No.*"

Bernadette's voice stopped him before he could make his escape. She looked around at her siblings.

"We'll take a vote," she said, raising her hand. "Who's in favor of bringing John inside?"

Marjorie's hand shot up. Amalia hesitated momentarily, then raised hers as well. Rachel, Edie, Bill and Lennox kept their arms at their sides.

"Three to four," Rachel said. "We leave him be –"

"Lennox doesn't get a vote," Marjorie snapped, "so it's three to three."

"Then we're tied," Rachel said. "Unless you want to go ask Cassandra."

"No," came Edie's timid voice, and she shakily raised her hand. "I agree: we should bring him inside." She leaned forward so that she could look at Rachel. "Mother wouldn't want to leave him out there."

Marjorie clapped her hands together.

"Good, then that's settled," she said. "Dig him out, Kneller. Alexa will show you where the body is."

I glanced up as she volunteered me, not happy to have to return to the dead body, but donned my outerwear and led Kneller outside to the uncovered face and red bow tie even so.

"This isn't exactly how I expected my day to go," he

said conversationally as he began to shovel around the body.

I murmured in agreement, unsure if I should retreat back into the house to leave him alone at his task or stay and watch the uncomfortable progression of events. John's face was such an unnatural shade of gray now that he no longer looked human. I wished that they had left his expression buried in the blanket of snow.

Kneller began to speak in a sing-song voice.

"*And the afternoon, the evening, sleeps so peacefully!*" he proclaimed merrily as though it was a routine thing to dig up his employers. "*Smoothed by long fingers, asleep ... tired ... or it malingers, stretched on the floor, here beside you and me ...*"

I kept my eyes on the blade of the shovel, watching as it scooped snow and moved it to the side, slowly uncovering more and more of the dead man.

"*Should I, after tea and cakes and ices, have the strength to force the moment to its crisis?*" Kneller went on, tossing snow to the side as though keeping the meter with the sound, "*But though I have wept and fasted, wept and prayed, though I have seen my head (grown slightly bald) brought in upon a platter, I am no prophet – and here's no great matter –*"

He uncovered the body and knelt down to brush the topmost layer off with his hands.

"*I have seen the moment of my greatness flicker, and I have seen the eternal Footman hold my coat and snicker – and in short, I was afraid!*" he finished, wiping his gloves off on his pants. "That's more of Eliot, by the way."

"I know," I said dispassionately, wondering how he could think it was the proper time to be reciting poetry.

"I thought you didn't read poetry?"

"I don't. I just recognized the imagery from the parts you recited this morning – and the meter." I stopped myself before adding *that you so wonderfully kept with your shovel,* and instead said, "It's an interesting choice of eulogy for an established man like Professor Marlowe. I don't suppose Eliot talks more about murder in the rest of the poem?"

"Nope." He leaned up against his shovel. "So – head or feet?"

"Excuse me?"

"Head or feet?" he repeated, indicating the body. I simply gaped at him.

"I – what?"

"Well I can't carry him up to the master bedroom by myself," he said, "and I doubt any of them are going to help me."

I wasn't sure it was a good enough reason to ask me, and I quickly regretted not going inside when I had had the chance. My stomach turned unpleasantly, and as I imagined grasping John around the wrists to tug him up, the feeling of his fingers on my own wrist came back to me and bile rose in my throat.

"Feet it is, then," Kneller said, deciding for me. He grabbed John below the arms. "Come on then."

I reached down and tentatively grasped the hems of the dead man's tuxedo pants, but upon giving it a pull, I realized that there was no way we would be able to lift him. Even if I had been capable of mustering the strength needed, the body was so stiff and weighed down that we would be lucky to drag him a few inches.

"You're going to have to try a bit harder, Alexandra," Kneller said. "Put your back into it."

"He's – stuck –" I replied, yanking on his ankles to no avail. Kneller watched me impatiently.

Snow crunched somewhere behind me, then a voice called over to us.

"Here – let me."

I turned to see Lennox walking toward us. He took

my place and wrenched John's legs from the snow to lift him. Kneller gave him an irritated look but, seeing as I was useless to him, agreed to his help.

I followed them to the house, hurrying around them to open the door, and then led them up to the Augustus Suite. As they maneuvered John's body onto the window seat, I looked over at where Mrs. Marlowe still laid upon the bed. Her hands laid at her sides and a large silver ring adorned with diamonds and sapphires caught the little light that was in the room. I blinked and snapped the rubber band around my wrist. When I had first seen her there, her hands had been clasped together. Someone must have moved her, I knew, though I couldn't help but imagine that she really was sleeping, just as I had first assumed, and that she would awaken at any moment and chide us for disturbing her slumber.

I ran my hands over my arms to ward off a shiver, then looked over the room to see if anything else had changed. The silk pillows and fur rugs were still in place, though there was an extra pair of women's slippers by the foot of the bed that I hadn't noticed before. They were askew as though someone had kicked them off to get into bed. Cold wind raked in from the window and I was no longer able to suppress my shiver. I clutched my arms, trying to think clearly rather than give into the notion that the house was haunted, but the alternative was no better: that there was something else going on in the house that was strange and frightening, and it would explain exactly how John Marlowe had wound up dead.

"Well, that was enough excitement for me for one day," Kneller said briskly, clapping his hands together as though to rid the death from his palms. "If you'll excuse me ..."

He exited the room and returned downstairs, leaving me and Lennox alone. Lennox was staring down at

John's body with the same troubled frown he had worn upon first seeing him dead. As I observed him, I wondered if he was beginning to suspect the same thing I was; I was certainly hoping so. For if someone truly had killed John, then that meant I was in a house full of people I neither knew nor trusted who might have been the ones to do it, and Lennox was momentarily the only one I had reason to believe was innocent because he had been locked in the nursery when John had died.

I pulled my swing coat further around me, not eager to let the cold creep upon my skin.

"The doors really were locked," I told him. "I'm not confused."

"I believe you."

I took a step closer to him.

"So he must have been murdered," I said.

Lennox hummed. He didn't seem quite as convinced, or perhaps he simply didn't want to believe it was so.

"Or someone else locked the door," he said.

"But if he was just locked out he could have rung the bell, like you said. And even so, why didn't anyone admit to it?"

"Perhaps they were frightened."

My mind flashed back to the odd look Bill had given him at the table, and though I knew that it was possible, it didn't stop me from thinking the worst. John Marlowe hadn't gone out and frozen to death in the snow: it was too coincidental. No, I corrected, too *convenient* for the people who would now hope to inherit his money.

"Perhaps they were frightened because they knew they'd done someone wrong," I argued. "To John."

Lennox glanced up at me, then returned his eyes to the dead man.

"I guess we'll find out," he said. "If there was any

foul play, it'll be found in the autopsy."

"Not if moving the body messes up the results, like you said." I took another step closer. I was now standing only two feet away from him. "Could you tell? You're a doctor."

"Technically, I suppose," he responded uncertainly. "But I haven't done anything akin to an autopsy since medical school, and I certainly don't have the supplies –"

"But you could take a look. See if he's been hit on the head or something."

Lennox stared at me. It was a patient look, though not without hesitation as to why I was so anxious.

"The family wouldn't like that," he said. "They're not particularly fond of me, as I'm sure you've noticed. I think it's best to wait for the police."

"But no one called the police: the phone's out."

"It'll come back on, I'm sure. And if not, then Kneller can go to the mainland and alert them himself."

"Not until the weather gets better." I took a final step toward him so that I was standing directly in front of him. I could feel myself becoming fixated on what had happened to John in a way that had only happened to me once before: when my mother had started to lose her memory. The intense urge to fix what had happened had gripped me for years – and still gripped me now – and I had a feeling that I wouldn't rest until I figured out what had happened to John, just as I wouldn't rest until I did everything that I could for her. And though I couldn't begin to wonder why it was happening now, I couldn't deny that it was exciting – almost freeing – to be able to focus on something new for the first time in over a decade. "Wouldn't you rather know now?"

"I'd rather not get into trouble for tampering with the body," Lennox responded. His tone was gentle but his voice was firm. I sighed.

"Alright."

I stepped past him to get to the window seat.

"Alright what?" he asked.

"Alright, I'll take a look myself."

I leaned over to gaze at the dead man. On the surface he looked more or less intact: there were no cuts or scrapes on his face, nor were any of his limbs bent at an odd angle. To all appearances there was nothing wrong with him – except, of course, his unnatural stiffness and the lack of color in his flesh.

"I don't mean to be rude," Lennox said from behind me, "but I rather doubt you have any idea what you're doing."

I ignored him. My heart was pounding as though I had just run a mile in the cold, and the urge to know what had happened was too strong to suppress. I ran my eyes up and down John's form, trying to detect how he could have been killed. Poison? Strangulation? Blunt force trauma?

"Even if something happened to John," Lennox tried again, "it won't change anything to know at this exact moment."

I put my hand on John's head, no longer repulsed by the thought of touching him as my resolve spurred me on, and pushed back his thinning hair to search for any cuts or bumps on his skin.

"If you're uncomfortable, Dr. Lennox, then you don't have to stay," I said as I forced the dead man's head to the side to check the back of his skull, "– but I'm *not* uncomfortable. I'm curious. I'm perplexed. I'm – quite frankly – a bit angry, because I was counting on John Marlowe staying alive. So if you'll excuse me, I'd like to find out if I should blame the universe for striking him down, or someone under this roof."

I fumbled with John's rigid coat, and the thin layer of ice that clung to it snapped as I pulled it open. The thick wool slumped away to reveal the dead man's chest, which was just a tuxedo coat, vest, crisp white shirt, bow tie and a gold bauble. I frowned and leaned in closer, knowing that he hadn't been adorned with any such ornamentation when I had seen him the previous night. The object upon his chest was surrounded by a dark brown stain.

"I know you have no interest in an autopsy, Dr. Lennox," I said slowly, "but you might want to take a look at this."

I didn't move my eyes from the gold spot on John's chest as Lennox leaned down to see what I was pointing at. The smell of cigarette smoke from his clothing wafted into my nostrils and made my eyes water, but the image of what was in front of me had burned itself into my memory and floated in front of my mind as clearly as ever. The golden bulb was so delicate and embellished that it looked like a Christmas ornament. But it wasn't an ornament. It was the hilt of a knife. The blade of which, I knew, was buried in the dead man's chest.

CHAPTER FOUR

The Marlowe women and Bill gathered around John's body for the second time that day, though this time there was an altered air about them that had nothing to do with the return to their usual attire. Their eyes went from the knife handle sticking out from beneath his tuxedo jacket to his lifeless face, and their breaths came out around them in puffs of white from the frigid air, seemingly waiting for Lennox to backtrack and announce that John had really died of alcohol-induced hypothermia after all. I stood by the dead man's feet with Mrs. Tilly. Her hand was clutched around her necklace and she was rocking back and forth. Kneller was further back in the doorway.

Finally Edie spoke.

"Who else is on this island?"

"It's just us, Edie," Marjorie said, her voice crisp. "You know that."

"No, there must be someone else," Edie said. "A vagrant, a wanderer – someone that Mum hired that we don't know about. That's who did this."

"I've been here for four weeks now," Bernadette said. "There's no one else on this island."

"There must be," Edie said. "None of us killed John!"

"What do you think happened?" Marjorie snapped impatiently. "A madman hijacked a boat, came to the island, stabbed John, then ran off again?"

"He might not've run off," Edie said. "He might still be here –"

"There's no one else on the island, Edie!"

"Maybe we should organize a search, just in case," Bill said, putting a hand on his wife's shoulder. She flinched and pulled away.

"You want to search the island, Bill? Be my guest," Marjorie said. "A foot of snow and thirty acres of woods sounds like great exercise."

"Maybe this isn't what it looks like," Rachel said. "Maybe – maybe John just fell – "

"Oh yes, maybe John just *fell* backwards while holding a knife in the middle of the yard, and it *plunged* into his chest, killing him – "

"You're not helping, Marjorie!"

"Neither is standing here pretending that this is something that it's not!" Marjorie countered, her cheeks growing redder than her hair. "Someone killed John, and last time I checked, there were only eleven possible suspects!"

"Twelve, actually," I corrected automatically.

The family turned to look at me.

"No, eleven," Marjorie said, "because I know it wasn't me!"

"Well, it wasn't any of us, either," Rachel said. "And James certainly couldn't have done it."

James was still downstairs in his wheelchair. As the siblings continued to echo that they weren't killers, either, I glanced around at everyone's faces. Marjorie was belligerent, Bernadette quizzical, Rachel pained, Edie terrified, Bill tense, Lennox rigidly composed, Mrs. Tilly disbelieving, and Kneller mildly amused. Amalia was downright livid.

As Lennox looked over and caught my eye, I quickly turned away. I had the feeling that he had been taking a similar survey of expressions, and I wondered what he had decided mine was. Unmoved, perhaps. Or unsympathetic, or uncaring, or unemotional, or detached. It didn't matter: I had heard them all numerous times before.

"It had to have been you," Amalia said, looking shakily at Rachel. "You've wanted this ever since – ever since what happened!"

Rachel looked half flabbergasted, half sickened.

"I would never –" she began, " – *never* have hurt John. He was my brother. My *twin*. It was – we all know it was a – an – an accident –"

"Everyone knows it wasn't you, Rachel," Bernadette said. "Amalia's just upset."

"Of course I'm upset!" Amalia exclaimed. "I'm – I'm – I'm too young to be a widow!"

"Don't flatter yourself: we all know you're nearly sixty, despite what you claim," Marjorie said. "And I, for one, think it's interesting that Lennox here just showed up out of the blue, and suddenly our brother is killed."

"It couldn't have been Dr. Lennox," I said, correcting her before I could stop myself. Lennox glanced at me, his mouth still open with the intention of defending himself. I avoided his eyes.

"Oh?" Bernadette said, looking toward me and drawing out the word for much longer than necessary, her large midsection swelling as she went. "And how do you know that, Alexa?"

"Because I locked him in the nursery last night."

Raised eyebrows met me from all directions, and Bill sent me an odd look as though he thought me a liar. Lennox closed his mouth. His expression shifted uncertainly for a moment, but then he appeared quite relieved.

"You locked his door?" Bernadette asked. "And where did you get the key? I don't remember issuing you one."

"I took it from the Pantry."

"Oh? So you *stole* it?"

"No, I just wanted to lock his door –"

"And why *would* you lock his door?" Marjorie asked.

"Because I wasn't about to sleep in an adjoining room with a stranger," I said. I folded my hands behind my back and then added, "I didn't think it would be proper."

Marjorie crossed her arms.

"You're in the nanny's room, you mean? Whose idea was that?"

"Tilda hasn't been able to collect all of her belongings from the maid's room yet," Bernadette said. "John didn't think it was fair to let her replacement rummage through her things, so he had me put her in there."

"Well, that's very close quarters," Marjorie said, her voice dripping with disdain. "You two must have been comfortable."

"I'm not sure it matters who's sleeping where," Rachel said quickly, though her ever-present smile was a bit tighter than usual. "The point is, Isidore had nothing to do with this."

"And who did, then?" Edie said. "It wasn't one of us!"

"Of course it wasn't," Marjorie said. She looked at Amalia. "It was you!"

"Me?" Amalia exclaimed. "I wouldn't – I had no reason to – I didn't kill my husband!"

"You're the one who gets his life insurance and newfound fortune," Marjorie said.

"Not if you contest the will!" Amalia returned. "We all know your mother wanted the money to go to a male heir, and I don't have any sons!"

"It's not my fault you stopped procreating after two," Marjorie said. "You were more worried about your figure than your lineage –"

"I never expected John to die right after Sylvia!"

"Come to think of it," Bernadette said, reaching down into the container of biscuits on Mrs. Marlowe's bedside table and taking one out to munch on, "wouldn't the Uniform Simultaneous Death Act come into play?"

"The what?" Amalia asked.

"The Uniform Simultaneous Death Act," Bernadette repeated, her words barely audible between the crunching of the cookie in her teeth. "It states that if two people die within 120 hours of one another, they're legally both said to have predeceased the other."

"What's that supposed to mean?"

"That John wouldn't inherit Mother's fortune."

Amalia's face twisted unnaturally in anger. Her hands clamped around the ends of her hair, and she looked ready to yank it from her head.

"He *what?*" she whispered dangerously.

"It's just the law, dear," Bernadette said unsympathetically. "No need to get upset –"

"So you did do this!" she screeched, looking around at her sisters-in-law. "This is exactly what you wanted! For the estate to be split up among the rest of you –!"

"It won't be split up among any of us if the will states it has to go to a male heir," Bernadette said matter-of-factly. "If anything, it would go to Bill."

Bill gave a startled shake of his head. He pushed his glasses up the bridge of his crooked nose and swallowed, suddenly looking like he wanted nothing more than to crawl next to Mrs. Marlowe and play dead until the conversation was over. From the way Amalia's eyes had narrowed on him, I hardly blamed him.

"Oh, well – I don't – I never expected –" he stuttered.

"She wouldn't leave it to Bill," Amalia said scathingly. "He doesn't have any children – nor will he."

She threw her brother-in-law a withering look, but it was Edie whose cheeks burned, sending red blotches over her white skin.

"Well, that's the only option –" Bernadette said, but Marjorie cut her off.

"No, that's not the only one," she said in a low voice. Her eyes went to Lennox. Her sisters' followed.

"She wouldn't leave it to *him,*" Amalia said in disgust. "He's not a part of this family!"

"You know how he wormed his way into Mother's good book –"

"Why don't we just wait until Mr. Brookings can go over the will with us?" Rachel cut in with her forced-calm tone. "I'm sure there's no point in getting upset over something until we know exactly what we're dealing with."

"I know exactly what I'm dealing with," Marjorie snapped, her eyes still on Lennox, but then she turned to Kneller. "Kneller, I'm ready to go home. Get the ferry ready, will you?"

"Yes, ma'am," he said, pushing from the door frame and leaving to do so.

"You can't just leave!" Amalia insisted. "Not until the police come! No one's leaving!"

"Feel free to give them my address," Marjorie said, already turning from the room. "I'm not staying here another night."

She plowed from the room, knocking Bill with her shoulder as she went. As we watched her disappear down the hallway and into her room, Edie gave a violent shiver. She clutched her bony arms, then briskly followed her sister out of the room.

"Get your things," she shot at Bill as she passed. "We're leaving, too."

"You can't leave!" Amalia screeched again, but Edie had already hurried off. Bill slunk after her. Amalia turned to the rest of us, daring us to announce our departures next, but no one did. Her hands had clenched into fists, and she shook with anger as she stormed from the room. Rachel muttered that she had to check on James before following, and then Bernadette gave a loud huff and left, too.

I looked over at Lennox. His face was still void of emotion. I tried to think of something to say to him, but before anything could come, a voice rasped from behind me.

"Why couldn't you have just left him out there in the snow?"

Mrs. Tilly was standing at the foot of Mrs. Marlowe's bed, clutching one of the posts with a white-knuckled hand. Her eyes were glued to John's body.

"What?" I said.

"Why didn't you just let him disappear? It would have been better that way." She uncurled her hand, but she was still quivering from head to toe. "You keep those curtains closed, now – or the Devil'll send a moonbeam down to steal Mr. Marlowe's soul."

"Assuming he has a soul," I replied, and Mrs. Tilly's eyes snapped up to me. She gave me a long, ugly stare and tore from the room. I crossed my arms and looked over at Lennox. He was staring at me with an odd look in his eyes.

"What?" I asked him. "Do you think she's right?"

"About the devil?"

"No. About leaving him out in the snow."

His gaze returned to John. I followed it, and for a moment as I stared at the body, I saw the juxtaposing images of how he had smiled so widely when he had offered me the job and how his expression had turned monstrous when he had rushed down the stairs toward me the night before. I couldn't contend with who he had been, nor with what had happened.

"I don't know what to think," Lennox said at last.

I started toward the door. Lennox's voice called after me.

"Are you leaving?"

"No." I pulled off the gloves I was still wearing and

shoved them into my pocket. "I'm going to check the phone line."

"Why?"

"Because I want to know what I'm dealing with."

I marched from the room and went outside, circling to the back of the house. The junction box was on the patio that Kneller had just shoveled. Yanking the door open, I ran my fingers down the various wires, searching for one that was no longer intact. It only took me a moment to find it: it was severed in two pieces. One piece came from the top, the other from the bottom. The entire middle section had been removed. My mouth twitched as I looked at it. We would have to go directly to the police station to get help after all. I went back to the house to inform Kneller.

He was already on the front porch when I arrived.

"I'd like a ride, too," I said, pulling out my gloves.

He shook his head.

"I need to," I said, tugging the gloves on. "I have to go to the police station –"

"No one's going anywhere."

"We have to. The phone line's been cut –"

Marjorie came out onto the porch. She was wearing her thick fur coat and had a scarf wrapped around her head to protect her ears from the cold, windy ferry ride.

"My bags are upstairs," she said to Kneller. "Second door on the left."

"I can't take you back to the mainland, ma'am," Kneller said.

"What are you talking about?" Marjorie said sharply. "What have Birdie and Amalia said? They can't hold me here against my will –!"

"The ferry's gone."

Marjorie and I stared at him.

"What do you mean, 'gone'?" she said.

"Gone, as in *not here*," Kneller said. "It's not at the

dock."

"Well, this is just – this is just –" She threw her hands in the air and marched back into the house. Her shrill voice rang out from the Foyer. "Birdie! Rachel! Edie! Get down here!"

I dropped my gloves down to the porch. My stomach sank with it. Marjorie was waving her arms around as she shrieked at her sisters.

"The ferry is gone!" she said. "Gone! Vanished!"

"Well, then that proves it!" Edie said, crossing her arms over her chest as though to protect herself from another impending knife attack. Bill had come out of the Study at the sound of their voices. He fumbled with his eyeglasses as he listened. Amalia stood in the doorway to the Parlor, her arms crossed rigidly. Out of the corner of my eye, I saw Lennox on the stairs, though he stayed on the second floor landing. "Someone else was here, killed John, then fled!"

"And how did they get here, might I ask?" Marjorie said. "Did they stow away on the ferry?"

"Well – yes! Yes, I imagine they did!"

"So a vagrant stowed away on Frank's ferry without him noticing – despite being as big as a Cord Cabriolet with no room to hide – and then came here, hid, killed our brother, and fled back on the ferry?"

"It's the only logical explanation!"

"Says the woman who was frightened of a ghost the other night," Marjorie said, her voice dripping with scorn.

"Just because you don't believe in things doesn't mean they're not real!"

"Don't get upset, Edie," Rachel said. "We're all under a lot of stress –"

"If I may, ma'am," Kneller said, stepping forward to cut her off. "It's possible that no one took the ferry, but that the storm set it off into the ocean."

"Just like the storm knocked the phone line out?" Marjorie retorted. "You've tied the boat up in storms hundreds of times, Frank! Someone set it out into the ocean!"

"On purpose?" Bill asked. "Why?"

"To keep us all here," Marjorie said, her eyes boring into her eldest sister's. "Isn't that what you wanted, Birdie?"

"That doesn't mean I set the ferry loose. I wouldn't even know how to do that."

"It can't be much more difficult than operating a car," Marjorie said. "You've seen Kneller operate it more than anyone –"

"This is getting out of hand," Rachel said. "We can't keep blaming one another for something that none of us would do –"

"Where were you last night, Kneller?" Amalia cut in. "You would have an easy time sneaking outside – no one would have heard you from the main house."

"I was in my bed, alone," Kneller said. "And in case you're hoping to accuse me further, remember that whoever killed your husband locked the doors of the main house with a deadbolt behind them."

Amalia drew herself up haughtily so that her nose was an inch above his.

"How did you know that?" she asked.

"Your maid told me," he replied.

"Did she?" she said, turning her cold stare to me.

"I told him what had happened when I went to get him earlier," I said. "I didn't think –"

"Don't worry, Alexa," Bill said kindly. "No one thinks you did this."

"Speak for yourself," Amalia said. "She's a more likely culprit than the rest of us!"

"Oh, for Christ's sakes –" Marjorie said. "She's the maid!"

"The maid that John hired!" Amalia screeched back. "Who knows where he found her! She probably got one look at the estate and – and –"

"Decided to stab him and take his wallet?" Marjorie finished blandly.

Amalia fumed.

"No one would hurt John," Rachel said, cutting in hurriedly. "I'm sure of it."

"But that's just it, Mrs. Langston," Kneller said. "We don't know that no one would kill your brother, so we're all going to be a bit on edge until we discover who did it."

"None of my siblings would kill John," Rachel said firmly.

"Well then, I guess that leaves you with five suspects," Kneller returned. "Me, Lennox, your sister-in-law, the cook and the maid ... and two of us have alibis. What do you propose to do about it?"

"I'm not sure either of you have an alibi," Marjorie said. "Just because the doors were locked doesn't mean anything. You might have gone through the window for all we know!"

"No one went through a window," Bernadette said with a tone that suggested no one could be so low class. "The shutters were closed and locked from the inside because of the storm. I oversaw Alexa do it myself."

"Not all of the windows have shutters!"

"All of the windows that *open* do," Bernadette said. "Mother made sure of it. She wanted to make certain that no one could sneak in without her knowing. And the nursery doesn't even have a window anymore, so Lennox would have had to have had a key to get out."

Edie gave a horrible shudder as though the thought of the nursery was too disturbing to stand.

"Well, maybe he did have a key," Marjorie said.

"There's the master key!"

"The master key went missing ages ago," Bernadette said. "So unless you think he's been hanging onto it for all these years –"

"He could have picked the lock," Amalia said. "And then re-picked it to lock himself in again!"

"That makes him sound like *quite* the criminal mastermind," Bernadette said. "I would think a man that clever would find a better way to kill someone."

"What's that supposed to mean?" Amalia said.

"Just that stabbing a man and leaving him in the snow is rather flagrant. If he was trying to kill John in the hopes of getting the inheritance, you'd think he'd want to make it look as though he'd died of natural causes – something a doctor ought to know how to do."

"Or a nurse like you, Birdie," Marjorie shot.

"It doesn't matter how he died!" Amalia said. "The fact is that he's dead!"

"It does matter, Amalia," Bernadette chided. "Millions of dollars aren't going to help Lennox if he's sitting in a jail cell."

"He probably thought he could get away with it!"

"I think I'll go check the phone again," Bill said hurriedly, but I stopped him.

"Don't bother: the line's been cut. I just checked it."

"I – what?" he spluttered. "No, it can't be –"

"Christ Almighty!" Marjorie shrieked. "When I find out who did this, I'll see you laying in the Augustus Suite next to John!"

"And when I find out who did it," Amalia added, "I'll help her!"

"Assuming it wasn't either of you," Bernadette said.

"I had no reason to kill John!" Amalia screamed, her golden skin deepening with red and her hair flying up around her face wildly, but her words were peppered by someone else's chuckle. Everyone turned to look at Kneller, who couldn't quite hide his amusement behind his hand.

"You think this is funny?" Marjorie asked.

"No, no," Kneller said, though the smile still tugging at his lips begged to differ. He nodded to Amalia. "I just thought your choice of words was ... interesting."

"And what's that supposed to mean?"

Kneller lifted his chin, and his skeletal cheekbones jutted out as he raised his eyebrows.

"I just think, if we're being perfectly honest," he said, "then we should all admit one thing: everyone here wanted John dead, for one reason or another."

Amalia's face twisted, but it was Rachel who spoke.

"You're out of line, Frank."

"And you're in denial if you think it's not true," he returned. "We all got something out of his death, whether it's the inheritance or just the lack of his presence on this earth."

"Get out!" Rachel said. She was white and shaky. Bill laid a hand on her arm in an attempt to calm her. "Go back to the guesthouse if you're – you're just going to – to –"

"To point out what everyone's thinking but no one will say?" he finished for her.

"Just because we didn't like John doesn't mean we wanted him dead," Bernadette said matter-of-factly. She ran her hands over her large stomach, smoothing out the wrinkles in her dress. "And the only person who would kill him is whoever's next in line to inherit."

"Unless John's death was only the first," Edie whispered.

"Don't be ridiculous," Marjorie snapped. "The killer can hope to get away with one murder, but they're not going to get away with slaughtering half the family!"

Creaking came from the staircase. Lennox had

moved from the landing onto the topmost step. He slowly made his way down the stairs, but Amalia moved to block him from the Foyer.

"You did this," she breathed. "You bring death wherever you go."

Lennox looked at her carefully.

"A gross exaggeration, Amalia," he replied. "Now, if you'll excuse me, I'd like to have a cigarette."

She glared at him without moving, holding her ground for so long that I thought for sure he would push past her, but he simply waited, and waited and waited, and finally she stepped aside. He crossed the room and went out the front door. As it shut behind him, the cold air that had slipped in rushed over us, and a collective shiver went around the room.

His departure ended the conversation. Edie rushed back upstairs, and Rachel turned on her heel and returned to the Drawing Room. I took my chance to escape next, crossing behind Bernadette and Marjorie to get to the stairs, and made my way to the third floor. I went to the nanny's room and took a seat on the bed instead, rubbing my palms against my temples as I tried to think of what to do. But there was nothing to do, I realized. The choice had been made for me by someone unknown, and I was staying on the island and in the house with a murderer for an indefinite period of time. The only thing to decide was what to do about it.

Hide, was my initial thought. Hide in my room, or in a separate part of the house, and hope that someone somehow knew to send help our way. Yet already the task made me feel useless, and something was tugging at me to do more – to help myself, *save* myself – though I didn't know what that would be. As Kneller's words floated back to me, suggesting that all of us had wanted John dead, I gripped my sheets tightly and tried to decide if that was true.

For if John had truly planned to go through on his promises to me, then his death was more disadvantageous than I could stomach; but if he had only brought me to the island in the hopes of having his way with me, then I was only sorry that he hadn't died before I had been dragged all the way out to the island.

The uncertainty of it all, though, made it feel as though a disease had settled in my chest and was eating away at me from the inside out. I reached for the bottle of prescription medication on my bedside table and uncapped it, then tapped out four pills even though it was too early to take any. My thoughts were running through what had happened, flooding me with the broken images of John's face swaddled by the snow and the ornate handle sticking out of his chest. I pulled off my cap and tossed it at the foot of the bed, changed into my nightgown, then undid my hair so that I could lay comfortably back on the pillow as I waited for the medication to take effect. A solution would come as soon as my mind had time to rest, I told myself.

The familiar feeling of ease came over my head several minutes later as though clouds had been piped into my brain to momentarily hide my thoughts from my mind's view, and yet I frowned. There was something bothering me about the knife that I had seen sticking out of John's chest. I had seen the ornate gold pattern somewhere before, though I couldn't place where. Not the dining room or kitchen: the former only had sterling silver utensils, and the latter's had wooden handles. Yet I was certain – certain – that I had seen the exact etchings somewhere. I tried to pull open the drawers to the filing cabinets in my head, but the fog created by the medication was too thick now, and I couldn't sort through my stored thoughts.

A knocked sounded on the door and Lennox called through the wood, asking if he could enter.

I didn't respond. My mind was elsewhere.

He stepped over the threshold and then halted in shock. For a moment I thought he might have been embarrassed to see me there in my nightclothes, but from the way his olive skin had paled and his pupils had dilated, his expression looked more frightened than anything. One of his hands was still on the doorknob, seemingly incapable of letting go, and when he spoke, there was a slight waver in his voice that contrasted sharply to his usual tone.

"Alexandra?"

I lifted my heavy eyelids slightly to look at him. The pills were rendering me careless.

"Yes?"

"I –" He wrenched his hand from the doorknob and folded his arms together instead. "Are you alright?"

I felt that I ought to have been the one asking him the question: he looked more unsettled than he had when he had first seen John dead.

"I found a man dead out in the snow this morning," I said tonelessly. "Then I found a knife in his heart. Am I supposed to be alright?"

"I only meant –" he began, but he was having trouble focusing on the words. His eyes kept running over my disheveled hair and face, searching for something unknown. Emotion, I guessed, judging from the fact that he couldn't seem to find it. "I just – you looked – never mind."

He glanced at the glass bottle on the bedside table.

"I'll leave you be," he said hurriedly, then crossed to the nursery. He was just a blur, and as his muddled form disappeared behind the door, I wondered what had brought him to Exeter Island. He wasn't family, so who was he? Mrs. Marlowe's psychiatrist? And why had Amalia said that death followed him wherever he went?

I let my eyes close completely. The family was too secretive, too closed off, to know what was going on at any given moment. There were underlying meanings in everything that they did or said, and I couldn't hope to understand them any more than I understood myself.

The room went black even though it was still daytime. Out of the shadows of my dreams, Mrs. Marlowe sat up from her bed in the Augustus Suite and scolded me for failing to save her. Her face was still frozen by death and only her mouth moved, and when I tried to apologize her lips parted to reveal fangs that threatened to sink down into my skin. I tried to run from her, but the windows in the room had been boarded up like the one in the nursery, and when I looked back at her she had become my mother, though she asked the same question: *Why can't you help me?*

It was nighttime when I woke. My head lurched and my body swayed as I got to my feet, and I fumbled to get to the door. My shoulder smacked the wall as I walked down the hall to get to the bathroom, and when I reached it and yanked the chain to turn the light on, it was so bright that I thought I would be sick. I quickly turned it off again and fumbled my way though the darkness to go to the bathroom, then turned the water on full blast in the sink to wash my face, wishing that I could wash away the image of my mother along with it.

Forget about it, I told myself, but the words didn't help. There was nothing worse than forgetting. I didn't lift my head, frightened that if I looked in the mirror, I would see her resemblance staring back at me in my down-turned eyes and frowning lips. John's words rang back at me. *Who will take care of her when your aunt no longer can?* Because he was right: it wouldn't be me – not if I had no money and no means of supporting her.

I straightened up and glared at the outline in the mirror. Whoever had killed John Marlowe had ruined my life. They had taken the last chance of many last chances that I had struggled to get, and I wasn't going to leave the island empty-handed. If I couldn't get back into my doctorate program, then the very least I could do was find out who had killed him and make sure, when the police finally arrived, that they would be imprisoned for the rest of their life the way that I refused to be imprisoned by what they had done.

I left the bathroom and went downstairs to have a cigarette, smoking quickly to avoid standing outside for too long. The wooden mermaid in the pillar beside me eyed me as I stood there, and I threw her a wary glance back. She looked more alive than I had felt in a long time – but that was because she was made of wood, I reasoned, whereas I, as far as anyone knew, was made of stone.

I returned to the Foyer and climbed the stairs to the second floor. The darkness was disorienting, and my head felt light and woozy from the nicotine and medication. When I reached the landing and turned to go to the next staircase, something opposite me flickered in my blurred vision.

A woman, covered from head to toe in a long black veil that fell over a gown of the same color, was gliding along the hallway. Her dress was adorned with beads that made a clinking sound as she walked as though she was chained at the ankles, and on her hands, diamonds and sapphires glinted from a ring that had caught the low light of the wall sconces. A ring that I had just seen, only hours before, on the hand of the dead woman in the Augustus Suite.

CHAPTER FIVE

"Mrs. Marlowe?" I asked.

The woman in black paused and looked over at me.

"Yes?" she answered. Her voice was soft and childlike – innocent, almost, but not quite: perhaps simply naive. It was the same partially British accent that the rest of the Marlowes spoke with.

"I ..." I began, having not expected her to respond. I wished I hadn't taken the medication. My head was pounding and the logical thinking that usually steered my mind had been pushed off course, and for a moment I felt truly unsure as to whether or not I was actually seeing a ghost. As I blinked, though, the uncertainty vanished. "Goodnight."

"Goodnight," she returned, then slipped through the door to the Augustus Suite and closed it behind her.

I turned and walked up the stairs to the third floor, then followed the hall to my room. Once inside, I took a seat on my bed, forcing myself to think rationally.

She was dead. I had seen her laying in the bed in the Augustus Suite on numerous occasions. I had seen her – I had *smelled* her. It was impossible for the figure in the hallway to be real, which meant one of two things: that I was seeing things, or that someone was playing a trick on me. And both of those thoughts, I found, made me very uneasy.

I fumbled for the bottle of pills on my nightstand and snapped the rubber band against my wrist to remember how many I had taken. Four, just like always, I was sure. Taking them early wouldn't have had such an adverse effect on my brain, and even if I had taken too many, they wouldn't cause hallucinations. I made to replace them on the table, but they slipped off the edge and fell to the floor with a shatter that rang out in the quiet of the night. Glass skated across the floor and the pills followed in every direction.

"Alexandra?"

Lennox was calling through the door. He twisted the handle and let himself into my room. I hadn't locked his door.

"I'm fine," I said quickly, hopping down from my bed and hurrying to pick up the pills, but it was so dark that I could barely see them. Lennox's footsteps creaked as he stepped further into the room, and a moment later the light flicked on. I didn't turn to face him, instead focusing on picking out each white pill from beneath the glass. He stooped to help me.

"I'm fine," I repeated, placing a handful of the medication on the nightstand.

He wordlessly added the remainder of the pills to the pile I had started. I grasped at the neckline of my nightgown, wishing that I had put on my dressing gown.

Lennox glanced around the room.

"I thought I heard someone come in here," he said.

"No, that was just me. I went out for a smoke."

I stood up. Lennox remained crouched on the floor with the glass. He raised his eyebrows.

"At this time of night?" he asked.

"I needed a cigarette."

"I'm sure you did; I'm just surprised that you would wander the house at this time, given what happened last night."

"Whoever killed John isn't going to kill me."

"You don't know what they might do. And everyone in the house is on edge: you might have startled someone and gotten attacked for it."

"I appreciate your concern, Dr. Lennox, but I

wasn't attacked, and I have no intention of being attacked, either."

Lennox put his hands on his knees and pushed himself up. His pants were wrinkled and his shirt was unbuttoned as though he had just thrown it on over his undershirt; he must not have brought nightclothes for what was supposed to be a short stay.

"I only meant that you might want to be more careful," he said, his voice low.

"Whoever killed John isn't going to kill me," I repeated. "They have no reason to."

"How can you be sure of that? You don't know who killed him: you don't know what they're after. I heard the cook tell you that you should have left him out in the snow – what if that was what the killer intended? And you found him and messed up their plans? Then, on top of that, insisted that he was murdered and found out how?"

"So I should have just kept my mouth shut? Funny how men always think that's the best thing for women to do."

Lennox leaned in closer to me. His voice was still barely more than a whisper.

"I have no qualms about your boldness: I think it's admirable. But there's a time and place for it, and this is neither. Someone on this island killed John, and if they're willing to do that, then they're probably willing to do whatever's necessary to ensure that their plan is successful."

He shifted slightly, his bare feet dangerously close to stepping on the glass. I lifted my eyes to his.

"That's good advice," I said, "though I don't know why you're giving it to me."

He didn't seem to understand. Perhaps it was the nature of his profession to offer guidance, though the way he said it made me uncomfortable. It was as though he thought he knew me well enough to do so. He certainly seemed to think he knew me well enough to walk into my room in the middle of the night.

"I'm trying to help you," he replied.

"Why? For all you know, I could be the killer."

"I –" he began, caught off guard by my bluntness. "I suppose you could be. Though if you were, then I don't know why you would have given me an alibi. If anything, you should have said that you saw me leaving the room last night and had everyone think I was the one who did it."

He turned away from me, carefully stepping around the broken glass to get back to his room. The strange figure from downstairs was still flitting in and out of my thoughts, and for the briefest of moments, I had the urge to ask him to stay.

"Do you think something else is going on here, Dr. Lennox?" I said suddenly, stopping him as he entered the nursery and made to close the door.

He glanced up at me, half-hidden in the shadows of his light-less room, and a frown pulled at his brow.

"Something other than a murder, you mean?"

I gave him a halfhearted shrug. I couldn't hope to explain it without sounding paranoid, but I was beginning to feel like everything that had happened since I had arrived on the island was all part of a plan that had been masterminded solely to toy with me: having my wages stolen, finding Mrs. Marlowe dead, knowing that John had lied to me about the job, being put in the room with Lennox, finding John dead, seeing a supposed ghost of the family matriarch ...

"It just seems like there have been an awful lot of odd coincidences since I arrived here," I clarified.

Lennox gave a slow, thoughtful nod.

"Yes," he said. "It certainly does."

He shut the door between us. I sat back on my bed, not bothering to turn off the light as I stared at the wood separating us. On the one hand, it eased my thoughts ever so slightly to know that he found something off about our current situation; yet on the other hand, it bothered me that he hadn't explained himself any further.

I snapped the rubber band against my wrist, hoping that my thoughts would organize and rearrange all of the strangeness into something that made sense to me. When they failed to do so, though, I let out a long sigh and leaned back against my pillow. And it occurred to me, as I drifted back into an uneasy sleep, that there was nothing straightforward about the Marlowe family.

***

"Wake *up*."

Someone was prodding my shoulder, and I leaped out of bed and fell onto the floor. Mrs. Tilly was standing at my bedside with a scowl on her face.

"The family is due to eat in ten minutes," she said. "You were supposed to be down hours ago – and I'm not covering your duties again."

"What?"

"I can't cook *and* serve," she said irritably. "Some of us actually work for our salaries."

I pushed myself to my feet and stood up, shaking myself from my grogginess. Someone had cleaned the glass from the floor, though I doubted that it was Mrs. Tilly.

"Really?" I said. "My mistake: I thought you just made money by taking it out of other people's wages."

Mrs. Tilly's coal-like eyes narrowed.

"Yes, and quite a bundle it was, wasn't it?" she said. "Mr. Marlowe must have been very pleased with your ... services."

She held up the worn brass key that locked my room.

"I'll be taking this back," she said. "Unless there's a particular reason you need to lock your door?"

I narrowed my eyes.

"Only to keep you out."

"Well, feel free to ask Mrs. Carlton if you can have it back – but I wouldn't waste your time. She was the one who told me to get it back from you." She nodded down to the key to the nursery that was still on the nightstand. "You can keep that one, though. No one minds having that man locked up."

When she left, I put my uniform on, shoving the frilly cap over my head and pulling my stockings up just beneath where the money was strapped to my thigh. I was glad that I had kept it there; she would have undoubtedly snatched the rest of it had it been laying in the nightstand drawer with the keys.

I hurried down the hallway and staircase, momentarily contemplating that the ghostly figure might have been Mrs. Tilly's idea of a joke – but as much as I would have liked another reason to despise her, she was far too short and stubby to be the figure beneath the black veil. All I could hope was that whoever was trying to scare me would give up after seeing my lackluster reaction to their costume.

Yet as I reached the Foyer and saw the ghost gliding down the opposite staircase to my left, it was clear that that would not be the case after all.

"Ah, so you've decided to come down," came a loud voice from below, and I looked over the banister to see Bernadette addressing the ghost from the Foyer. She didn't seem remotely frightened by it, and instead cast a disapproving look in its direction as though she was often met with the inconvenience of the dead getting up from their funeral beds, and was simply wondering if she should shepherd it back to its room or wait until after breakfast.

"Well, I suppose that means the table will need to be set for nine again," Bernadette said. "Such a shame: an even number is much more pleasant on the eye ... Though lovely to see you, of course, Cassie."

The ghost gave her a nod and waltzed past her in the direction of the Breakfast Room. As Bernadette made to follow her, she finally took notice of where I stood on the steps.

"Well?" she berated. "Don't just stand there, you lazy girl – come set the table!"

She waddled off, though I didn't follow her immediately. I was too busy feeling foolish for thinking with such certainty that someone had been trying to delude me when I ought to have realized that it was Cassandra: she was the only person in the house whom I hadn't yet met. It occurred to me now that I had heard her high, clear voice on the first day I had arrived at the house. I snapped the rubber band against my wrist several times, harder and harder, angry with myself for being so stupid and for forgetting such a recent memory, and fearful of how befuddled the pills had made me that I hadn't realized it right away. I had to be more careful, especially given the circumstances. The medication was just to give me enough reprieve from my thoughts to let me sleep, and I couldn't take advantage of taking them without them taking advantage of me in return.

I descended the remaining stairs and went to the buffet table to retrieve plates and silverware with which to set the table, still debating if I ought to have been following orders anymore at all when all I wanted to do was find out who had killed John. The fact that the family was still eating meals together rather than actively trying to find a way off the island and away from which one of them had killed him irked me and disturbed me all at once, as though each one of them was acting that way on purpose to conceal the fact that were the murderer. My hand clenched around the bundle of forks and knives and I peered over my shoulder to where the family was settling down at the table to eat, and as my eyes ran over them, I opened the files for them that I had created in my head in which I stored every memory of them, more determined than before to figure out which of them had done it.

"I see Mrs. Tilly's making quite the elaborate breakfast," Bernadette said as I laid the silverware. "I suppose I should be happy that not all my staff have succumbed to laziness."

She indicated the unfinished table.

"She's probably just worried that the murderer will do her in if she doesn't cook well enough," Marjorie replied. She looked over at her black-veiled sister. "I see you've decided to join us, Cassie."

Cassandra turned in her direction.

"I felt, given the circumstances, that it was best for us all to be together," she said. "What with losing both Mother and John."

"That and the fact that I banned Mrs. Tilly from sending any more food to her room," Bernadette said in her carrying whisper, leaning toward Marjorie.

I went and filled the coffee pot, poured Bernadette her usual cup of cream and tablespoon of coffee, then approached Cassandra.

"Would you care for some coffee, *Mrs. Marlowe?*" I asked politely, emphasizing the name that she had responded to when I had addressed her twice before.

"*Miss* Marlowe," Bernadette corrected. "Cassie's not married – and she's a Marlowe by birth. *Mrs. Marlowe* would be incestuous."

"She was Mrs. Marlowe last night," I said, causing Bernadette's eyebrows to raise. Cassandra gave a little chuckle.

"You must be mistaken," she said.

Marjorie waved her empty cup at me. I quickly poured Cassandra a cup and left it on the table, then went to fill her sister's. When I looked back, the cup had disappeared under her veil. I wondered what else she was hiding under there: certainly the secret of what she had been doing in her mother's room the night before.

When I returned to the room with the platter of crepes and oatmeal, Edie was just taking a seat. Her pale skin had turned nearly transparent, and the blue of her veins was visible beneath her eyes.

"I think we should discuss John's death before the rest of them come down," Marjorie said, taking a sip of her coffee.

"The rest of them meaning my husband?" Edie asked.

"If that's what you're calling the man whom you no longer have relations with, then yes," Bernadette said in her infamous whisper.

Edie's cheeks went from white to red.

"No one thinks it was Bill," Marjorie said impatiently. "And we know it's not Rachel or James."

"I'm glad you can be so certain," Bernadette said. "Who knew you held us in such high regard?"

"It had to have been Amalia or Lennox, despite his excuse of being with the maid," Marjorie carried on, not seeming to care that I was in the room. "It's the only thing that makes sense."

"You mean because murders often make logical sense to you?"

"Why are you being so unhelpful, Birdie? Don't you think it was one of them?"

"I think it's just as likely it's you," Bernadette said indifferently.

"And why would I kill John?"

"I don't know," Bernadette said. "I don't

understand the mind of a murderer."

"I'm not a murderer!"

There was a clatter and a crash, and broken porcelain scattered across the floor. It took me a moment to realize that it had come from beneath Cassandra's veil; she seemed to be swooning.

"Is everything alright, Cassie?" Marjorie snapped. "Not having flashbacks to the execution, are you?"

"Oh, no, but ... I think I'd better go lay down," Cassandra said. "All this talk of murder ..."

"Well, don't let us stop you," Marjorie said, turning back to Bernadette and Edie.

Cassandra was flailing an arm in my direction. I went to her side.

"Can I assist you, Miss Marlowe?" I said.

"Oh, yes, dear ... I don't think I can make it on my own ..."

I took her arm and led her back to her room. Perhaps it was the heavily sequined dress acting as a type of armor, but she seemed quite strong despite her insistence on putting her weight on me. I trudged up the stairs with her hanging from my side, not certain if I was more pleased to get away from the Marlowe women's argument or displeased at being stuck with a woman who seemed to think that walking around beneath a large black sheet was perfectly acceptable, though the opportunity to speak with her was too great a chance to miss. I wondered if she had seen anything on her nighttime strolls the night that John had been killed.

"I'm so sorry," she said as I helped her into her bed, though her tone suggested otherwise. She pulled back the pink satin sheets and pointed for me to bring her another tufted pillow. "It's just that John and I were so close, you know. My only boy ..."

"Oh, that's – how horrible for you, ma'am," I said,

though it seemed an odd way to refer to one's brother. I stuffed the pillow behind her back.

"What beautiful hair you have," Cassandra said, reaching out to pull at a piece that had come loose beneath my cap. "Like a worn penny, isn't it? Is this your natural color?"

"Yes, ma'am," I said, though I wasn't sure that being likened to a dirty one cent piece was much of a compliment. Copper would have sufficed.

"This was my natural color, too, before I went gray, of course."

"I see."

"What did you say your name was again?"

"Alexandra Durant, ma'am."

"Alexandra," Cassandra repeated. "You don't look like an Alexandra."

"I didn't realize that."

"No, I don't think the name Alexandra suits you at all ... Perhaps I could find a better one for you."

"That seems like a waste of your time, Miss Marlowe. Especially given everything else going on here."

"Oh, I always have time for you."

I paused, not bothering to attempt to decipher what she meant, then said as carefully as I could, "In that case, do you have time to discuss what happened to your brother?"

"Pardon?"

"Professor Marlowe," I said, though the clarification didn't seem necessary. "I wondered if you saw anything the night he died."

"Why would I have seen anything?"

"No reason. I just thought ... since you were visiting your mother's room so late last night ... maybe you did the same the night before."

I couldn't see Cassandra's expression, though from her sharp intake of breath, I knew that I had hit a nerve. Her arm twitched.

"If I knew what happened to John," she said after a long moment, and I was surprised to hear that her voice was still high and even, "I would destroy whomever had harmed him."

She patted my arm for a moment, letting her fingers run up and down my sleeve. I straightened to pull myself away.

"You can leave now," she said, turning away from me as she laid down further on the bed. "Turn the light off on your way."

I nodded and retreated from the room, gently snapping the door shut behind me. As I stood staring at the wood, I couldn't decide whether or not she was unhinged. Come to think of it, I realized, I couldn't decide if any of the Marlowes were unhinged or just eccentric, and unlike Marjorie, I wouldn't rule out any of them as suspects until I had solid reason to do so.

When I returned downstairs, the rest of the family had joined the table.

"... as soon as we can. James can't be away from his nurse for too long," Rachel was saying.

"We'll all get out of here as soon as we can," Marjorie replied, "but you don't get first dibs just because your husband's a cripple."

"Marjorie!" Edie said, her eyes wide.

"What? I can't pretend that he's not."

Rachel's eyes had turned down. She scooped up a spoon of porridge and fed it to James; it dribbled down his chin, and she quickly cleaned it away with a napkin. I forced my eyes away.

"Maybe Kneller can radio for help," Marjorie said. Bernadette and Edie threw her warning glances. "What? Now I can't bring up Kneller, either?"

"I'm sure if there was a way to contact the mainland,

Frank would have done it already," Rachel said.

"I'm not," Marjorie said dryly. "I wouldn't be surprised if he thought it was funny that we're all stuck here."

"Alexa will go ask him," Bernadette said. She flicked her fingers at me without so much as throwing me a glance, which might have been a good thing: my face had adopted a scowl. She might have gotten me to stay on the island, after all, but between John being murdered and the ferry being gone, I was no longer content to be the demure, compliant servant that she assumed had been hired for her. Just as I opened my mouth to ask if there wasn't an easier way to summon Kneller, though, I stopped myself, letting my eyes scan the people who were tucking into their breakfast, mostly unfazed by the dead body that laid in the room upstairs. Someone in the house had done it, and if I hoped to find out who, I was doing myself no favors by getting on their nerves.

Bernadette looked up from her plate at last and, seeing me still standing there, gave an impatient huff.

"Go, Alexa!" she repeated, and I took my cue and left, stomping through the heavy, wet snow to get to the guesthouse with a cigarette clutched in my hand to ward off some of the chill that my coat and boots could not.

Mr. Kneller looked mildly amused to see me standing on his porch.

"I never knew maids ran so many errands," he said.

"That makes two of us," I replied, pulling off my gloves. "How did Mrs. Marlowe use to contact you? By phone?"

"No, no: Sylvia never cared much for those, hence why there's only the one. She used to ring a bell for me."

I raised my eyebrows. Somehow I couldn't imagine Kneller responding to a jingling bell anymore than I could an unruly dog doing so.

"You must have loved that," I commented.

"Oh, yes. Too bad my hearing *unexpectedly* took a turn for the worse at the *exact* moment of Sylvia's passing, forcing her children to find a new means of communication – a terrible, terrible pity, really – so the bell remains *woefully* out of use ... I'm as heartbroken as anyone." He gave me a wide, toothy grin. "So: what brings you down here?"

"They want you to radio for help."

"With what? Do they think I have a walkie-talkie hiding beneath my bed?"

"I'm just relaying the message," I said. "There must be some way to contact the mainland. Can you repair the phone line?"

"I could have, had the person who cut it not removed most of the wire."

"But couldn't you just add more?"

"Oh, sure," he said sardonically, clearly unimpressed with my line of thinking. "Let me just hop in the ferry, go to the general store on the mainland, and get some more!"

"You don't have any laying around?"

"Unfortunately I didn't think that the need to repair a phone line would arise this weekend. Sorry to disappoint you."

He turned and wandered back into his house. Given that he had left the door open, I took it to mean I could follow him. I found him in the kitchen reading and drinking coffee, seemingly unconcerned with the entirety of the situation.

"Well – do you at least have any idea who it was?" I asked.

"Admittedly I left my post last night, so I didn't complete the junction box stake-out," he replied. "So sorry."

"But there's got to be footprints. Tracks in the snow –"

"Which would tell us ... what? That whoever cut the

wire came from inside the main house and wore boots? Shocking! All the evidence leads to *everyone!*" He shook his head at me and went back to his book, chuckling as he read. *"I should have been a pair of ragged claws scuttling across the floors of silent seas."*

I crossed my arms.

"Why are you acting like this? Why aren't you concerned?" I said.

"On the contrary, I'm very concerned, Alexandra. I just know that there's nothing I can do."

"So you're making jokes instead? Snickering when the Marlowes fight – reciting poetry when you're digging up John's body? Because that doesn't sound like someone who's indifferent: it sounds like someone who thinks this whole situation is entertaining!"

Kneller raised his eyes from the pages of his book. He considered me for a long moment before responding.

"Maybe I do find it entertaining," he said. "Do you?"

"No!"

"Really? Then what do you find it?" he asked. "Certainly not sad: I saw your expression when you looked at John. There was no pity. There was no regret."

"I didn't know what to think," I argued. "I was – I was shocked –"

"You were cold. You're still cold. Maybe even angry. So don't lecture me about not shedding any tears for the man when you certainly haven't wept for him, either."

He returned his eyes to the poem he was reading. As the insinuation that I had wanted any of this to happen sunk in, I grabbed the book and yanked it down again, forcing him not to ignore me.

"Whoever killed John Marlowe ruined my life," I told him. "I didn't want him dead."

Kneller looked at me steadily.

"I'm willing to believe the first part," he said. "But I'm not so sure about the rest."

"I didn't want him dead," I repeated more forcefully. "Maybe everyone else did, but I didn't – I *don't*."

Kneller glanced at where my hand was still gripping his book. He nodded for me to release it, then placed it down on the table.

"Then you're not doing a very good job at showing it," he said.

My mouth dropped open. I struggled to find a way to defend myself, but before I could, Kneller carried on.

"Let me tell you something, Alexandra: maybe you're right. Maybe whoever killed John ruined your life, as you say. But here's what you don't understand: had John Marlowe stayed alive, he would have ruined your life, too. So maybe instead of harping on about how you wish he was still here, you should just be grateful that he died before you could find out what he had in store for you."

I shut my mouth, no longer interested in trying to reason with him, and turned and marched from the house. He might have been as crazy as the rest of the family, and any hope I had had that he might have given me some insight as to who had killed John vanished. I would have to figure it out on my own.

Halfway across the yard, I slowed my pace and pulled out another cigarette, lighting it as I looked up at the house. From where I stood, the boarded up window of the nursery was visible on the turret. A snow-covered yew grew beneath it, large and round like a pillow. I wondered what Lennox was doing, then – as quickly as the thought had come – I wondered why I was thinking of him at all.

I returned inside and told Bernadette that Kneller had no way to contact the mainland. Her huge midsection swelled as she took a deep breath in, and she waddled away to tell the others. I considered following her to see how they reacted, but then a separate idea struck me, and I went upstairs to the third floor to find Lennox. He wasn't in the nursery, nor the surrounding rooms. I went back to the first floor and circled through the rooms until I found him sitting in the library. A book lay open in his lap and reading glasses were perched on his nose. He looked up as I approached.

"I wondered if I could ask you something," I said. "About what you said last night."

"Which part?"

"When you said you were trying to help me."

"I was. Though I don't understand what your question is."

"I want to know –" I began, wishing I had planned what I was about to say more carefully ahead of time, "– if you would be willing to help me again."

Lennox stared over the tops of his lenses at me, a frown pulling at his brow. I wished he wouldn't look at me so intently – not without announcing what he was trying to see.

"I guess that would depend," he said cautiously. "What is it you need help with?"

I moved forward and took a seat on the ottoman so that I was sitting directly in front of him. He made a movement as though he was about to pull away, but stopped himself before doing so.

"I wondered if you'd help me figure out what happened to John."

One of his eyebrows raised ever so slightly, though if he thought that I was completely mad, he did a good job of hiding it. I supposed that was why he was a therapist and I – with my bluntness and tactlessness – would likely never be one.

"You already found that out," he said. "Someone stabbed him."

"I know, but I want to find out who did it."

"And you want my help?" Lennox looked as though he wasn't sure whether to be flattered or perplexed, though he settled on the latter. "I'm not sure I understand. Why would you need me?"

"Because you know the family better than I do. I can listen in on their conversations, but you can actually be a part of them. If we worked together, we might have a shot of figuring out who the killer is."

Lennox took his glasses off and pocketed them. Laying his book on the table, he folded his hands together and gave me a long, patient stare.

"Are you studying to be a forensic psychologist, Alexandra?"

"No," I said, mildly annoyed that he couldn't remember the topic of my dissertation.

"Then don't you think it would be best to wait for the police to show up?"

"No."

"Do you care to share why?"

"Because when they do show up, I'd like to be able to point at whoever killed him and say, 'There they are. Take them away.'"

"And when will that be?"

"In a few days, I imagine."

"In a few days it'll be Christmas Eve. As far as anyone knows, the family is just spending the holidays together."

"Well, when they don't show up for work, then," I said, but Lennox was already shaking his head.

"Who? Bernadette? Marjorie? Edie? Cassandra?" he asked. "None of them work. John was the only one of them who had a profession, but the university won't start its next term for weeks. Mine and Bill's colleagues will note our absences, of course, but that's unlikely to alert them until the New Year. Our biggest hope right now is that James' nurse gets concerned when he and Rachel don't return home, but – again – she might just assume they've decided to stay longer with the family."

"Well, someone must be coming to bring Mrs. Marlowe's body back to the mainland, right?"

"Not that I know of."

"They can't just leave her up in the Augustus Suite," I said, growing frustrated with the way he shot down all of my ideas. If he didn't want to help me, just as he hadn't wanted to help me in the Augustus Suite when I had asked him to look at John's body, then he ought to have just said so. And though I had a feeling that was exactly what he was planning to say anyhow, I still thought I could convince him otherwise. "That would be illegal."

"Leaving her in the suite would be," Lennox said. "But she doesn't have to leave the island. In Maine you can bury people in your backyard, if you so choose."

"What?"

"It's perfectly legal, provided you have a proper death certificate and a fence around the burial area. And the Marlowes have a plot on the south end of the island. So, like I said, the police might not show up for quite a while."

I hesitated, mildly concerned that I had lived in Maine for eighteen years without ever hearing of such a thing, but then returned to the real issue.

"So that's even more of a reason to figure this out," I said. "If we're going to be stuck here for weeks, then wouldn't you rather know who the killer is?"

"It's not that I don't want to know, Alexandra – I do. But let's not be foolish."

"I'm not being foolish," I said crossly. "What do you think I should be doing? Serving the tea and scones at four o'clock sharp every day, acting as though everything's perfectly normal?"

"Perhaps. If you don't get involved, then there's less of a chance you'll get hurt."

I shifted my jaw. The action didn't go unnoticed by Lennox.

"Does that offend you?" he asked.

"Yes – because you wouldn't be saying it if I was a man."

"Of course I would. I've already given myself the same advice that I'm giving you: stay out of it. Don't give them any reason to suspect you."

I had already formed my response when I paused, thrown off by his choice of the word *suspect*. I looked into his dark eyes for any sign of what he wasn't saying and wished that I could read him a fraction as well as he seemed to read me. For I could tell there was something hiding behind that perfectly composed stance and carefully placed expression, and I needed to know what it was.

"What are you doing here?" I asked. "And don't tell me it's for the wake – you didn't even visit Mrs. Marlowe's body."

He shifted, sitting up a bit straighter.

"I was invited for the wake," he said. "I was informed it would be held in the evening."

"But why would you come?"

"Because I wanted to pay my respects to the family."

"Even though they don't like you?"

"Sylvia liked me. If her children had a problem with that, then there's nothing I can do about it."

I paused again, trying to find a way to get him to say what I wanted to hear, but couldn't think of how to do so other than outright asking him.

"So you were Mrs. Marlowe's psychiatrist?"

Lennox opened his mouth and then closed it. For a moment he appeared to be thinking, but then his face smoothed back into its composed expression.

"If I was," he said carefully, "it wouldn't be ethical to tell you."

Though I would have preferred a better affirmation, I couldn't argue with him. He couldn't tell me who his patients were, dead or alive.

"So why does the family hate you?"

Lennox scanned my face. I wondered if he was put off by my bluntness. I hardly blamed him, and yet I had no time to skirt around our predicament with pleasantries and politeness. Perhaps he understood as much, because he leaned back in his seat and folded his arms, seemingly deciding on what and how much to say.

"There's a painting that Sylvia promised to give me when she died," he said. "I've come to collect it."

"How much is it worth?"

"It's worth quite a bit to me, which is presumably why the family doesn't want me to have it."

"So they know that's why you're here?"

"I assume so. That's why it's been moved."

"What's it a painting of?"

His eyes ran over my face, searching for something unknown.

"A woman," he said shortly. "A ... very beautiful woman."

"And you thought the Marlowes would let you show up and take it?" I said skeptically, thinking of how they had sent me out to watch him so that he wouldn't steal the Tiffany lamp.

"John invited me here under the pretense of giving it to me – so yes, I thought I would be able to show up and take it."

I frowned, briefly wondering why John hadn't admitted to his siblings that he had been the one to invite Lennox.

"So you're more interested in finding your painting

than you are in finding the killer?" I asked.

"No," he said, his tone becoming firm, "I just don't want to get involved in something dangerous."

"But *why?*"

He stared at me for a long moment – so long, in fact, that he seemed to be playing out the conversation, complete with my reaction, in his mind before he spoke.

"Because," he said, and his voice dropped so low that I had to strain to hear him. "When the police do show up and start questioning everyone on what happened, you can bet that the Marlowes – including whichever one of them is responsible for killing John – are going to protect themselves, and the only way to protect themselves individually is to protect the family as a whole."

"So you think they're going to pin it on you?"

"There's only a handful of choices, and I'm well aware that I'm at the top of the list."

"But you have an alibi. I already told them you didn't leave the nursery."

"It's not airtight, and you can be sure the family won't hesitate to pick you apart to discredit what you've said. It'll be five against one."

"So there was no point in saying anything, you mean?" I asked coolly. "I'll remember that the next time I have the urge to correct them for falsely accusing you."

He pushed himself to his feet. I instinctively leaned back, wary that he might reach out and grab my arm as John had done as he whispered a threat that masqueraded as a jest.

"Don't think that I don't appreciate it," he said. "I do. But I'm trying to impress upon you the gravity of the situation we're in."

"A situation that won't get any better if we sit around and do nothing."

Lennox let out a sigh. He ran his hand through his

hair.

"You seem to be an intelligent person, Alexandra, and I don't doubt that you might be able to work out what's happened here. But I can't work with you. I simply can't."

"Because I'm difficult?"

"No," Lennox said. He paused, his eyes darting between either of my own as he searched for what to say. "I'm afraid I'm just – not bold enough."

He gave me a curt nod and left the room. When the door shut behind him, I stood and went to the window to stare out at the endless white. I wasn't sure that I believed his excuse: the genuineness that I had heard in his voice on previous occasions had been absent from his tone. He more than likely did find me too difficult and simply wanted to spare my feelings.

I leaned my head up against the cool glass, letting the conversation file itself away into my mind as I altered the plans I had made to not include him. The more my head filled up with the words, the more I felt the space beneath my rib cage emptying. I could only imagine that it was making room for the loneliness which was growing within me by the day.

CHAPTER SIX

Amalia and Marjorie had begun another screaming match, this time choosing to have it in the Ballroom, and as their voices reverberated against the walls and boomed out into the rest of the house, I crept upstairs to make the beds and avoid them. I started in the rouge Baxter Room where Bernadette liked to have a plate of biscuits laid out each night, then went to the yellow Mabel Room that was far too bright and sunny for Edie's frigid demeanor, then the green Eleanora Room that smelled strongly of smoke despite Bernadette's insistence that Marjorie smoke outside, and finally the navy Fletcher room where Amalia now slept alone. As I made up the beds and refilled the water pitchers, I half-expected to find some incriminating evidence that would point me to who had killed John, but the rooms betrayed nothing out of the ordinary. I lifted up the mattresses and rummaged through the closets, unsure if I was looking for a bloodied article of clothing or Lennox's painting. Maybe if I found it, I reasoned, he would change his mind about helping me. Not that I needed his help, I reminded myself. I was perfectly capable of solving John's murder on my own.

In the pink Lillet Room where Cassandra had holed herself up for the first few days of her stay, I repeated my search, even running my hands over the walls as though a secret door might pop out and reveal a hiding place to me, but there was no sign of the painting or anything else. I wondered if Lennox was right in saying that I was being foolish, and if I would be better off keeping my head down and acting like nothing more than the maid. I let out a breath and took a seat at the vanity. The heavy silver ring adorned with diamonds and sapphires sat among

Cassandra's other jewelry. I picked it up and turned it beneath the light, trying not to think of her pulling it off of her mother's rigid, cold finger.

"It was a gift."

I dropped the ring and spun around. The black, ghostly figure of Cassandra was standing in the doorway, her expression hidden beneath her veil. I faltered for an excuse as to what I was doing.

"You can try it on, if you like," she said, stepping over to where I sat at the vanity.

"Oh – no," I said hastily. "I was just –"

I moved to stand up, but she put her hands on my shoulders and guided me back down. I sat staring into the mirror, her shadowy image behind me and her satin-gloved fingers stretching over my neck.

"Look at that face," she said, stroking my cheek. "It's like a Raphael painting, isn't it?"

I didn't answer, still expecting her to chide me for going through her things. Her high voice was nearly unnatural from the depths of her veil, and I simply didn't know what to make of her. It was one thing if the family found her charades permissible, but I wasn't quite convinced that she was wholly sane. Perhaps her veil was hiding the guilty face of a woman who had stabbed her brother.

"You're so pretty," she went on. "Do you have a boyfriend?"

"No."

"You must chase them away like flies."

"Not really," I said, unable to keep from correcting her. "Usually they chase me away."

Cassandra gave a little chuckle.

"Oh, most boys just think you're out of their league," she said. "I was the same. Men have a difficult time being inferior."

I made to stand up again.

"I should really –"

"What beautiful hair you have," she said, her hands holding my shoulders and keeping me down as she pulled a piece down from beneath my cap. "It's such a waste to wear it like you do."

"Mrs. Carlton prefers if I –"

"Birdie's never had an eye for beauty," Cassandra said, tossing my excuses away. She pulled off my cap to reveal my hair, running her hands over it as she hummed to herself. My skin prickled beneath her touch.

"I should really finish cleaning, Miss Marlowe –"

"Is this your natural texture?" she cut in, letting my hair down. It was wavy from the way it had been tied back, with odd bends and crinkles in it. "It would look so much more beautiful straight ..."

I didn't respond. She reached forward to pick up the sterling silver brush on the vanity and ran it through my hair. The soft bristles melted against my skin. She continued to brush, humming a sad tune as she worked, and her strokes were slow and deliberate. As I watched her in the reflection, I got the impression that she was crying.

I clicked my teeth together, unsure of what to do. Her hands continued to run up and down my head, and there was more than kindness in her touch: there was tenderness. I tried to tell myself it was my curiosity that was keeping me from breaking away.

"There," she said, finishing and setting the brush back down. My hair was smoother now and fluffier; it almost made my rigid expression appear soft. "It's no wonder he chose you."

"What?"

My muscles immediately tensed, though Cassandra didn't seem to notice. She leaned her cheek up against mine, the veil scratching at my face as she did so, and I could smell the rose soap on her skin.

"John," she said, letting her hands slide down my arms as she continued to stare at me in the mirror. Her voice was airy and far-away. I wasn't even sure she knew what she was saying. "It's no wonder he chose you, is it?"

My jaw cramped.

"I don't know what you mean," I said.

"I saw you two on the stairs the other night," she said. "I've never seen John get so ruffled. You must have been having quite the disagreement."

My mind flashed back to the figure who had stared down at us, watching as John grabbed me and doing nothing. My skin turned cold as though I had been doused in icy water and my heart was pounding so hard that I couldn't have counted the beats if I'd tried. She let out a soft laugh, and as I squirmed, her grip on me tightened.

"Don't worry, I won't tell anyone," she cooed. Her hot breath was right in my ear. "It'll be our little secret ..."

Her arms wrapped around my chest, locking me in place in something akin to both a stranglehold and an embrace. The heavy ring jabbed me in the collarbone.

"I don't know what you mean," I said, forcing myself to remain unaffected.

"Oh, I think you do. I don't believe in coincidences. You being here, John dying ... it's a life for a life, isn't it?"

"I don't know what you mean," I repeated, though my voice was wavering now and I couldn't keep the fear away anymore.

"Maybe you don't right now, but you will. We'll work it out, once we're together and the rest of them are ... gone."

Her hand moved over my throat. I ripped myself from her grasp.

"I have to go."

I snatched my cap up and stood with such haste that

I knocked the stool over and tripped over it. Quickly regaining my footing, I bolted from the room and ran up the stairs to the third floor. As I reached my room and shut the door, anxiety pierced my skin and the need to know what was going on became stronger, though no amount of snapping the rubber band around my wrist gave me any explanation as to why she wanted to be alone with me.

I went to my bed and sat down, my feet tapping the floor sporadically as I tried to make sense of it. She had seen me arguing with John the night he had died. Had I been wrong to think that she hadn't helped me? Had she thought, for a reason I didn't understand, that he was going to hurt me, and so she had been the one to sneak out and kill him? Or did she think that I had been the one to kill him – and she wasn't sorry about it, just like no one else seemed to be?

Who was John Marlowe? Certainly not the man I had thought he was. But if he had never been planning to get me back into my program so that I could finish my doctorate, then what had been the point of bringing me to the island? To ruin my life, just as Kneller had claimed he would have done? It didn't seem to fit, especially since being kicked out of my program had already done that.

Or maybe that was only the beginning. I shook my head and snapped the rubber band again, but it did no good. John Marlowe had had no reason to want to ruin me: he didn't even know me. Was I here just to make his family uncomfortable with my brusqueness? There was certainly no way of finding out now, unless he had shared his plans with someone. I returned my thoughts to the task at hand: finding out who had killed him. Cassandra was seeming more and more likely, though Marjorie and Amalia weren't far behind.

When the police do show up and start questioning everyone on what happened, Lennox's words rang in my head, *you can bet that the Marlowes are going to protect themselves, and the only way to protect themselves individually is to protect the family as a whole.*

The family knew it wasn't Kneller, and I doubted anyone would suspect Mrs. Tilly, which left me and Lennox. And he had an alibi. I had given him an alibi. Which meant that I had left myself open as the prime suspect.

I ran through everything I had said or done that might lead them to believe I had killed John. Cassandra had witnessed our argument. Bernadette and Mrs. Tilly were wary of how much money he had paid me. Kneller, if no one else, had noticed my indifferent expression when I looked at the dead body. The reminder of Amalia's voice screeching that I had been the one to stab her husband made me flinch, and once again I had the eerie feeling that John had planned this all to trap me despite knowing that he couldn't have possibly realized he was going to die when he had hired me.

I numbly stood up an hour later and went downstairs to serve cocktails in the Parlor, my mind so packed with words and phrases that I didn't realize I had poured digestifs instead of aperitifs until Bernadette loudly scolded me. I snapped the rubber band against my wrist, angry that I had forgotten and trying to clear my head enough to focus on gathering information. The family started on the incorrect drinks as I made the proper ones. Cassandra was sipping Drambuie beneath her veil. I wished that I could tell if she was looking at me.

By the time dinner was served, there was so little alcohol left on the bar cart that it was a wonder any of them were still capable of walking. Though I had set the table for nine, Lennox was nowhere to be seen; it was as though he knew that everyone was particularly on edge and had avoided mingling with them at all costs. Mrs. Tilly had concocted a soup consisting of far too much dill, and the smell was stifling when mixed with the scent of Bernadette's hot breath as she ordered me around.

"I asked for soda water with lemon, Alexa, not lime," she said, waving her glass in my direction as though she was really going to drink anything but more wine for the remainder of the meal. I went to fix it for her, but I didn't think there were any lemons left, and there certainly wasn't a way to get more. The Pantry had only been stocked for the month, and December was quickly coming to an end.

"Oh, Alexa, you continue to be a disappointment," Bernadette drawled when I informed her of as much.

"Stop beating her up about it," Marjorie snapped. "She's just a girl ..."

"That didn't stop you from beating up your children," Bernadette said, her voice not even bothering to drop to a whisper in her inebriated state.

Marjorie's nostrils flared outwards.

"I – never – *touched* – my children!" she screamed, banging her fists down on the table with such force that Rachel and Bill's glasses toppled over. "That's – how dare – ?"

"That's enough, Birdie," Rachel said, but Bernadette only responded by taking another slug of her Merlot.

"Take her wine," Bill said to no one in particular, but no one paid him any mind. "Someone – just take her wine –"

"Everyone knows that what happened was just a terrible tragedy," Rachel said pointedly to her eldest sister.

"Well, obviously not everyone," Bernadette said, moving to put her wine back down and knocking over the unwanted soda water with lime, "or else they wouldn't have dragged you through that trial, would've they?"

"Maybe you should call it a night, Birdie," Rachel

advised, not seeming to realize that her sister would never miss a meal. "We don't want anyone getting upset."

"Yes, we certainly don't need any more murders in this family ..." Bernadette said. "We break all the odds, don't we? Three murders in one family ... Four if you count Mary."

There was a clatter of silverware: Edie had dropped her fork and knife.

"No one's counting Mary," she said, her face whitening to match the tablecloth.

"Are we counting the six in Cassandra's 'real' family?" Marjorie asked, her voice dripping with sarcasm that barely covered her anger. Her face was still twitching. "Or have you all forgotten her true lineage that she jabbered on about nonstop at the last family gathering?"

Bill's eyes rolled up to the ceiling and he drained the rest of his glass of Claret, appearing to give up on the idea of staying sober.

"Oh, yes, we mustn't forget how she escaped the execution of nineteen-seventeen ..." Bernadette agreed.

"Why don't you take off that ridiculous get-up, Cassie?" Marjorie snapped. "You're not fooling anyone."

"I'm in mourning," Cassandra said. "There's no need to question my grief."

"I question anyone who didn't even bother to visit her own mother in the past ten years –"

"Says the woman who killed her children," Bernadette muttered loudly.

"I didn't kill my children!" Marjorie screamed, her face redder than her hair and the knife and fork clenched so tightly in her hands that her knuckles looked ready to burst through the flesh.

Bill grabbed me by the arm.

"Take her wine!" he ordered. "Take it!"

I stared over at Bernadette's wine glass, safely

fastened in one pudgy hand, and I didn't move.

"If anyone's the killer, you are, Birdie!" Marjorie shouted. "You're the one whose husband died mysteriously after marrying you –!"

"Let's just calm down, everyone," Rachel said ineffectively. "There's really no need to –"

"My husband was very sick," Bernadette said, speaking before swallowing and sloshing wine all down her front. "It was lucky he had me to take care of him –"

"You were poisoning him for years –!"

"No one killed Edgar," Rachel said. "No one killed anyone –"

"Someone killed John!" Amalia said, so outraged at the suggestion that she finally joined the conversation. "Someone killed my husband, but no one seems to care!"

"Why would we care about your husband's death when poor Cassandra here had her entire *biological* family slaughtered by Russian Revolutionaries –?"

"She is *not* the long-lost Grand Duchess Anastasia!" Bill exploded, seemingly unable to hold it in a moment longer as he threw his hands up in the air. "She – is – not! So stop egging her on!"

"Of course she is, Bill," Marjorie continued. "Don't you remember the cold, hard evidence that she produced to prove it to us at Mother's seventieth birthday –?"

Edie flinched and knocked her knife off the table. It fell to the floor and stabbed into the wood, quivering in its spot.

"She was executed with the rest of the Romanovs!" Bill exclaimed. "Everyone knows it! For Christ's sake, there are photos of her from when she was an infant in the family album!"

"There's no need to get so upset, Bill," Bernadette said.

"Besides," Marjorie added, "I like this story better

than the last few. Remember when she insisted she was married to King George the Sixth?"

"Or when she claimed to be the Lindbergh baby," Bernadette agreed, "despite being thirty at the time ... and the wrong gender."

Cassandra gave a little chuckle. It sounded haunting from beneath the depths of her veil.

"You're all very silly," she started, "to believe such guff. I've always known who I truly am –"

"Kill me!" Bill roared, jumping to his feet. "Somebody kill *me!* That's what happens to the men in this family, isn't it? They meet untimely ends?"

"That's because all of the Marlowe women are insane," Amalia said, standing up as well.

"Speak for yourself, you manic-depressive wench," Marjorie said, throwing down her napkin and rising from her chair, too. "John told us all the stories about you going off the rails – we all had plenty of good laughs over you when you were 'away on a retreat' every other year –"

"Those were – those were health retreats!" Amalia said. "I never – I'm not crazy!"

"Maybe not after all the electro-shock therapy," Marjorie countered, "but I wouldn't bet on it!"

Edie and Bernadette stood up next, and there were so many voices ricocheting off the walls that I ducked down as though one might come down and strike me like a bullet to the head. As the screaming continued, another sound joined into mix.

"Gaaahhh! Gaaaaaaah!"

James was pounding the arms of his wheelchair. Rachel was frantically trying to calm him.

"Be quiet!" she shouted at her family members. "Be quiet! You're upsetting him! Be quiet!"

But if anything, their voices just got louder. They were overlapping and twisting together, no longer separate streams and tones but a horrible cacophony of sounds that I couldn't interpret. I shook my head desperately, trying to pick the words apart so that I could memorize each one and file it away for future reference, but it was impossible to do. And I couldn't miss what they were saying: not when Bernadette might drunkenly admit whether she had really killed her husband, or Marjorie her children, or any one of them John. I had to get them to stop shouting and go back to the usual bickering that I could understand.

I turned and exited the room, unsure of where I was going. The voices were still booming from outside and inside my head, and I had to muffle them if I hoped to work out a plan. My eyes were glued to my feet as I hurried down the hallway past the Billiard Room and Smoking Room, and it wasn't until I weaved past the Study that I realized where I ought to go: the kitchen. Maybe if I brought them their dinner they would quiet down, like angry lions being thrown large slabs of steaks.

"Ah – escaped, did you?" said a voice as I stepped into the kitchen, and I looked up to find Kneller sitting at the small table with a plate of chicken, potatoes and root vegetables smothered in gravy set before him. A beautifully placed tray of Cornish hens was on the table waiting to be brought out and Mrs. Tilly was checking on a souffle in the oven.

"You have to do something," I said automatically, changing my mind about bringing them their food. Perhaps if he went in, he could mediate the situation – or at least shock them to their senses with the sight of him in his darned socks walking over the polished floors.

Kneller raised an eyebrow.

"About what?"

"About them screaming! They're – they're – someone's going to get hurt!"

If I had thought that might compel him to set his

fork and knife down, I was terribly inaccurate. He took a large bite of chicken.

"Well, it won't be me. Smart of you to get out of there while you could, though."

"But – someone's got to do something. I can't calm them down, and Mr. Langston's about to explode –"

"*We* don't have to do anything," Mrs. Tilly said, shutting the oven door and turning to me. "*You,* however, will serve them the dinner I made. Mrs. Carlton won't like it if it gets cold."

Her indifferent expression mirrored Kneller's. It was the same look they all wore, more or less: the one that said that properness overrode everything else, and that the only way forward was with routines and formalities regardless of the situation.

"But ..." I started again, not willing to explain why I needed the family to stop shouting. Kneller waved me off.

"Alexandra, this isn't the end of the world. It's not even the end of the Marlowes: they get into these fights more frequently than the three of us get paid, I imagine."

"Well, you didn't see them this time –"

"I've seen them plenty of times," Kneller said impatiently, throwing out his arms and sending a forkful of mashed potatoes soaring across the room towards Mrs. Tilly's feet. "Every month when the kids didn't visit. Every birthday when Sylvia threatened suicide. Every Christmas for the past forty years. It's gotten old. If they're ever in there having a nice discussion, then feel free to run and get me. I'd like to see it."

"But ... I can't just ..."

"Hide from them? Sure you can. It's what I do. It's what Frances does," he said, nodding at Mrs. Tilly. "It's what any rational person would do – not that I'm convinced any of us is rational, mind you, given that we work for them." He took another bite of food, chewing it in one side of his mouth as he added, *"I should have been a pair of ragged claws scuttling across the floors of silent seas ..."*

I crossed my arms as he slipped into his poetry. He reminded me of someone, but I couldn't place whom. Before I could dwell on it, though, a separate thought occurred to me.

"You know them all pretty well, don't you?" I asked.

"I do."

"So which one of them do you think did it? Who killed Professor Marlowe?"

"Don't you go speaking of that in here!" Mrs. Tilly cried, hurriedly crossing herself, but I ignored her. Kneller made an odd face. It was something like a smile, but his mouth twitched so much that it was impossible to call it anything at all.

"They all did it. To themselves," he said.

"Can't you just give me an honest answer?" I asked. "Instead of your roundabout, insightful, poetic ones?"

"My answers are always honest," Kneller replied. "Except when they're lies, of course."

"You're as bad as they are."

Kneller's face darkened. He was bristling with a thousand unspoken horrors.

"Oh, no," he said, pointing his knife at me, "I'm not. But maybe you'll find that out for yourself, the longer you're trapped here."

Mrs. Tilly cut between us, brandishing her apron at me and covering me in a dusting of flour.

"My dinner is getting colder by the minute!" she said. "You're paid to serve, not chat!"

I could feel myself seething – seething from her attitude, seething from Kneller's, seething from the family's, and seething from how hypocritical they all were for their talk of formality which was juxtaposed by their complete inability to speak in anything close to a civilized way to one another.

I reached forward and snatched up the tray of Cornish hens, making an alteration to my initial plan to distract them with the food.

"There are worse things than it getting cold," I said.

The voices got louder and louder as I walked back down the hallway towards the snippets of shouted epithets.

"Gahh! Gahhh!"

"Shut up! Shut up, you disgusting old cripple –" Amalia was screeching, her words intermixed with Rachel's pleas for her to stop. "John should have done you a favor and let you bleed to death –!"

"He would've let him bleed to death, you bitch!" Bill returned. "It was a passerby who had the decency to run for help –!"

"Decency? You call *this* decency?"

I reached the Dining Room and stepped inside. Amalia was leaning over James' wheelchair, her face right in his as she shouted at him, and Bill was trying to pull her back as Rachel held her husband across the chest to keep him away from her.

"Let her go, Bill!" Marjorie said. "Let her do what she will –"

"No! Stop this!" Edie's voice rang out. "Stop this! Someone will get hurt –!"

"Let them! Let them tear each other's throats out!"

"Do it yourself," Bernadette slurred over to her sister. "Show us how you beat your children until they stopped crying out for Mummy to stop –"

"I'll kill you, Birdie!" Marjorie said, throwing herself halfway across the table at her and crushing glasses and appetizers beneath her. "I'll kill you –!"

I couldn't stand watching them for a moment longer, all dressed in their finest and acting their worst. My fingers briefly tightened on the handles of the tray. Then –

I let go. The tray struck the floor with a horrific scream that seemed to reverberate through the house like the cry of the mythical banshee and surely would have caused the overly superstitious Mrs. Tilly to run screaming from the house decrying the theft of another Marlowe soul. Chickens rolled in every direction, looking like deformed little beings coming to chase the inhabitants from the room, as the lights escaping from the crystal chandelier suddenly seemed to reflect a myriad of dancing evil sprites and malevolent fairies. Edie leaped back, so startled that she tripped over her chair and fell to the floor, and Bill and Rachel ducked down with their hands to their ears. Marjorie and Amalia, however, both abandoned their prey to snatch up their knives. Pounding footsteps came from the hallway, and from the corner of my eye I saw Kneller appearing in the doorway behind me. A panicked Mrs. Tilly stood behind him, her hand clutching her necklace to her chest and her breathing harsh and irregular. Stunned faces met me from all directions. There was a long moment of silence, then –

"You *clumsy* girl!" Marjorie shouted, the knife still clutched in her hand, and her blotchy face turned completely red. "What do you think you're doing?"

I only looked at her.

"My mistake, Mrs. Pickering," I said tonelessly. "It slipped."

"You stupid, arrogant little –"

Thwack.

Mrs. Tilly had strode forward and struck me with her apron. The thick canvas cut against my cheek as though I had been whipped.

"I'll put your hands on the burner!" she cried, cutting into Marjorie's obscenities. "I'll put 'em on the burner, you hear?"

"I think that would make her more likely to drop

the tray in the future, Frances," Kneller said, his face twisting as though he was trying hard not to smile. Mrs. Tilly let out an indignant growl and swatted me once more with her apron before storming from the room. Kneller's eyes briefly caught mine before traveling over to where Bernadette had left her chair to crawl beneath the table, her large backside sticking out as she attempted to retrieve the fallen food.

"I hope you weren't planning on keeping this job," Marjorie spat, throwing down her silverware. "What an idiot John was to hire you –!"

"Don't you dare insult my husband!" Amalia cried.

"He hired an imbecile!"

"He would have controlled her if he hadn't have been murdered!"

"I'm sure even John couldn't prevent inevitable mistakes from happening," came Lennox's voice from the door, and I turned to see him standing behind Kneller. He was watching us carefully. "Perhaps Mrs. Tilly should make the trays a bit lighter next time."

"Perhaps you should mind your own business, Lennox!" Marjorie said. "And as for you, Frank, you can go back to your squalor of a house and wipe that smile off of your face!"

Lennox's expression didn't change, though Kneller's darkened. He gave Marjorie a glowering stare.

"I think we'll go to bed," Rachel said hurriedly, only then seeming to realize that James had stopped shouting. She grasped the handles of his wheelchair and pushed him from the room.

Bernadette grabbed the edge of the table to haul herself back up, huffing from the endeavor of retrieving the chicken. She put it on her plate, oblivious to the argument, and began to eat. Marjorie threw her an appalled look.

"I think I'll go to bed, too," Bill muttered, hurrying

after Rachel and James. Edie gave him an irritated look as he left.

"Well, don't just stand there!" Marjorie said to me. "Clean up this mess!"

"Of course, Mrs. Pickering," I said, my tone still as bland as ever. "Shall I get the souffle first?"

Marjorie fumed; Kneller chuckled. I saw Lennox make a movement as though he was going to step forward, but on second glance he was still again.

"Just get out! Out!" Marjorie screamed. "You're a complete waste –!"

I turned and left the room before she could finish, sliding between Kneller and Lennox to make my escape. As I turned down the hallway to go to the Foyer, Lennox's footsteps sounded behind me.

"Alexandra."

I paused and turned back to him. Kneller was watching us from his spot outside the Dining Room.

"Yes?" I inquired.

Lennox glanced back at Kneller. The older man crossed his arms, his angular face looking more skeletal than ever in the shadows of the house.

"Let the girl go, Isidore," he said. "She was dismissed. Unless you're giving orders now?"

"It was a request," Lennox corrected, though he looked a bit abashed. He stood sideways as he looked between the two of us, then added in a firmer tone, "which I believe I'm still allowed to ask. Unless *you're* giving orders now, that is."

Kneller gave a soft laugh, though he certainly didn't look like he found the response funny. He nodded his head at me before turning back down the hall to retreat to the servants' door. Lennox faced me once again.

"May I speak with you?"

Though I nodded, he waited until we had reached

the Foyer. As I took one step up the staircase, he reached out and put his hand on my arm to stop me. It was the lightest of touches, and yet it held me in place as though he had grabbed me – but not, I realized, in a bad way.

"You need to be careful."

He was staring at me intently. It was the same look that he had used the first time I had met him that made me feel as though I was being examined rather than observed, and I still didn't know what to make of it.

"So you've said," I replied.

"And you're evidently not heeding my advice."

"I'm trying to figure out what's going on here: I can't do that by standing in the corner, waiting for someone to ask for a drink refill."

"What if you could?"

I raised my eyebrows.

"Meaning?"

"Meaning that I know the Marlowes better than you do," he said. "So if we were to – as you've suggested – work through this together, then perhaps we could do it in a different way. A safer way."

I simply looked at him. His tone made it sound as though he was only doing it out of concern for me rather than concern for the situation we were in.

"I thought you didn't want to get involved," I said.

"I don't. But I also don't want to see you get hurt."

"Why would that matter? You don't know me."

"I'm not of the belief that you need to know someone to care about them, Alexandra."

I brought my arms up to my chest to cross, breaking from his touch.

"While I appreciate your valor, Dr. Lennox, it's not necessary. I would welcome your help if you were interested in solving John's murder, but if you're only offering it to be chivalrous, then I decline."

"Why?"

"I just said why," I told him, readying to repeat my statement word for word.

"No, why would it matter what my reasoning is?" he asked. "Either way you're getting help."

"Yes, but –" I faltered, unsure of why I was truly turning him down. There was something about him that made me nervous, though not in the sense that I didn't trust him. It was the idea that he was as genuine as he seemed, and that, for a reason I didn't want to explore, I couldn't be the recipient of his kindness. "It's the principle of the matter."

"Are your principles the most important thing to you right now?"

"No, I just –" I began, "I just – I just think you're doing this to be – to be nice. And I'm not ..."

"Comfortable with that?" he finished, but it wasn't the correct guess.

"No. I just think – you have to be doing this because you want to solve John's murder, and nothing else, or else you'll just be – disappointed."

"I'll be disappointed if you come out of this unharmed?"

"You'll be disappointed that you wasted your energy on me," I said, trying to put into words what he ought to have figured out by now. "I'm not – I'm – I'm difficult."

"I think 'strong-willed' might be a better word," he said with the hint of smile.

It was easy for him to say, with his perfectly poised lines that streamed into faultless answers for whatever question was thrown his way. He was the picture of compassion and thoughtfulness: a man who always knew what to say in stark contrast to the habitual bluntness and presumptuousness that my professors had advised me to break from. And standing so close to him, I realized that I was looking at an image of who I was supposed to be and yet whom I would never be able to mirror despite all of my efforts and trials.

"No, I'm difficult," I corrected. "I'm too critical, too outspoken, and too unfeeling."

Lennox stared at me. For a moment I thought he might provide some sort of antidote for the way I acted, or even suggest a diagnosis that he assumed would explain the way I was, but then he cocked his head slightly to the side, his mouth a frown, and simply said, "I'm not sure that's a good enough reason not to help you, Alexandra."

"Well –"

I was cut off by the sound of thundering footsteps heading in our direction. Lennox quickly stepped aside, hiding behind the shadows of the staircase, and I followed. A streak of bright red hair flew past us and went upstairs, indicating that Marjorie had decided to go to bed. As the door to her room slammed from above, Lennox turned back to me.

"Let's get something straight, Alexandra: I do want to know what happened here. I also don't want to get into trouble – nor do I want you to. The most logical way forward, then, appears to be us working together to figure this out as discretely as possible. Does that work for you?"

"Well, I – I guess that would be fine," I said.

More footsteps sounded from down the hall. We retreated into the shadows once more. Amalia hurried up the stairs after her sister-in-law, but barely halfway up she dropped something, sending it back down with a *thump, thump, thump* to the black-and-white tiled floors. As she staggered back down the stairs to retrieve it, I knew that she would spot us, and so I stepped out from my hiding spot and picked it up for her.

"Give me that!" she snapped upon reaching the bottom step, snatching the heavy bottle of scotch from my hands. "It's my husband's!"

She clutched it to her chest as though frightened. I blinked.

"I was only trying to help you, Mrs. Marlowe," I replied.

"I don't need your help," she seethed, though she teetered dangerously in place as though she might pitch down the stairs in a drunken stupor at any moment. She leaned her face into mine. "And if I find out that you had *anything* to do with my husband's death, I won't put your hands on the burner – I'll put your *face* on it."

She grasped the banister and pulled herself up the stairs, swearing at me under her breath as she went. Lennox stepped out from the shadows, sending a worried frown at her back as she went before turning his attention to me.

"I know, I know," I said, not nearly as bothered by Amalia's threat as he appeared to be. "I'll work on being more discreet."

"I would settle for you being even slightly wary," he returned, though there was the hint of a twinkle in his eyes. I held his gaze for longer than I had intended to, staring at him as I filed his words away for later. I imagined myself returning to the sentence and ruminating over the playfulness in his tone, knowing that I would wonder and deliberate over why he seemed fascinated by me rather than frustrated; and for a moment, before I realized what I was doing, I hoped that he was thinking of me with as much adoration as I found myself feeling for him.

"I think you'll find that I'm very wary, Dr. Lennox," I said, breaking eye contact as I reminded myself that there was no place for such thoughts. "I'm just not as diplomatic about it as you."

"That's alright. I don't think I'd like you as much if you were."

I felt a sudden heat rise to my face, and despite telling myself that he had meant it in another way, my stomach churned uncomfortably.

"I'm hungry," I said abruptly, sidestepping him to force myself to break eye contact with him. "Should we see if there's anything for dinner?"

"That's a good idea," he said, but then his mouth turned to a sly grin. "Assuming you haven't dropped it all, that is."

CHAPTER SEVEN

We both stopped short upon entering the kitchen. Though Mrs. Tilly had retired for the night, she had chosen to take her anger with me out on the room. The over-spiced soup had been dumped over, its contents filling every crack in the coils on the stove and dripping down onto the floor, the carving utensils were sticking out dangerously from various drawers as though she was hoping I might brush past them and slice open my arms, and broken dishes filled the sink to create a mosaic on the cast iron. I surveyed the damage with a raised eyebrow, imagining that she expected me to spend the night scrubbing up the mess in penance for my wrongdoing. I shook my head and opened the refrigerator. I had more important things to do than appease her, though I might consent to help her with the floors if she handed me my money back.

"Cheese, bread, olives," I listed, looking through the contents, "or I could go get one of the Cornish hens from the Dining Room, though I haven't cleaned the floor in there in a few days."

"What about that?" Lennox said, nodding to the souffle that was sitting on a tray, beautifully dusted in powdered sugar and waiting to be brought to the Dining Room. I glanced at him. He didn't strike me as a man who ate dessert in place of dinner.

"I'm saving that for later," I deadpanned. "In case another argument breaks out."

"Ah. Well, then, I promise to be on my best behavior." He scooped up the souffle and moved it to the table. "But I simply can't resist."

He retrieved plates and spoons from the cupboards to serve it. It had already deflated, but I couldn't deny that it smelled wonderful – especially considering that Mrs. Tilly usually left me burnt or otherwise undesirable food to eat.

"So I take it I missed an exciting dinner," he said, handing me a plate.

"And an informative one. Should I fill you in, or could you hear it from the third floor?"

"Only pieces, and those were mostly expletives."

I took a bite of the souffle. It was still warm and decadently rich: I ought to have been raiding the kitchen for food since my arrival.

"Let's see ..." I began, "Bernadette accused Marjorie of murdering her children, Marjorie accused Bernadette of murdering her husband, Cassandra apparently believes she's the Grand Duchess Anastasia, Amalia's upset that no one cares that her husband was murdered, though she's not bothered that he apparently gave James brain damage ..."

"You make it sound rather blasé," Lennox said, his troubled frown reappearing to pull at his brow.

I shrugged.

"I'm just telling you what was said," I replied. "Apparently there have been questionable deaths in this family before – or did you know that already?"

"I'd heard about Marjorie's children, though not the bit about her being responsible. And I knew that Bernadette's husband passed away unexpectedly, but not that there was any reason for concern."

"So you knew nothing, then," I confirmed, albeit a bit ungraciously.

"Well, I –" Lennox began, but then he stopped and offered me a smile. "Is this the part where we begin to argue?"

"Not necessarily. I just don't want to waste time pulling teeth to get answers out of you."

He didn't look offended. If anything, he looked rather amused.

"I'll try to be more direct, then," he said. "I didn't know about any mysterious deaths in the family."

"Do you think what Bernadette said was true? Amalia might not get any of John's money?"

"It's possible. The Marlowes have always been very careful about keeping their money in their bloodline."

"So one of the siblings must have killed him, then – to get the estate."

"Not necessarily. They didn't seem certain about Sylvia's will. She may have very well said that the money has to go to a male descendant."

"But they said there were no more male heirs."

"Not in the immediate family, but I'm sure that they have distant cousins who are twice-removed who would fit the bill. It's an old family: they'll find someone."

"What about the Marlowes' children?"

"Well, there are no males. Not anymore."

"So Marjorie had sons?"

"A son and daughter."

"And they were beaten to death?"

Lennox sat back. Perhaps my tone had once again been too conversational, or perhaps it was becoming difficult for him to remain a confidant with the questions I was asking.

"Yes," he said.

"Possibly by her?"

"Her husband went to jail for it."

"So possibly by her," I affirmed in the same tone I had before telling him I didn't want to pull teeth.

"I suppose it's possible, yes," he said diplomatically. "Marjorie's always had ... outbursts. But even so ..."

"You don't think a mother could kill her children," I finished for him.

Lennox lowered his spoon and stared at me from across the table. His eyes had gone darker, and not even the orangey kitchen light would reflect in them.

"It's very difficult thing to consider," he said. His voice had dropped very low. The sound of it made me uncomfortable.

"What about the rest of them?" I asked.

"Amalia and John have daughters, Bernadette, too. Rachel and James never got the chance to have children because of the accident."

"Was it really an accident?"

Lennox sighed.

"I don't think any of us knows what John truly intended," he said. "But from what I've been told, John, James, and Rachel were on a trip together – this was before he married Amalia – and at some point they were up on a cliff overlooking the water. John tried to convince James to jump in, and James – being a cautious man for starters, and undoubtedly knowing that it wasn't a good idea – refused. So John gave him a push." Lennox grimaced. "Anyhow, James went down head first and cracked his head against the rocks, and ... well, you know the rest."

"Doesn't sound like an accident."

"John always maintained that the water looked deeper than it was, and he couldn't possibly have known there were rocks under the water: they weren't visible from where they were standing."

I raised my eyebrows in skepticism, but had no desire to discuss it further.

"So if Mrs. Marlowe had granddaughters, why aren't they here?"

"I doubt she ever met them more than once, if at all, or had any sort of close bond with them. She never left the island, and it's not like any of them made any effort to come visit her."

He almost sounded bitter. I got the odd sense that he might have cared for the dead woman, though I couldn't imagine why. Occupational hazard, I decided.

"And the Burtons?"

Lennox set his spoon down. He had barely eaten, though he no longer seemed to have an appetite.

"They tried," he said. "Many times. Edie had a dozen pregnancies, at least."

"Miscarriages?"

"And stillbirths."

"That's ..." I began, but I didn't know what word I was trying to find. Terrible? Awful? Nothing seemed to convey what I actually thought, and searching for feelings was far too difficult a task for me anymore.

"Unbearable," Lennox finished for me.

I swallowed.

"Do you have children, Dr. Lennox?"

"No. And you can call me Isidore, Alexandra."

"Right," I said, though I doubted that I would. It was easier to hide behind formality than it was to be exposed through friendliness. I ran my eyes over his face. I was probably mistaken, but I got the feeling he wasn't being truthful about the children, though I didn't know why he would lie about such a thing. Perhaps he was just being overly careful about what he said to avoid breaking doctor-patient privilege. I tried to picture him in a room with Mrs. Marlowe, listening as she told him whether or not she thought her daughter had killed her children, or if her other daughter had poisoned her husband and so on, and I wondered if the Marlowes' reason for hating him was because they knew he was privy to all of their secrets.

"Who do you think did it, if you had to guess?" I asked.

"It would be easier to say who I don't think did it. Not Rachel, obviously not James. Not Edie or Bill. I wouldn't think Cassandra, either."

"I'm not so sure," I said. "She's ..."

"A character," Lennox agreed, though it wasn't the word I would have chosen.

"She said something to me earlier about wanting us to be together once the rest of them are gone."

Lennox startled.

"Wanting us to be together?" he repeated.

"No – her and me."

"Ah – of course." He cleared his throat. "Well, I certainly don't know what the explanation would be for that."

"What about Mary?"

Lennox's eyes snapped up to meet mine.

"Excuse me?"

"Mary," I repeated. "Bernadette said something about her being murdered. Who is she?"

"Was," he corrected unnecessarily. He pushed his spoon around his plate, the frown returning with more prominence to his brow. "She was their sister."

"And she was murdered?"

"No."

"Well, are you sure? Because they seemed to think –"

"No." He looked back up at me. "No, she wasn't murdered. Can we move on?"

I paused. It wasn't lost on me that I had struck a nerve with him, though I wasn't certain how I felt about doing so.

"I'm just trying to get a clear picture, here," I said. "Bernadette specifically said, *We break all the odds, don't we? Three murders in one family ... Four if you count Mary.*"

"And you asked me to give you direct answers, so I am. Mary was not murdered. She did, however, die in a very horrible and tragic way that I'm afraid I have no interest in discussing."

I surveyed him carefully. His voice was sharp, but not out of anger. As I ran my eyes over his face, noting how his skin had paled, I got the impression that the subject was too personal for him, though I couldn't pinpoint why.

He stood and carried his plate to the trashcan, sliding the rest of his dinner into the bin with the serving knife.

"Listen," he said without facing me, though his voice had softened back to its usual tone. "I want to answer your questions – I do. But I just can't talk about that. I hope you understand."

I shifted my jaw, debating whether or not to push the subject.

"You're certain she wasn't murdered?" I asked.

"Yes."

"And there's no chance it has anything to do with what happened to John?"

"None," he said, turning back to me with a hint of exasperation in his voice. He brandished the serving knife as he tried to convince me. "She died sixteen years ago, and there was nothing mysterious about it. She wasn't beaten to death. She wasn't poisoned. She wasn't stabbed with a knife –"

Stabbed with a knife, I repeated to myself, fixing my eyes on the knife in his hand. It was nothing like the gold knife that had killed John, and yet the remains of the chocolate that clung to its blade were eerily reminiscent of dried blood and the way Lennox was gripping the handle so firmly jogged something in my memory.

I stood up and left the kitchen, not bothering to tell him why as I rushed through the house to get to the Study. Reaching the door, I yanked it open and hurried to the desk, rummaging through the contents until I produced what my memory had already found: a golden sheath with an ornate pattern that matched the handle of the knife in John's chest perfectly. Only it wasn't a knife, I knew now: it was a letter opener.

"What are you doing?"

I jumped and hurriedly shoved the sheath into my apron pocket as Bernadette's voice rang out from the hallway. I squinted my eyes through the dark room, wondering how she could see me when I hadn't even turned the light on, when I realized she wasn't speaking to me.

"I was just on my way to bed," came Lennox's reply.

"The Foyer is in the opposite direction," Bernadette said. "So let me repeat: what are you doing?"

"I'm heading to bed. I just got a bit lost."

"A likely story: you were here long enough to know which corridor leads where."

"And I've spent a great deal of time away, in which I've understandably put this house out of my mind."

Bernadette huffed.

"Well, carry on then," she said unhappily. "And if you see the maid, tell her the Dining Room is a right mess."

The sound of Lennox's oxfords retreating down the hallway had faded to silence before Bernadette moved away from the door. I peeked out in time to see her heading in the direction of the kitchen, then hurriedly made my way in the opposite direction to follow Lennox, not in the mood to hear her shouting that someone had taken a bite of her souffle without permission. I climbed the stairs up to the third floor, trying to make sense of what I had just learned.

Why had John been killed with a letter opener when there was an array of knives – not to mention a gun – in the house? It didn't make sense, and I didn't like it when things didn't make sense. The mind was a sensitive thing when it ought not to have been: too easily manipulated and changed, rewired or broken. And I knew how it worked – at least the medial temporal lobe, with its hippocampus, amygdala, cingulate gyrus, thalamus and hypothalamus, epithalamus, and mammillary body. I knew how to remember when others forgot, and store thoughts away like files in a cabinet that could be sorted through and produced later; but I didn't know people, and I didn't know how to read them, or what to think of them, or how to be around them, and I didn't know what they were capable of. And so for all of my knowledge, I didn't know what to do with the information I had found. My only hope was that Lennox could make sense of it.

He was in the nursery when I came into my room. His door was open and he was sitting on his small cot, his chin resting on his hands as he stared off across the dark room, though he jumped up upon seeing me.

"I didn't mean to offend you," he said. "I was only –"

"It was a letter opener that killed him."

"What?"

I leaned against the threshold between our rooms and crossed my arms, realizing that he had taken my abrupt departure as a sign that he had upset me. I was surprised to find the fact that he would care meant something to me.

"That's why I left. I remembered where I saw the pattern before."

"A letter opener?" he repeated, looking both confused and relieved. "Are you sure?"

"I found the sheath in the Study," I said, taking it out of my pocket and tossing it over for him to see. "Does it mean anything to you?"

"No, not at all," Lennox murmured, turning it over in his hands. "Well – except that it would have been much more difficult to kill someone with such a short blade."

"So they must've known what they were doing."

"Or gotten very lucky," he agreed, standing and bringing it back to me.

"Do you have any ideas why someone would use a

letter opener when there's a gun in the Parlor?"

"Well, a gun would've made too much noise. They didn't want to wake the whole house, did they?"

"So why not use a kitchen knife?"

Lennox hummed to himself.

"Well, I don't know," he said. "Maybe the killer didn't think anyone would notice if a letter opener was missing and was hoping the body wouldn't be discovered with the snowfall."

Mrs. Tilly's words flashed through my mind. *Why didn't you just let him disappear? It would have been better that way.*

"And everyone would think he wandered off?" I asked.

"Perhaps. The ferry was gone, after all: they might have assumed he had taken it back to the mainland."

"They could've done a better job hiding the body, then. Half the island's woods: why didn't they kill him in there?"

"Maybe they couldn't lure him that far out. And it would be difficult to drag him all the way once he was dead, at least undetected. Especially for the women."

"How did they lure him outside, then? It's not like he smoked."

"Maybe he was with someone who did."

"Marjorie?"

"She's the only one who smokes, as far as I know. Apart from us."

I thought of how quickly Marjorie had grabbed for her knife upon hearing the clatter of the serving tray when I had dropped it to the floor, as well as her evident distaste for her brother's inheritance when she had spoken about it the night of the wake.

"So she invited him out for a smoke, walked halfway around the house with him, then took out a letter opener and stabbed him?" I asked. "But why the letter opener?"

"It could have been spur of the moment. Maybe their conversation escalated into an argument."

"After she was what? Checking the mail?"

"Perhaps it has some sort of significance to her or the family," he suggested.

"And how do you propose we find out?"

He gave me a look, understanding what my question was suggesting.

"I'm not going to ask them if any of them had a special connection to it over morning coffee," he said.

"I don't know how else we're going to get the answer."

"You think the killer is going to do what, exactly? Jump up and tell me?"

"No, I think that someone *else* is going to jump up and tell you. If it's Marjorie who had a reason for choosing the letter opener, then I'm sure Bernadette will gladly tell you – especially if she's had a couple of cocktails."

Lennox raised his eyebrows, clearly not impressed with my line of thinking.

"Are you forgetting that only an hour ago you said you'd work on being more subtle?" he asked.

"I'll be plenty subtle. It's you who won't be."

As he gave me another stern look, I attempted to come up with a different plan, but I didn't think he would be pleased with any alternatives that I thought up. In a way he was rather like them: wanting to go on as though everything was normal and never let anyone know he was up to anything indecorous. And that was fine, I knew, because I could certainly be indecorous enough for the both of us.

"Well, if you don't want to, you don't have to," I said, pushing away from the door-frame as I resolved to think something up in the morning after my mind had had a chance to rest. "I'll try to think of something less conspicuous. No promises, of course."

"I would appreciate that," he said with a smile. As I turned to go back to my room, he added, "Goodnight, Alexandra."

I gave him a wave in return, then shut the door between us and followed the light that pooled beneath it across the floor to my bed. Taking four pills from my nightstand to swallow dry, I changed into my nightclothes and crawled into bed.

I laid my head on the pillow and stared down at where the soft yellow light gathered at my side. As my eyes began to shut, though, it was interrupted by a shadow: Lennox must have been standing on the other side of the door. I waited a moment, thinking that he might knock so that he could tell me another thought he had had about the murder, but then his shadow retreated and the light in his room flicked off. I let my arm hang over the side of my bed, touching the spot that it had left. And for a moment before I closed my eyes and fell into a sleep filled with notions of what else he might have come in and said to me, I didn't feel alone.

**

The sun was just a blur of murky reds and purples over the horizon when I went out for a smoke the next morning. I watched as it hit the ocean and sent diamonds of light over the surface, sparkling in innocence or apathy, and was just considering take a quick walk down to the dock while I finalized the plan I had come up with when the front door opened. Marjorie had come out for her morning cigarette.

She took out her lighter, which was a heavy, solid gold, and flicked it open to light her cigarette. It made a *ching* sound that rattled through the air. Her eyes trailed over to me as she took a deep drag, and from the way she was looking at me, it seemed as though she was formulating a plan of her own as to how best to get back at me for disrupting her dinner the night before.

"You look familiar," she accused. "Where have I seen you before?"

I blinked, wondering if she was so hungover from the previous night that she had forgotten who I was.

"Just around here, Mrs. Pickering."

"No, there's somewhere else. I *know* you."

She narrowed her eyes, but I only shrugged.

"I'm really not sure what you mean, Mrs. Pickering. My apologies."

She took a step closer to me, pulling her fur coat around her as a gust of wind skated across the porch.

"You're pretty," she said, though not in a complimentary way. She looked from my face to the cap covering my hair. "What are you doing working as a maid?"

"I ... just needed some money, Mrs. Pickering."

"What were you doing before?"

"Studying. In college."

She eyed me suspiciously.

"How old are you?"

"Twenty-nine."

"Twenty-nine is too old to be a college student."

"I'm in graduate school."

"Oh, graduate school? So why aren't you there now?"

"I'm ... taking some time off. To write my dissertation."

"While also working as a maid?"

"Yes," I said, my tone turning rigid. "Because I need the money."

It didn't appear that she liked the response. She

flicked her cigarette impatiently to rid it of ash.

"You know what I think?" she asked, but didn't bother to wait for an answer. "I think you're here because you had your eye on John."

"Excuse me?"

"Why else would you take this job? You could get medial work almost anywhere, and yet you chose this one. Maybe you were hoping my brother would take an interest in you, is that it? Maybe that he would leave his wife for you? You'd be set for life."

"I'll be set for life once I complete my degree –" I began angrily, but Marjorie cut me off.

"So what happened? Did he reject you? Toss you out of his bed? So you got your revenge by stabbing him in the dead of the night, then pretending you'd just found him out there –"

Something sharp hit my hand and I started. A large piece of ash had fallen from my cigarette and struck my finger. I dropped it and stomped it out, trying to calm myself.

"I was told I would be working for your mother, Mrs. Pickering – so I in no way took this job because of Professor Marlowe."

Marjorie came closer to me. She leaned forward until her face was right in mine.

"Let me tell you something," she whispered, blowing smoke into my face as she went, and it took all of my willpower to resist the compulsion to smack her. *"I don't believe you.* Not one bit."

She tossed her cigarette over the porch railing and returned inside. It took me a moment to follow her, for her accusation seemed to press against my lungs and halt my breathing. Her tone was so careless that I hardly believed she seriously thought I had killed her brother, and yet I didn't wholly believe she had said it just to get a rise out of me, either. Lennox's words flashed back across my mind: *you can bet that the Marlowes – including whichever one of them is responsible for killing John – are going to protect themselves, and the only way to protect themselves individually is to protect the family as a whole.* My chest tightened uncomfortably, but not out of fear. For if she been the one to kill John and was working out a way to weasel her way out of it by putting the blame on me, then perhaps I would need to be more careful. Or maybe, I realized as I returned inside, I would have to be more forceful in my actions to expose whomever had caused the mess we were all in.

The family behaved as though the disagreement from the night before – along with the murder – had never happened, though Amalia, at least, was at the other end of the table with Lennox and didn't speak to anyone. It appeared that, despite her dislike for the doctor, he was less offensive to her at the moment than her in-laws. The normalcy of them taking their seats and unfolding their napkins to drape over their laps before helping themselves to the sugared berries and diced apples was rather jarring, and even though I sensed that it was largely feigned to cover their true reactions to John's death, I couldn't help but think that it would be nice to put it to an end. I narrowed my eyes at Marjorie as she took a sip of juice. I wanted to see how she reacted to what I was about to say most of all.

Just as I opened my mouth to speak, though, the bell jingled to alert me that the next course was ready to be collected. I set down the coffee pot and went to the kitchen.

I was barely over the threshold when a finger jabbed me in the chest, halting me in place. Mrs. Tilly glared at me. The kitchen was still a right mess, though she had had to clean it a bit in order to cook.

"Did you forget something?" she asked.

"No."

"It took me an hour to scrub the stove this morning. You were supposed to do it last night."

"Was I?" I replied, wiping off the spot of flour she had left on my dress. "My mistake. I thought the kitchen was your job."

Her face turned to a sneer.

"If you *ever* ruin one of my meals again, I'll make sure you regret it."

She turned away from me and went back to the counter. Without her form blocking the table, I could now see that she had laid out a dozen or so platters, each one carrying a singular scone, in attempt to prevent me from dropping more than one serving in the future. I had half a mind to inform her that I was going to ruin the meal in a completely different way, but decided against it. Instead, I swept all of the scones onto one tray and left the room.

As I crossed through the East Room, I took in the sight of the portraits with greater attention than I had before, as though doing so might give me some insight into who the family members really were. In the first frame was a striking man with dark hair and a matching beard. He had a wide smile and clear green eyes that were the same shade as mine. It must have been John's father, though it was difficult to imagine that that could have been the man who had raised such bitter, unhappy children. In the next frame was Mrs. Marlowe with her narrowed brown eyes, pursed mouth, and dark red hair, though her birthmark hadn't been painted on her face; then Bernadette, only eighteen or so when the portrait had been done, with her fluffy hair sticking out in a triangular shape around her chubby cheeks; Rachel and John, who shared a frame – her smile withering and his an unctuous smirk; Marjorie, her bright orange hair down past her shoulders in a thousand ringlets; and Edie, with rosy cheeks and a timid smile that I had never seen her wear before. The last portrait must have been of Cassandra.

She had dark hair like her father, despite her telling me that it had been copper like her mother's, and wore a wide, almost infectious smile, though it seemed misplaced on her face as though it was part of a mask. There was a hook on the wall and a square of dust that was the same size as the other portraits: it must have been where the portrait of Mary had hung, yet the fact that it was missing suggested it was the same one that Lennox sought. Could I have been mistaken to think that he had been Mrs. Marlowe's psychiatrist? Had he really been Mary's – and she had died under his care?

I hurried onward to the Breakfast Room.

"... really no need to bring it up again." Lennox's voice was saying as I entered.

"It just must be so lonely for you," Bernadette said unsympathetically, "being in there with the ghosts of the past –"

Edie flinched and dropped her cup. It broke against the table, spilling coffee everywhere. I put my tray down and moved forward to collect the pieces, putting them on the still-intact saucer and carrying them away, then began to serve.

"That room –" she muttered, her voice nearly inaudible as she jumbled the words. "It should have been – closed off. Years ago."

"Well, yes, but then poor Lennox would have nowhere to sleep," Marjorie said. "Besides, I wouldn't be so sure he's so lonely ..."

I stooped to let Bernadette take her food. She selected three scones and doused them in clotted cream and jam. As she finished arranging them on her plate and licked her fingers, I took my chance to speak.

"I realized something last night," I began, keeping my view on the entire table to watch everyone's expressions. "About –"

"Alexandra." Lennox cut me off. His eyes were fixed on me from his spot across the table. He slowly raised his cup. "Would you mind refilling my coffee?"

"I –"

"Would you mind serving me my breakfast first?" Marjorie said, sending a glare in his direction. "Since I believe you work for me, not Lennox."

I shifted my jaw and brought the tray over to her, irritated that he had stopped me from speaking. It was clear that he didn't need more coffee: his cup was still three-quarters full. He evidently knew that I had been about to tell them about the letter opener and, just as I had presumed, didn't agree with it.

"What was that you were saying, Alexa?" Rachel asked kindly as I brought the tray over for her to select a scone. I threw Lennox a glance, my stubbornness telling me to take the chance to go through with my plan, but I stopped myself. He knew the family better than I did, I reminded myself, that was why I had asked for his help. If I found his reasoning as to why he didn't want me to tell them too faulty for my liking, then I could still inform the family about the letter opener later.

"I just realized," I said carefully, feeling his gaze on me as strong as ever, "that everyone has been calling me by the wrong name. It's not 'Alexa.' It's 'Alexandra.'"

"You told me your name is Alexa," Bernadette said exasperatedly from the head of the table.

"I can't imagine why you think it's appropriate to correct us now," Marjorie agreed. "There are much more important things going on in this household than your name."

"My apologies, Mrs. Pickering," I said tonelessly.

"Well, I think Alexandra is a lovely name," Rachel said, nodding to me that she was finished getting food for her and Mr. Langston. "I'll make sure I call you that from now on."

"I think I prefer Alexa," Bernadette said. "Alexandra is far too many syllables. No one should have a name that's such a mouthful."

She concluded her statement by taking a large bite of scone and jam. I brought the tray to Lennox.

"Did you still want more coffee, Dr. Lennox?" I asked in a would-be polite voice, trying to see if he was satisfied with what I had said.

"Oh, no," he replied. "I think I'm just fine now."

"Well, I'm not fine," Amalia said angrily. "Because – in case you've all forgotten – my husband is dead!"

"Yes, dear, we're well aware," Bernadette said. "Though I'm not sure what you'd have us do about it."

"I'd have whichever of you did it admit to it!"

"That's a marvelous idea," Marjorie drawled. "Why don't you do it now? We're all listening."

"I didn't kill my husband!"

"I don't know who else would've," Marjorie said, but her eyes moved over to me, seeming to silently confirm my suspicions that she planned to accuse me of being the murderer as soon as her other accusations fell through.

"Really?" Amalia said. "Because I can think of several people – starting with you!"

"Let's not get into this again," Rachel said. "I truly don't believe anyone here killed John –"

"And what do you think happened?" Amalia snapped. "He committed suicide?"

"I probably would have," Marjorie said into her coffee cup as she raised it to take a sip, "if I was married to you ..."

Amalia's eyes flashed in rage.

"You just wait until the police get here," she seethed. "I'll have them drag you away in shackles!"

"No one's going to be dragged away in shackles,"

Bernadette said. "If anything, whoever did it will be taken as subtly as possible to avoid bringing any further shame on the family –"

"If the killer's worried about shame, they should have considered that before killing my husband!"

"Well, there's nothing to be done about it now," Bernadette said. "So might we continue our breakfast in peace?"

Edie set down her silverware.

"I agree with Amalia," she said. "Something has to be done – I can't go on like this!"

"Whatever do you mean, dear?" Bernadette asked.

"I can't sleep at night! Not with – not with two dead bodies inside the house!"

"Well, we could put them both outside, I suppose," Bernadette said. "Though there's only one pedestal ready in the mausoleum at the moment ..."

"No one's touching my husband again," Amalia said. "Not until the police come and prove which of you did it! I'm locking the door!"

"Alright then, we'll keep them inside," Bernadette said. "So long as the room's properly chilled there shouldn't be a problem."

"Oh, Birdie," Rachel said, looking revolted. "Please: that's our mother and brother you're talking about."

"It's just science, dear," Bernadette said. "Bodies decompose at a much faster rate in warm temperatures –"

"I can't sleep knowing that there's a killer in the house, either!" Edie exclaimed.

"Well, then the killer can sleep outside," Bernadette said.

"Oh, yes," Marjorie said dryly. "Whoever it is, just drag your comforter outside at night ... *Alexandra* will help you ..."

"Can you two be serious for one minute?" Edie said.

She was nearly crying. Her fingernails dug into her arms as she grasped herself tightly, looking frightened of coming apart. My mind went back to her twelve dead children, and suddenly she didn't seem as ridiculous as her siblings made her out to be, but rather sorrowful. I tore my eyes away, unable to look at her a moment longer. "Can't we just – just say who did this?"

"Oh *that* should entice whoever killed John to come forward," Marjorie said. She looked around the table. "Everyone, Edie is uncomfortable, so whichever of you stabbed dear John to death, please admit it now – no hard feelings, she just wants you to sleep over at the guesthouse until she's able to leave –"

Rachel flinched violently, though no one else seemed to notice. I frowned, trying to place her reaction. Perhaps she was just fearing another argument like the one the night before.

"There you go again!" Amalia said. "John wasn't dead a day before you started making jokes about him –!"

"I made jokes about him his whole life – why stop just because he died?" Marjorie returned.

"Yes," Amalia said, nodding as though she had just realized something that made her dislike her sister-in-law even more. "Yes, you did make fun of him all his life – and it hurt him very deeply! I can't begin to tell you the pain he suffered at yours and your sisters' hands –!"

"Oh, get over it. He could dish it but couldn't take it, couldn't he?"

"My husband was never as cruel as you've all been –!"

"There's no need for this fighting," Rachel interjected, trying to placate her siblings despite her shaking voice, "so let's not jump on one another –"

"Oh, easy for you to say," Amalia said. "You're happy that he's dead, aren't you? Just admit it!"

"I am not!" Rachel breathed. "I don't understand how you could think –?"

"Stop acting like you're better than all of us! Always playing the saint when we all know better! You're glad he's dead! You've been waiting for this since he – since James had his accident!"

"She's been waiting for someone to stab him outside on the night of our mother's wake?" Marjorie asked skeptically. "Goodness, what a specific wish to be miraculously fulfilled –"

"She's been waiting for him to die!" Amalia screeched. "Even before what happened to James! Ever since he showed your mother those love letters that Frank used to send you and revealed what a whore you are!"

Rachel's expression froze as though she had been turned to marble.

"Now hold on, Amalia –" Bill started, but Amalia cut him off.

"She has! She wanted him dead, and she wants me to suffer for it by being stuck here with all of you –!"

"Believe me when I say this," Marjorie cut in, "no one wanted you here. We were all hoping you'd be on another of your supposed 'retreats' –"

"You wanted me out of the way, more likely!" Amalia said. "You knew if I wasn't here you'd have an easier time covering the whole thing up –!"

"Oh, for Christ's sakes," Marjorie said, "if we were all in on it together, don't you think we would have been able to think up something a bit more clever?"

"You – you were probably all bickering too much to decide on something proper!"

Marjorie downed her orange juice as though it was vodka, her eyes never leaving Amalia's face.

"Oh, yes," she said caustically. "Rachel wanted to push him off a cliff, Birdie wanted to slowly poison him,

Lennox wanted to throw him out a window –"

Lennox's hand twitched and he splattered coffee over his plate. Edie put her face in her hands, unable to listen to anymore talk of death.

"You undoubtedly wanted to beat him to death," Bernadette whispered loudly in Marjorie's direction, and Marjorie's nostrils flared out as though about to spout fire.

"Somebody had better admit something," Amalia said shakily, her beautiful face contorted in rage and her dark hair flying out around her head like the snakes of Medusa's, "or I'll – I'll – I'll kill myself!"

Whatever reaction she might have been hoping for, it certainly wasn't the one she received. Silence met her words, and there was no hint of worry on anyone's face.

"Would you like my knife?" Marjorie asked, holding it out toward her while taking another bite of her scone.

Amalia let out a shriek. Picking up her plate, she flung it across the table. It hit Marjorie in the shoulder and cracked in three, then fell to the floor and shattered.

"You bitch!" Marjorie fumed.

"Stop it – both of you!" Rachel said. "This isn't helping anything!"

"I don't need your advice!" Amalia seethed. "Go back to caring for your crippled husband, why don't you? That's the only purpose you have in life!"

"Now hold on," Bill interjected, pushing his glasses up on his nose in what appeared to be an attempt at gaining valor. "That's not fair: Rachel's the only decent person at this table!"

"Is she?" Edie asked sourly, her blue eyes bulging as she looked up from her hands.

"Well, no, I didn't mean –"

"You can't work your way out of that one, Bill," Marjorie said briskly, taking a sip of coffee. "And I'll remember that sentiment, thank you very much."

"The only decent one?" Amalia echoed, ignoring her sisters-in-law and staring at Bill with rounded dark eyes. Her anger was rendering her a bit unhinged, and though she was fuming, she was almost smiling, too, as though she found the process either amusing or liberating. "I'm not sure 'decent' is how I would describe a woman who had an affair with the help while her husband was incapable of stopping her –!"

"Well," Bill spluttered. "Well, that's none of my business –"

"How is dear Frank doing?" Amalia said, rounding on Rachel again. "What does he do over there in the guesthouse, other than pine away for you?"

Rachel looked as though she was on the verge of tears. Her mouth and jaw were quivering, and from the greenish tinge that had taken over her skin, I readied myself to throw the breadbasket in front of her to use as a basin.

"What's your plan now?" Amalia continued. "Going to move in with him now that your mother's not here to disown you? I'm sure James won't mind: just wheel him into the corner while you throw yourself into another man's arms –"

"That's enough, Amalia!" Lennox said, but Amalia had gained too much momentum and there was no chance of stopping her now. Her face broke into a smile as she watched Rachel's crumble.

"Go on," she goaded. "We all know you want to. You've been dying to do it for years –!"

Rachel stood up. For a moment I thought that she might strike the other woman, but then she sucked in a breath and stood from the table. Taking the handles of James's wheelchair, she pulled him back, not caring that he had been trying for several minutes to pick up his scone, and they left the room.

"There was no need for that, Amalia," Lennox said

as the door snapped shut.

"I can do without your input, too!" she replied. "Don't think I've discounted how you might be involved in John's death!"

"I didn't kill your husband."

"Really? Because I'm finding your presence here odder and odder. You just happened to show up the night he was killed –"

"Which was also the night of the wake," he interjected.

"And you're the only one with an air-tight alibi?"

"It's better than not having an alibi at all, I would think."

Amalia's lips thinned into a tight line.

"Yes, but you seem to have a funny way of being around when people mysteriously drop dead, don't you?"

"Not that I'm aware of," he returned, and for the first time his tone turned harsh as she wore away at his patience. "But if you keel over unexpectedly in my presence, I'll be sure not to be alarmed."

Amalia leaned toward him.

"You're not getting any of the money," she warned. "I don't care what the will says: you won't get any of it."

"I'm not interested in the money."

"Really? Still have enough from your last inheritance, do you?"

Lennox stood up. Amalia mirrored him.

"Your husband invited me here," he said.

"And why would he do that?"

"You can ask him," Lennox said angrily, "when you see him in Hell."

He turned and left the room. Amalia's mouth was twitching as she watched him, and a moment later she slammed down her napkin and stomped out through the other door. I stood in my spot by the wall rather than retreating to the kitchen, still holding the coffee pot as though there was a chance that someone might ask for a refill. I had to hand it to whichever of them was the killer: they all did a very good job at feigning innocence.

The remaining family members eyed one another. Marjorie was the first to speak.

"Though I would never admit it in front of her," she said, "Amalia has a point. Why would John invite him here?"

"Probably for the sole purpose of sticking him in the nursery to sleep," Bill said. "Or have you forgotten your brother's sense of humor?"

"John didn't have a sense of humor," Marjorie retorted. She scooped more butter onto her knife and spread it over her scone. "He had a sadistic sense of self-worth that he insisted on sharing with the world. And knowing that, why would Lennox show up?"

Bill didn't respond. Marjorie raised her eyebrows at him, waiting for an answer.

"To kill him," she said for him.

"He had no reason to," Bill said, but his uncertain tone didn't agree with the words.

"Of course he did: for the money. And we'll know soon enough what Mother's will said once we get out of this place. Why shouldn't she have left it to the closest thing to a male heir she had?"

"I think I'm a closer male heir than he is!" Bill exclaimed.

"Oh, yes," Marjorie tutted. "But you have no children, nor will you. Lennox, at least, has the time and means to procreate, and so long as the children don't die ..."

Edie stood and ran from the room. I could hear her sobbing as she ran through the empty East Room.

"Well," Bill said unhappily, rising from his chair, "I guess I'll go check on my wife."

Marjorie, Cassandra, and Bernadette remained at the table. From the look in the former and latter's eyes, they seemed to be in a contest to see who could stay the longest.

"I bet you're glad you came down to breakfast today, Cassie," Marjorie finally said.

"I'm afraid I haven't been glad in many years," Cassandra said. She wasn't wearing quite as an elaborate get-up as usual, though there was a pillbox hat perched on her head and a double-layered veil over her face. Given her silence during the family's heated discussion, for once she almost seemed to be the sanest person in the room. I rather thought that didn't bode well for the rest of us. "And I doubt I'll be glad for years to come, what with losing John —"

"Oh, for Christ's sakes," Marjorie said, and threw down her napkin and left.

I cleared my throat.

"Should I clear the table, Mrs. Carlton?" I asked.

Bernadette gave me a withering look.

"No, you should certainly not," she said, and indicated for me to bring the platter of scones back over. "I'll not be made to starve just because of my siblings' inability to sit properly for a meal ..."

CHAPTER EIGHT

When they had finished and I could finally slip away, I hurried up to the third floor to find Lennox, but found the nursery empty. I returned downstairs and checked outside, thinking that he might have gone for a smoke, but there was no sign of him out there, either, and it was such a frigid day that it didn't seem likely that he would stay out for so long. I continued my search on the first floor, weaving in and out of the rooms. As I walked, the dimness of the house greeted me with shadows, and the unseen ghosts that I didn't believe in but couldn't get out of my mind followed me like a stranger.

I slid my fingers over the top of the baby grand piano in the Music Room, drawing a line through the thick dust that I hadn't bothered to clean yet. No one ever entered the room anymore, and the windows were covered over in dormant vines that blocked out the sunlight. Photos of the Marlowes as children littered the top of the mantle: they were young and wild-looking, with starched play-clothes that were stained with grass and mud, and wiry little smiles that seemed to hide devious intentions. Mrs. Marlowe wasn't in any of the photos, but several different nannies were. Their black-and-white faces stared up at me from the paper as though warning me that the house had chased them away.

As I reached the last picture frame and looked down at a thirty-something year old Edie with an infant child in her lap, I pulled myself from the room. There was nothing to find in there except the loneliness that I had been hoping to outrun.

The wall in the Lounge had partially come down, revealing the rot behind the wallpaper, and it was so drafty that it was normally kept tightly closed off. I gave it a glance and then headed down the hall to the Ballroom, which was nothing more than a huge empty space with golden chandeliers and gilded stucco walls, an ornately painted ceiling, and tiled mosaic flooring that served as a reminder of the glory of the past. I shut my eyes and tried to picture the children from the photographs dancing around the room, or the older ones from the portraits in the East Room waltzing with suitors, but the image wouldn't come. It was as though the house was doing everything in its power to protect its inhabitants' identities, and the more I searched, the darker and colder the rooms became in the hopes of chasing me away.

Spider-webs like silvery curtains hung down from the ceiling as I entered the Smoking Room, and I ducked to avoid them. Forgotten furniture reeked of smoke and a large container of butane sat in the middle of the floor. Mrs. Marlowe must have used it to refill her lighter, which – by the state of my surroundings – got more use than anything else in the house. I coughed into my sleeve and patted my hand against the wall behind me in search of the light switch, but the push-button wouldn't budge against my thumb. I moved into the room even so, thinking that Lennox might have holed himself up in a corner to brood over Amalia's accusations, but before I could take a proper look around, a voice spoke.

"Who's there?"

I jumped and looked around. Rachel was sitting in the far corner of the room at a small table, though I could barely see her.

"Oh – I – sorry, Mrs. Langston," I said. I cleared my throat. "I was just – I thought I might do some cleaning in here."

She surely knew I wasn't telling the truth: the lie sounded false even to my own ears. She didn't move from her spot.

"That's all right, Alexandra."

I couldn't see her face, and without the ever-present smile on it, her voice sounded sorrowful. Something tugged me toward her despite my senses telling me to leave.

"Can I bring you anything?" I asked. "Some coffee – or a lamp?"

I had meant to say *or a cup of tea,* but the idea that she was sitting in the dark had overtaken the words.

"No, no thank you," she said. "I'm just taking a break."

I didn't ask what from. Caring for her husband, I assumed, or else from dealing with her family's explosive fights. As I moved closer to better see her, though, another thought crossed my mind – one that I didn't wish to believe but that I couldn't discount, either – and I found myself wondering if she was sitting in the dark contemplating a horrid guilt she held for killing her brother. The thought made me shiver.

"Isn't there somewhere more comfortable for you?" I asked. I moved around the boxes so that she was at least in my line of sight, though she was still just a dark shape on the chair now. "It's – smoky in here."

"You're sweet," she said softly. "But, really, I don't mind."

I hesitated. I couldn't remember the last time someone had called me sweet, which meant it had either been before I had properly trained my memory or simply had never happened at all. I was leaning toward the latter.

"I should get back to James," she continued, though she didn't sound like herself anymore: she sounded like someone broken. Or perhaps that was who she really was, and who I had been seeing was simply a woman wearing a mask for the outside world. "He might need me."

"I doubt he'll know one way or the other," I said

before I could stop myself. I bit my tongue too late to stop the words, then faltered for an addendum. "I mean – because he – because of –"

"Because he's damaged," Rachel said for me. She smoothed her skirt over her legs, staring down at the thick wool fabric. "We don't really know how much he understands. Sometimes I think he knows everything we're saying. And other times ... nothing at all. But since I can't be certain, I have to assume that a part of him is still here."

She raised her eyes to me, and I felt that I ought to say something: to tell her that I understood what it was like to love someone who couldn't love me in return, or that I had spent the past decade of my life trying to fix the damage that had been done to my mother's mind. Yet as the seconds ticked by, I couldn't get the words out. Words only came to me when they were straightforward and harsh, and never when they carried any sentiment or understanding.

Rachel stood up and moved around me to get to the door. I listened to her footsteps disappearing down the hall, still wishing that I had said something. It felt as though every chance that I missed to prove I still had a heart chipped away at me with a chisel, and the deeper it dug, the more it exposed my insides to be made of stone.

Something silver on the table caught my eye: a cross hanging on a chain. It was the same one Rachel had worn the night of the wake. I picked it up and turned it over in my hands. The back was etched with delicate letters. *To RMM, love FEK*. To Rachel Marlowe, I guessed, from Frank Kneller. I stuffed it into my pocket and leaned down to press my jaw onto my balled hands, suddenly feeling defeated. If she had killed John, I wouldn't have blamed her – and I wouldn't point the police at her, either, regardless of whether she had ruined any chance I might have had at returning to the university.

I stood and left the room, making my way to the

Drawing Room in the hopes of finding her to return the necklace. Perhaps she had left it behind on purpose, but I didn't think so. She wouldn't have been wearing it to her mother's wake if it meant nothing to her, so there seemed to be no reason to leave it behind now. I reached the Drawing Room, took the necklace from my pocket, and raised my hand to knock, but –

Voices murmured from inside the room. I leaned in closer, thinking that she might be speaking to Mr. Langston.

" ... really shouldn't be talking about it," Rachel was saying.

I felt my breath catch at the thought that I had been right: she had killed John and was confessing to her husband. But then –

" ... so just don't say anything," she continued. "You know what they'd do."

"But I have to," came a second voice. It took me a moment to recognize it as Bill's: it was strained and gruffer than usual. "I can't just pretend it didn't happen ..."

"You can pretend. You should pretend. Let them think it was someone else. Please, Bill. *Please.*"

"What if it's not someone else?"

"It *is* someone else," she said, and her voice cracked unnaturally. "I'm certain it is. So please don't say anything."

There was a long pause. I sucked my breath in, waiting for Bill to ask her how she knew such a thing, but then he said, "And what about the fact that she's lying?"

"You don't know that for certain. She could just be mistaken –"

I moved to lean closer to the door, but the slight shift in my weight caused the floorboards to give an awful squeak. I jumped back, but the necklace chain caught on the door handle and yanked me forward again. I grappled to untangle it, but footsteps were already coming toward me and before I decide what to do the door swung open,

snapping the chain at the clasp and releasing it into my hand
–

Bill's face appeared in front of me. His expression was nearly wild, and his startled eyes zeroed in on me standing there. I held up the necklace.

"Mrs. Langston left this in the Smoking Room," I said rigidly, forcing my tone to be neutral and hoping that my expression matched.

Bill eyed the cross dangling from the chain. It spun ever slightly as I held it out between us, turning in an imperceptible breeze.

"You shouldn't disturb people when they're in their rooms," he said.

"I'm sorry, Mr. Burton – I just didn't want her to worry that she'd misplaced it."

"I think she'd be more worried to know that you're sneaking around outside her room – I certainly am."

"I'm not sneaking," I said carefully, but then my brashness got the better of me. "And if I was, I don't know why you'd be concerned. Unless you had something to hide –"

"Me? I have *nothing* to hide!" he said angrily. "It's you who's – who's –"

He struggled to find the word he was searching for, his spluttering getting the best of him as he swayed in his spot, but before he could finish, Rachel appeared by his shoulder.

"What's going on here?"

Bill jumped and looked over at her.

"She was listening at the door!" he exclaimed.

Rachel glanced at me, then down to the necklace in my hand. She turned back to Bill.

"It looks like she's just returning my necklace," she said. She reached forward and took it from me. As Bill began to protest, she cut him off. "Alexandra – can you put the ramp out? Bill and I are going to take James for a walk."

"Of course." I moved my eyes away from her face over to Bill's. Holding his gaze, I added, "That's why I'm here, after all."

I turned to cross the Foyer to get my coat from the rack by the door, knowing Bill's eyes were following me as I went. I tugged on my boots and opened the front door to escape his distrusting eyes.

Cold air greeted me when I stepped out onto the front porch. The large piece of wood that Kneller had brought from the shed was resting on the far side beneath a layer of white from the last two days of snowfall. I heaved it across the porch, the weight of it protesting against my efforts and the rough edges sending splinters into my hands. When I finally reached the stairs, I gave it a firm kick to get it down, and it slid down and stopped in front of a familiar pair of oxfords. Lennox took a step back.

"There you are," I said, not bothering to apologize for jabbing him in the toes. "I was trying to find you."

"I was just having a cigarette."

I had half a mind to tell him that he must have had a dozen or so cigarettes in the time that I had been looking for him, but instead I shuffled down the ramp to him and took out a cigarette of my own.

"Why'd you stop me from telling the family about the letter opener?" I asked as I lit it.

Lennox heaved a sigh.

"Because it's not a good idea," he said firmly, "and I don't know what you're expecting you'll get out of it if you do."

"I'm expecting to get a reaction out of them – maybe one that will point at whoever did this."

Lennox stuck his cigarette in his mouth and took a long drag, his eyes not leaving my face as he did so.

"Let me ask you something, Alexandra: did you

observe the family when you brought them outside to show them John's body?"

"Well, not exactly."

"What about after we told them he'd been stabbed?"

I thought back to when the family had collected in the Augustus Suite, picturing Marjorie's belligerent manner, Bernadette's quizzical air, Rachel's pained eyes, Edie's terrified grimace, Bill's tense form, Mrs. Tilly's disbelieving shaking head, and Amalia's livid expression.

"I noticed how they looked," I said.

"And?"

"Do you want me to recount it?"

"No, because I observed them, too, and do you know what I saw?" He waited for me to shrug. "Nothing. No signs of guilt, nothing incriminating – nothing remotely out of the ordinary as far as reacting to such news goes."

"So what's your point?"

"Someone in that room killed John, unless Edie's right about a madman hiding out on the island. And if the killer can feign normalcy so well, then there's nothing you can say that will shock them into giving themselves away. Whoever did it chose the letter opener for a reason, and maybe it does have some sort of significance – or maybe it was selected specifically to draw attention away from them and to point to someone else."

I took another drag of my cigarette, considering what he had said. For all of my stubbornness, though, I found that I agreed with him.

"Alright, well ..." I said, "then I won't say anything about the letter opener."

"Thank you."

A thumping sound came from the front porch, and we both watched as Bill and Rachel brought James's wheelchair down the ramp and onto the path. They pushed him down in our direction. Bill threw us a look as they passed but said nothing. When they were a safe distance away, I turned back to Lennox.

"I think Bill and Rachel know something," I said, then briefly relayed the conversation I had just overheard. Lennox finished his cigarette and lit another as he listened.

"Well, it sounds fairly generalized," he said when I was done. "They could have been talking about anything."

"She specifically said, *Let them think it was someone else,*" I repeated. "What else do you think they'd be talking about in these circumstances? Who forgot to turn the lights out in the Parlor?"

"I don't know. It seems unlikely, but if either of them knew who killed John, I don't know why they'd keep it a secret."

"Unless it was one of them who did it."

Lennox raised his eyebrows.

"Well, that I wouldn't believe for a second," he said.

"Bill sounded like he wanted to confess something: he either knows who did it or he did it. And like you said, why would he protect the killer?"

"I don't know. But I don't know why he would kill John, either."

"Maybe he thought he'd be the one to get the estate."

"I highly doubt it. I don't think anyone expects Sylvia to have left him anything."

"Bernadette thought it was possible. She said, *It won't be split up among any of us if the will states it has to go to a male heir. If anything, it would go to Bill.* Remember?"

"Well, not word for word, no," he replied, looking mildly intrigued.

"And just this morning when they were all talking about how you might get the estate," I went on, "Bill said that he's a closer male heir than you."

"Well, he is," Lennox said. "But again, I doubt either of us were left anything. I'm sure Sylvia would have left everything to a blood relative."

"But if there aren't any male blood relatives who aren't third cousins twice removed, then she might have picked him. And if he's next in line, wouldn't that make him a likely suspect?"

"Outwardly, yes. But it sounds to me like the conversation you heard was out of context."

"I doubt it. He sounded upset."

"He could be upset about anything."

"Such as?"

"Perhaps his marriage is failing," Lennox guessed. "He and Edie might be separating and they haven't told the family yet."

"Seems like a funny time to bring it up," I said, growing impatient that he refused to even entertain the idea. "We're all trapped in a house with a killer, and you think they're hiding in the Drawing Room talking about whether or not he's going to get divorced?"

"You're talking about people who still sit down for formal meals three times a day despite knowing that someone among them is a murderer," Lennox replied. "So, yes, I think it's possible."

"And yet you don't think it's possible that he killed John?"

Lennox sighed. He flicked his cigarette to rid it of ash.

"No, quite frankly, I don't," he said. "I've known Bill a long time. He's a good, hardworking man. He wouldn't kill someone in the hopes of inheriting some money."

"But it's not 'some money,' it's a load of money. How much is this island worth? A million? What's the family's shipping company valued at? Twice that?"

"More, I would think," Lennox said mildly, and I wanted to scream at him to wake up.

"You can't just say he didn't do it because he's nice!"

"I didn't say that: I said your reasoning is too flimsy. If it was set in stone that he was next in line to inherit, then I'd consider the possibility – but it's more likely that Amalia is getting the money, or *thought* she was getting the money, or one of Sylvia's biological children."

"You didn't see him when he realized I'd overheard him. He was frightened."

"I'm sure he was. John's dead. No one knows what happened. If anything, I think that Bill's frightened for his life, not frightened because he's guilty."

I crossed my arms.

"Just because you like him doesn't mean he didn't do it," I said. "People do horrible things all the time, and it's the people we like who disappoint us the most."

Lennox's cigarette was drooping in his mouth. I took several quick drags of my own, trying to look unaffected, but he was giving me that searching look again as though he was reading the thoughts running through my head, and I got the feeling he knew exactly what I was talking about.

"That's a very cynical point of view," he said after a few moments. "Especially from someone so young."

"It's not cynical: it's factual," I replied. "There's a difference."

Lennox dropped his cigarette and pushed it into the snow with his shoe.

"I could be mistaken," he said after several moments, his diplomatic tone returning. "You're right: it could be him. But you asked me for my help because I know the family better than you, so I'm just telling you that I find it much more likely that it was Amalia, Marjorie, or Bernadette."

"And your reasoning?"

"Because Amalia thought she would inherit from John, Bernadette is the oldest, so she might be the next in line, and Marjorie –" He paused, searching for a word. "Marjorie is ... volatile."

I could still see Bill and Rachel in the distance. He was pushing James' wheelchair down the path at a slow pace, periodically getting stuck in the snow, while she stood by his side. I frowned.

"What if he did it for Rachel?" I asked.

"Excuse me?"

"The night of the wake, when the family was arguing about how John inherited everything, Marjorie said that Rachel was out of money and had asked John for more."

"She did?"

"Marjorie said, *Then why were you practically on your knees begging him for money yesterday to help you out of your debt? I'm surprised you would bother to humiliate yourself. You ought to have known he'd say no.* And Rachel was pretty embarrassed. So what if Bill knows – or assumes – he's the next to inherit, and so he killed John to get the money for Rachel?"

"And they were just casually discussing it in the Drawing Room, in full earshot of anyone standing outside the door?"

"Like I said, he wasn't happy to see me standing there."

"But if he was truly talking about killing someone, then why didn't he go somewhere where no one could overhear him? And what was the bit about someone lying?"

"He said, *And what about the fact that she's lying?* And Rachel replied, *You don't know that for certain. She could just be mistaken.*"

"So Bill killed someone, told Rachel, and now

someone's lying about ... what?" he challenged.

I shifted my jaw, trying to come up with a good argument.

"Maybe he's talking about Edie," I said. "If Bill sneaked out and killed John, then his wife probably noticed him getting up from bed. She's lying to protect him from blame, but maybe not for much longer. You saw her at breakfast: she looked like she was ready to fall apart."

Lennox made an odd face as though he was frightened but trying desperately not to show it. I smiled inwardly at my victory: he couldn't deny the possibility of the murderer being Bill any longer.

"Well, that's ... that's ..." he started. "I don't think that's right, but ... we can certainly observe him more closely, since you've brought up a good point."

Rachel, Bill and James had disappeared beyond the clusters of trees. As they left my view, I tried to think of what it would mean if my assumption was correct. Bill would inherit the money – go to prison, depending on whether or not it could be proven that he did it – and then his wife and Rachel would split the millions depending on what their deal was. I shook my head. I could see why Lennox didn't want to entertain the possibility. The three of them seemed to be the best of the Marlowe family.

"What happened to them?" I asked. I didn't expect him to outright tell me given the ethics of it all, but perhaps, given the circumstances, he would bend the rules to tell me about his client's children.

"Who?"

"The family. The Marlowes. How'd they all wind up so ...?"

"Maladjusted?" he finished. He heaved a sigh. "I could guess, but I don't know for certain."

"Give it your best shot. It might explain who killed John."

He shifted in his spot and crossed his arms, staring off across the snow as he thought. I had the feeling he was planning what to say carefully to avoid being unethical.

"Well, I would think the way they were raised explains the most," he said. "Sylvia and Malcolm wouldn't win any awards for parenting."

"Meaning?"

"I don't really know: it's not like I was around when they were growing up. But Sylvia had her issues, and her husband sounded like he was a piece of work."

"You're going to have to be more specific," I said. "I get that they were bad parents – but what actually happened to make their children – like *that?*"

"I told you: I really don't know. Anything I do know is hearsay. Apparently Sylvia came from money. A lot of money. She was the daughter of an earl or something similar, but she always had ... problems. Anxiety. Phobias. Her parents couldn't marry her off in England so they married her off in America, and it certainly wasn't because Malcolm found her charming. He wanted her money, and she knew it but couldn't do anything about it. I don't know whose idea the island was, but she either trapped herself here because of her fears or was trapped here by him and developed more fears. By the time she was middle-aged she was a full-blown agoraphobic and her husband had turned her money into a fortune that was, by society's standards, his."

"Was he abusive?"

"I wouldn't know. He died long before I came into the picture. But ... Sylvia always said that John reminded her of him."

My mind went back to the portrait of the red-haired man with the wide smile in the East Room. He looked friendly enough, especially in comparison to Mrs. Marlowe's scowling face in the portrait next to him. It was, however, the same smile that John had given me on the occasions when he had reassured me that he was going to help me.

"Maybe we're going about this all wrong," I said, dropping the butt of my cigarette to the ground.

"How so?"

"Maybe it has nothing to do with an inheritance at all. Maybe someone just killed him because they hated him so much."

Lennox raised his eyebrows. I shivered, suddenly remembering how I had let slip the words, *I'd see him dead before I let him* mere hours before John had been killed. My mind traced over the wet floorboards and my misplaced shoes that I had found the next morning when I'd awoken, and a terrible thought came over me that I quickly pushed aside. I hadn't killed John Marlowe. The pills knocked me out: I couldn't have possibly gotten up and done such a thing.

"Someone just happened to kill him after he'd inherited everything?" Lennox repeated. "It seems highly coincidental."

"But it's still possible. Maybe the killer was seething when they heard John got all the money, or maybe they didn't want to do it while Mrs. Marlowe was still alive, or maybe it was the first time they'd seen him in years and they didn't want the opportunity to pass by."

"Maybe," Lennox said, though he didn't sound convinced. He took out another cigarette and lit it, stowing the lighter back in his pocket as though trying to cram his distaste for the other man down with it.

"I'm just trying to think of every possibility," I said, taking the cigarette as he offered it to me. "He was probably killed because of the inheritance – but he might have been killed solely because he was a bastard."

"And I'm inclined to agree. I just think that – if he someone was willing to kill him solely because he was a bastard, as you've so delicately put it – then he probably would have been murdered years ago. John was cruel. The only thing I ever saw him derive joy from was other people's pain."

I shifted my jaw, considering his point, but before I could ask more, crunching footsteps came from behind us, and we both turned around. Kneller was walking toward us.

"Enjoying the outdoors, Isidore?" he called.

"I'm enjoying my cigarette," Lennox replied.

"Yes, I can tell," Kneller said, eyeing the cigarette still clutched in my hand as he came closer. He gave Lennox a wide, almost goading smile. "Taking another walk over to the cemetery?"

"No; the snow's a bit too deep. Maybe if you shoveled a path."

"Did you see the yew? Or do you need me to shovel a path to that, too?"

"I saw it."

"Sylvia had me plant it."

"Well, you did a good job, judging from its height."

"Yes, I gave it a lot of love and care ... something you wouldn't know about, of course."

Lennox's jaw clenched; Kneller smiled triumphantly.

"Am I missing something?" I asked as bluntly as possible, for neither man seemed to realize that I was still standing there.

"No, nothing at all," Kneller said, not moving his eyes from Lennox's face. "Though Frances was looking for you."

"Well, she'll have to wait," I said, finding myself rather unconcerned with what Mrs. Tilly needed.

Kneller shrugged.

"Suit yourself: I'll tell her to haul over the coals while she waits for you. It'll be good practice for when she reprimands you for skirting your duties." He turned and sidled back to the house, reciting as he went. *"And would it have been worth it, after all, after the cups, the marmalade, the tea, among the porcelain, among some talk of you and me, would it have been worth while to have bitten off the matter with a smile –"*

I shook my head as he departed and took another drag of Lennox's cigarette. When I tried to hand it back to him, though, he waved it away.

"You finish it. I think I've had enough." He put his hands in his pockets and looked off into the distance. "I think I'll take a walk down to the water ... The optimistic part of me hopes I might see a boat in the distance that I can flag down."

He didn't invite me to join him. Giving me a nod, he quickly departed, leaving me alone. I dropped the cigarette and stamped it out, then begrudgingly went back to the house to see what Mrs. Tilly wanted.

She wasn't in the kitchen when I returned. I glanced around the vacant room, then went to the Pantry to see if she was getting something off the shelves. Not seeing her, I heaved a sigh and turned away, but then a voice spoke out of the shadows.

"You should stay away from him."

I jumped and swung around. Kneller was leaning up against the radiator by the door, his form mostly hidden by the shelf and shadows.

"Excuse me?"

He turned his hands over, warming them over the hot steel. He didn't turn toward me.

"You should stay away from that man," he repeated, and there was a harshness in his voice I seldom heard. "I'm surprised at you: aren't you concerned that he might be the killer?"

"No."

"Oh? Why not? Because he's handsome?"

"No, because I locked him in his room that night," I said evenly, though I couldn't deny that his tone had shaken me. In the low lighting, he looked more like a skeleton than ever, and his worn, element-stained clothes gave the impression that he had crawled out of the earth from a grave. "– which I told everyone already, in case you've forgotten."

"He's taken quite an interest in you," he hummed. "I wonder why."

I crossed my arms.

"He's not interested in me," I said. "He's interested in proving who killed John so he doesn't get the blame."

"Ah, yes – poor Isidore is always trying to outrun blame, isn't he?"

"Do you care to explain yourself, or is this just one of your poetic reflections that you throw out in the air to provoke me?"

"No, it's because *I have known the eyes already, known them all – the eyes that fix you in a formulated phrase. And when I am formulated, sprawling on a pin – when I am pinned and wriggling on the wall, then how should I begin to spit out all the butt-ends of my days and ways? And how should I presume?*"

"If that was actually a question, then I don't have the answer."

"It wasn't a question: it was an analysis – of you. You in your little maid's uniform, trotting around the Dining Room while they're all shouting and arguing, nothing more than a moth that's been pinned to a specimen board, still alive and wriggling and desperate to get out."

"I don't wriggle – and I'm not a moth."

"Oh, my apologies. I would have said a butterfly, but a moth seemed more appropriate. Attracted to the light, you know. Or in this case, a certain doctor."

He pulled his hands away from the heat. Taking his gloves from his pocket, he put them back on and readied to go outside.

"Let me give you some advice," he said. "A man never wants a woman for any reason other than *wanting a woman*. You'd do well to remember that."

When he disappeared through the door, I stalked away to find Mrs. Tilly. Upon checking the nearby rooms and going to the third floor, though, I found her in her room taking a nap. She evidently hadn't been asking for me at all: Kneller had just wanted to get me away from Lennox. I went to the second floor to make up the rooms, feeling myself seethe from his antics, though his distaste for the other man unsettled me, and I began questioning the household's dislike of Lennox with more seriousness than I wanted to.

Only the door to the yellow Mabel Room where Edie and Bill slept was open, indicating that I could clean it. I set to work getting it in order, hoping that the mindless work would steer my thoughts away from trusting Lennox. It was its usual mess: the sheets were strewn around the bed, the blanket was piled in a heap at the foot, and the comforter was hanging off the side, half dumped onto the floor. I yanked everything back in place, crossing from side to side as I worked to ensure that it was perfectly symmetrical, though I doubted that either of them would complain. When I had finished refilling the water pitcher and straightening the shoes beneath the tufted bench, I took the maid's cap from my head and wiped at my brow, then loosened my hair from the knot at the nape of my neck, wishing that I was still outside in the cold.

Floorboards creaked behind me, but I didn't register them until a startled gasp pierced the air, too. I turned around in time to see Edie in the doorway, though I nearly didn't recognize her. She had shriveled in on herself as though she had taken ill, her entire form hunching in a pose somewhere between a recoil and the fetal position, and she was gurgling as though the words she wanted to say had gotten locked in her tightened throat. Her pale face was frigid and even her lips had drained of color.

"Are you alright –?" I began, but I had barely spoken when she bolted from the room. I followed her to the hallway, catching sight of her as she fled down the stairs, and was just debating whether or not to follow her when a giggle sounded from down the hall.

I turned my head. Cassandra's veiled form was peeking out of the Lillet Room.

"What?" I asked harshly as she let out another giggle.

Cassandra drummed her glove-covered fingers over the door-frame.

"Mary, Mary, quite contrary," she said in a sing-song voice. "How does your garden grow? With silver bells, and cockle shells, and pretty maids all in a row ..."

I opened my mouth to inquire none too politely if she was feeling alright, but was saved from making the comment by Lennox coming up the stairs. He paused on the landing and looked over at me, his eyes running over my hair, but as Cassandra let out a third giggle, his eyes snapped away to focus on her.

"Is everything alright?" he asked, though his tone was still tense.

"Yes, Isidore," Cassandra replied. "Is everything alright with you?"

"Just fine," he said carefully, throwing me an inquiring look. "Alexandra, I was hoping you could show me where the washing machine is: I'm afraid I'm running out of clothes. Unless you needed her, of course, Cassandra."

"No, no," Cassandra said sweetly. "She's all yours ...

for now."

She slunk back into her room and shut the door. I glanced at Lennox, then hurried upstairs with him to the nanny's room. He shut the door behind us.

"And you think she's just a character?" I said, raising my eyebrows at him.

"I don't know what else to call her – other than something ungracious, that is."

He came to stand at the end of my bed. The hems of his pants were soaked from his walk to the dock.

"I take it you didn't see a boat heading our way?" I asked.

"No, I'm afraid not. Though it gave me a chance to think more about how John died, and it's still bothering me to think that such a short blade could have killed him."

"Alright, but the handle matches the sheath perfectly."

"But it's – what? A three inch blade at the most?"

I took the sheath from my nightstand drawer and let him judge for himself. He turned it carefully in his hands.

"This just doesn't make sense," he murmured.

"Is it not big enough to kill someone?"

"Not where he was stabbed – at least not immediately."

"So you think I'm wrong?" I said, irritated that he was questioning my memory.

"I think that it might be possible that we have the wrong murder weapon."

"So you think I'm wrong."

"No, I – well, I'd like to be certain. It just seems very unlikely that the knife belonging to this sheath would have killed him."

"So maybe he died of hypothermia like Bernadette said."

"But that would mean that the killer left him there

still alive and trusted that the cold would take care of him. That seems a bit risky to me. What if he had stumbled to his feet and gone back to the house?"

"Well, they knew he couldn't get back inside. The door was locked."

"He could have rung the bell, though. I think there has to be something else."

"Like what?"

"Like ... something that we could find if we take a closer look at the body."

I stared at him. He was so collected, so nonchalant, that had I not heard the words he had spoken, I might have guessed he was discussing his favorite medical journal.

"You're rather bolder than you give yourself credit for, Dr. Lennox."

He smiled the smallest of smiles.

"Not as bold as I'd like to be, I'm afraid," he replied, and his tone left me with a hammering in my chest and a warmth on my skin that had nothing to do with the heat in the house. I quickly cleared my throat, hoping that my voice wouldn't give me away.

"I did tell you to look at the body two days ago, if you remember," I said. "And now it'll be harder to do. Unless you have a theory of how to convince Amalia to let us, that is."

Lennox handed me the sheath back.

"I thought, perhaps, we wouldn't ask for permission," he said.

"Didn't she say she was going to lock the door?"

"Yes. But I have the key."

"So she didn't lock the door?"

"No, I believe she did. I just ... happened upon the key when I went into her room."

He put his hands into his pockets. I continued to stare at him, marveling at his nerve and yet unable to keep

Kneller's warning from echoing in my mind.

"Mr. Kneller says I should stay away from you," I said, running my thumbnail over the intricate birds decorating the sheath.

I had thought that he might look affronted, or perhaps scoff at the ferryman's advice and tell me why it was incorrect, but he barely changed his expression.

"And what do you think?" he asked.

"I think it's possible that you somehow sneaked out of your room and killed John that night, just like I think it's possible that someone killed John for a reason entirely separate from getting any of the inheritance."

"And I suppose it's possible, as well, that you sneaked out of your room that night and killed him," he replied, and though it was clear from his tone that he was teasing me, I couldn't help but think of the puddle that had been on my floor the morning after John had been killed. It had been in the exact spot that he was now standing at the foot of my bed. "I suppose we'll just have to trust one another."

The bell by my door jingled, indicating that someone from downstairs was looking for me. I sat up straighter and swung my legs over the side of the bed, then tossed the sheath up onto the bureau.

"I'm afraid I can't do that, Dr. Lennox. I know better than to trust men I hardly know. John Marlowe taught me that."

"Why take the chance of working with me then?"

"I don't know," I said, standing up and fixing the maid's cap back over my hair. *Because he's handsome?* Kneller's voice said in my head, but I pushed his words away. "Maybe I just like the adventure of it all."

CHAPTER NINE

"You rang?" I asked Mrs. Tilly blandly as I stepped into the kitchen. She glanced up from the table where she was rolling out dough without responding.

"Yes, I did," came a voice to my left. Marjorie was standing by the stove. She had a kettle on the burner, though I had never seen her drink tea, and I had certainly never seen her anywhere near the servants' corridors. She crossed her arms as she looked me up and down. "Mrs. Tilly has informed me that you've been slacking on your duties."

I felt my jaw clench, though I didn't look at the cook. I gave Marjorie my most feigned polite smile.

"I didn't realize that, Mrs. Pickering," I said. "She didn't inform me of any problems."

"It's not her job to inform you of anything. You saw the kitchen was a mess this morning and didn't think to clean it up? What exactly did you think you'd been hired to do?"

My smile tightened, becoming strained.

"My mistake, Mrs. Pickering. I'll try to be more ... aware."

"Don't think I haven't had my eye on you," Marjorie said. "I think we all know that John didn't hire you because Tilda was getting old. Birdie said he paid you quite generously, and yet you clearly have no work ethic. Do you care to explain why?"

"It's my first time being a maid, Mrs. Pickering. I guess I just don't understand all of the rules."

The kettle began to whistle, but Marjorie didn't so much as glance at it. Her eyes were fixed on me.

"I think you understand quite well what you're doing here," she said in a low voice. "Better than any of the rest of us, undoubtedly. So let me ask you again: do you care to explain yourself?"

The kettle whistled louder. The screech filled the room as steam poured from the spout.

"I really don't know what you're talking about, Mrs. Pickering," I said evenly. "I'm afraid this is all just a misunderstanding."

"Do you like working here, Alexandra? Do you like cleaning rooms and serving food? Being a maid?"

It was clear that she already knew the answer. I saw no reason to pretend anymore.

"Not especially, Mrs. Pickering."

"Would you be more comfortable retiring from your duties? John already paid you, after all. It's no skin off of my back if he wasted his money."

Out of the corner of my eye, I saw Mrs. Tilly look up from her work, though I couldn't make out her expression.

"I've already spoken to Mrs. Carlton about it," I said carefully. "She insisted that I stay on."

"Birdie's not the one in charge here, however much she likes to think she is. So I'm asking you: do you want to retire from your duties?"

I knew from her tone that she was baiting me, but I didn't react. I knew that she was tricking me and would still have me serving her lunch in half an hour's time, so whatever game she was trying to play, I had no qualms about playing along. I gave her a shrug.

"If you're giving me permission, then yes," I said.

"Alright, then: I'll let you go. But do me a favor before you take your apron off ... pour me a cup of tea."

I gave her the slightest raise of my eyebrow, then dutifully stepped forward and lifted the kettle from the stove. Turning slightly, I looked for where she had put her mug, but the counter-tops were empty. She hadn't even taken the tea canister out.

"Is there a particular type you prefer –?" I began, but I never finished the sentence. Without warning, Marjorie reached forward and grabbed my free hand, slamming it down upon the burner. I let out a horrible, mangled cry and wrenched my arm from her grasp, but the excruciating sting of hot coils searing into my flesh remained. My knees buckled and I dropped to the floor, smacking my head against the corner of the counter as I went. My right hand released the kettle, sending it crashing down to the floor beside me. It sprayed me with boiling water, but I was unaware of anything except for the sickening feeling of the ruined flesh on my hand.

I let out a wail, clenching my hand to my stomach and pressing it to stop the pain, but to no avail.

"Jesus, Mary and Joseph –" Mrs. Tilly said from somewhere behind me, followed by the sound of her rolling pin falling from the table and hitting the floor.

"There you go," Marjorie tutted from somewhere above me, and the hem of her skirt brushed against my cheek as she stepped over me to get to the door, "no more work for you ..."

I could hear the sound of her footsteps change as they stepped off of the kitchen tiles and onto the hardwood in the hallway, though somewhere in my mind I believed that she wouldn't leave me there to suffer. I rocked back and forth in my place, the pain rendering me senseless.

"Please," I called over to Mrs. Tilly. "Please – cold water –"

The cook's outline was just a blur of black and white through my watering eyes. She stooped to retrieve her rolling pin, then brought it back up to the table.

"The sink's right there," she said gruffly. "Get it yourself."

I let out another hoarse cry, readying to beg her if

only she would turn the faucet on for me, but then instead I rolled to my knees and pushed myself to my feet. With my hand still clutched to my stomach, I staggered blindly to the Pantry and ran out the servants' door, falling down the steps and onto the path. I pressed my hand into the snow, letting out a wailing moan as the cold hit my hand. My vision was marred by spots of blackness that grew and grew until I couldn't see, but I stayed in my place, gritting my teeth so I wouldn't shout.

"No, no, no – no, no, no –" I repeated over and over again, wishing that the words would numb the wound faster than the snow. "No –"

I pressed my face into the ground, forcing myself not to lose consciousness. I couldn't tell if it was the pain or the blow to the head that was threatening me to pass out, but I knew that I couldn't allow it. A concussion would render me confused – or worse, cause memory loss. *Stay awake, stay awake,* I repeated over and over in my head, though the pain was so intense that it would have been easier to blackout. Instead I swore under my breath: cursing Marjorie, cursing the household, cursing John. I cursed until I went numb from cold, and only then did I lift my head. The snow was stained red with blood. I pulled my fingers from beneath the white: they were an unnatural shade of gray, not unlike the color of John's skin when I had discovered him, and whatever pain I had experienced was gone: there was no feeling in it anymore.

"Mmm. Mmmm."

The sound came from my throat, but I didn't know what word I had been trying to say. I staggered to my feet, my legs wobbling so much that they could barely hold me, and my stiff cheeks wouldn't allow me to move my face. I clutched my left hand to me as I stumbled back up the steps to go inside. It felt as though it had been turned to metal.

Mrs. Tilly wasn't in the kitchen. The scattered

remains of lunch dishes were piled by the sink, though it was difficult to believe that an entire meal had passed while I had been outside. I knocked into them on my way to the door. I couldn't tell if it was dark already or if my vision had been impaired, and I couldn't think clearly enough to care about the answer. With every ounce of concentration I could muster, I forced myself to remember how many steps it was to the staircase in the Foyer, then led myself upstairs to the third floor.

"Alexandra?"

I didn't quite register Lennox's voice; I barely remembered walking from the stairs to my room.

"Alexandra – what's happened to you?"

I felt his hands on my face before I had even noticed he was next to me. His skin was hot in comparison to mine, and it was only then that my body seemed to realize how piercingly cold I was. I shivered violently.

"Here – here," he said quickly, ripping the blanket from my bed and wrapping it around me before returning his hands to my face. "What happened to you?"

I slumped up against him, wishing that I could get warm again. My frigid hand lay like a stone at my side.

"What happened to you?" he repeated. As my eyes began to close, he gave me a firm shake to keep me awake. "Alexandra – what's happened?"

"My – hand."

He grabbed for my wrists, lifting my right hand and then my left.

"Jesus – what in the world ...?"

I was partially aware of him laying me down in the bed, and sometime later he held my arm in his lap as he wrapped my hand. Blankets were piled on top of me, though I couldn't seem to stop shivering. His voice spoke to me from somewhere, but I couldn't make out the words. Every time I tried to respond, gurgling sounds came out instead.

"Let's see this," he said, the words finally intelligible to my ears. Something wet touched my forehead; he must have been dabbing at the cut with a cloth. The sting of alcohol against the open sore jolted me. I blinked up at the ceiling for several minutes, still halfway in a daze and uncertain of what had happened. As I reached to snap the rubber band on my left wrist and found a bandage covering it, though, it all came back to me.

"Don't try to move," came Lennox's voice. He was standing by the side of my bed, his image stronger now that my vision had cleared. "You hit your head, and your hand has a very severe burn."

I groggily pushed the blankets off of me. My skin was covered in a sheen of sweat.

"I figured that out, oddly enough," I muttered.

"Don't try to move," he repeated, putting a hand on my shoulder to ease me back down. "You're probably in a fog. You struck your head. You might have a concussion."

"I don't."

I pushed his hand off of me. He gave me a stern look.

"You can't *refuse* to have a concussion: it doesn't work that way."

"It's just a bump." I pushed myself up to a sitting position with my right arm. My head swayed and a wave of nausea came over me. "What time is it?"

He gave me another look that suggested he didn't care for my stubbornness, but then seemed to decide there was no point in fighting it.

"Quarter to six," he said. "I asked Rachel to tell Mrs. Tilly not to expect you for dinner."

"Don't bother. She knows." I could tell he wanted to know what had happened, a part of me hesitated to tell him. "What did you tell Rachel?"

"Just that you were unwell. She saw me getting things out of the medicine cupboard ... She didn't seem surprised. She said you'd missed lunch."

"You didn't eat?"

He ought to have: with neither of us there, there was no telling what we had missed of the family's conversation.

"I wasn't hungry," he said shortly. "If I had known that you were hurt, I would have come looking for you."

"It wouldn't have mattered," I said, my voice dull and void of emotion. "Marjorie decided to go through on her promise. She put my hand on the burner."

He didn't respond for a long moment. His expression was unreadable.

"She ... did what?" he finally managed, and there was venom in his voice that I hadn't heard before.

"She wanted to teach me a lesson."

I was surprised at how indifferent I sounded; it was as though Lennox's anger was enough for the both of us.

"A lesson for what? Did you – you didn't accuse her of killing John, did you?"

I shook my head.

"Does she expect you had something to do with it, then?" he asked.

I surveyed my bandaged hand. He had wrapped each finger individually except for my thumb, which was bound with my palm. It was throbbing now, though I preferred the feeling to the odd sensation of not feeling it at all.

"The odd part is, I don't think she does. She just wanted to hurt me." I looked back up at him. "I'm getting more and more convinced that it wasn't her husband who beat their children to death, though."

Lennox didn't seem to care for my nonchalance. His face was set in a grimace.

"That does it," he said, moving to go around the bed. "This has gone on long enough –"

"Don't," I said, calling him back from the door. "It won't help anything to confront her. It's not like she'll suddenly have remorse."

"Not her, but the others –"

"The others won't do anything: you know that. They'll berate her or congratulate her, depending on who it is, and then they'll argue for a while and forget all about it. It won't do anything in the long run, and it certainly won't help us figure out who killed John."

Lennox stared at me.

"I'm not just going to stand here and pretend that it didn't happen –" he began, but I didn't let him finish. His upset was rendering me calm in return, and I was finally able to think clearly.

"Dr. Lennox, you were the one who told me not to draw attention to ourselves, so let's not. Let her think that she's won. It'll make it easier to do what we have to do to solve this."

"I'm not remotely concerned with solving anything right now. She needs to be –"

"She needs to think that she's won," I repeated. "Now, the family will be having dinner soon, and since I don't think I'm going to be carrying anything, you need to go down and keep up with what they're saying to one another. Then after they're all asleep, we'll go to the Augustus Suite and examine John."

"We're not still doing that –"

"Yes, we are. Either we'll do it together, or I'll go down and poke around his body and relay every detail to you in what will probably be a very unfortunate waste of time for the both of us." I stood up, grabbing at the nightstand as I swayed in place. "We need to find out who killed John. And if Marjorie's willing to burn my hand because I didn't clean the kitchen, then I don't want to think about what she'd do if she suspected either of us is the killer – so let's figure it out before she gets any reason to, alright?"

He gave me a begrudging stare, though I took his silence as acquiescence.

"Now," I said, "if you don't mind, I need some privacy."

He didn't move. By the look in his eyes, he seemed to think that perhaps I was going to trick him and go down to confront Marjorie myself despite everything I had just said to him.

"I think I should stay. You don't look very steady."

"I'm not, but I need to change my clothes, and I imagine we'd both be a bit uncomfortable if I did it with you standing here."

He opened his mouth and closed it.

"Ah, of course," he said, a hint of embarrassment in his voice. "Well, in that case ..."

He retreated to the nursery and shut the door. I struggled with the zipper on the back of my dress, my bandaged hand throbbing with every move I made. I tossed the uniform to the ground and put on my spare one, then made my way down the hall to wash my face one-handed. A part of me was seething, but the other part was largely numb. I had underestimated Marjorie despite everything I had heard and seen of her, and a trickle of trepidation was coming over me that I had underestimated the rest of the family, as well. Perhaps I ought to have heeded Lennox's advice to keep my head down days ago.

But unfortunately, I thought as I lay back on the bed to rest, I didn't think I was capable of doing anything of the sort – and I feared that by the end of this adventure, or lack thereof, I would have far more troubles than a bandaged head and hand.

CHAPTER TEN

I waited for Lennox to return from dinner, anxiously tapping my feet as I surmised what the family was discussing. He wouldn't be able to repeat it word for word, and I feared that he might forget a crucial piece of information that I would have been able to use.

He came back just after nine, far earlier than I expected him.

"That was quick," I said as he came into the room and shut the door.

"Well, after they opened the seventh bottle of wine, the conversation turned to more of an exchange of slurs, so ..." He came to the end of my bed and hesitated. For a moment it looked as though he was considering sitting down, but then thought better of it. "They're all in their rooms now. I waited for them to go up."

"They're probably not asleep yet, though."

"Judging from how much they staggered going up the stairs, I doubt it will take long – and they'll undoubtedly be there until morning."

"What did they talk about?"

He sighed and put his hands in his pockets, looking as though he wished he had taken notes.

"Well, Edie was very upset," he said. "She didn't want to stay for the meal, nor did she want to be alone, so Rachel left with her midway through cocktails in the Parlor. Then, of course, her other sisters had a good time mocking her for being frightened. She's convinced she's seen another ghost."

I clicked my teeth together, recalling how she had run from her room. It didn't make sense that she had thought I was a ghost: I was wearing my maid's uniform, just as always, after all. Perhaps she hadn't expected me to be in there cleaning, or perhaps it had been the sight of Cassandra's form peeking out into the hallway that had caused her fright.

I glanced up at Lennox. He was wearing a troubled frown, not unlike the one he adopted when he spoke of the late Mrs. Marlowe, and it struck me that he would have such empathy for Edie's faint-hearted nature.

"Do you believe she saw a ghost, Dr. Lennox?" I asked skeptically.

He hesitated.

"I believe she thinks she did," he said. "Edie's experienced a lot of death in her lifetime. She's understandably ... haunted." He waited to see if I would question him further. When I didn't, he went on. "Anyhow, the rest of them had a fairly normal dinner. There were the usual tiffs: Bernadette commenting on Marjorie's drinking, Bill getting exasperated with Cassandra's antics, Amalia accusing everyone of murdering John ..."

"How was Marjorie?"

Lennox shifted his jaw.

"She was in a very good mood," he said darkly. "I think she was ... rather pleased with herself. She made a few comments about you taking ill. She advised the others that you were probably faking it."

"Wonderful."

"It might work out for the best. Now you have a legitimate excuse for not working anymore."

"I'm not going to stop working."

"You can't possibly –"

"Dr. Lennox, we've discussed this. There's no way I can figure out which of them is the killer by sitting up here doing nothing."

"I doubt you'll fair much better serving them their meals. If someone admits that they did it, I'll certainly tell you."

"But no one's going to admit to it. They might, however, let slip something that gives us reasonable doubt. Besides, it's not just the meals I'm interested in. Working means that I have access to their rooms."

"If there was a bloodied shirt hiding in their laundry, I think you would have found it by now."

"Or I might just not know what to look for yet." I stood up and held my hand out for the key. "So let's do this. I'll go unlock the door."

"No, *I'll* go unlock the door."

"If you go and someone sees you, you won't have a good excuse about what you're doing. If I do it, I'll say I'm feeling much better and was checking to see if anyone needs their rooms turned down for the evening."

He hesitated, not seeming to like the idea of me going down alone.

"This is no time to be chivalrous, Dr. Lennox. I have a bandaged hand and a slight headache: it's not the end of the world."

He murmured in halfhearted agreement and handed me the key, and I slipped down the stairs, my slippers padding my footsteps into silence. The hallway was quiet and the doors to the bedrooms were tightly shut. I circled around the floor, glanced over the banister to the Foyer below, then, seeing that all was clear, went to the Augustus Suite and unlocked the door. It swung open, pulled by the breeze drifting through the room. I hurried back to the staircase and waved Lennox down. Just as we reached the Augustus Suite together, though, a horrible *crash!* came from one of the rooms down the hall.

We darted inside and shut the door, so hasty in our efforts not to be seen and anxious to know what the sound was that we had pressed ourselves to the door, momentarily unaware that we were all but pinned together. Lennox jumped back from me, removing his hands from my shoulders, and cleared his throat.

"What do you think that was?" I asked, hoping to sound casual. My uninjured fingers had curled into a fist in my fright, and as I un-clenched them, I realized that the key had left a mark against my palm. I slipped it into my skirt pocket.

"It sounded like someone fell out of bed," he replied.

I tried to nod but gave an involuntary shiver instead. I had underestimated just how cold the room was; my maid's uniform was too thin to offer much warmth.

"Would you like my coat?" Lennox asked, not waiting for an answer before setting down the lantern he had brought and taking it off.

I pulled it on, muttering a thanks. It was far too large, and the herringbone material was permeated with cigarette smoke.

"Would you like my cap?" I offered in return, taking it off for him as the smell of death slipped over to where we stood from the mother and son laying in their temporary resting places. It was mild due to the breeze blowing through the room, but unpleasant enough to notice, and I certainly didn't like the idea of breathing it in. I pulled my turtleneck up to cover my mouth and nose.

He accepted it and placed it over his face as a makeshift handkerchief, then lifted up the lantern again. Soft light spread over the room. After going over to the window seat where John was laying, he set the lantern next to the body.

"Here we go," he said, his voice muffled through the fabric. He squinted at me through the dim lighting, his gaze moving up from my eyes to my hair. I wondered if it was disheveled from being under the cap all day.

John's body was covered in a thin layer of snow. In

the darkness, it looked as though someone had put a sheet over him. His lifeless eyes stared up at me: no one had bothered to close them. I kept glancing at the enlarged pupils, half-expecting them to slide over to stare at me accusingly. Though his form was cold and hard like the marble counter-tops in the kitchen and his skin had turned a grayish-purple color that matched the silk trim on pillowcases in the room, it was somehow difficult to understand that he would never move again. Every time I looked away, I thought I could feel his fingers circling around my wrist.

Lennox fumbled with John's wool coat, pulling it back to reveal where the letter opener had stabbed him through his crisp white shirt.

"Let's see here," Lennox mumbled, lowering himself to the handle's eye-level.

"It's exactly the same pattern. See there? Where that bird's tail ends, it continues onto the sheath."

"But it can't be: it wouldn't be long enough to kill him. There must be a longer one with the same pattern."

"No one has matching letter openers for different sized envelopes," I told him. When he didn't agree, I lost my patience. "Look –"

I reached forward and yanked the blade upwards. It popped from John's chest to reveal a two and a half inch blade, the silver stained with blood. Lennox gaped.

"Alexandra – you can't just pull it out –!"

"I'll stick it back in," I said, ignoring his complaints and shoving it back down. It protested against the frozen body, and as I pushed it down so that the handle was exactly as far down as it had been before, a grotesque feeling came over me. I quickly released the cold metal, lessened only slightly from how I had held it with my shirt sleeve rather than my bare fingers, and wishing that I hadn't been so rash solely for the point of proving that I was right.

"We can't tamper with the body," Lennox said, eyeing me over the top of the cap.

"Well, it's too late now, so let's just get on with it."

He turned back to John's body. I was fairly certain I saw him roll his eyes as he went.

"Something's not right here," he said a moment later. "This shouldn't have killed him."

"Sure looks like it did," I replied. "It's plunged right into his heart."

"No, the blade's too short for that. And the heart's difficult to stab anyhow because it's protected by the sternum and ribs, not to mention all the connective tissue you'd have to get through. Unless the attacker was extremely strong and either very knowledgeable of where to strike or extraordinarily lucky, there's not a good chance that this would have killed him – especially not quickly."

"Maybe it wasn't quick. Maybe they wanted him to suffer."

"And did what? Stood over him to make sure he didn't crawl away?" Lennox raised his eyebrows skeptically. "If they wanted to be certain he would die, then they should have either stabbed him multiple times or in a more efficient spot."

"What's more efficient than the heart?"

"The carotid artery or the spinal cord would be best," he said. "There's also the axillary artery in the armpit: that probably would have been the best choice with a blade like this. If you know what you're doing you can aim for the liver – that's almost always fatal – or the femoral artery."

I stored the information away in the back of my mind, hoping that I would never need to use it.

"Well, then, it obviously wasn't someone who knows anatomy," I said.

Lennox hummed, seemingly unsure.

"You just said they didn't hit the right spot," I said,

almost annoyed.

"But that's just it: he's dead."

"So it was the right spot?"

He sighed in frustration.

"I guess it's possible, but it just doesn't seem right. One stab and he's dead? Even knowing the most efficient places to stab someone, I think I'd hit them multiple times just to make sure."

"Well, maybe they didn't want to get too messy."

"What?"

"You know – with all the blood. Can you imagine any of the Marlowe women ruining her coat by staining it?"

"I ... hadn't thought of that."

"It'd be a bit of a giveaway if they brought me their laundry and asked me to get a bloodstain out."

Lennox thought about it, then said –

"I suppose they could have done it naked."

I had the briefest vision of a nude Bernadette waddling out into the snow with the letter opener clutched in her hands, and I didn't know whether to be repulsed or amused.

"I'm all for exploring every possibility, Dr. Lennox, but I think we can both agree that no one walked out into a snowstorm naked to murder John Marlowe."

"But they stabbed him once to avoid making a mess? It just doesn't seem like a wise plan."

"That's because you're thinking like a doctor. You might have stabbed him in an artery, but someone like Amalia wouldn't know better, so she stabbed him in the heart without realizing that she should have used a knife with a longer blade and got lucky."

"But that's just it ..." he said. "What did you say before? About being messy?"

I clicked back several sentences in my head to retrieve it.

"I said, *Well, maybe they didn't want to get too messy. You know – with all the blood. Can you imagine any of the Marlowe women ruining her coat by staining it?*" I repeated blandly.

"With all the blood," Lennox echoed, and his frown deepened. He turned slowly back to the body, his eyes running over the opened tuxedo jacket and crisp white shirt, and then he said, "There's not enough blood."

I glanced over at John's chest.

"Meaning?"

He turned to look at me, and despite the fact that he seemed to have made a discovery, he looked more puzzled than ever. Out of the corner of my eye, something moved by the four-poster bed; a curtain must have caught the wind. I didn't look over at it. My eyes were still on Lennox.

"Meaning that either I'm totally confused and this short blade somehow did reach his heart, then plugged up the wound so that barely any blood escaped, or – and more likely, I believe – he was already dead when he was stabbed."

I blinked. The movement by the bed caught my eye again, but I couldn't seem to break my gaze with Lennox.

"But that doesn't make sense," I said. "Why stab someone who's already dead?"

Lennox looked up and down John's body, searching for something unseen.

"To hide what really killed him," he said. "We have to do a full examination."

His eyes were hungry now, just dark orbs quivering in the light from the lantern. He tossed down the maid's cap to work better, and as his hands began to undo the buttons on the dress shirt, I watched how delicately his fingers moved as though he was playing the piano rather than undressing a dead man, wondering if he had been a surgeon before becoming a psychiatrist. My gaze was transfixed on his hands as they finished undoing the buttons and opened the shirt, and as he shifted, the lantern light caught something that I had failed to see before: a thin golden band, nearly the same color as his skin, circling his ring finger and nearly imperceptible if not for the light making it gleam. My heart sank before my mind could forewarn it not to feel. He was married.

"He might have been struck, choked, poisoned –"

I could barely focus on what he was saying. Every part of me felt deflated as though someone had squeezed the air from my lungs, and I wished that I could transport myself back outside into the snow and remain there until I went numb.

"Can you hold the light up more?" he said, throwing the words over his shoulder at me, and I wordlessly obliged. The lantern sent patterns dancing over the curtains and floor, illuminating the darkness and sending it retreating back to hide. I felt the truth settle in my stomach like a huge, empty hole. I trained my eyes on the squares of yellow that stretched over the room, boring into them to keep the tears from escaping onto my face and making me feel even more ridiculous. He was married. How could I have missed that? Why had I failed to notice the wedding band before now?

Yet whatever answer I had hoped for would have to wait, because in the soft lantern light, I saw something that momentarily pulled me from my thoughts.

"Dr. Lennox."

"A little higher," he said, not paying attention to anything but the way my arm had slumped back down.

"Dr. Lennox," I repeated, this time more forcefully. I wasn't sure what I was seeing: perhaps I truly did have a concussion and the shadows of the room were playing a trick on my eyes.

"Higher, Alexandra. It needs to be over my shoulder or else he's thrown into shadow ..."

"*Dr. Lennox.*"

I had dropped the lantern fully back to my side, and as the light stretched across the floor to the bed, the image became clearer. Lennox turned to look at me, but I didn't see if he was irritated or concerned. As I pointed behind him, he followed my gaze.

"What the ...?"

There, in the middle of the four-poster bed, was the form of a woman – but whereas Mrs. Marlowe had been laying down before, she was now sitting bolt upright and staring directly at us.

Lennox grabbed me by the wrist and hoisted the hand holding the lantern up, throwing the bed into light. My shoulder cracked painfully from the sudden movement.

"What are you *doing?*" said the coarse, gravelly voice of a woman, but I was too shocked to respond. My eyes blinked against the bright light flooding into them from the too-close flame, trying to regain focus on the sight in front of me, and though Lennox's grip on my wrist tightened, I could feel him shaking. *"What are you doing?"*

My head was pounding even harder now and I couldn't think to process what was happening, let alone respond. She was dead. I was positive she was dead. The chill in the air had become more intense, and I was shivering despite Lennox's warm coat as I tried to make sense of how the sight in front of me could be possible. For I knew it couldn't be Mrs. Marlowe, but it was certainly someone, and that someone could very well be the killer – keeping watch over her victim's resting place.

And then the answer hit me. For surely enough, there was a woman sitting up in bed, though it wasn't Mrs. Marlowe, who still lay dead in her spot. Cassandra was glaring at us from beside her mother.

"We were just examining Professor Marlowe," I said. "To see what killed him."

If I had thought that the truth might appease her, then I had been sorely mistaken. Cassandra's veiled form sprung up like a black cat and crawled across her mother's body to get nearer to us.

"You shouldn't be in here," she hissed at Lennox. "You have no right to be in here –"

She hopped down to the floor and lurched forward. Her black, ghostly form neared us, getting closer and closer like a stain moving across the carpet.

"We were just trying to help, Cassandra," Lennox said soothingly. "We want to find out what happened to your brother –"

"You had no right!" Cassandra yelled. "Don't touch him! Don't touch my boy!"

"I apologize, Cassandra," Lennox said in the same calm tone, though the hand holding me gave me a slight tug in the direction of the door. "We didn't mean to startle you. We'll go –"

"What's wrong with you?" Cassandra said, but from behind her black veil it took me several moments to realize that she was speaking to me. "Didn't I teach you better? What do you think you're doing running around with this man you hardly know –?"

She reached forward as though to grab me, but Lennox yanked me sideways across the room. I danced around the head of the polar bear rug to avoid stepping on it, then narrowly managed to avoid slamming into a floor lamp –

"You have no right –!" Cassandra yelled again, but now we were at the door. Lennox gave my arm a final wrench and pulled me out into the hallway, hurriedly shutting the door behind us.

"Jesus," I said, unsure of whether I felt more confused by her actions or irritated that she had interrupted our work. I leaned my head against the door, listening for the sounds of following footsteps, but all was quiet. I took out my key and locked the door for good measure. After all I had seen of Cassandra, I didn't put it past her to come up to my room, even if it was just to brush my hair again or else snuggle up beside me as I slept. I shoved the key away and grimaced at the thought.

Lennox's arms were crossed. He was staring at the lock on the door, his teeth clicking together as he thought. Then, much to my surprise, he let out a swear.

"*Damn.*" He briefly turned away from me to face the wall, then spun back around. "Well – now what are we going to do? She's going to tell the others – they're going to want to know what we were doing in there."

"So we'll tell them the truth," I said.

"That we were examining John's body? And how are we going to explain that we're working together?"

"I doubt we'll need to. They'll know as soon as Cassandra tells them she saw us."

"Oh, wonderful."

I wasn't sure why he was so upset. Logically speaking, the fact that he was working to solve John's murder would indicate that he hadn't been the one to kill him – though, I reasoned, the Marlowes weren't known to be very practical.

"This was exactly what I didn't want to happen," he muttered. "If they think we're working together –"

He broke off without finishing the sentence. I raised my eyebrows at him, unwillingly becoming more and more wooden as I listened to him.

"I didn't realize you had stated that condition so clearly," I said coldly. "My mistake. Had I known, I wouldn't have agreed to go to the Augustus Suite with you."

I took a seat on the side of my bed and scooped four pills onto my bandaged hand, then popped them into my mouth and swallowed them dry. It was two hours past the time when I normally took them, and I could feel my mind starting to flood with all of the things I didn't want to think about anymore. What would it matter if Cassandra told everyone? Surely they would either not believe her or be more concerned that she was sleeping beside their dead mother than they would be that we had been examining John.

I reached down and pulled off my shoes. My toe had poked a hole in my stocking, sending a run up the front of my leg. I was down to one good pair. I patted my thigh to make sure that the bundle of money was still strapped there.

"Just tell them Cassandra's lying," I said. "It's not like it would be hard to believe."

"Even with Cassandra's mantra of fabrications, I doubt they'd believe us over her," Lennox said. "And a quick look at John's body will tell them someone was examining him, so I don't see the point in denying it."

I sent a glare over at him, hating the way the word *us* sounded coming from his mouth. There was no *us*: there should have never been an *us*. How foolish I had been to go against all of my better instincts and ask for his help. My eyes went to the ring circling his finger again, and I focused on the anger I felt at him rather than the other feeling that threatened to push it out of the way: the disappointment – the brokenness – that I had allowed myself to be attracted to him.

"What do you think she was doing in there?" Lennox asked.

"Sleeping," I replied irritably, no longer interested in having a conversation with him.

"Why in there?"

"Maybe she misses her mother."

"Plenty of people miss their mothers – that doesn't mean they snuggle up to their corpses."

"You're talking about a woman who's convinced

that she's a grand duchess. Are you really surprised by anything she does?"

"Making up an identity and laying with a decomposing body are two different categories. And why did she call John her boy? He was older than her."

"I don't know. You're the psychiatrist – you figure it out."

Lennox gave me a stern look.

"There's no need to be short with me, Alexandra. I'm sorry if it sounded as though I was blaming you: I'm just upset because I specifically said I didn't want the family knowing we were working together."

"You didn't *specifically* say that. Believe me: I remember. The only thing you *specifically* said was that you were doing this because you didn't want me to get hurt."

"Which is true –"

"Really? Because you only seem concerned about yourself at the moment."

"You want me to be concerned about you?" he said heatedly. "Fine. I'm concerned that you've gotten yourself far enough on Marjorie's bad side that she's willing to openly hurt you the way that she did. I'm concerned that you continue to act rashly without remotely considering the consequences first. And I'm concerned that you just took *four times* the recommended dose of an anxiolytic and you'll probably pass out before the conversation ends."

My jaw clenched.

"I won't pass out," I said. I would be dead asleep in thirty minutes, of course, but for the moment I was still perfectly functional.

"How often do you take them?"

"None of your business," I said automatically.

"They're highly addictive – do you know that?"

"I know exactly what they are," I said tersely, and in the moment it no longer mattered what we were truly arguing about, because the only thing of importance was the fact that he had allowed me to make a fool of myself by falling for him when he was married to someone else. I tried to snap the rubber band around my wrist, but the bandage was in my way. I tore it off, not caring that the burn throbbed harder and harder with each tug of the gauze, angry beyond belief at myself for failing to notice the wedding band before and wondering if – in my desperation to have him fill the loneliness that had made its home in my chest – I had simply pushed the sight of it from my mind. I tossed the bandage down and snapped the rubber band. No, I thought with certainty, I wouldn't purposefully forget something no matter what the reasoning was.

"You're going to mangle your hand further," he told me, then nodded to my wrist. "Why do you do that to yourself?"

"I don't know what you mean," I said, putting my hands behind my back.

"It looks painful."

"It's not."

"Not compared with other things, you mean?" he said, and heat flushed my face. His dark eyes were steady, and, against all my logic, I was positive he could see right through the skin and bones into my thoughts. I didn't like what he was going to find.

He had managed to revert back to his composed tone, yet I couldn't do the same. There was something intrinsically easier with being angry with him than there was with being comfortable, especially now. I looked away from him, trying not to linger on how it had felt to be so close to him in the Augustus Suite and instead on how irritating it was that he always asked me if I was alright as though he was just waiting for me to tell him that I wasn't. I wished that I could shake him and make him as unsettled as I always felt.

"No, I mean it's not painful," I repeated. "And for

the record, I don't need your concern."

Lennox stepped away from my bed.

"I'll let you get some sleep. You're not yourself."

"How would you know?"

He shifted his jaw. I could tell that I was cracking him, and the image of the hard shell that surrounded who he was being shattered and falling to the floor spurred me on despite my better sense telling me to stop.

"You're right," he said shortly. "I wouldn't."

He turned to go to the nursery, but at the door he looked back, seemingly unable to contain himself anymore.

"Sixteen-hundred milligrams is an unprecedented amount of Meprobamate, especially for someone of your size," he said. "I'm shocked that any licensed doctor would prescribe it, and I'm equally as shocked that someone who's educated in psychology would take it."

"I take it to sleep," I said.

"If you want to sleep, you might as well take a horse tranquilizer – it's less dangerous than what you're doing."

"If you're worried about danger, then you shouldn't have suggested we go to the Augustus Suite," I shot back. "Don't blame me for decisions you made yourself."

His expression was locked, preventing me from guessing what he was thinking. I waited for his response, counting the seconds with my pounding heart and throbbing hand, but it never came. He surrendered to his room without another word.

As the door shut between us, I realized that I was still wearing his coat. I took it off and chucked it toward his room. It hit the door frame and slid down the wall, barely making a sound as it crumpled into a heap.

I leaned back on my bed, tense and anxious again even though the medication ought to have taken its effect. I reached over to my bedside table and picked up two more pills. Fuck him, I thought angrily as I swallowed them dry.

He didn't know anything about me.

But worse, I thought as I stared up at the blotchy ceiling and finally succumbed to sleep, was the idea that I knew nothing about him – and despite everything, I still desperately wanted to.

CHAPTER ELEVEN

When I awakened, it was to the sight that I wasn't alone in bed. A woman slept peacefully at my side, her dark red hair swept away from her lined face and her hands gracefully resting beneath her head.

"Mom?"

Her eyes opened, blinked twice, and her face broke into a smile.

"Alexandra," she whispered. "There you are."

"How did you get here?" I wanted to sit up, but my body felt too heavy. I could barely keep my eyes open. "How did you know I was here?"

"Don't you remember?"

I thought back, trying to retrieve the information from my memory, but I was unable to. I shook my head.

"No."

Her smile turned downwards.

"Me neither," she said sadly, and before I could say more, her body became transparent until she vanished into the air.

I jolted from my dream, my arms flinching violently and my fingers curling into fists. The familiar sight of the empty nanny's room greeted me, bathed lightly in cold winter light, but my skin prickled with sweat and my head pounded and burned against the pillow. I had taken too much medication.

I tried to sit up, but just as in my dream, my body wouldn't allow me to. The entirety of it ached as though I had a case of the flu and my stomach gurgled in discomfort.

"Well, *finally,*" came an irritated voice from behind me, and I forced myself to roll over. Mrs. Tilly was standing next to my bed. "Sleeping in, are we?"

"What?"

"Your were supposed to be in the kitchen an hour ago!" she said. "I had to set the table and serve the coffee myself! I couldn't wake you!"

I glanced around the room. The door to the hallway was open, as was the one to the nursery; Lennox was nowhere in sight. I groggily flopped my legs out of bed and pulled myself to my feet to get dressed, but I could barely think. I snapped the rubber band against my wrist to recall the previous day's events: Marjorie. The burner. The Augustus Suite. The letter opener. Cassandra. Lennox.

"I thought Marjorie said –"

"*Mrs. Pickering* expects you to serve. Or are you really so foolish that you think she was letting you off the hook?"

I shifted my jaw. I wasn't sure what I thought anymore.

"It might be a bit difficult for me to hold the tray –"

"Don't make excuses," Mrs. Tilly snapped. "Get up and get downstairs: I don't want my food burning."

She stomped from the room, and though I was glad to see her go, I wasn't pleased to be alone. I glanced back at my bed, fearing that the sight of my mother would greet me. Perhaps I had hit my head harder than I'd initially thought, or perhaps it was just the sight of Cassandra laying next to Mrs. Marlowe that had made me dream of her. I got down on the floor and patted around for my shoes. Yet even as I settled on the idea, I couldn't shake the feeling of anxiousness that had come over me, as though my mother had somehow entered my dreams to warn me about something. I pulled my shoes on and brushed the thought aside. No, I reasoned, I had just taken too many pills. My mother couldn't watch out for me anymore, and certainly not through the impossibility of dreams.

I grasped at the banister to ease myself downstairs,

feeling as though I wouldn't get through the Foyer without vomiting. When I made it to the kitchen, Mrs. Tilly had the tray waiting for me. I took it from her hands, shoving it up against my hip to hold it in place with my good hand, then slowly made my way to the breakfast nook. It was safe to assume that Cassandra was going to tell the family that she had seen me and Lennox in the Augustus Suite, assuming she hadn't already; and I – with my head hammering and stomach contents threatening to come up at any moment, didn't know how I was going to defend myself.

No one spoke of the incident when I entered the room. I glanced at Lennox. He gave the slightest shake of his head. Cassandra was sitting at the head of the table, her long veil trailing down to the floor like a puddle.

I brought the tray around the table to serve them, certain that they could hear my head pounding as I stooped to their level. The smell of ham wafted up from the tray and into my nostrils, and I clamped my mouth firmly shut as another wave of nausea came over me.

"Oh, feeling better?" Bernadette asked as I lowered the tray for her.

"Yes, Mrs. Carlton."

"Had a bit of an accident, did you?"

"Yes, Mrs. Carlton."

"It looks quite painful," Rachel said from down the table.

"Yes, what a nasty gash," Marjorie agreed. "I hope it knocked some sense into you."

I waited to respond until I reached her. A part of me hoped that, if I was truly going to be sick, I would do it on her lap.

"It did, Mrs. Pickering. I'm going to be more careful in the future."

She only smiled. I stole another glance at Lennox, but he was busy drinking his coffee. I wondered if he was doing so because he didn't agree with my response, or if he was just concerned about Cassandra.

She stayed silent as I worked my way around the table, but when I reached her and stooped down to lift some meat and eggs onto her plate, her veiled head turned in my direction.

"Oh, Alexandra – your cap," she said, noting that it wasn't on my head. She reached beneath her veil and produced it, the black fabric barely distinguishable from her satin gloves. "Here you go. You left it behind last night."

My mouth opened but no words came out. She gave a little chuckle before pulling it down over my head, brushing my hot cheeks with her gloves as she went. As her index finger came to rest against my lips, she leaned toward me and whispered, "Shh. It'll be our little secret."

"Is everything alright down there, Cassie?" Marjorie called. "Or should I assume there's a good reason that you're dressing the maid?"

"Oh, everything's fine," Cassandra giggled. "I was just telling Alexandra not to worry ... I won't get her into trouble."

"I don't think any of us would give her a hard time for losing her hat," Bill said, though he threw me a look as he said it, and his eyes were still distrusting of me.

"Oh, no, it's not that," Cassandra said with another giggle. "It's something *much* bigger ..."

"Well, either tell us or shut up about it," Marjorie snapped, "and send her over with the juice."

I pulled away and went to serve Bill, then maneuvered the tray onto the buffet before getting the juice for Marjorie. When I was done, I took my place against the wall, hoping that that was the end of it, but –

"Alexandra did something quite naughty last night," Cassandra said, seeming to realize that no one was going to drag it out of her as she had hoped they would. She put her hand over her mouth to hide another giggle. Her dead mother's ring gleamed up at me like a wicked smile.

"What's this?" Bernadette asked. She glanced from her sister to me. I opened my mouth and closed it. Two seats away, Lennox took a sip of coffee, his back straight and his eyes fixed on his saucer.

"Oh, yes," Cassandra went on. "She and Isidore had a *very* exciting time."

She lifted her veil from her lap so that she could bring her food underneath it. I stood in my spot, wanting to explain myself in my usual direct way but only managing to focus on the searing pain in my head.

"They ... had what?" Bernadette asked.

Marjorie had her fork raised to her mouth, but the scrambled eggs slipped off of it and back down to her plate with a *plop*. She raised her eyebrows in disgust.

"Would you care to explain, Cassie?" she called. "Or will our imaginations suffice?"

"Oh, I'm not sure if I should share the details," Cassandra said. "It was highly unsettling ..."

Lennox put his coffee cup down. It clattered against the saucer.

"Alexandra and I were in the Augustus Suite last night," he said wearisomely. "It was my idea. I wanted to examine John."

The family's faces went from one shocked expression to a completely different type. I raised my eyes to look at him, but his gaze was on Marjorie.

"You wanted to what?" she asked.

"To examine him," Lennox repeated. "I was curious about his cause of death –"

"You had no right to touch my husband!" Amalia said. "How dare you disturb him without my permission?"

"I'm sorry, I must not have heard correctly," Marjorie cut in. "You wanted to *examine* him? For what?"

"His cause of death," Lennox said again. "It's been troubling me that he was killed by a – by such a short knife. I was hoping to –"

"You mean you were doing an autopsy?" Marjorie said. "My God – and you didn't think of discussing it first with all of us?"

"I admit that it was wrong, though in the circumstances –"

"How do we know you weren't tampering with evidence?" Amalia exclaimed. "Wiping your fingerprints from the blade? Covering your tracks?"

"If anything, there will be more of my fingerprints on him now than there were initially," Lennox replied calmly. "But the point is –"

"The point is that you shouldn't have been in there!" Amalia said. "I suppose you were hoping you'd get away with it? You and your little roommate?"

"I thought it might be best to do it privately, yes," Lennox said.

"But Isidore," Rachel said, "you must have known that it wasn't your place –"

"I'm not sure that regular rules apply at the moment," Lennox said. "And, quite frankly, I doubt that you all would have allowed me to look at him had I asked –"

"For good reason!" Amalia exclaimed.

"How is it that you caught them, Cassie?" Bernadette inquired.

Cassandra's veiled head turned up in surprise. She faltered for a moment.

"Well, I was in there checking on Mummy –" she began.

"Oh, Cassie," Marjorie said. "You weren't sleeping in her bed again, were you? It's bad enough you've been wearing her clothes."

Cassandra made an indignant sound, and I was

certain that, had I been able to see her face, she would have been blushing.

"I certainly wasn't –"

"Really, Cassie," Rachel said. "It was odd enough when she was alive –"

"I was checking on her! And it was a good thing I was, or else –"

"It's highly unhygienic," Bernadette stated. "Once a body begins to decompose, all sorts of toxins are released –"

"Poor, poor Cassie," Marjorie went on. "Never got enough of Mother's love in life so she has to take what she can get now …"

"I was checking on her!" Cassandra said, her voice still fairly calm despite being raised. "And Mummy and I were the closest, so I certainly never wanted for her love and affection –"

"How did you even get in there?" Amalia asked. "I locked the door!"

"Well, you obviously didn't do a very good job," Bernadette said. "Considering that both Cassie and Lennox were able to walk right in –"

"I locked it! I have the key!"

"There are two keys to the Augustus Suite," Marjorie said. "One was Mother's, one was Father's."

"Well – well –!" Amalia spluttered angrily. "Well someone might have mentioned that!"

"It wouldn't have done you much good: it's not like Cassie would have handed the one in her possession over," Bernadette said. "Not if it meant she couldn't snuggle up to Mother's corpse …"

"Well, you might have at least locked the door behind you!" Amalia said angrily as she rounded on Cassandra, but before the veiled woman could counter that she had indeed locked the door, Bill cut in.

"Perhaps we should get back to the point," he said.

He looked at Lennox, whose shoulders had tensed. I watched him, thinking that he would relax now that he didn't have to tell them he had taken the key from Amalia's room, but the uneasiness didn't leave him. "What exactly did you discover when you ... examined John?"

Lennox glanced my way. I stared down at my hands, focusing on the shiny, purplish skin on my left palm and fingers rather than the fact that he was taking the majority of the blame for what we had done.

"Well, I didn't get to finish –" he started.

"And you certainly won't now!"

" – but it seems," he carried on, ignoring Amalia, "that John was stabbed postmortem."

The family stared at him, not understanding.

"He was stabbed after he was dead," Lennox explained.

"But that doesn't make any sense," Bill said. "He couldn't have been dead before he was killed."

"You must be mistaken, Lennox," Bernadette agreed. "He didn't just drop dead of fright upon seeing someone come at him with a knife –"

"That's not what I'm saying," Lennox said. "It would appear that whomever stabbed him did it for – shall we say – show. To cover up how he really died."

"This is ludicrous," Amalia said. "My husband was murdered!"

"Yes, he was," Lennox said. "But not in the way we initially thought. I'm very confident that something else killed him first."

"Something else like what?" Bernadette said. "Hypothermia?"

"If I could take another look at the body –"

"You certainly may not!" Amalia said.

"It's the only way we're going to discover what happened to him," Lennox said. "I can guess, but conjecture won't do us much good."

"Neither will having you poke around my husband's body!"

"Afraid what he might find, are you?" Marjorie asked.

Amalia drew in a breath, her chest puffing out as she seethed.

"It's Lennox I'm worried about!" she said. "He could be doing all sorts of things to John – trying to cover up how he died –!"

"I would be happy to finish my examination under your watchful eyes," Lennox said.

"Oh, *now* you don't mind an audience," Amalia snapped. "Quite a different tune than you had last night when you were sneaking around with the maid!"

"Admittedly it does look rather bad," Bernadette said conversationally.

"I know I didn't kill John," Lennox said. "But – unfortunately – I can't say the same for any of you. That's why I chose to do it without telling you."

"You seem very trusting of little Alexandra, though," Marjorie said.

Lennox glanced at her.

"I don't think she had anything to do with it, no," he said. "She has no connection to him, after all."

"No connection that we know of," Cassandra said, folding her hands in front of her. "Though perhaps there's one that she hasn't revealed to us yet."

The pain in my skull was so intense that I didn't even try to respond.

"There is something funny about her," Marjorie said, eyeing me suspiciously. She put down her fork and leaned closer to me as though trying to detect what it was, but the only fear I felt was that I was going to vomit.

"I'm sure Alexandra is innocent in all of this,"

Rachel said.

"Oh, you're sure everyone is innocent in all of this!" Amalia returned. "You seem to be under the impression that John was struck down by the heavens!"

"No, I just think –"

"If John wasn't killed with the knife," Bill cut in, "then what was he killed with?"

Everyone looked at Lennox. He slowly laid both hands on either side of his plate.

"It could be a number of things," he said. "A blow to the head, strangulation ... poison."

The family's eyes went from Lennox's face to their glasses of juice. Edie looked horrified that she had finished hers, Marjorie looked relieved that she hadn't yet taken a sip.

"Poison?" Edie said. "But where would anyone get poison –?"

"Where wouldn't they get poison?" Marjorie said. "There's rat poison in the cellar! There's cleaning solution under the sink! There's a goddamn pharmacy in Mother's medicine cabinet!"

"But how would John be poisoned?" Bill asked. "It would have had to be in the food, and none of us is dead."

"Well, maybe the killer only added it to *his* food," Marjorie said impatiently, and Bill quickly adjusted his glasses to avoid holding her gaze.

"No, it was the scotch," Edie said. She shook her head. "It must have been in that horrible scotch that none of us was allowed to drink."

Bill put his hand to his throat as though imagining the poison going down into his stomach. Edie had put her hands on her face, her fingernails digging into her cheeks. Amalia made an odd gulping sound.

Marjorie turned toward me.

"You poured him his scotch nightly, Alexandra," she said coldly. "Perhaps you noticed something ... *off* about it?"

I blinked but didn't respond.

"Anyone could have poisoned the scotch," Lennox said. "It's right out in the open. And we're not even sure that's what did it."

"Really? Then why don't you take a swallow?" Marjorie shot.

"I don't drink," Lennox said simply.

Marjorie's nostrils flared.

"Well, *that's* very convenient –"

"And even if I did," Lennox continued, "I believe it's in Amalia's possession now. Or somewhere in her digestive tract."

He gave Amalia a look. She squirmed in her seat.

"You drank John's scotch?" Marjorie asked her. Her face lit up in delight. "Goodness, kudos to the killer ..."

"Considering that John died on the second night of his arrival, I would assume that Amalia will live," Lennox said. He turned to her. "Though if you *do* start to experience any symptoms, at least we'll have some confirmation of what happened to the both of you."

Amalia seethed.

"You slimy, slithery piece of –"

"Let's all just calm down," Rachel said as the others chimed in to add to the bickering. "Arguing won't solve anything –"

"Neither will sitting here getting along!" Amalia said, slamming her napkin down to the table with a bang. "In case you haven't noticed, nothing's going to change the fact that someone poisoned my husband! Someone at this table!"

"That's pure speculation," Bernadette said. "It could have been Mrs. Tilly ..."

"She *was* rather upset that John let Tilda go," Marjorie agreed thoughtfully.

"It wasn't her!" Amalia screeched. "It was one of you! I know it was one of you!"

She stood and made a thrashing motion with her arms to knock the plates and glasses within her reach off the table and onto the floor. They clattered loudly onto the wood, half of them smashing to bits, and Bill gave a wild jump that dislodged his glasses again. For a moment Amalia stood and surveyed the damage she had caused, and then she threw her head back and let out a long, wailing scream. It pierced the air and vibrated off of the walls, raining down upon us like fire from the sky, making my head pound harder and harder until I thought that my head would crack open. I was rather convinced that she wasn't half as upset at John being killed now as she was the thought that she might succumb to the same fate, though she had enough dignity left not to openly say it. When she finally stopped, she stormed from the room, but not before the full extent of her damage was done: my head gave one last resounding pound, and then I lurched forward and vomited onto the floor.

The family turned to stare at me.

"Well, that ruined my appetite," Marjorie said briskly, tossing her napkin over her plate.

"Oh, Alexandra," Rachel said kindly, "are you still not feeling well?"

"Either that or she had whatever did John in," Marjorie muttered.

I couldn't stand for a moment longer. Dropping to my knees, I fell to the ground – barely managing to avoid landing in the pile of sick in front of me. I barely registered the sound of a chair scraping across the hardwood, but a moment later someone was helping me to my feet.

"Oh, yes, you take care of her, Lennox," Marjorie called. "Put that degree of yours to some use."

"You can bring her to the Drawing Room, Isidore," Rachel suggested. "If you don't think she'll make it up the stairs ..."

"I think she just needs some fresh air," he responded, holding me up by my elbows.

"Oh, no, Isidore," Cassandra cooed. "Why don't you take her upstairs? She looks like she needs you to tuck her into bed ..."

Lennox ignored her.

"Come here," he told me gently. "Let's get you outside."

"And who's going to clean up this mess?" Bernadette asked as he led me to the door. "I can't eat with the smell of bile filling up my nostrils, you know –"

"You're welcome to clean it up yourself," Lennox said. "I believe the mop is in the front hall closet."

Bernadette huffed indignantly, but it was Cassandra who spoke.

"Don't worry, Birdie," she said. "Lennox is just very protective of her. Aren't you, Lennox?"

His head moved as though he was throwing her a look, but I didn't see. He led me to the door and down the hallway, then bundled me up in my coat and brought me outside. The pounding in my skull had lessened slightly, but I sank down to sit on the porch even so. I leaned my head up against the mermaid pillar. Lennox crouched down next to me.

"Now, despite your attempts to will it away, you're exhibiting symptoms of a concussion," he said. "May I look in your eyes?"

"No." I shifted away from him. I was embarrassed enough, and I certainly didn't want him anywhere near my face. I wiped at my mouth with my apron. "It's not a concussion."

"Forgive me, but I believe I'm the doctor."

"And I believe I'm the one who took an extra eight-hundred milligrams of my medication last night, so I know that's what's made me sick." I leaned my head back, finally consenting to look him in the eye. "I'm sorry."

The words were muffled, and I wasn't even certain that I knew what I was apologizing for. Being sick? Not helping him explain to the family what we had been doing the night before? Fighting with him? Maybe all of it, or maybe something else entirely. I let my eyes wander back over to his wedding ring. My heart gave another rueful pang.

"That wasn't as bad as I thought it would be," he commented.

"It was pretty bad for me," I replied, though I was grateful that he didn't chide me further for the pills. "I seldom apologize."

"I was referring to the conversation with the family," he said with a smile. "The apology was unnecessary, especially since I'm the one who owes you an apology. I spoke out of fear and I was wrong. Please forgive me."

"Ah – well, alright," I mumbled, avoiding his eyes. I tried to think of anything else to say to lead the conversation back to the murder, but every thought was about him. They raced through my mind as though mocking me, trying to get me to admit what I hated to believe. I shut my eyes as they pinged off one another, bounding back and forth within my skull: the fact that we had both been brought here by John Marlowe, both been promised things we would likely never see now, both been stuck together in the adjoining rooms in the servants' corridors. It had made me feel a kinship with him that I otherwise wouldn't have felt, for if we hadn't been stuck here on the island with no chance of getting off until someone noticed our absences, then surely I would never have felt that way about him. Surely ...

I lifted my head slightly. A thought had just occurred to me – one that conflicted with the little information I thought I knew about him. He had told me that his colleagues would only notice his absence when the New Year came, but his wife must have noticed by now seeing as he had only planned to stay on the island for a night.

"Won't your wife wonder where you are?" I asked.

Lennox's head turned to me in surprise.

"What?"

"Your wife," I repeated, indicating his ring. "Won't she wonder where you are?"

Lennox looked down at his hand, a frown appearing on his face as though he hadn't realized that his ring held any such symbolism. After a moment, he stuck his left hand in his pocket, seemingly to rid it from sight.

"No."

"But you said you were only staying for the night," I said. "So won't she –?"

"I'm not married," he said shortly. "Not – anymore."

"Oh." A part of me knew that I was supposed to add some sort of sentiment to my statement and offer my condolences for the breakdown of his marriage, but all I felt was a sense of relief that I was far too worried I might accidentally speak aloud if I tried to say more.

"Perhaps we should head back in," Lennox said. "I don't want the family to think we're out here conspiring."

He insisted on re-bandaging my hand when we got inside, then tried to get me to go to bed, but I declined. I was hoping that having something to do would keep me from thinking of him, but as I returned to the now-empty Breakfast Room to clean up, I couldn't stop the thoughts from coming. My mind was battling with itself as it tried to come to grips with my feelings, which it so seldom had to deal with, and I ran through every possibility as I mopped up the floor and swept the broken dishes into the trash. It was the danger that was drawing us together: scientifically speaking, the increase in my heartbeat due to all of the unsettling events was simultaneously tricking me into believing that I was falling in love. Or it could have been transference: I was substituting feelings that I had pushed aside and dumping them onto him, thereby believing that I actually had feelings for him. Or ...

I stopped midway through stacking the breakfast plates, trying to come up with another excuse. Or it could have just been that he was kind to me. It had been so long since I had had a conversation that wasn't met with irritation at the way I constantly challenged and corrected people. If anything, he seemed entertained by it. But even if that was true, and even if my feelings were somehow requited, the only thing I ought to have been focused on was finding out who killed John and getting off the island, after which Lennox and I would never see one another again. Yet even with that knowledge, I couldn't get him off my mind.

The house seemed even warmer than usual, and I found myself tugging constantly at my turtleneck and cap as I worked. I wished that they would turn the heat down, or at least stop telling me to light the fireplaces, but no one else seemed to mind the unbearably stuffy air. I went to my room to change into something lighter, tossing my dirty apron into the laundry chute on the way. Not caring if Bernadette scolded me for not wearing my uniform, I put on the dark green skirt and blouse that I had traveled to the island in, grateful to get the fabric off my neck. As I perched on the edge of my bed, I had the urge to lay down and shut my eyes, but forced myself up again. Cleaning the rooms would give me another opportunity to look through their belongings; and this time, rather than searching for a blood-soaked article of clothing, I would be searching for anything that could have been used as poison or a blunt weapon.

Once again, only the door to the Mabel Room was

open, though it was the others that I longed to search. My hands shook as I began to clean, and the bright yellow walls were glaring in the morning sun. I couldn't imagine Edie feeling comfortable in there: it seemed as though someone ought to have painted it a dull, drab gray decades ago. As I made up the bed, I shook the sheets harder than usual in the hopes that something would come tumbling out, but they only rose up like a parachute before gracefully falling back down; likewise, when I fluffed the pillows, there was nothing hard hidden within the down feathers that waited for me to uncover it. Nor did I truly think there would be, I reasoned as I finished making the bed, as I suspected by now that the killer was intelligent enough not to stash evidence in their room – especially if they were willing to let me in to clean it.

And yet, even with that thought, I continued to stoop and look beneath the bed, then carefully went through the contents of the bureau, slid my hands inside Edie's shoes, opened the suitcase at the bottom of the closet to ensure that it was still empty, checked behind the curtains, and crawled up onto the foot of the bed so that I could peer onto the top of the canopy. Finding nothing, I repeated my search in the adjoining bathroom – going so far as to lift the back off of the toilet and look into the water tank. I was readying to leave when I saw the faintest hint of a dark brown bottle peeking out from behind the clutter of toiletries and makeup on the sink. Snatching it up, I quickly read the name: *Chlorpromazine*. A quick shake of it told me that it was still nearly filled with pills, though I didn't recognize the name to know what they were for. Anxiety, I guessed, or depression. Lennox would be able to tell me.

So what had happened, I wondered as I carefully wiped the bottle down and replaced it in its spot. Had John been poisoned – possibly by Edie's or someone else's pills – or had he been murdered another way? Words were skimming the surface of my mind, but I couldn't slow them enough to read them, and my shaking form was rattling me and making it difficult to think at all. All I knew was that I didn't know the people inside the house, and more than ever I didn't know why John had brought me here. What game had he been hoping to play by hiring me? What game had been stopped by whoever inside the house had killed him?

My skull pounded as I tried in vain to figure it out. Who had killed him? Marjorie – who might've lured him outside by saying she needed a cigarette? Bill, who wanted to say something that Rachel had begged him not to? Amalia, who may or may not have been set to inherit his life insurance as well as the Marlowes' fortune and island? Bernadette, the eldest child who thought nothing of sitting down to breakfast moments after seeing her brother's body in the snow?

Who killed Professor Marlowe? said my own voice in my ear as I spoke to Kneller about John's death.

They all did it. To themselves.

I squeezed my eyes shut, trying to think of what he meant. Were there multiple assailants? Was it possible that the family – either two of them or more – had conspired together to kill John? And now they were playing us, hoping that we'd believe their game of charades at the dinner table that covered their true feelings of glee that they could all share in the inheritance they thought they ought to have received?

I set the water pitcher back on the nightstand and then took a seat on the bed, staring at the yellow walls as I tried to think. If the whole family was in on it, then perhaps Lennox and I had simply gotten in the way. Lennox was never supposed to have shown up, and – now that I thought about it – neither was I. John had hired me on his own, kicking out the previous maid without warning. Had the servants been in on it, too? And John had messed it all up by promising Lennox a picture and promising to get me back into my program? Or had he inadvertently helped them, as now they had two people who, despite being innocent in all of this, could take the blame for what they had done?

And if that was true, then Lennox and I truly were in trouble. The fear that I ought to have felt days ago descended upon me all at once. I had been blinded by the Marlowes' eccentricities when I ought to have been mistrustful. They were people who discussed murder no differently than what type of wine would go best with their meal, and who, as far as I had seen, would readily and easily band together to say that I had been the one to plunge the letter opener into John's chest. The image of Lennox and myself being marched from the house by the police floated before my mind before being replaced by another one: our bodies, rigid and blue, disappearing beneath the falling snow, never to be uncovered again. Because if either of us had figured it out, I knew, and they had any inkling that we knew what they had done, then that was surely what they would do to us.

And it would be so simple for them to succeed in killing me, at least – so easy to do away with me like a soiled rag. If my aunt didn't hear from me for weeks, then she would undoubtedly assume that I saw no point in trying to call again given how poorly my mother reacted to my voice on the phone. It would only be weeks from now when I was due to return home that she would finally realize something had happened, and even then she wouldn't have the means to do more than report my absence to the police. She couldn't come looking for me – she had to watch over my mother.

My heart gave a horrible pang. Which was worse, I wondered? That my mother would continually ask for me when I didn't show up to see her every weekend, or that she wouldn't ask for me at all – because she no longer remembered me at all?

I pulled my sleeve against my forehead to wipe my brow, then stood and collected the extra blanket to put away in the chest at the foot of the bed. I yanked it open, intent on tossing it inside and leaving, but –

"Jesus."

The word had barely escaped my mouth when I leaned forward into the chest, sure that I was mistaken in what I was seeing. For there, at the bottom of the chest, was a tiny, pale, and motionless baby. It had been stabbed through the chest with a jagged piece of green and blue stained-glass.

"What the ...?"

As I moved closer still, I could see that it was only a doll, though it was possibly the most realistic – and frightening – doll I had ever laid eyes on. It was dressed in the long white Christening gown that I had seen once before on my first day at the Marlowe house – though then it had been laying in the crib in the nursery. It must have belonged to one of Edie and Bill's children, but if that was so, then I didn't understand who had shoved the glass into it – or why. I reached in and pulled it out with my good hand, holding it by one arm as though it might sudden wake up and bite. The glass had pierced through blue stitching, and when I squinted, I could read the word *owl*. My stomach turned unpleasantly, though I knew it had no relation to the extra medication I had taken the night before.

"Alexandra?"

I jumped and dropped the doll, slicing my finger on the glass as it fell through my fingers. A splatter of blood jumped from my skin and onto the white fabric, reaffirming how realistic it looked. As it landed with a *thump* at the bottom of the chest, I turned quickly to the door.

Rachel stood in the doorway. Her eyes were focused

in the spot where the doll had been suspended from my hand. I got to my feet, squeezing my hand shut to stop the bleeding from the cut on my palm.

"What are you doing?" she asked.

"Cleaning."

She raised her eyebrows, silently suggesting that she knew the only reason I was keeping up with my duties was so that I could snoop through the rooms. I rearranged my face, hoping to feign innocence.

"I just wanted to let you know," she began, "that I'll be in the Augustus Suite for a little while, so you can clean the Drawing Room."

"How are you going to get in?"

My voice betrayed a hint of my concern. After all, if she was planning to ask Amalia to unlock the door, then Amalia would realize that her key was gone and know that Lennox had taken it from her room.

"Cassie's going to unlock it for me."

"Oh, good." I paused. "Where's Mr. Langston?"

"He's down there. I'm sure you won't disturb him." Her mouth twitched as though she was trying to smile but found herself unable to. "Unless that makes you uncomfortable?"

I squeezed my hand tighter. John's voice whispered in my ear. *Does this make you uncomfortable?* The sound of it still made me shiver.

"No, Mrs. Langston. It doesn't make me uncomfortable."

I tossed the blanket inside the chest with my good hand and closed the lid, then started toward the door to leave. She was still staring at me oddly, and I wondered if she could have possibly thought that I had planted the doll there. Given that she was so adamant that none of her siblings could possibly be violent, I didn't put it past her. As I tried to pass her, she didn't move.

"Was there something else, Mrs. Langston?"

"No," she said, saying the word a bit too quickly. She paused, then started again in a slower voice. "Just ... just make sure you look after him while I'm not there."

"Alright. I won't leave until you're back downstairs."

She nodded, though she didn't seem content with my answer. I raised my eyebrows as she retreated down the hallway to her mother's room, then made my way downstairs, stopping at the front hall closet as I went to get a bandage so that I could wrap my hand, though it was difficult to do with my maimed left hand. Instead I pressed the gauze to the cut until it stopped bleeding. I couldn't afford to lose function of both hands, after all.

James was dozing off when I entered the Drawing Room. I worked as quietly as I could so as to not disturb him, then perched myself on the edge of one of the cots as I waited for Rachel to return.

The door opened half and hour later and Rachel slipped into the room, her eyes rimmed with red. It seemed odd that she had chosen now to revisit her mother's deathbed, and I couldn't help but think back to her conversation with Bill, then to the doll that mimicked the way John had died. I didn't care what Lennox had said about Bill being a good man: I didn't believe in coincidences, and I didn't believe that she and Bill had been discussing anything other than John's murder when she had begged him not to tell anyone what he knew.

"Thank you," she said quietly, avoiding looking at me as she busied herself dusting off the front of James's sweater.

"May I ask you something, Mrs. Langston?"

"No." She took a seat on the chair next to her husband and poured herself a glass of water. "I'm afraid I have a bit of a headache. I'd like to be left alone."

I shifted my jaw. I knew that I ought to wait to ask her later when she was in a better mood, but the question on the tip of my tongue didn't want to be swallowed back into my throat.

"If you knew who had killed your brother," I said quickly, "you would say something, wouldn't you, Mrs. Langston?"

She didn't look over at me. She seemed nearly frozen.

"I told you I want to be left alone, Alexandra," she said, and her voice was dull and toneless. "Please don't try my patience – I'm afraid I have very little left."

I believed her, and yet I couldn't let it go.

"Because if you knew," I continued hurriedly, "I would hope you'd say something. I would hope you would want the killer to pay."

Her head turned slightly toward me so that it was a profile over her shoulder.

"I don't want anyone to pay," she whispered. "I just want it to be over."

She stood and went to the door, opening it and sweeping me out with a wave of her hand, and I reluctantly obeyed. The door shut behind me so quickly that the hem of my skirt got caught in it, and I yanked it free and returned upstairs to check on the other bedrooms. Every door was shut – including Bernadette's, who was usually so particular about me refilling her biscuit jar – indicating that no one was in need of cleaning. I wondered if the family was holing themselves up for fear of the poison that had been discussed at breakfast, or if they didn't want me snooping around in their rooms anymore.

I returned to my room and laid back on my bed. They all had something to hide, that much was clear, though I wavered back and forth on whether that meant that they had conspired together to commit murder. It seemed that they would have to be far too good at acting to keep up such a front, especially since they were only performing for me and Lennox. Or maybe it was just a handful of them who had done it, I considered, thinking of the forlorn note I had just heard in Rachel's voice. And I didn't blame her: the senseless arguments had gone on long enough, and I wanted it to be over, as well. How to achieve that, though, I didn't know.

The bell jingled for me sometime later, and I shook off my thoughts and trudged downstairs to collect the serving tray from the kitchen. My hands stung as I gripped the handles, and by the time I reached the Dining Room my left one was throbbing horribly. I went around the table to let the family members spoon beef stew into their bowls, waiting impatiently for the tureen to lighten and get the pressure off of my palms. I had barely finished and set the tray down when Bernadette called me back from my place by the wall.

"Fetch the port, Alexandra – I fear we're going to need it."

"And make sure it's unopened," Marjorie added darkly.

I went to the bar cart where one was waiting to be uncorked.

"I wouldn't trust her to do that," Amalia said from behind me. "She could easily poison the whole bottle from over there –"

"She could just as easily poison us at any time," Bernadette said. "Who knows what she does with the food between here and the kitchen. A little sprinkle of rodenticide with the powdered sugar and we're all on the floor ..."

"Given an awful lot of thought to how to poison someone, have you, Birdie?" Marjorie asked.

"It's just science, dear. And rodenticides can only

poison in multiple doses, so it very well might be too late already."

She tucked into her meal, adding heaps of butter to her roll before dipping it into the stew as though the thought of dying whilst eating was not an unhappy one. Marjorie rolled her eyes.

"So that's how John was killed, was it?" Amalia said angrily, seemingly taking Bernadette's words as an admission of guilt. "Rat poison?"

"I doubt it," Bernadette said, speaking before finishing her bite and giving the table at large the view of the half-masticated food in her mouth. "He was probably killed with Mother's tranquilizers. A couple of those crushed up and his central nervous system would be more depressed than Edie's been since her last stillbirth –"

Edie burst into tears, showering her food in salty water. Bill threw Bernadette an irritated look.

"Was that really necessary?" he asked. "For Christ's sakes – especially when she spent all morning at the cemetery –"

"I was merely illustrating a point," Bernadette replied indifferently. "Besides, I didn't say there was anything wrong with being depressed after losing a child – or twelve. Though it has been twenty years ..."

"Let's get back to how you poisoned John, shall we?" Bill said pointedly as his wife let out a sound akin to a howl. Bernadette held up her hands.

"I'm only trying to be helpful," she said. "The real murderer, of course, is welcome to jump in tell me if my speculation is accurate."

"Technically I never said that John had been poisoned," Lennox said carefully from the far end of the table. He set his glass of water back down and folded his hands together. "I just said that it was a possibility. He might have been strangled or taken a blow to the head –"

"Oh, it was poison," Amalia said blisteringly as she looked around at her sisters-in-law. "They didn't have the strength to fight him, or the guts. I'm surprised he was stabbed in the chest rather than straight in the back!"

"I'm surprised he was stabbed at all," Marjorie said. "Though I suppose since there are no cars here, the option of running him over was out –"

"Is that one of the ways you considered killing your children?" Bernadette asked while indicating me to bring over the basket of rolls. "Odd that you didn't settle on it: I would have thought it would be easier to claim it was an accident that way."

"You'd know all about claiming someone's death was an accident, wouldn't you?" Marjorie snapped. "What was Edgar's official cause of death? Morphine overdose?"

I held the basket out for Bernadette to choose from, and she took her time deciding between a plain one and one covered in poppy seeds, humming as she thought.

"It's much more common than you would think," she said, turning back to her sister after deciding on both. "And it was the doctor who prescribed the morphine, so it was his fault if anyone's –"

"Yes, but it was you who administered it to him!" Marjorie said.

I returned to my spot by the wall, feeling that I finally understood them. They were wired for the insanity that they created around them, and murders and unfounded coincidences were slotted into their schedules right between afternoon reading and tea time, only to be spoken of at select moments after discussions of politics and literature had run dry.

"Let he who is without sin cast the first stone," Bernadette said evenly, then added in her loudest of whispers, "child-killer."

"I *did not* –"

Yet before Marjorie could deny it once again, a roll went soaring across the table and promptly smacked Bernadette straight between the eyes. It bounced off of her and fell with a *plop* into her soup. There was a stunned moment of silence as everyone looked with disbelief at where it had come from: James had flung it from his spot at the opposite side of the table.

"He can move?" Amalia asked, looking as dumbfounded as I felt. I had only ever seen James use his arms to painstakingly feed himself, or else bang the arms of his chair.

"Of course he can move," Bill responded.

"Sometimes he loses control of his movements," Rachel said hurriedly, grabbing onto her husband as though he was having a spasm, but his arm was quite still. My eyes went from his now-empty hand to his face, which was still the same glazed expression as always, and yet I got the distinct impression that he had known exactly what he was doing: casting the first stone.

"But if he can move –" Amalia started, "then it might have been him! He killed John!"

"Oh, for Christ's sakes, Amalia," Marjorie said, "the man is in a wheelchair. You think he rolled down the steps and out into the snow, then somehow managed to overtake John?"

"Maybe he's just faking! He might not have been injured by John at all, and he's just been – just been pretending all these years to – to – get some remorse out of John!"

"*Remorse* out of *John?*" Marjorie asked. "Did you even *know* your husband? And I thought Cassie came up with farcical ideas ..."

"You saw what he just did! Even I couldn't have hit Bernadette with such precision, especially from that distance!"

"Well, he might not have been aiming for me at all," Bernadette said. "It's possible he was trying to throw it at Marjorie –"

"Oh, get bent, Birdie," Marjorie snapped. "He was aiming at you. Luckily the target is *exceedingly* large –"

Amalia opened her mouth again, looking as though she was still desperately hoping to find a way to prove that it could have been James. I returned my gaze to the wheelchair-bound man. Though Amalia was clearly grasping at straws, I couldn't help but think back to what Rachel had said to me. *Sometimes I think he knows everything we're saying ...*

"James did *not* mean to throw anything at anyone," Rachel said firmly. "Like I said, sometimes he just loses control of his functions –"

"Well, maybe he lost control of his functions and killed my husband!" Amalia returned. "And then – and then *you* stabbed him with the knife to divert attention off of him!"

"That's the most absurd thing I've ever heard," Bill said.

"I'm inclined to agree," Lennox said. "James did not kill John."

"Though if he had –" Bernadette commented, digging the soggy roll from her stew and popping it into her mouth, "– I doubt any of us would blame him."

Amalia ignored her and rounded on Lennox.

"How would you know?" she asked. "Because *you* killed him?"

"No," Lennox replied, almost sounding bored as she accused him for the dozenth time, "because I don't believe that throwing a piece of bread is indicative of one's ability to plunge a knife through layers of connective tissue. The killer would need to be extremely strong, and James – well, James is not."

"Extremely strong like you, you mean?" Amalia asked.

"Amalia, I did not kill your husband."

"You think I'm going to just take your word for it? Just because the maid says she locked you in doesn't give you an alibi, Lennox – not one that I'll accept, anyhow! Especially since you seem to be very adept at finding ways to unlock doors despite not having a key!"

"She has a good point," Marjorie chimed in. "You seem to be finding your way around the house with exceeding ease – and the maid's help. It's beginning to get a bit ... suspicious."

"And –" Amalia continued, building steam, "– and you would have had an easy time knowing what poisons to use on John! You probably brought them with you, then killed him right away in case we searched you!"

Lennox's jaw shifted, though for the first time, he betrayed a hint of apprehension.

"In fact," she went on, seeming to recognize the same thing I had, "it's all beginning to make more and more sense! You poisoned him hoping it'd look like he'd died accidentally, but then realized that we'd know it was you, so you stabbed him to throw us off your scent! I know it!"

"Really?" Lennox asked, barely managing to maintain his calm tone. "Because only two minutes ago you were convinced that James had done it –"

"Yes, but that was before you pointed out one crucial bit of evidence: the killer had to have been *strong*. So it *must* have been a man – it *must* have been you!"

"He's not the only man in the room," Bill said indignantly, seemingly more affronted that he had been forgotten than he was concerned about being accused, but Amalia paid him no mind. Her torso rose up like a snake readying to strike its prey. Savagery was dripping from the pores of her cheeks, and she looked as though she wanted nothing more than to destroy someone, though it didn't seem to be exceedingly important to her whom it was.

"Don't try to deny it anymore, Lennox. We all know how slippery you are –"

"Am I? I wasn't aware."

"Really?" Marjorie threw at him from down the table. "I don't think your *wife* would agree."

Lennox looked over at her, a dangerous look in his eyes.

"You can leave her out of it, Marjorie," he said in a low voice.

"Why? Still sensitive to how she *slipped* right out of your life –?"

"Marjorie!" Rachel interjected. "Come, now – there's no need for this –!"

"Oh, shut up," Amalia snapped at her. "Don't act as though he knows what it's like to be a good husband: I think we'd all agree he never had a clue."

"Well, then at least you'd all agree on something," Lennox replied. I had never seen him so on edge: his hands were clenched into fists on either side of his plate, and his mouth was twitching. "That and the fact that you're a miserable, self-loathing excuse for a woman."

Amalia's face went red. I looked from her to Lennox, wondering if I could somehow silently remind him of his tactic to stay out of the Marlowes' line of fire, but it was evident he had lost too much of his composure to regain it.

"Forgive me if I don't trust your diagnosis, *Doctor!*"

"That wasn't a diagnosis," he returned. "And if you're looking for one, I can assure you it won't please you."

"I wouldn't trust you to psychoanalyze a screwdriver," Marjorie said, cutting off Amalia's retort before it could come. Her eyes were glinting in the same way they had before she had burned my hand, and all at once I got the feeling that she didn't act on her violent impulses in moments of anger, but – as she had done with me – planned out her attacks methodically in periods of calm. I tried again to catch Lennox's eye to warn him, but he was too busy glowering at her.

Marjorie took a deliberate sip of broth, her eyes not leaving Lennox's face as she watched him seethe.

"No wonder your wife couldn't stand it, really," she went on. "What did you do? Go on and on about what you assumed was wrong with her until she finally couldn't take it anymore? Or was being married to you enough to send her over the edge –?"

Lennox looked ready to explode. His form was rigid and yet he was shaking all over, and his teeth were bared in an unnatural grimace. He forced open his jaw, readying to reply, but –

"Maybe Mr. Langston was just trying to point out who did it," I said from my spot by the wall.

Every head in the room turned toward me.

"What are you talking about?" Marjorie demanded, clearly vexed that I had interrupted.

"When he threw the roll," I clarified. "You know – maybe he was just trying to point out who the killer was."

"Are you completely asinine? How would James know who killed John?"

"Well, the Drawing Room connects to the Foyer," I said, trying to sound contemplative even though everything I was saying was ludicrous. "Maybe he saw whoever locked the door."

"Then why would he have thrown it at me?" Bernadette said.

"Well, I would assume his aim isn't as accurate as Mrs. Marlowe and Mrs. Pickering think," I said, nodding at each woman in turn in feigned penitence for disagreeing with them.

"I'm sorry, I'm not sure I'm understanding you," Marjorie said. "You think James just sprang out of bed at the sound of footsteps on the porch and peered through the keyhole, spotting the killer as they tromped inside? And now he's a roll-flinging vigilante?"

"I think it's possible," I said.

"Oh you do? Well, good on you, you foolish girl." She gave me a look of utmost loathing, but it wasn't enough to keep her attention off of Lennox. She turned away from me to look down the table at him. "Now let's get back to what a horrible husband Lennox was –"

Lennox's jaw tightened again. I took a step forward toward the table.

"Actually, Mrs. Pickering, I think it's *very* possible," I said. I set the basket of rolls down next to her with my bandaged hand, using my good hand to grip the sterling silver serving tray more firmly. Marjorie turned her eyes back to me, and though I could see the same venom in them as I had before she had burned me, I didn't care. "Though I agree with Mrs. Carlton's earlier assessment."

"What earlier assessment?"

I readied myself for her reaction, then let the words fall from my mouth.

"That Mr. Langston was probably aiming at you."

She jumped to her feet and reached out to grab me around the neck, but this time I was prepared for her. Raising the serving tray like a shield, I blocked her hands, letting them clang off of the metal as I pushed her back down. She fell back into her chair, momentarily startled, but then her face contorted in complete rage.

"Why, you little –!" she roared, grabbing for the knife resting on the edge of her bowl.

"Alexandra!" Lennox exclaimed, and his chair clattered as he rushed to his feet.

Marjorie swiped at me, but the blade only hit the

tray with a screech of metal on metal. Behind her, Edie let out a frightened squeal and dove sideways into Cassandra's lap.

"What?" I challenged Marjorie. "You don't think my reasoning is justified? Because as far as I can see, you're the only one violent enough to have done it –"

Marjorie grabbed onto my tray, trying to force it down.

"I'll slit your throat!" she screamed, brandishing the knife over it, and I leaped back as she came perilously close to slicing me.

"Stop this!" Rachel yelled just as Lennox grabbed Marjorie from behind, pulling her away from me. He seized her wrist and forced her hand down, squeezing her fingers until she released the knife. "Stop this! Please!"

"I'll stop when she's dead in the ground!" Marjorie shouted, and from the look in her eyes, I believed her.

"Stop this –!" Rachel said again. "Stop! Stop!"

"See?" Amalia joined in, pointing at Lennox. "See? That's probably how he got John – by sneaking up on him from behind –!"

"No, he didn't!" Rachel cried. "He didn't!"

"Go ahead, Lennox!" Amalia goaded. "Pick up her knife and plunge it in her chest, just like you did to John –!"

"He didn't do it!" Rachel screamed. "I did it! *I did it!*"

There was a startled silence as everyone looked at her in shock. Marjorie had stopped flailing, and as Lennox's grip on he slackened, she slipped from his arms down to the floor.

"What?" Amalia said.

"I did it!" Rachel cried, tears streaming down her face, and she grabbed onto the cross on her necklace as though it would make the admission easier. "I killed him! I poisoned him and stabbed him! *I did it!*"

She threw her hands over her mouth, sobbing into her fingers. Her eyes were wild with pain, bright and strange, and there was nothing but sheer sorrow in her cracking voice. For a moment she stood quivering from head to toe in front of us all, but then she turned and bolted from the room. The distant sound of a door slamming jolted everyone from their shock.

Edie pushed herself up from Cassandra's lap.

"What did she say?" she asked disbelievingly. "She – she killed John?"

"Don't be ridiculous," Bill snapped at her. "Of course she didn't!"

"She just admitted it!" Amalia said.

"Well, it's not true!" Bill returned. "She just said it so you'd all stop fighting!"

No one else seemed as certain. Edie's face was startled and white, Amalia was twitching in affirmation and rage, and Bernadette had finally set her silverware down, seemingly realizing that there was something more important than her food. Marjorie clambered to her feet, shoving Lennox away from her. She pushed her disheveled red hair from her face.

"Well, my God," she said. "Of all the people ..."

"We don't know if what she said is true," Lennox cut in. "Bill might be right: she just said it to keep this from escalating."

He stooped to pick up Marjorie's fallen knife, placing it on the windowsill behind him. Bill gave him an odd look that I couldn't read. It was almost as though he questioned why the other man was agreeing with him.

"Quite right, Lennox," Bernadette said. "We don't know why she said it, so we'll just wait for her to get back –"

"No one admits to murder as a distraction!" Amalia exclaimed. "You saw her! She said she did it – she said she poisoned and stabbed him!"

"This is Rachel we're talking about!" Bill countered. "She wouldn't hurt anyone!"

"She'd hurt John! It's just like I said: she's wanted him dead since James' accident!"

"It does make sense," Marjorie said. "And John wouldn't give her any of the money to help with James' care –"

"That doesn't mean she'd kill him!" Bill argued. "Rachel has no animosity toward anyone – you all know that! She didn't suddenly turn into a murderer overnight!"

"She might have," Edie whispered from between her fingers. "You know what Mummy used to say – we all carry the curse."

"What in the world are you talking about?"

"The curse. The family curse. She said it plagues all of us – that we'll all meet untimely ends –"

"That's the most ridiculous –"

"Remember what she used to do to us?" Edie said, looking around at her siblings for affirmation. "She had to lock herself in her room to stop herself ... She said she wanted to drown us every time Papa left and let him return to find our bodies dressed up in our Sunday best –"

"Well, she didn't," Bill said. "And in case you've forgotten, your mother didn't meet an untimely end. She was eighty-six."

"But Papa was only fifty-five when he died," Cassandra said, her innocent, nearly child-like voice made ominous from the depths of her veils as she joined into the conversation. "And Mary –"

"Stop it, both of you," Lennox said from the window. "This isn't the work of a curse."

"Oh, Lennox, you don't believe that, do you?" Cassandra asked. "You can't tell me you haven't felt a presence up there in the nursery late at night –"

"I don't care what caused her to do it," Amalia cut

in. "The point is that we've got the confession, so let's bring her back and deal with her!"

"Deal with her how?" Marjorie shot. "We're not going to lock her in the Drawing Room until the police come."

"We must! We have to restrain her! Tie her up! Anything to keep her from killing again –!"

"No one's getting restrained," Bernadette said firmly. "We'll wait for Rachel to come back, and then we'll discuss this calmly and civilly."

"I'm not going to be calm or civil! She killed my husband – and the only way you'll convince me otherwise is if someone else admits to it, too!"

Everyone glanced around, seemingly waiting for another person to pipe up and claim that they were the true killer. I studied their expressions, my eyes darting from one face to the next, and it perturbed me to see that they all wore the same expectant expression that maintained their innocence more than their silence did.

I caught Lennox's eye and gave him the slightest shake of my head, unsure of what to do. It was unbelievable to think that Rachel had done it, and yet I couldn't stop my mind from putting all the pieces together: the conversation with Bill where she had begged him not to tell the family something, how she had proclaimed that none of her siblings was the killer, the way she had spoken about wanting all of it to be over ...

The bell on the wall jingled, indicating that Mrs. Tilly wanted me to come and collect the dessert course. I threw one last look at Lennox and then darted from the room, but instead of going to the kitchen, I hurried to the surrounding rooms to check for Rachel. Though there was still doubt racing through me, I couldn't shake the look on her face as she'd admitted to killing John. There had been more than sadness in her eyes: there had been remorse. And people, as far as I knew, didn't feel guilty for no reason.

CHAPTER TWELVE

I searched the house for her, but to no avail: the Drawing Room was empty, as were the unused Smoking and Music Room. I hurried from floor to floor, trailing in and out with the expectancy of finding her, but upon reaching the third floor and checking even the storage rooms, it was clear that she had gone outside.

I donned my coat and boots and went out into the snow, hoping to see footprints that would lead me to her, but the compressed snow on the paths allowed no such thing. I looked down the one that led to the dock, then the one that circled to the back of the house and branched off toward Kneller's, trying to guess which way she had gone. The one leading to Kneller's, I decided, setting off. The need to find her was gripping at my chest, and every word she had spoken was running through my head as I tried to put the pieces of John's death together. *You can pretend. You should pretend. Let them think it was someone else. Please, Bill. Please.*

I had barely reached the back of the house when a figure caught my eye: Kneller was shoveling out in the distance. I hurried along the path to get to him.

"Oh-ho, another errand?" he called as he noticed me. "It'll have to wait. I told Edie I'd have a path to the cemetery shoveled for her by this afternoon."

"I was just wondering if you'd seen Mrs. Langston."

"Rachel? Not out here. She's probably back at the house."

"I checked."

"Well, there's thirty-seven rooms. You might've missed her."

"There's thirty-eight rooms, and I looked

everywhere."

I glanced over my shoulder, thinking that I might see her approaching in the distance, but only the white landscape greeted me. I sighed and turned back to Kneller. A ways behind him, the faint outline of a wrought iron fence was visible beneath heaps of snow, indicating what must have been the family's cemetery plot.

"What's your hurry?" Kneller asked.

"Well, for starters, she just announced that she murdered Professor Marlowe."

Kneller's eyebrows shot up, disappearing beneath his hat. He stuck his shovel into the ground and leaned up against it.

"Why on earth did she do that?" he asked.

"Presumably because she did it."

"Nah, she didn't," he said, waving me off with such certainty that I raised my eyebrows as well.

"And how do you know that?"

"Because I know Rachel. She didn't kill John."

"Then why did she say she did?"

"Maybe she's taking the blame for someone she loves."

"Someone like you?"

Kneller gave me a toothy grin, but it didn't extend to his eyes.

"Nah, not me. She chose her family over me a long time ago, I'm afraid."

He plucked up his shovel and restarted his work.

"When you do find her, though," he called over his shoulder, "tell her to come talk to me."

"Why?"

"So I can talk some sense into her before her family takes her seriously."

I trudged away from him back toward the house, pulling off the maid's cap and shoving it into my pocket as I went. I never knew what to make of conversations with him, and they seemed to instill me with more doubt than anything. Perhaps, at least, he was right that she was somewhere in the house and I had simply missed her. I stopped beneath the branches of the yew tree to light a cigarette, still contemplating whether or not I believed her admission. Before I could get anywhere, though, Lennox came down the path front the front of the house.

"Is Rachel back yet?" I asked.

"What? No – not that I know of. I was more worried about you."

He moved closer to me, throwing a wary glance at the yew as he went. As he came to stand on my other side, he gave me a pointed look.

"Yes?" I inquired.

"I'm not sure where to begin, really. Perhaps when you speculated that James was trying to point out the killer, or accused Marjorie of being his target, or goaded her until she was livid enough to kill you, or – most recently – when you left the Dining Room and never came back, leading me to think you might've – might've –"

I flicked my lighter again, letting the flame catch as I inhaled, then turned my head as I answered in a breath of smoke.

"Gotten jumped by Edie's curse?" I finished blandly. Lennox didn't appear impressed.

"I had no idea what happened to you," he said. "And Marjorie and Amalia left shortly after you, so when you didn't return I thought that Marjorie might've followed you to the kitchen and finished you off with one of Mrs. Tilly's cleavers."

"Well, she didn't – lucky me – and I only left because I was trying to find Rachel."

"And the rest of it? Because, correct me if I'm wrong, you said you were going to be more careful – and provoking Marjorie until she grabbed her knife is anything but that!"

I took a drag from my cigarette. His tone was harsh, though it was clear he wasn't angry with me: I could still see the worry in his eyes.

"I wasn't trying to make a scene," I said. "I just did it so they'd leave you alone."

"What?"

"Come on, Dr. Lennox: it's not like I actually believe that James was trying to indicate the killer by throwing his roll. I just saw how uncomfortable they were making you, so I tried to divert their attention – and it worked."

"I –" he stammered. "Well, I – still, you shouldn't have –"

"Provoked Marjorie? Hard not to, considering that she flies into a rage over just about anything. Besides ... I figured you wouldn't let her kill me."

His mouth twitched, though his expression had softened. He nearly looked abashed.

"No, that's true," he said. "I wouldn't have."

"Thank you. Now, let's get back to finding Rachel."

I indicated for him to follow me down the path that led to the front, thinking that she might have taken a walk down to the water like she had with Bill and James the day before. Lennox followed me.

"You're not actually considering that she did it, are you?" he asked.

"I'm considering everything, Dr. Lennox. Let's put it this way: from a logical standpoint, Rachel's husband was incurably damaged by John and her life was ruined by having to play caregiver. Now, if Bill's really next in line to inherit, and he obviously cares about Rachel, then they might have devised a plan to kill him. They poisoned him – using the pills I found in his and Edie's room, by the way –

and then stabbed him so no one would trace it back to the prescription bottle."

"What kind of pills?"

"Chlorpromazine."

"Chlorpromazine is an anti-psychotic," he told me, saying the name with the correct pronunciation. "It's rarely fatal, even when overdosed on. How full was the bottle?"

"Mostly," I admitted begrudgingly.

"Then I think it's safe to assume that – unless John had an allergy to the drug and suffered anaphylactic shock – neither of them murdered him with that. Nor, I presume, did they murder him at all."

"Well, that's not all I found in their room," I said, then briefly relayed the eerily life-like doll that was hiding in the chest at the foot of their bed. Lennox's frown got deeper and deeper as he listened. "You have to admit, Dr. Lennox: it's a bit too fortuitous to ignore."

"Well," he began, and I could tell that he was still ready to argue with me. "I –"

"The doll was stabbed through the chest. You're telling me you think that's a perfectly normal thing to have laying around someone's bedroom?"

"Bill and Edie lost twelve children. Bill might have just been – getting his frustration out on the unfairness of it all."

"Well, he might have been *getting his frustration out on the unfairness of it all* on John, too."

He shook his head at me. We reached the front of the house and continued down the path toward the water. With every other step, his arm brushed up against mine, and my skin was growing warmer and warmer despite how frigid the air was.

"Alright, that's logical," he said. "Do you actually believe it?"

I released the smoke from my lungs, watching as it

created a cloud of white in front of me.

"To an extent," I replied. "But this family's just too weird. Too secretive. I can't discount any of them, really. The way Amalia accuses everyone might be because she's trying to divert the blame off of herself, and Marjorie's certainly crazy enough to have done it. Cassandra, too. It's like Kneller said: *If we're being perfectly honest, then we should all admit one thing: everyone here wanted John dead, for one reason or another.*"

"I don't know that I wanted him dead," Lennox mused.

"That's only because you wanted him to give you your painting. If he'd done that then keeled over, you probably wouldn't have blinked an eye."

Lennox murmured to himself, though he didn't argue. As we turned around the clusters of trees that led to the dock, he turned to me with a thoughtful gaze.

"How do you do that, by the way?" he asked.

"Do ...?"

"Repeat things from memory."

I finished my cigarette and dropped it to the ground, pausing to stamp it into the snow even though it would surely go out on its own. Lennox waited for me to join him again.

"I just do," I said.

"So you have an eidetic memory?"

"No. I'm not even sure that those exist." I chewed the inside of my cheek, thinking of whether I wanted to go on or not. "I just trained myself to remember things."

"How?"

"You've heard of Simonides?"

"The Greek philosopher?"

"Poet," I corrected. "He was the one who came up with the idea of the Memory Palace. That's sort of what I do – only I do it better."

"So what types of things do you remember?"

"Lots of things."

"Conversations? Things you've seen or read?"

I nodded. Lennox stared.

"Which one were you nodding to?" he asked.

"All of the above."

"So –" he started, still looking utterly lost, " – how long do you remember it for? Just until you decide you don't need it anymore, then you forget it?"

"No. I don't forget."

"You don't forget the important things, you mean?"

"No, I don't forget. Anything."

He stared at me so long that it made me uncomfortable. I took out another cigarette and lit it.

"You can't possibly remember everything," he said. When I didn't answer, he added, "What was the first thing I said to you when we met?"

I didn't even need to snap the rubber band around my wrist to give him the answer.

"I'm here for the wake."

He made a humming sound. I had a feeling he probably didn't remember what it was he had said himself and was trying with difficulty to match the words with his arrival.

"But how do you do it?" he asked. "You can't have a room for everything you've seen or read or heard – even the Marlowe house isn't big enough for that."

"That's why I don't use a house: I used a filing cabinet. Sixteen, actually – at the moment. I use the words to make up the scene that I'm in, like little tiny pen markings that form an ink picture, then I file it away in one of the drawers depending on its category to be retrieved whenever I choose."

Lennox stared.

"That must be incredible," he said.

"It beats the alternative."

"And that's what your dissertation was about? Memory?"

"Understanding and preserving the way information is encoded, stored, and retrieved in the adult brain," I recited.

"You must be popular among your peers. I imagine they come to you for help memorizing their class notes."

"Not really. And that's not the point of my research."

We reached the dock and paused, watching the water move back and forth against the shore. It looked as though it was made up of millions upon millions of sapphires and onyx stones, all glistening beneath a sunless white sky.

"What is the point, then?" he asked, and his voice had gone soft again. Perhaps he could tell what was coming from the way my tone had become clipped and my sentences had shortened.

"To prevent chronic brain disorders that cause people to forget," I said.

Lennox waited for me to say more, but I didn't go on. I knew what he was going to ask me: I could tell from the way his eyes ran over my face. But then –

"Can I have a drag of your cigarette?" he asked. I was so surprised that I only stared. He offered me a smile. "I left mine at the house."

I numbly handed it over. He put the cigarette to his lips as he stared off over the water, leaving me waiting for the question that I was sure he would ask and that I wasn't sure I wanted to answer.

"Mother or father?" he said as he exhaled. "Or is it a grandparent?"

"Mother."

"When did it start?"

"Thirteen years ago."

"She must have been very young," he commented, and I shrugged, trying to look anything but as affected as I felt, though I didn't think that I was successful.

"She was forty-three."

Lennox coughed as he took another drag and turned his head away. When he faced me again, a frown pulled deeply at his brow.

"Did something cause it?" he asked. "A stroke? A head injury?"

I stared at the water, trying to force my eyes to see the deep blue waves gently rocking back and forth rather than the memory playing in my head. The loneliness was filling me up just at the suggestion of it, and I didn't want it to overtake me. Not now. Not when I had held it off for so long.

"No. Nothing the doctors can pinpoint, anyway. One day she just ... stopped remembering."

"Does your father take care of her now?"

"No, his sister does."

"Where's your father?"

"He went to war. And never came back."

Lennox was silent for so long that I wondered if I had finally said something that he couldn't think of a response to, but then he shook his head.

"There's too much tragedy in this world," he said quietly.

He held the cigarette out for me, but when I reached up to take it back, my fingers closed over his hand instead. All the cold in the air disappeared, replaced with a warmth that spread up from him and overtook my skin, and all at once it was as though the murder and the fights and the insanity of the Marlowe household had been erased, leaving us alone in the peacefulness and serenity of one another's company. I stared at where our gloves tangled in a ball of black leather, wondering what had made me do it, and then lifted my gaze to stare into his eyes. He had the same genuineness that I had noticed the first night I had met him. It was an odd thing to see in a person – and odder still when it made me want to lean in and whisper everything into his ear that I was too frightened of admitting – and I hoped with everything in me that what Kneller had said wasn't true: I couldn't have just been a moth who went toward a flame.

A breeze skated over the water and whipped my hair up to dance around my shoulders. Lennox followed its movement with his eyes, and something akin to sadness fell upon his expression, though he gripped my hand tighter.

"I should tell you something, Alexandra," he said quietly, his eyes still on my hair rather than my face. I stepped closer to him, telling myself that it was to better hear him and not for any other reason, and I was so close to him that I could see every fleck of gold in his brown eyes. I counted them as I waited for him to speak – *twenty-one, twenty-two, twenty-three* – but he seemed to have lost his nerve, and contrarily I seemed to have gained mine. Because if I was going to get rejected, I reasoned, then it might as well have been now, because later was becoming further and further away the longer that we were trapped here.

I stood up on my tiptoes and pressed my mouth to his, feeling heavy and weightless all at once. My heart hammered as I waited for him to push me away and tell me that I had made a mistake, but his arm had moved around my back to hold me closer, and my mind seemed to be floating somewhere outside of my body, staring down at the two people in the snow as it watched something that couldn't be true except in the wildness of my imagination.

When we broke apart I was nearly too lightheaded to stand, and for once my mind was completely blank. The incessant drumbeat to remember had vanished, as though the only thing worth knowing was that moment.

He took both my hands in his and pressed them to his chest. He stared at them for a long time, and it felt as though if I just moved a little closer, I would finally be able to see into his head the way that he always seemed to see into mine.

"I ..." he began, but his attention had moved to something else as he lifted his chin to look up at me, and his olive skin paled as though he had taken ill. I waited for the words that he had been about to speak, nearly irritated that he could be distracted at a moment like this, but then his mouth dropped open and his eyes widened in horror.

I turned to search for what had disturbed him. Gulls were squawking in the distance, flailing and pecking at something floating in the water. I squinted momentarily, but it only took me a moment to recognize what it was: a body, skin stark white and clothing pure black, bounding back and forth just off the shore as it was rocked by the waves.

We both raced off the dock, but his legs carried him far faster, and by the time I was halfway to the spot he was already waist-deep in the water and moving with broken, painful steps to reach the body. He swiped at the gulls, smacking them away, and they opened their huge beaks to screech at him for stealing their prize. He shouted for them to get away, grabbing onto the body and pulling it toward him protectively.

I rushed to help him, wading knee-deep to meet him and grab hold of one of the rigid arms, and we tugged it together to the shore.

"C-coat," he said to me through chattering teeth. "Give me – c-coat!"

I stripped it off and pushed it into his outstretched hands. He wrapped it around the body, and I barely had time to register the sight of Rachel's gruesome gray face before he turned her onto her stomach so that he could pound on her back, trying to force the water from her lungs.

"Go!" he shouted at me. "Get –"

He hadn't finished the sentence before I turned and ran, my boots pounding into the snow and flattening it down beneath me as I rushed to get back to the path. The house seemed farther away than ever, and I raced alongside the clusters of trees that shielded it from my view, ignoring the way my breath hitched from the icy air. Rachel's face was burned into my vision. What had she done? I thought frantically, but no sooner had the thought come than another followed: what had been done to her?

When I finally made it to the front porch, I threw myself at the stairs, tripping halfway up and banging my shins against the step, and then clambered back up and tore through the front door.

"Bill!" I shouted, my voice booming through the Foyer as I called for him. "Bill!"

He emerged from the Drawing Room, a wild and uncertain look on his face. The sound of doors opening came from above us, and footsteps pounded on the upstairs hallway as the others scrambled to see what the shouting was about.

"What on earth –?" came Marjorie's voice, but I ignored her and gave Bill a yank.

"What's wrong with you, Alexandra?" Bernadette said, huffing as she came downstairs.

"Come with me!" I said, tugging him toward the door. "It's Rachel! Go to the dock!"

His perplexed face morphed into an expression of understanding, and he freed himself and shot through the door. I raced after him, but the exertion from sprinting such a distance already rendered me far slower than usual, and by the time I turned around the cluster of trees he and Lennox were staggering toward me, Rachel's body hanging between them. They pushed past me wordlessly to get back up to the house.

"Rachel!"

Edie's strangled voice rang out as we entered the Foyer. Bill and Lennox laid the body down.

"Get something warm," Lennox demanded. "Coats, blankets – go!"

He put his mouth over hers and held her nose, blowing air into her lungs. It made a *whooshing* sound as he tried to revive her.

Coats were brought from all sides of me, though no one dared to get closer to the body. I pulled the large overcoat from Bernadette's hands, moving toward Lennox while my eyes remained on Rachel's paralyzed face.

"Dr. Lennox," I said, crouching down so that I was next to him. He didn't respond. I gently laid the coat over Rachel's form, tucking it over my own even though I knew it would do no good. "Dr. Lennox ..."

No one was rushing around now. The only movement in the room came from Lennox's continued efforts, and he was adamant as he went, certain that she would take a breath at any moment. His hope outlasted the rest of ours, and he kept going far past the time when everyone else's eyes had dropped to the ground, and Edie had started to sob into her hands, and then her sobs grew louder and filled the room, huge gulping and gasping sounds that rang out beneath the chandelier and fell back down upon us like rain drops, and puddles formed at our feet from the snow dripping off our shoes, and everyone knew it by then: even Lennox, though he continued on anyways, his movements getting more frantic and frustrated the longer that he went on, before he finally stopped.

Rachel was gone.

CHAPTER THIRTEEN

For the first time, the house was freezing. The front doors were still open, drawing cold over the black-and-white tiled floor that circled around our ankles and under the necks of our shirts. The air in the room had changed, and the breathing had changed with it. Short, shallow breaths came out all around the Foyer; nonsensical shakes of the head; fingernails digging into skin, twisting it around as everyone tried to wake themselves out of what could have only been a nightmare.

"Just like Mary," Cassandra said.

"This can't be," Edie whispered. "This – this can't be."

There were no jokes this time. No one dared it, and no one wanted it. And then, from somewhere else in the house, a strange howling rang out. Everyone looked up, then –

"It's James."

Bill was the one who spoke. He looked at Lennox as though he might have the answer to what to do about Rachel's husband, but Lennox only shut his eyes in response.

"Someone should go get him," Marjorie said. "Birdie – it's got to be you."

"I'm not bringing that man in here," she said. "Hasn't he suffered enough?"

"We can't just leave him there," Bill said. "What's he going to think happened?"

Marjorie ran her fingers over her mouth.

"Nothing," she said. "Nothing at all."

No one could think of a way to respond. Lennox was still shaking, and he didn't look like himself anymore. It was as though the water had washed off the exterior he had so carefully painted onto his skin, and underneath it all was a man who had cracked in numerous places and was quickly coming undone.

"Why would she do this?" Edie asked, her voice muffled through her hands. "Why?"

"Isn't it obvious?" Amalia said. She was standing with her arms crossed, and her eyes were narrowed to slits. "Guilt."

"She didn't kill John!" said an angry voice, and it took me a moment of looking around to realize whose it was. Bill had his hands balled into fists; he was shaking nearly as much as Lennox.

"She admitted it," Amalia returned. "If that wasn't proof enough, then this is!"

"Rachel wouldn't kill herself!" He was so distressed that it was rendering him senseless. His glasses had slipped down his running nose and his eyes were bright with tears. Even his hair, or the little that remained, was standing up as though he had raked his fingers through it to push it toward the ceiling. "She wouldn't! And she didn't kill John! I know she didn't!"

"You don't *know* anything!" Amalia spat.

"Yes, I do! I know – because on the night John died, I saw who locked the door!"

A cold breeze skated through the door, opening it further and sending it banging against the wall. Everyone was frozen in place: even Lennox had stopped shaking, though his chest rose and fell heavily. It was so quiet that all I could hear was my heartbeat thumping against my rib cage, and the air was thick with tension as everyone waited for Bill to speak.

"Well?" Marjorie demanded. "Spit it out! Who?"

Lennox slowly stood from the floor. He was staring at Bill intently, moving his lips ever so slightly, but the meaning was unintelligible.

Bill raised his chin.

"It was Lennox."

Marjorie's back straightened. Amalia went stiff. Lennox shut his eyes. It was just as he had feared, I knew: that the family would put the blame on him. I glared at Bill, and my uncertainty that he had been the one to kill John turned to sureness as I put it all together. He and Rachel had killed John, then she had gotten cold feet about what they'd done, and so he had had no choice but to kill her, too –

"*You?*" Amalia breathed, her eyes narrowing in on Lennox. "You killed my husband?"

"No," he said. He was shaking his head: his hand was on his brow, and beads of sweat appeared on his olive-toned skin. "No, I didn't –"

"You just *happened* to lock the door after my husband was brutally murdered?"

"It couldn't have been Lennox," I cut in. "He was locked in."

"I saw him!" Bill said. "He was out that night! You're lying!"

"You're the only one lying," I returned, stepping forward so that I was standing between him and Lennox. Despite my soaked stockings and boots, I felt a sudden rush of heat come over me as I looked at him, wishing that I had told the family my assumptions about him earlier. "I locked him in – so there's no way you could have see him go out or in!"

"I did! I'd gotten up to go to the bathroom, and when I was walking back –"

"That makes no sense, Mr. Burton," I interrupted. "There's a bathroom connected to the Mabel Room: you weren't anywhere near the Foyer."

Bill's mouth opened to gape at me. It was clear that he realized he had said something wrong, but saw no way to correct his mistake. He spluttered as he pushed his glasses up the bridge his nose.

"Well, that's – that's because –" he started, but Edie cut him off.

"Bill – *don't.*"

He looked at his wife. His thin lips were twitching. As his eyes went back to Rachel's lifeless form, though, he put his hand to his mouth and went on.

"I haven't been sleeping in the Mabel Room," he said.

"Ridiculous," Bernadette said. "Where've you been sleeping, then?"

Bill pointedly looked away from Edie as he answered.

"In the Drawing Room."

Marjorie stared.

"With Rachel?" she exclaimed.

"No – it wasn't like *that*," Bill said. "There's a couch in there to sleep on, and since nothing was going to happen –"

"My God," Marjorie said. "Lennox upstairs with the maid and Bill down here with our sister –"

"No! There was no affair, and the point is that I saw Lennox –"

"I can't seem to think of another reason why a married man would sleep in another man's wife's room," Marjorie said. "Edie, did you know about this?"

Edie looked at Bill. She had nothing but contempt in her eyes. I tried to fit her into the line of events that had happened. Was she in on it, too? Did she know what Rachel and Bill had done, and now she was deciding whether to save her husband or let him take the full blame?

"I didn't know the details of his sleeping arrangements, no," she said.

"Don't be like that," Bill said angrily. "You're the

one who kicked me out of my own bed –!"

"I didn't tell you to sleep with my sister!"

"I wasn't sleeping with her! I was sleeping on her couch, for Christ's sake!"

"There are forty rooms in this house!" she screamed back. "You couldn't have picked an empty one?"

Bill grabbed at his hair, yanking it so that it stood up even straighter on end. He let out a frustrated growl.

"Don't act like this is my fault," he said, jabbing a finger in her direction. "You're the one who told me to go. You're the one who's so frightened of every creak in the night that you jump out of bed screeching –"

"I – I do not!"

"You swear you see ghosts and then vilify me when I don't agree with you!" he said. "But there are no ghosts, Edie! You're haunting yourself! You've been haunting yourself for decades!"

"I – I have not! Why would I –?"

"Because you feel *guilty!*"

Edie looked as though she had been slapped across the face. She startled backwards, crashing into Cassandra and jumping as she turned and saw her black-veiled form. My heart pounded harder, waiting for her to lose it and tell us the truth, but –

"I – I –" she sputtered. "I don't – I have nothing to – I don't feel guilty –"

"Of course you do!" Bill said, and from the tone of his voice, it sounded as though he had been waiting years and years to tell her as much. "You talk in your sleep! You beg for forgiveness!"

"Stop it!" Edie said, and she was frantic now, her fingernails digging into the banister as she began to back up the stairs away from him. "Stop it, Bill: stop it –!"

"You think it's your fault – no, you *know* it's your fault – that all of our children died!" he shouted. "The doctors told you that you couldn't have any, and you tried anyway, and they all died – even the ones that weren't mine – because of you!"

Edie let out a wail that echoed around the room and lingered in the air long after she had run up the stairs and shut herself in her room.

"Well," Bernadette said into the awkward silence that followed. "That was more than I needed to know about your marital problems –"

"Stop it, both of you!" Marjorie said. "That's not the point! Did Lennox kill John or not?"

"Of course he didn't," I said. I glanced at Rachel's body, knowing that it was neither the time nor place for the conversation, but I couldn't hold back when I felt so close to finally hearing the confession. "Bill did!"

"Now hold on –!" Bill said angrily, turning back to me. "I never –!"

"I heard you and Rachel in the Drawing Room talking about it: I heard her begging you not to tell anyone what you'd done!"

"She was begging me not to tell them that I saw Lennox!"

"And why would she do that?" I said, fed up with his string of lies. "If you'd really seen him, then she would have told her family about it!"

"That's – that's what I tried to tell her to do, but – but she –"

"She brings up a good point," Marjorie said slowly. "If either of you knew it was Lennox, why didn't you say something?"

"I wanted to!" Bill tried again. "I wanted to tell everyone, but – but Rachel wouldn't because she didn't think it could have been him –!"

"That's because it wasn't him!"

"No, it's because she was too trusting! She was

always too damn trusting!" he bellowed. He looked around at the family, frantic desperation in his wild eyes, and there was such conviction in his gaze that it caused me to take a step back from him. "He killed him! I *know* he killed him – and he killed Rachel, too!"

"Now, Bill –" Bernadette began, but Bill was having none of it.

"He left right after Rachel did, didn't he? And then she just happens to end up drowned in the ocean?"

"Amalia and Marjorie left, too," Bernadette said. "So did the maid –"

"But Lennox was *there!* He found her! What was he doing down by the water?"

"He was with me," I said.

"Doing *what,* exactly?"

"We were taking a walk!"

"Oh, just taking a *stroll* down by the *water,* were you?"

"It's not like there's anywhere else to go!"

"He was gone for ages! It's awfully cold outside for that amount of fresh air!"

"Sure beats being inside with all of you!" I said, but Bill's face was such a mask of accusation that my confidence wavered. My mind involuntarily flashed back to seeing Lennox walk up the path from the front of the house, but I pushed the thought away. He *hadn't* killed Rachel, and he *hadn't* killed John. "Where were you all this time, then?"

"I was staying with James!"

"Oh, *that's* a solid alibi: should we go ask him to verify that?"

"I was in the Drawing Room when you came in screaming about Rachel!"

"Yes – and I'm sure you had plenty of time to get back here after *you* killed Rachel!"

"I would have never hurt Rachel! She was the only

good part of this family!"

I took a step toward him, but hands on either of my shoulders held me back. I glanced around to see Lennox.

"Alexandra," he said quietly. "There's no point in —"

"Yes there is!" I said, turning back to Bill. "If Lennox had killed her, why would've he tried so hard to resuscitate her? Why not just leave her out there?"

"It was for show! To throw us off!"

"I was with him! I know he didn't kill her!"

"Just like you know you locked him in his room? Because it's sounding more and more to me like your sole purpose here is to be his alibi!"

I opened my mouth to respond, but my clipped words were interrupted by a giggle. I turned wildly around. Cassandra stood over Rachel's body, her hands folded neatly in front of her, looking like the angel of death who had come to take her away.

"Oh, that's not why she's here," she tittered.

"Knock it off, Cassie," Marjorie warned. "This is no time for your inanities – Rachel is dead!"

"Oh, yes, I know," Cassandra said sweetly. "That's why I'm bringing it up: because she'll come back too."

"Cassie –"

"No, it's true – I've seen it. Someone passes but then someone else comes to take their place so their life can go on. No one's ever really gone."

She said it was such innocence that it was difficult to believe she was anything but horribly naive. As her sisters gaped at her, she got down on her knees and brushed Rachel's wet hair from her face.

"Just look," Cassandra continued, her hand still brushing her dead sister's hair, and there was something so sinister in the sight and sound together that it felt as though they pierced straight into my bones. "Mary came back."

"What in God's name are you talking about?" Marjorie said.

"Oh, don't act like you haven't noticed," Cassandra replied, her voice becoming sweeter and sweeter with each passing second, and she finally stopped stroking her sister. She looked up, then pointed her finger directly at me. "She's right there."

Everyone turned to look at me.

"That's the *maid,*" Bernadette said.

"No, no," Cassandra said. "Look again."

"For Christ's sakes," Bill growled as Marjorie and Bernadette peered more closely at me, "are you actually going to listen to her –?"

Marjorie's sharp intake of breath cut him off.

"Wait a minute: she's right."

"Oh, not you, too," Bernadette said. "Mary is dead!"

"I know that!" Marjorie snapped. "But look at her! She looks just like her!"

There was a look of utmost horror on her face, and yet as she took a step closer to me, it became mixed with accusation.

"I knew there was something funny about you," she said. "I knew it from the moment I laid eyes on you –!"

"Well, you obviously didn't," Bernadette said, "or else you wouldn't be realizing it now –"

"That's because her hair was covered! Look at her, Birdie! Don't you see it?"

Bernadette teetered in place. Her eyes ran over me as though she had never really noticed me before, and her double chin wobbled beneath her open mouth.

"Well, she has the same hair color – but she's not nearly as pretty, and her nose has that awful bump on it ..."

"She looks damn near close enough for me!" Marjorie said. "Her height's the same, and her build, too.

And the eyes – they're that same green –"

"What does it matter?" Amalia said, echoing the thought going through my head. I had noticed that I had the same hair and eye color as their father when I had seen his painting, after all. I looked to Lennox, but he had turned away from me, ignoring my request for him to tell me what the others wouldn't.

"It matters because it explains why Lennox has been so cozy with her!" Marjorie exclaimed.

"I don't care who he's been cozy with unless it has something to do with my husband's murder!" Amalia returned.

"Wait –" Bill said slowly. He looked from me to Lennox and then back again. "Wait – that's just it, then, isn't it? That explains it."

"Explains what?" Bernadette said exasperatedly.

"Everything!" Bill said. "Why she's been lying for him! Why she said she locked him in and was with him when Rachel was killed!"

"I'm not following you," Bernadette said evenly. "Just because she looks like Mary doesn't mean she'd give him an alibi."

"Maybe it's the other way, then! She – she killed John, and Lennox is – is covering for her!"

"That's completely asinine: she's the maid!"

"The maid who's a dead ringer for your sister!"

"This is getting us nowhere," Bernadette said. "Alexandra, are you going to explain how it is you look like Mary?"

I raised my eyebrows at her. The situation was rendering them all completely senseless.

"No," I said shortly.

"See?" Bill exclaimed. "See? Now she's denying it!"

"I'm not denying anything!" I said. "I didn't know I looked like anyone – and I don't know why it matters!"

Bernadette's stomach swelled as she took a deep breath and Amalia let out a stream of curse words, but it was Marjorie whose expression changed from irritation to understanding.

"Oh, wait," she said, her mouth twitching. She looked at Lennox. "Does she not *know?*"

I stole a look at Lennox, as well, but he had shut his eyes behind his hand.

"I know who Mary is," I said. "I just don't know why it matters –"

"No, I don't think you do," Marjorie said, inching closer as she continued to stare Lennox down. "I don't think he told you."

"She was – she was your sister," I said, but Lennox's reaction was throwing me off. "Your youngest sister."

"And that's all he said?" Marjorie tutted. "Oh, Lennox. Poor, poor, broken Lennox, always trying to avoid blame ..."

Lennox didn't remove his face from his hand. His chest was rising and falling heavily again, and his soaked clothing was making him shake violently –

"Well, it's not too late," Marjorie said. "Go ahead, Lennox. Tell her the rest. Tell her who Mary really was."

She couldn't hide the maniacal glee that his discomfort was causing her. Bernadette was huffing in indignation and Amalia had a look of contempt on her face as she stared at him. Only Bill shifted uneasily, clearly not eager to watch the conversation unfold. A sense of dread began to stir in my stomach, and I tilted my head to the side as I stared at the doctor, not understanding.

"Dr. Lennox," I said, barely moving my lips. "Just tell me."

He pulled his hand from his eyes, lowering it shakily to his mouth. He ran his knuckles against his lips, back and forth and back and forth as though in a trance.

"Dr. Lennox?" I said. "Did Mary drown, too?"

He shook his head.

"No, she … she jumped from the nursery window."

I swallowed, feeling the family's eyes on me as they waited for the reaction that I didn't want to give them, so I tried to put it all together in my head: John inviting the both of us here, putting Lennox in the nursery for a reason that everyone was privy to but me, the missing painting from the East Room that he had hoped to inherit, the family's hatred of him for an unspoken reason –

"Mrs. Marlowe wasn't your patient, was she?" I asked.

"No."

He finally looked at me, and in his eyes I could see the plea for forgiveness, but I still didn't know what I was supposed to be forgiving.

"But Mary was?" I said, taking a hesitant step closer to him as I felt I had figured it out. "And she – she died under your care?"

Lennox's face cracked. He put his hand to his mouth again, trying hard to pull himself together before he shattered completely. His fingers tightened as though he could force the emotions back down his throat to make way for the words, and his breathing came in several gasps before he was able to calm it.

"No," he said. "No – she was my wife."

My stomach dropped. I opened my mouth and closed it, trying to think of something to say and trying to understand what to think all at once, but nothing came. I just stood in my spot, neither frozen nor thawed, and stared at him, not believing that I hadn't figured it out, not believing that I had been so blind to miss all of the pieces that I normally would have put together – normally, if I hadn't let myself be so infatuated with him.

"I know I should have told you," he whispered.

"But I – I didn't know what to think, and I didn't want *you* to think –"

"Tut, tut," came Marjorie's voice from somewhere behind me, but then I felt her hands on either my arms, holding me as though to comfort me, though the effect was ruined by her long, painted nails digging into my flesh. "You see, Alexandra? Lennox was just too *sad* to tell you the truth ..."

I swallowed again, keeping my eyes on Lennox's face as I tried with everything within me to hold off the emotions threatening to appear on mine. Marjorie rested her head on my shoulder, her cheek right up against mine.

"But you missed the best part, Isidore," she said. "Tell her the rest."

Whatever it was, I knew I didn't want to hear it. There were tears in his eyes, and as he tried to speak, a strangled sob came out instead.

"She –" he said, and if Marjorie hadn't been holding me I would have run from him before he had to say it. "She had our six-week old son in her arms when she did it."

"And there they went together," Marjorie said, no hint of sympathy in her voice even as Lennox continued to shake with tears. "Splat on the ground –"

I wrenched myself from her grip and spun around, my burned hand curling into a fist, and before I could think of anything at all, I punched her squarely in the face. Blood splattered across her white cheeks and she stumbled backwards, tripping over Rachel's lifeless form and falling to the floor. And as I surveyed the damage that had been done, not just by me but by all of them, I knew that the family was filled with too many secrets to uncover, and I knew that every word out their mouths were lies in one way or another, and every expression was feigned. And the worst part was that Lennox was one of them: not an outsider like he had had me believe, but a part of the family, so there was no way for me to pull it all apart, or to put it all together, so all I could think to do was run from them – out the door and into the snow – and hope that my feet would take me somewhere where I could make sense of it all again.

I didn't know where I was going until black, jagged lines came into view on the white horizon. My mind was reeling and my thoughts wouldn't slow, and I was more desperate than ever to know the truth, but it was impossible.

I stumbled up the freshly shoveled path, my eyes stinging from cold, stopping only briefly when I hit the frozen cemetery gate before throwing my leg over it to get inside. The tombs were all covered in snow, looking like nothing more than huge mounds coming out from the earth as though giants had laid down to slumber beneath starched blankets. I clutched my arms as I walked in front of them, somehow freezing and numb all at once, and followed the overlapping footsteps to the end of the line. The last tomb in the row had only a dusting of fresh snow upon it, and beneath it I could see the statue of a woman holding a child gently in her arms. The sight of it made me shake harder. I hastily brushed off the plaque with my sleeve, revealing the words etched into the stone underneath.

MARY ELIZABETH LENNOX 1916 – 1939
OLIVER WINSTON LENNOX 1939

"Too warm out here for a coat?" called a voice, and I wiped at my eyes and turned around. Kneller was leaning over the fence, a toothy smile on his face as he surveyed me. He forced the frozen gate open with one strong push and made his way over to me, noting the grave that I had stopped by. "Ah – quite the tragic death of his wife and child, wasn't it?"

"Yes." I paused. "They said I look just like her."

"You do. I imagine it's rather jarring to discover you look like the dead wife of the man you fancy."

He came to stand next to me. I crossed my arms.

"It doesn't matter," I said.

"Ah, that's where you'd be wrong," he said, not understanding what I meant. "Contrary to what women like to believe, Alexandra, it *always* matters what you look like."

He cocked his head at me when I didn't respond, his smile turning crooked.

"What? You don't believe me?"

"No – I just don't care," I snapped. "Not when – not when there's a house full of crazed maniacs waiting for me –"

"Oh, that's rather harsh: they're not all bad. You must like Rachel, at least."

I opened my mouth and then closed it, faltering as I realized that he didn't know what had happened.

"I – well, I –"

"Did you give her my message?" he asked, cutting into my stammering.

"I – I – I didn't get the – the chance –"

"You're shivering, Alexandra. You're going to catch your death if you stay out here."

"I – I – I should – I should –"

"Should have been a pair of ragged claws scuttling across the floors of silent seas?" he chuckled, repeating the line from the poem for the third time to me. "Believe me, you already are. I am, too. We're both bottom-dwellers. The lowest of the low. That's why people like them –" he nodded back toward the house, "– will never see us."

The image of Rachel's body bobbing up and down on the waves flashed across my mind and made my legs weak. I grabbed onto the statue of the woman and child to keep upright, then – realizing what I'd done – immediately let it go again.

"I – I need to tell you something," I said shakily, though I didn't feel capable of doing it. My palms were sweating and my heart was beating frantically, and though I knew I was physically capable of speaking the words, I also knew that they would come out jumbled and wrong, and there were so many thoughts in my head about what had happened between the time Rachel had fled the Dining Room and wound up on the Foyer floor that I could barely speak.

"Well, go ahead. I'm listening."

I shut my eyes, once again seeing Rachel's lifeless body imprinted against the back of my eyelids, and all I could see was her flailing as she was pulled beneath the waves of the ocean until the water filled her lungs, and yet for all of the bluntness that normally plagued me, I couldn't tell him, though I didn't know why. Because I thought that he might still love her? It wasn't like me to care. Perhaps everything that had happened between me and Lennox had shifted something inside of me, or perhaps I was just didn't want him to hurt the way that I was hurting.

"No, I – I can't. I – I need to think."

"Oh? What about? Whether or not you're still in love with Lennox?"

A gust of wind circled through the statues and stones and leaped up upon me, making my teeth clatter together. I imagined instead that it was me who was floating face down to stare through the blue-green water, and then my body became heavy and I sank down and down until I was sitting cross-legged on the sandy floor, staring through the nothingness and trying to discern if anything was waiting in the darkness. And no one was coming for me, I knew, letting the idea of Lennox slip away as the realization that perhaps all he had seen in me was the wife he had lost. And that was where I belonged: with the seaweed and the sand, away from the voices up above.

"N-no," I said, stuttering from the chill.

"I should hope not," he said, taking his coat off and draping it over my shoulders, either in an act of chivalry or simply because he couldn't stand hearing my teeth chatter any longer. "Because you don't seem to know who he is."

"He – he told me everything."

"Oh, I very much doubt that."

"He – he told me in front of the whole family. So – so they would've –"

"They barely knew Mary – she was born fifteen years after Cassandra, so they were grown up."

"What's that supposed to mean?"

"It means that Sylvia was too old to be having children. Malcolm dropped dead of a heart-attack within the year. And there was Mary, all alone in a big, empty house with no one but her mother for company – unless you count Frances, Tilda and me. She used to come down to see me and read poetry – she appreciated it, at least. All of the other children had been sent off to boarding schools when they were that age, but not Mary: Sylvia had realized that she was the last thing she had to hold onto, and she held her very, very tightly. Keep in mind that Sylvia was severely agoraphobic by this point – so when Mary was eighteen and ready to leave ... Sylvia was devastated."

"And then?"

"And then she went off and came home a few years later with Lennox. Sylvia was in a craze: I could hear her screaming from my kitchen. Apparently she felt that Mary's abandonment of her had ruined the last bit of her health. The siblings weren't too happy, either, because Sylvia was hoarding her money when she ought to have been, by their standards, giving them proper allowances. But Sylvia was paranoid and insisted that no one loved her, and refused to give anyone a nickel for fear that once they got her money, they would abandon her completely."

"So what's this got to do with Lennox?"

"I'm getting there: be patient," he chided. "So when Mary returned home with Lennox and saw how broken up her mother was, she didn't want to leave her again. She insisted to Lennox that they stay here on the island. You can imagine how well he took it: what newly wedded man wants to live with his crazed mother-in-law? But for whatever reason he agreed, and then Mary got pregnant, and then –"

"She jumped out the nursery window," I finished, still not understanding why I needed the dead woman's backstory to understand it all.

Kneller watched me. His eyes were just slits in their narrowed state, and the toothy grin was gone from his face.

"She didn't jump out of that window," he said. "Lennox pushed her."

CHAPTER FOURTEEN

"What're you talking about?"

My heart was thumping painfully in my chest, though I didn't quite register what Kneller had said. Lennox hadn't pushed her: she had jumped. He had just told me.

"Why do you think the family hates him?" Kneller asked. "He killed his wife and got off scot-free, claiming some bullshit that she had depression even though there wasn't a single sign!"

"Just because there weren't signs didn't mean she wasn't depressed –"

"She wasn't depressed! She was happy – the happiest she'd ever been! She had a beautiful son and a full life awaiting her!"

"But that doesn't mean –"

"She went backwards *through the glass,*" Kneller cut in, and his words were in timing with another gust of wind that rattled me off balance. "Backwards. Who jumps *through* a window *backwards?*"

"Maybe – maybe she twisted mid-air –"

"Not according to the cuts all over the back of her arms and head!"

"Well – well, she might've – might've just –"

"Alexandra, listen to yourself!" he exclaimed, grabbing me by the shoulders and shaking me so hard that the coat fell from to the ground. "You're blinded by infatuation! You see a man who's promising to sweep you off your feet, but you know nothing about him!"

I stared at him for a long, steady moment. He was wrong. I knew he was wrong. I had seen Lennox when he spoke of his wife – had seen the way his expression crumpled and heard how his voice wavered – and it wasn't the look of a man who didn't feel anything but the utmost guilt for what had happened to the woman and child he had loved.

I pulled myself away from him, then hurried from the cemetery and back down the path, knowing that I had to go back to the house before I got any colder, but my thoughts were pulling me in every direction and I was getting disoriented. I staggered on and off the path, half-blinded by tears and sick to my stomach.

When I finally returned to the house, it was as though I had been anesthetized. My limbs were barely working and my brain was even worse, and I trudged through the now-empty Foyer, barely registering that Rachel's body had been moved because I was too lost between half-composed thoughts and fractured sentences that had tangled in my head. With each footstep that hit the black-and-white tiled floors, Kneller's words pounded against my head. *Lennox pushed her.* Yet the further that I walked, the more the words became interspersed with murmuring voices that filled up my ears. I shook my head, trying to pull the thoughts apart again, when it occurred to me that the voices weren't in my head at all: the Marlowes were talking in the Parlor.

My ears perked up as I tried to discern who was inside.

"– it's the only way –!" Amalia's voice rang out, followed by Marjorie's.

"– mind blood on my hands –!"

I crept closer, putting my hand over my mouth so that they wouldn't hear my labored breathing, but –

Footsteps creaked on the stairs. I jumped back from the Parlor door, looking for a place to hide, but then a low gurgling alerted me to who was there. I hurried up the stairs two at a time.

"Mr. Langston – hold on," I said.

James had one hand grasping the banister as he tried to move his shaking leg down upon the topmost step, but he was far too unsteady to do so. I couldn't imagine he had gotten all the way up there without help, but there was no one else in sight. I grasped his arm to steady him. I hadn't realized he could walk.

"How did you get upstairs, Mr. Langston?" He only gurgled in response, and I heaved his weight onto me as I helped him slowly descend the stairs. It took us several minutes to reach the Foyer, and I paused instead of leading him over to the Drawing Room, unsure if Bill was in there or with Amalia and Marjorie in the Parlor.

"Can you get back to your room alright?" I whispered, though I didn't know what response I'd hoped to receive. He gurgled again and shuffled forward, clutching something tightly in his hand. The hint of gold glinted from beneath his fingers, catching my eye.

"What do you have there?"

I tried to pry it away from him, but his grip was unyielding.

"Raaah, Raah," he said angrily, holding his arm rigidly to his abdomen to keep me from discovering what he had. "Raa Raah –!"

"Okay – okay," I said quickly, trying to shush him before he alerted anyone that I was there. I glanced over at the Parlor door, but my heart was beating so loud that I could no longer hear the family's voices. "Just – just go back to your room –"

I darted up the stairs away from him. As I threw one last look at him standing all alone in the empty room, the reality of Rachel's death finally hit me, breaking through the barrier of shock I had felt since seeing her lifeless body. I pulled myself away and hurried up the stairs to the third floor, then locked myself inside the bathroom. Perching on the edge of the tub, I peeled off my stockings. The material was sticking to my shins, which each had a gash in them from where I had banged them against the porch steps. I turned on the faucet and waited for the water to turn warm, then dabbed at the injury. The soapy water barely stung. I couldn't feel much at all.

Rachel was dead.

I couldn't quite process it. It wasn't like the emptiness I had felt when John had died. For Rachel was something else: kind when she needn't be, graceful where most would be bitter, and sorrowful in a way that I thought I understood. She had been kind to me, and yet all I had done in return was degrade her for choosing to stay with her husband. The sound of James's cries came back to me and I shut my eyes. What would happen to him now? Or did it matter, since he would still be trapped regardless of what went on around him?

And as I realized it, I finally understood what bothered me so much about seeing him there in his wheelchair, the saliva dripping down his chin and his sunken, hollow face: it was my own fear, reflected in his form, that despite all of my efforts, my memories would start to slip away just as my mother's had, slowly at first and then faster and faster until I couldn't grasp them, and then I wouldn't know who I was or what I had been, just as he had no sense of the man who had lived before he had been confined to his chair.

I ran my hands over my thighs. The money John had left for me was still safely strapped there, sticking out like a tumor beneath my skirt. And what had it all been for? Had he hired me solely because I looked like his sister – and Lennox's wife – and he wanted to toy with the other man's emotions? Or had he known how Lennox would stare at me, and known that Lennox wouldn't tell me the truth about who he was, and he surmised how uncomfortable it would make me – the girl who didn't feel anything, being cared about for once?

I hit my palms against my skull, willing myself to think about the situation at hand. I needed the pills on my bedside table. My brain was no longer functioning: the words were too jumbled and quick now, too persistent and crazed. I hurried to my room, turned on the light, went to the bedside table, but –

The pills weren't there. The neat white stacks had been cleared away, leaving the nightstand bare. I stared in disbelief. They had just been there that morning. I had had a month's supply left – they couldn't be gone.

I dropped to my knees and checked to see if they had fallen on the floor, then tore off the wool blanket on the bed and opened the drawer to the nightstand to search for them, but they were gone. I laid my hand on top of the bureau, trying to calm myself before I became overwrought, but as my palm brushed over the wood, I realized that something else was missing: the sheath for the letter opener.

I jumped back from the spot and clutched my arms across my chest. I was being ridiculous, I told myself. There was no reason for anyone to take the medication or the sheath. I had just misplaced them and couldn't remember.

I snapped the rubber band against my wrist but nothing came. I must have put them somewhere, perhaps after taking the extra pills last night. I grabbed my uniform from the floor and shook it, convinced that the missing items would spill from the pockets, but only the key to my room clattered out and onto the floor. I snapped the rubber band again, certain that I was forgetting what I had done and would remember at any second –

I halted. A memory was clawing at my mind, frantically trying to escape the jumble of thoughts. It slipped and skirted around the mess I had made of my brain, moving closer and closer to the forefront. But rather than explain what had happened to my medication and the sheath, it focused on the key in front of me. I reached down and picked it up, opening my fingers and staring down at the worn metal, finally understanding what the problem was. Mrs. Tilly had taken the key to the nanny's room back days ago: the one in my hand was the one Lennox had given me that supposedly went to the Augustus Suite ... so how had I locked my door with it last night?

I crossed the room and shoved the key into the lock, turned it to hear the *click*, then twisted the knob. The door was firmly locked shut. I turned around and went to the nursery door and did the same. The door locked, as well. I unlocked it again, then stared down at the key in utter disbelief before tossing it onto my bed as though if I held it a moment longer it would burn my hands. It had been a lie when he had said he'd taken Amalia's key to get into the Augustus Suite: he had a skeleton key. No, I corrected myself, searching for the word in my memories: a master key. A master key that, as Bernadette had said, *went missing ages ago,* and that she had assumed Lennox hadn't stolen and kept for all those years, but evidently had. Which meant ...

That Lennox could have gone out on the night that John had been killed. I thought back to the morning I had woken up, unable to explain why the floor was wet and my shoes were strewn around, and then to the look of certainty on Bill's face when he had told us that he'd seen Lennox locking the front door. But what did that mean? That Lennox had been the one to murder John? Had he killed his wife and child, too? Had he tricked me, seeing how lonely and desperate I was for companionship, into believing that it was anyone but him? And now that his facade was falling apart, he had stolen my pills because he knew that I wouldn't be able to think straight without them?

Snap. Snap. Snap. Snap. My thoughts bounced in time with the rubber band smacking against my wrist, but both were useless to me. I needed the pills. The house, the island, the deaths, the uncertainty – it was all too much to deal with on my own, and now that I was truly on my own, more so than ever, I needed something that would help me.

"Dammit!" I said aloud, pounding my palms against my

head. And then, from somewhere in my jumble of thoughts, came Marjorie's voice in my ear. *There's a goddamn pharmacy in Mother's medicine cabinet!*

I snatched up the key and unlocked my door. Bernadette had said that her mother had taken tranquilizers, and Mrs. Marlowe surely wouldn't miss them now ...

Hastening out of the room and down the stairs, I flattened myself against the walls for fear of being seen. The house seemed oddly empty, and though I hoped that the family was gathered downstairs, I kept my footsteps as light as possible as I went past the bedrooms.

I reached the Augustus Suite and unlocked the door with the master key, then slipped inside. My eyes immediately swept over the room to check that Cassandra wasn't in there again. Mrs. Marlowe was on her bed alone, and Rachel's body had been laid next to John's on the window seat. My coat was still wrapped around her like a blanket, and her fingers had been intertwined with John's in the most unnatural hand-holding I'd ever seen.

I crept across the room, maneuvering over the polar bear rug and around the floor lamp, then felt along the wall for the bathroom light switch. As soon as it was on, my frantic state of mind overtook me. I hurried to the cabinet and fumbled with the various prescription bottles, twisting their labels toward the light as I read the drug names. My hands got more and more shaky as I searched, and in my carelessness I knocked one of the bottles from the shelf, sending it shattering into the basin, but I hardly had time to care as I found the one I needed: Meprobamate.

Relief flooded over me. I twisted the cap off the bottle and emptied the contents into my hand, but there were only three two-hundred milligram pills: less than half of my usual dosage. I swallowed them hurriedly and searched for another bottle, but to no avail. They would be enough, though, I tried to convince myself as I bathed myself beneath the bright overhead lights. All I needed was to slow my thoughts so that I could think.

I stepped back into the bedroom and started toward the

door. The first thing I needed to do was hide until I could work out who to trust. The Smoking Room or Music Room would be the best places, or maybe even one of the storage rooms on the third floor.

I slipped back past the bodies of Rachel, John, and Mrs. Marlowe, debating and deciding all at once, but just as I reached the polar bear rug I realized that something was wrong. A chill ran down my spine that had nothing to do with the open window, and head turned slowly back to the bed. Mrs. Marlowe was gone.

"Shit –"

I spun around just in time to see Cassandra raising her arm, and I barely had time to register the heavy book in her hand before it came crashing down against my cheek. I fell sideways onto the rug.

"So it *was* you!" she hissed. "Stealing more medicine, are you? To kill the rest of us?"

"What –? No, I –"

She swooped down upon me again, wielding the book like a hammer and taking aim at my face again. I ducked down and put my arm up to shield myself. The hardcover struck my forearm instead.

"Don't lie!" she said. "I saw you sneak in here! I heard you going through the bottles!"

"No – that's not –"

She struck me again and again, smacking the book against any part of me that she could. As the corner of it caught my eye and jabbed into the socket, I let out a cry of pain and flattened myself to the floor, covering my face.

"I knew I shouldn't have trusted you!" she screeched. "I knew you wouldn't be what I wanted!"

I turned to get onto my hands and knees but the book crashed into my back, flattening me down again. Gripping the soft white fur, I yanked myself away from her, but she grabbed me by the hair and pulled me back.

"Ah!"

I twisted around and aimed a kick at her stomach, catching her off guard and sending her doubling over with several of my hairs still clutched in her hand. I scrambled to my feet, but my shoe caught the head of the polar bear and I went crashing back down to the ground next to the bed –

"Jesus –"

The utterance barely left my mouth. My chin had hit the floor, but that wasn't what had stunned me. For there, staring out at me from the darkness beneath the four-poster bed where she had been hidden, was the sunken, dead face of Mrs. Marlowe.

Cassandra gave a furious cry from behind me, and I rolled to my side just in time to avoid her pouncing on top of me. As I scrambled up to crawl over the bed, though, she caught me by the ankles and yanked me back down. My shoulder crashed into the ground and I rolled onto my back, my right arm pinned beneath me, and no sooner had I registered her hands leaving my ankles than she was on top of me, her knees pressing into my chest and making it hard to breathe and her veiled head hanging over me like a phantom.

I raised my untrapped hand and shoved it up into her face, trying to break her nose. She caught it in between her teeth instead and bit into my burned, bubbled skin, and I let out a cry of pain as the wound gave a terrible, forceful throb. I tried to yank it from her clamped jaw, but she was relentless now, and in her crazed costume made up of her deceased mother's clothes, she looked so monstrous that I thought she might very well eat me alive.

"You – crazy – bitch!" I said, closing my fingers around her mouth to force her jaw open, but I only caught a fistful of the opaque fabric of her veil instead. Grimacing, I tugged my hand away from her with all of my might, my burned skin tearing from my palm as it scraped through her teeth, and as I flung my arm away with a howl of pain, it tore the veil from her face.

For a moment all I saw was long, silvery hair that fell down upon me. At first I didn't know who – or what – I was looking at. For the reason Cassandra wore the veil had nothing to do with being in mourning, but rather because she had done something to her face to change the wide smile and big eyes I had seen in her portrait to a thin, pursed mouth and narrowed, angry slits of eyelids, and there was now a large mark on her face running from her right eye over her cheek and down to her mouth like a stain. Suddenly the long black dress decorated with beads and the heavy silver ring adorned with diamonds and sapphires that she had plucked from her mother's hand made sense, and the reason her appearance had caused me to confuse her with the dead woman became clear. She looked just like

—

"Mrs. Marlowe."

CHAPTER FIFTEEN

I hadn't meant to say the name aloud. Cassandra's tightened eyes tried to widen, but the action was unnaturally stopped by whatever surgeries she had had done. For a moment she simply looked as horrified as I felt, but then her face morphed into a livid, twisted scowl and she bared her teeth like a madwoman.

"You."

Her arm shot out and snatched me, trying to get me to release the veil, but the damage was done.

"You wicked little thing!" she cried, crawling further up my chest with her hand still locked like a shackle around my wrist. Her voice was no longer the sweet, unknowing one that piped her fantasies into conversations, but a harsh, frightened woman who had been discovered. She shook me by the arm, repeating, "You wicked, *wicked* thing!"

"I – I didn't –"

"You had no right!" she said, and her knees were so far up my chest that they were pressing into my neck and choking me. "You had *no right!*"

"I – I – didn't –"

"Liar! You think you're so clever, do you? So clever for seeing beneath my veil?"

The words barely audible from her shaking voice, and her hands sprung out to wrap themselves around my throat. Even if I could have spoken, I wouldn't have known what to say.

I squirmed beneath her and grabbed at her hands, trying to yank them off, but her fingers squeezed tighter in response and her sharp nails dug into my bare neck. My eyes watered until my vision blurred and my chest thumped and thumped as it waited for the breath that wasn't coming, struggling violently to fill with air again –

"Well guess what?" she hissed. "I've seen beneath

your veil, too, and I know who you really are – and you're not my daughter, no matter how much you've tried to look like her!"

I pulled at her fingers one by one, trying to break them off of my throat, but she was growing stronger and I was growing weaker, and I couldn't see anything anymore except the bright white light of the moon flooding my wide open eyes, and I was certain that it was ending, certain that it would be over soon and I wouldn't have to fight anymore –

I have seen the moment of my greatness flicker, I thought as my eyes rolled back into my skull, and could see inside my head to where the words were endlessly built up inside, stored and useless, remembered and soon to be forgotten for good. *And I have seen the eternal Footman hold my coat, and snicker, and in short, I was afraid ...*

"No!"

A muffled sound came from above me and Cassandra's weight was thrown from my body. I gasped and choked, blinking frantically to get the blurred shapes around me to sharpen back into things I recognized.

Lennox was grappling with Cassandra. He had her pinned to the floor, but she was wriggling like a rabid animal beneath him that had been caught in a trap. As he tried to hold her hands down, one escaped and came up to slice him across the face with the sapphire and diamond ring –

"Ahh!"

He grabbed at where she had torn his flesh and she took her chance to escape. She pulled herself out from beneath him and shot back over to where I was still laying on the rug, but –

He grabbed her and yanked her back. As she kicked and flailed her arms, I scrambled backwards away from both of them, hitting into the window seat where John and Rachel's bodies laid.

"What in God's name –?" Lennox started, finally noticing her face, but his voice was drowned out by a wail that erupted from her mouth like a flood. He clapped his hands over her mouth to stop her.

"She's trying –" I croaked, "to look – like – her mother –"

"Like Sylvia –?"

His question ended in a shout: she had bitten his hand, too. He shook it frantically, cursing as he went. Cassandra bared her teeth at him.

"I am Sylvia!" she shouted. "I – am – Sylvia!"

Lennox's face reflected the shock that I was feeling, though mine wasn't just due to Cassandra's appearance, but the revelation of what he had done, too. I wanted to run, but my hand was throbbing and my chest was heaving, and I couldn't seem to move. Instead I reached back, and in a split's second decision, I plucked the letter opener from John's chest and shoved it into my pocket.

"Cassandra," Lennox said, adopting his calm, patient tone, "Sylvia is dead –"

"Lies!" Cassandra said, and her eyes – fighting so hard to widen that they looked ready to burst – went from anger to dejection in an instant. "Lies made up by my children to get my fortune!"

She swiped at his face but he pulled back just in time. He grabbed her by the wrist to keep her from trying again, and from the way his knuckles had turned white, it looked as though he was holding her more tightly than he needed to.

"You can't replace your mother, Cassandra," he said. "It won't help your grief –"

"My grief?" Cassandra echoed. "My grief is that my baby is dead! My poor Mary – the only one who really loved me – pushed from the window with my grandson!"

Lennox's face hardened.

"She wasn't pushed!"

"You think I don't know? You really think you know better than her mother what happened to her?"

"You are *not* her mother!"

"You couldn't stand how close we were! You couldn't stand it when she wanted to come home! You wanted to keep her all for yourself! But Mary loved me more than anyone – *anyone* – and she would have never left me here alone! Never! So you pushed her!"

Without warning, Lennox raised his hand and struck her

across the face. I jumped back, nearly as stunned as Cassandra ought to have been, but a huge demented smile came over her face instead.

"You're insane," Lennox growled.

Cassandra let out a laugh. It filled the room like a haunting cry, sending chills up and down my skin. Lennox shoved her back down to the floor. He looked nearly as deranged as she was: his mouth was twitching and his teeth were grinding, and for a moment as he bent over her, I was certain that he was going to hit her again, beating her into the floor until the smile left her face, but then –

He stood up and took me by the arm, pulling me from the room. Cassandra's laughter followed us. I was too numb to react as he brought me upstairs, but as we reached the nanny's room and I saw into the nursery where the boarded up window was, my senses kicked back in.

I yanked myself from his grip and tried to run, but he grabbed me around the waist, holding me back. The breath was knocked from my lungs and I fought to get away from the grip, twisting and turning violently –

"Alexandra – what're you doing?"

"Let – go!" I said, still trying to fight him even though it was a useless cause. He was far stronger than me, and if he had been able to overtake John then I certainly stood no chance –

"What's wrong with you?" he said, wheeling me around to face him. "What happened?"

I pulled away with every ounce of strength I contained, and my arms slipped through his grip with a jolt. Shocked at my success, I teetered off balance and fell back onto the floor with a *thump*, my arm breaking my fall and twisting painfully beneath me.

"Alexandra, what's happened? What's wrong?"

He was still playing his game, thinking that he could win me over to his side by manipulating my feelings and getting me to believe he was anyone but whom he said he was, but there was nothing in his voice that I trusted anymore. I could feel the cold metal of the letter opener against my leg through the fabric of my skirt, waiting for me if I needed it.

"You killed John!"

"Alexandra, you know that's not true –"

"I know you did it! I know about your key!"

Lennox stiffened. As he took a long breath, the scent of alcohol wafted over me, and I noticed that his eyes were a bit brighter than usual. He had evidently been helping himself to liquor while the family was gathered in the Parlor, despite the fact that he had claimed he didn't drink.

"I – yes, I have a master key, but ..."

"But you didn't use it? You just carry it around as a keepsake?"

He stood up straighter.

"I took the master key with me years ago when I left the island," he said. "It was an accident: it was in my pocket."

"And you saw no reason to return it? You just held onto it for all these years?"

"I brought it back many times: unlike the rest of the family, I actually visited Sylvia several times a year, and it made it easier to have my own key when I stayed here. And then when John invited me back –"

"You thought you'd just bring it along in case you had to sneak out at night and kill him?"

"I thought he might not be planning to give me the painting, so I figured I'd bring it in case I had to search the house for it myself."

"So that's why you sneaked out of the nursery that night?"

"I didn't sneak: I knocked for five minutes and you didn't answer because you were knocked out from those pills you take!"

Cold came over my skin as he admitted it, and the last bit of hope that I had harbored left me. My breathing was quick and shallow, and his own had turned labored.

Floorboards creaked from outside the room, and we both turned in time to see Mrs. Tilly's white apron whipping out of sight as she dashed past the room.

"We need to keep our voices down," Lennox said,

turning back to me.

"Why? Afraid that the family will find out what you've done –?"

He grabbed me and yanked me to my feet. For a moment I thought that he might strike me as he had Cassandra, but instead he glared at me in his disappointment that I hadn't fallen for him the way he had wanted me to. He marched me over to the bed and pushed me down to sit upon the mattress. I looked up at him steadily, rearranging my face so that I didn't look frightened.

"You're being ridiculous," he said, his tone a forced calm. "You're forgetting that I've been the one helping you find out what happened to John since he was killed."

"You've been pretending to figure it out, you mean."

"Why on earth would I do that?"

"So that I wouldn't think it was you! You said as much when I was trying to convince you to help me: that there were only a handful of choices of who killed John, and you were well-aware that none of the family cares what happens to you! So you realized I would be your only ally!"

He gave a frustrated growl; he was unraveling. His perfectly poised answers and calm demeanor were slipping faster than the seconds ticking by.

"You're being impossible," he said. "I had no reason to tell you that I was out that night – not after you'd given me an alibi, and not when I knew it was the only reason you were trusting me. I would have been a fool to throw all that away!"

"So why were you outside?"

"I went to the cemetery,. I knew the family wanted me to leave first thing in the morning, and I couldn't sleep without going to see Mary and Oliver's graves first."

"What – suddenly feeling sentimental about the family you pushed through the window?"

Lennox's cheeks hollowed.

"It's one thing to accuse me of killing John," he said quietly, "but don't you dare say I killed my wife and son, especially when you know that Cassandra says things – and does things – that bear no resemblance to the truth."

"It's not her I believe. Mr. Kneller told me."

"Did he? Well, I'm not surprised: he's been very adamant about it since the trial. I'm a bit surprised that *you'd* believe it, though."

"She went through the glass."

"Of course she did! It was a stained-glass window: it didn't open!"

"She fell backwards," I hurried on, desperate to keep him from changing my mind. The medication and the fight were rendering me dizzy, and I longed to put my head down and shut my eyes, blocking out everything that had happened today. "Who would do that?"

"Someone who wasn't in her right mind! She was depressed! She couldn't think clearly!"

"Kneller said she was happy –"

"Really? Well, that surprises me, since all I ever heard from him was how miserable and unhappy I made her!"

His voice broke as he said it, though he quickly covered it by coughing into his shoulder. I surveyed him with a shaky gaze, trying to see through his facade, but he was either too good a liar or he truly was telling the truth. All I knew was that I couldn't afford to make the mistake of believing it was the latter.

"And did you?" I asked. "Make her miserable and unhappy?"

Lennox stared at me for so long that I didn't think he was going to answer. His chest rose and fell with each breath he took, and though there was clear anger etched into his face, there was something else there, too, that I couldn't place.

"I was very ... displeased ... when Mary said she wanted to live here," he said after a moment. "We left our home. I left my practice. We went from starting our lives together to mollycoddling her mother, all because Mary was made to feel guilty for having a life of her own. And yes, I didn't always take it well – being stuck here, not working, not even being able to leave without asking Silvia for permission to have Kneller ferry me to the mainland – and that put strain on us. I was too hard on her: I realize that now. We were both desperate to escape, only she couldn't bear the thought of abandoning her mother again – so she abandoned everything, and she took our son with her."

He took a long, deep breath, pausing as he searched my face for an emotion that I couldn't give.

"I was with Sylvia when Mary jumped," he said. "It was her seventieth birthday. The whole family was here at the time, and Sylvia was having a fit because she insisted – once again – that nobody loved her. Mary was putting Oliver to sleep so I went to calm her down. And if I hadn't – if I had just stayed with Mary instead – then –"

His voice cracked again and he turned away.

"If it was Mrs. Marlowe's fault that you weren't there with your wife when she died, as you say, then why'd you come back to visit her so much?" I asked.

"It wasn't Sylvia's fault: she was a sick woman. And she loved Mary; I never doubted that. So for all of our differences and resentments for one another, both feeling like the other was stealing her away, when she died we only had complete understanding for the other's grief. The last few years when Sylvia stopped leaving the house, she would still let me take her out to the cemetery to see Mary's grave. I would carry her there because she couldn't put her feet out the door. And no, it wasn't to butter her up so that she'd put me in her will."

I rubbed my hands over my forehead, fighting to stay awake and file away each word into my head, but I wasn't even sure it mattered anymore. I had no way of knowing if he was being honest or not, and I didn't trust myself enough to know if I should trust him.

"Say something, Alexandra. Please."

I only shook my head. My hand was throbbing with pain from the ripped flesh and my thoughts were whirring, and I felt sick.

"Please," he repeated.

"Just – just give me a minute to think."

I shut my eyes as my memories pushed themselves to the forefront of my mind, wild and out of control. They replayed when John had called me into his office at the university to tell me that I had been dismissed from my program, smiling widely at me as he told me that my professors were kicking me out before gallantly offering me a chance to fix my mistake, before the scene changed and I was opening the door to let Lennox into the Foyer on the night of Mrs. Marlowe's wake. The two memories smashed against one another, splintering and breaking to form a horrid picture in my mind. I must have taken the wrong dosage of medication, I thought, or perhaps I was losing my mind. Or –

The sound of wood creaking cut into the air, but I only squeezed my eyes tighter, trying to concentrate on where my thoughts were pulling me. Maybe the memories were supposed to go together. Maybe I was missing something that I ought to have caught days ago – but what? John had called me into his office. Lennox had shown up at the house. John had told me I was being kicked out. Lennox had said he was here for the wake. John had offered me the job to work for his mother ...

"Alexandra," Lennox said, but I ignored him.

John hadn't called me to his office because my professors had dismissed me, I realized: he had *told* my professors to dismiss me. It had been no coincidence that I had been asked to leave the day after his mother had died, just as it was no coincidence that the previous maid had been conveniently fired, leaving a spot available for me. He had done it all solely so that he could lure me to the Marlowe house in timing with Lennox, so that he could put us in the adjoining rooms upstairs, so that he could haunt the other man with my image and torture him with my presence. All that time I had been trying to figure out why he had brought me to the island, but it had never been about me at all – it had been about Lennox. The only reason John had singled me out was because of the resemblance I bore to Mary. It had just been another of his sick jokes, only someone had killed him before he could deliver the punch line.

And had that someone been Lennox? There was still nothing to suggest that it wasn't. He had more than enough motive, after all, between the fact that he might have been Mrs. Marlowe's next heir and how angry he would have been at John if he had realized upon seeing me what kind of trick had been played on him. And yet even with that knowledge, something was pulling me in the other direction. Something in his voice, something in his face, and – more importantly – something within me.

"Alexandra."

"Alright, I believe you," I said, rubbing the bridge of my nose in an attempt to lessen the pounding in my head. I had no desire to explain it all to him now: not when I could so easily fall into the sleep I so desperately needed. "Let's just leave it at that."

"I really don't think we can."

His voice had gone low and tense. As my ears perked up at the sound of it, I dropped my hand from my face and opened my eyes.

He had gone very rigid – his hands slightly raised and his breathing shallow – though for a moment I didn't realize why. Then, as I blinked through the semi-darkness to clear my blurred vision, I saw that we weren't alone. Marjorie was standing behind him, a bandage awkwardly plastered to her nose and dried blood clinging to her nostrils from when I had punched her, and her face a mask of livid excitement.

The gun that normally hung over the mantel in the

Parlor was clutched in her hands, and she was pointing it directly at the back of Lennox's head.

CHAPTER SIXTEEN

Every bit of drowsiness abandoned me. It was as though the muzzle of the gun was pressed up against me, too, and if my chest rose and fell too much Marjorie's finger might slip on the trigger and –

"Do you recognize this?"

Bernadette's voice came from the doorway. She squeezed her way into the room, flanked by Amalia and Edie. In her hand was the sheath from my nightstand.

"Mrs. Tilly found it in here," she went on. "She wondered why you'd have it ... until we realized what it was. No need to ask where the letter opener is, of course."

My mouth went dry. I parted my lips to speak, but no explanation came out.

"I ... I ..."

"Get up, Alexa," Marjorie said.

I slowly got to my feet. Marjorie prodded Lennox's back with the gun, pushing him closer to me.

"Come on now – both of you. We're going to get to the bottom of this ..."

They pushed us over to the nursery door.

"Inside," Marjorie said. "Go."

We awkwardly maneuvered through the door, knocking shoulders as we went. Marjorie indicated for us to take a seat on the cot. My legs shook as I lowered myself down. The four women glowered from above us. Marjorie's eyes were narrowed; Edie's were wide. Amalia looked as though she would like nothing more than to be the one holding the weapon.

"Now," Bernadette said, her midsection swelling as she took a deep breath in, "let's discuss what's going on here."

Lennox shifted out of the corner of my eye. My back was so rigid that I didn't think I could have moved if I tried.

"I'm not sure what you mean," he said carefully.

Marjorie's face turned to a sneer.

"Don't play that game, Lennox," she said. "We know what's going on now. Mrs. Tilly found Alexandra's pills. I suppose she poisoned him and you did the rest?"

"No –"

"And which one of you stole my lighter?"

"What?"

"No one cares about your damn lighter, Marjorie," Amalia snapped. "My husband's death is a bit more important!"

"It's solid gold!" Marjorie returned. "I think the police will be interested to know that they're thieves as well as murderers!"

"I can't see why they'd be interested in the least," Bernadette said with a roll of her eyes, then she turned her attention back to Lennox. "Now, you really think you can continue to deny what you've done? Even after what you just did to Cassie?"

"Cassandra?" Lennox said. "I didn't do anything to her –"

"You nearly killed her!" Marjorie said.

Lennox let out a sound like a scoff; he covered it by clearing his throat. Edie sucked in a breath. Her pale form began to shake and she crossed her arms over her chest, sending a frightened glance around the room.

"I believe," Lennox said, "that your sister might be embellishing the truth –"

"Is she now?" Bernadette said. "And what would you call it?"

"Cassandra was very upset," he replied. "There was a slight scuffle –"

"Lies and more lies," Marjorie said. "Not that we expected anything different."

"I'm not sure what your sister told you, but –"

"She didn't have to say much!" Marjorie said. "We saw her!"

"Can't we do this somewhere else?" Edie said, throwing another glance around the nursery. "I can't stand this room –"

"She just came to get us – though she could barely walk," Bernadette said, ignoring her sister's plea. "She said you attacked her. So, what exactly were you doing in her room?"

"I wasn't in her room," Lennox said. "And I certainly didn't attack her. She –"

"We saw her!" Marjorie repeated. "We saw what you did to her!"

"What are you talking about? I barely touched her –"

"Just like you barely touched Mary before she fell out the window?" Marjorie scowled. "I admit, Lennox, I've been buying your story that she jumped for all these years, but now –"

"Cassandra was upset – she was out of her mind: all I did was try to control her –"

"That's not all you did!"

"She's done something to her face – take off her veil and you'll see for yourself –"

"We did see her face!" Marjorie insisted. "We all saw – at least what's left of it!"

Lennox leaned back. I didn't need to see his face to understand his apprehension.

"What're you talking about?" he said, and his voice had gone low as though he dared not hear the answer.

"You beat her within an inch of her life! I barely recognized her, her face is so sliced up and swollen!"

"No," Lennox said, and there was a note of panic in his voice. "No, that's not –"

"She said you went crazy and started shouting about wanting Mother's money, then got violent – *again*. Birdie could barely get the glass out of her face from you smashing it against the window!"

"This is – this is ridiculous. That never –"

His voice broke off and he didn't finish the sentence, though I doubted it would have made a difference if he had. I kept my eyes ahead of me rather than glancing toward him, having realized what he, apparently, had failed to: it didn't matter what we said to the Marlowes now. They had made up their minds about accusing us, and there was nothing we could say to alter it.

"She must have done it to herself," Lennox tried again. "You don't understand: she changed her face – she's trying to be your mother."

Amalia let out a laugh. It rang out coldly in the room.

"And why would she do that?" she said. "We've already got an impersonator here: Mary's perfect doppelganger, showing up just in time to greet you at the door –"

"Your husband hired her!" Lennox said.

"And he's dead now, isn't he?" Amalia seethed. "A lucky coincidence for you: we'll never know how she really got here. You planned it out perfectly, didn't you? Always have an alibi to cover you, just like you did with Mary –"

Lennox made a movement as though he was going to stand, but Marjorie swirled the gun over to point directly at his face. He halted midway through rising and then sat back down.

"I was with Sylvia when Mary jumped," he said, forcing a quieter tone. "Or are you really going to dispute what your own mother said at the trial?"

"She was senile and blind: she had no idea what time you were or weren't there," Marjorie said.

"I was standing *right next to her* when Edie came in and – and said that Mary had – had –"

"No one knows how long she'd been laying there when Edie found her," Marjorie said, cutting into his shaking voice. Edie turned away with her hands pressed over her mouth. "You probably pushed her then ran to find Mother before anyone knew what had happened!"

As Lennox's hands formed into fists, I looked at each of the Marlowe women. Nothing in their faces suggested that they didn't truly believe we had worked together to kill John. For a moment I wavered, thinking that perhaps I had been wrong to believe Lennox after all, but there was no denying the certainty in his own voice, either. But someone had to have done it, and if not someone in that room, then whom?

"This is a witch-hunt," Lennox breathed. "You don't care what the truth is: you just want someone to blame."

"This is exactly what it looks like, Lennox," Bernadette said. "Everything has fallen into place. I'm only sorry we didn't see it in time to protect Rachel and Cassie."

"Don't be ridiculous," Lennox said angrily. "Rachel killed herself – and it was because of all of you."

BANG!

The deafening sound filled the room and disappeared before I could react more than to jump, and it was only in the moments after when I held my ringing ears that I realized the gun had gone off. Smoke poured from the barrel as everyone stayed frozen in place. Marjorie's face was livid; her sisters' were shocked. As Lennox let out a strangled sound, I turned to look at him, realizing what had happened –

"Jesus!" he said, his hand clasped over his shoulder.

"Marjorie!" Edie gasped. "You weren't supposed to shoot him!"

"I don't see why not," Marjorie replied. "Get it over with now, I say –"

"We have to wait for the police!" Bernadette said sharply. "How are we going to explain what happened if he's dead?"

"He threatened us!" Marjorie said. "He attacked Cassie and he'll be after us next!"

"You can't just shoot a man who's sitting down," Bernadette said. "If he was standing, maybe –"

"It only grazed him," Marjorie said, aiming the barrel at Lennox's chest. "But not this time –!"

"No!" Edie said, her hands still over her mouth and her fingernails digging into her skin. She was white and shaking, looking like a porcelain pot that was about to shatter into a million pieces. "I can't – this room is – I can't watch someone else die in here –"

"Then leave!" Marjorie shouted..

"We should all leave," Bernadette said. "We'll lock them in and wait for the police to come."

"That could be days! Who knows what they'll do in that time!"

"Starve and defecate on the floor, I imagine," Bernadette replied, "seeing as they won't be able to leave the room."

"They might find a way out! They could – could pick the lock in the middle of the night and murder us in our beds!"

"Well, at least we'll never know," Bernadette replied. "As long as I'm in a deep sleep I won't have any idea it's coming ..."

"But if we hand him over to the police, he'll just slither out of the trial like last time!" Amalia raged. "You want him to get off scot-free?"

"That won't happen: there's enough evidence against him."

"Of course it might happen!" Amalia said. "It happened before and it'll happen again, and I'm not letting the man who ruined my life get away!"

"The justice system will take care of him –"

"And who will take care of *me*? Who will pay for John's death? Who will pay for me losing out on *my* inheritance?"

"It's not our fault," Bernadette said. "You might have known he would die –"

"Of course I didn't know! And now I'll probably only get his flimsy life insurance while the rest of you get the island –"

"I've had enough," Marjorie cut in. "I'm not waiting any longer. Birdie, if you want no part in it, then go have a brandy. Otherwise, you can all stay and watch!"

"No –!" Edie squealed, dashing to the door and fleeing through it. She disappeared through my room without so much as a glance back.

"You should at least do it outside –" Bernadette tried, but Marjorie was having none of it. Her face had stretched widely with a smile. Blood still clung to her teeth.

"Oh, no – this is the perfect place, isn't it, Lennox? Right in the room where your precious Mary and Oliver died. And how appropriate to have little Alexandra here ... it'll be like watching Mary die all over again –"

"I really don't think –" Bernadette started again, but Marjorie cut her off.

"Either stay or go, Birdie – but shut up!"

Bernadette tottered in place, her belly swelling as she took a deep breath in. She looked over at me and Lennox., but I didn't meet her gaze. My eyes were fixed on the open door behind them, though my mind flashed with images of the boarded up window, and my hand had closed over the letter opener in my skirt pocket.

Bernadette waddled away into the nanny's room.

"It won't do you any good," she called to Marjorie as she left. "Not that that's ever stopped you before ..."

"What about you?" Marjorie shot at Amalia.

"Oh, I'm staying," she said, crossing her arms over her chest. "I want to see it."

"Good – then stand back."

Marjorie adjusted the gun on her shoulder. Amalia gave a wide smirk and moved to get behind her sister-in-law's back. I pressed my toes into the floor, readying myself.

"I warned you," Marjorie said to Lennox. "I warned you – and now you're going to pay."

"I can't pay for something I didn't do," he replied.

"Go ahead and deny it up to the end, then. But don't think that I won't tell the police that you admitted everything before I was forced to shoot the both of –"

But she never finished the sentence, because I leaped up from the cot and plowed myself toward her, stabbing the letter opener as hard as I could into her arm. She let out a wail and swung toward me, her hands tightening on the gun, but –

Lennox seized the barrel and shoved it down just as she squeezed the trigger. Another shot rang out, disappearing into the floorboards next to my feet, and Amalia screamed and jumped back.

"Shoot, Marjorie! Shoot!" she demanded, but Marjorie was fighting for control of the weapon with Lennox, both of them grappling with their uninjured arms. I swiped the blade of the letter opener against her fingers so she'd release her grip, but then –

Amalia grabbed the gun from between Marjorie's slipping fingers and wrenched it back from Lennox. She barely had it in her hands a second before –

BANG!

My eardrum exploded from the sound and the smell of burnt hair filled my nostrils. The bullet had barely missed my flesh. I stumbled back, one hand on the side of my head to stop the ringing and the other searching for something that would help me regain my balance.

"Can't you *aim?*" Marjorie screamed. "Stick it in her stomach if you have to!"

But as Amalia started forward, Lennox launched at her and grabbed her around the middle, then threw her with all his might toward the wall. She hit the door frame and rolled onto her back, shrieking with pain. The gun rolled from her hands.

"No!" Marjorie yelled as I dove toward it, and no sooner had my fingers closed over it than her foot slammed into my head. I howled in pain as my ear ruptured further, my eyes watering before I could stop them. She seized the gun and swirled it around as Lennox charged toward her, then –

BANG!

I heard him give a brief cry before he fell to the floor, and I jumped up and plowed into Marjorie, knocking her backwards over Amalia's body. She fell with a *thud* and a curse into the nanny's room, the gun still clutched in her hands. I lunged forward to grab it away, but my foot caught on Amalia's tangled form, knocking me down and giving Marjorie enough time to turn the gun toward me. Amalia scrambled between Marjorie's leg to get out of her line of fire, but I jumped back into the nursery and shoved the door closed, then grabbed for the key in my pocket and locked it shut.

"Lennox –" I started. "How bad –?"

"I'm – fine." He staggered to his feet, his hand now clutching his side. Blood was pooling through his shirt. "But we – they'll get in –"

"I know." I rushed to the heavy metal crib, shoving

it across the floor. "That's why – we – have to – get *out.*"

Once the crib was at the door, I hooked the metal frame beneath the doorknob to ensure it stayed closed, then went to get the cot.

The doorknob rattled and then a fist slammed against the wood.

"They locked the door!" Amalia shouted.

"Forget it!" Marjorie returned, and a moment later another bullet rang through the air. She was shooting off the lock.

I yanked the mattress from the cot and folded the frame in half as though preparing to put it back in storage, then lifted the whole thing up. My left hand throbbed from the burned, bitten skin and I dropped the frame momentarily.

BANG! Another bullet struck and the lock clattered, bursting free, but as they tried to open the door, it hit against the crib.

Lennox appeared at my side, grabbing up the end I had released.

"To – window," I told him.

"What?"

He faltered and gave a grimace, dropping the cot and slapping his hands over the wound in his side. I tugged it toward the window.

"We've got to –" I said, heaving the frame up and bashing it against the boards, "– break through –"

"You are *not* jumping out of that window!"

"Yes, I am," I told him through gritted teeth, giving the boards another bash. The large, sprawling branches of the yew tree that were covered in thick snow would break our fall. "And you are, too!"

His face was pale and streaked with blood from his fingers, but as the crib scraped against the floorboards and the door opened a few inches, he lifted the cot and helped me slam it against the boards. They cracked against the metal. We pulled it back and slammed it harder, forcing the boards back. The nails screeched as they were shoved outwards. We slammed the cot one final time and –

Cool air poured into the room through the glass-less window and struck our faces. I clambered up to the windowsill, my mind blank and scattered all at once. Another shot rang out behind me and I glanced back to see the barrel of the gun sticking through the partially open door. I nearly lost my footing and fell, but my fingers grasped the window frame held me in place. Then –

BANG!

Lennox was thrown to the side, crumpling as the bullet hit him in the back of the leg. As he slumped against the wall, I jumped down from the windowsill. There was blood seeping through his pants from a large wound in his thigh.

"Lennox –" I said, pulling at his arm to right him, thinking somewhere in my mind that if I just got him to stand, he might be all right. His skin was covered in a sheen of sweat and his eyes were wide and confused. I pulled him harder, forcing him to use his good leg and get up from the floor. "Lennox, come on – we've got to go –"

BANG!

I didn't know where the next bullet struck. My eyes were fixed on him, willing him not to be hurt, and as though it was possible that they had such power he grasped at the wall to pull himself to his feet.

"Come on –" I said again, steering him to the window, but his stare had filled with a sudden flash of sadness and he didn't move farther.

And before I could speak – before I could think – he gave me an apologetic look, the sorriest look I was sure I had ever seen, and then he raised his hands and shoved me backwards out the window.

CHAPTER SEVENTEEN

I didn't feel myself falling. For the briefest of moments, I didn't feel anything at all, then my back slammed against the snow covering the yew and I plunged downwards into a tangle of branches and needles, twisting one way and then the other and smacking every part of my body as I fell further and further until –

My arm latched over a branch. I grasped it with every bit of strength I had remaining, willing myself to remain upright. The bark scraped against my skin, digging lines into my flesh, and as I slowly began to slip down again, I braced myself to fall. My feet slammed into the ground and my knees buckled, and I fell forward onto my hands, sinking into the snow.

For a long moment I stayed still, certain that every part of me must have been broken. Pain crept up upon me from each direction, throbs and aches that shook my body, and my ragged breathing filled the air. The yew blocked my view of the nursery window above, but the sound of gunshots had ceased. Perhaps they had run out of bullets, or perhaps ...

I forced myself to my feet. My legs wobbled as I took off blindly toward the guesthouse, hopeful and hopeless all at once. I stumbled onto the path, nearly losing my footing and falling back down.

I had barely made it to the guesthouse when I spotted Kneller. He was standing on his front porch staring at the main house, dressed in flannel pajamas and boots. As he caught sight of me approaching, he gave a start.

"What's going on over there?"

I didn't respond. I wasn't sure that my voice was working, and I could only hear out of one ear. I limped closer to him.

"Alexandra – what's going on? Why's there gunfire?"

"Please – help," I managed, my voice strange and distant sounding.

"What happened to you?"

"They're trying to – kill us."

"Who?"

"Marjorie – Amalia –"

"Trying to kill who?"

"Me – Lennox. They shot – him –" I reached out and grabbed his arm to steady myself. "Please – help. They – they think we killed John. They think –"

My ear was ringing so loudly that I could barely hear my own voice. I tried to focus on him, but spots were clouding my vision.

"They think Lennox killed him, you mean?" he asked.

"No, the both of us. They think we're in on it together."

He stared at me as though he thought I might be joking.

"Please," I tried again. "Please, you've got to help. You've got to stop them – to see if he's okay –"

"Come here," he said, taking me by the arm and leading me inside. He put me on the couch and tossed a blanket over me. "Now, get yourself warm. I'll go over there and talk to Rachel –"

I looked up, hardly believing that he didn't know. But of course he didn't know: no one had told him. *I* hadn't told him.

"– and see if we can make some sense out of all of this. Alright?"

He made to leave, but I couldn't let him go to the main house – not without telling him first.

"Mr. Kneller," I said to his back, then spit the words

out that I knew would never come otherwise. "Mrs. Langston's dead."

Kneller froze. For a long while he stood there, then, slowly, he turned back to me to stare blankly into my eyes. His wrinkled face was expressionless, not dumbfounded, but possibly expectant, waiting for me to backtrack as though I had said it out of confusion rather than actuality. He waited several moments, his chest rising up and down beneath his plaid nightshirt, and then his face turned downwards and he shook his head.

"What?"

"She's dead," I repeated, knowing that there was no way to go back now. "There was an argument, and she was upset –"

"No," Kneller said. His voice was shaking and his eyes were dangerous. "What are you talking about? They shot her –?"

"No. We found her in the ocean."

"No!"

He threw his hands up to his head, a look of utmost distress on his face, and then he aimed one firm, hard kick at the coffee table. The top of it split and it went scratching across the floor. As I watched him, I knew I ought to offer him some sort of condolences, but there was no time for it. I needed to help Lennox.

"Mr. Kneller – please. I need your help. I need to get to Lennox –"

He looked up at me, his face turning to a snarl.

"I'm not helping that man," he said angrily. "The world's better off without him."

"But –"

"If you want to get yourself shot, then so be it: serves you right for being so foolish."

"He didn't do it!"

"And you know this how? Because he *said* so?

Because you *trust* him?"

His anger was contagious. It came over me in a wave of heat, welling up inside me at his refusal to help. He was no better than the rest of the Marlowes: content to blame anyone and everyone else for their sorrows instead of realizing that if he had tried to figure out who had killed John rather than making jokes and snide remarks, the situation wouldn't have escalated the way that it had.

"No – because Mrs. Langston already admitted she did it," I told him.

"That's ridiculous," he snapped. "Rachel didn't kill John."

"And you know this how?" I said, throwing his words back at him. "Because she *said* so? Because you *trust* her?"

His scowl deepened.

"Rachel never hurt anyone," he said. "Lennox, on the other hand –"

"She had every reason to do it! John crippled her husband, he refused to give her money to help with his care – and she knew Lennox was out that night and didn't say anything!"

"It means nothing."

"She drowned herself in the ocean – you don't think that's an admission of guilt?" I challenged, no longer worrying about sparing his feelings but instead giving him cause to see that it wasn't Lennox who was the murderer.

"Rachel wasn't capable of killing her twin – something everyone else seems to realize but you, or else they wouldn't be trying to shoot you!"

"If Lennox did it, then why was John killed with a letter opener?" I shot back. "Seems like an odd choice of weapon, doesn't it? Unless you count that Amalia said John revealed Rachel's affair to the family when he opened the love letters that *you* had sent –"

I stopped short as I made the connection that I had failed to notice before. Kneller was looking at me oddly, though I didn't dare guess what he was thinking.

"And so –" I went on ineffectually, "– so it was – was most likely her."

"You really think so?"

I didn't answer. I was too busy trying to put together what my mind had already started.

Enjoying the outdoors, Isidore? Kneller's voice said in my memory as he goaded Lennox. *Taking another walk over to the cemetery?*

At the time I hadn't known the significance of it, but now that Lennox had admitted to me that he had left the house to visit his wife and child's graves, it made sense. What didn't make sense, though, was how Kneller knew – unless he had seen Lennox go there that night. The way to the cemetery didn't go past the guesthouse, though, which meant that Kneller would have had to have been outside, too. Which meant ...

My heart hastened again, throbbing against my throat until it was painful to swallow. I ran my hands slid down my bare legs, carried by the sweat on my palms. No, I thought quickly. No, I wasn't thinking rationally. It hadn't been Kneller who had killed John: it was someone inside the house. Only ...

Lennox had locked the door. The detail that Bill had brought up on the morning I had found the dead body was irrelevant. It all seemed so obvious now that I didn't understand how I had missed it. Just as I had given Lennox an alibi, he had given one to Kneller by locking the door and making everyone believe that the murderer was someone inside the main house.

My brain was working faster than ever to put the pieces together. Kneller had been in love with Rachel. They might have run off together had it not been for the accident that had caused James's brain injury – the accident that John had caused. Kneller had killed him out of sheer resentment for ruining the life he might have had with Rachel had she not been tied to her reliant husband. The letter opener was either chosen to make a statement about John opening the letters Kneller had sent Rachel or simply out of convenience to make it seem as though he had been killed in a different manner. It had just been luck that Lennox had locked the door that night and that the attention had been thrown off of Kneller, with the family certain that his death had to do with money. And Rachel ...

She must have realized it was Kneller who had done it: that was why she had begged Bill not to tell the family that he had seen Lennox, because she knew they would wrongfully accuse him and couldn't say as much without telling them it had really been Kneller. So instead she had taken the blame, and she had drowned herself in the ocean to cement her claim.

I licked my lips, my eyes clinging to Kneller as I realized the magnitude of my problem. I was caught between a household that wanted me dead and a man who had killed before and shown no remorse for it. The way that he had laughed and recited poetry as he dug John's body from the snow came back to me and I swayed in place. Would he dig out a hole for me to lie in, too? Kill me and then tell the Marlowes he had done it for them, just to save himself from being found out or ousted from the island?

"I have to go to the bathroom," I said suddenly. "I – I think I'm going to be sick."

Kneller looked over at me.

"It's just down the hall," he said.

I limped from the room, my mind racing as I tried to decide what to do. I could steal some blankets and extra clothes and then hide out in the woods. Bypassing the bathroom, I headed toward the coat closet and yanked it open, ready to sift through the items hanging inside, but –

My lungs flattened within me, halting my breath, and had I not still been grasping the doorknob, I might have fallen backwards to the ground. For a brief moment I thought that I had come face to face with a mirror, because there, nestled between a few sweaters and scarves, was a portrait of a calm, collected young woman with copper-colored hair and emerald eyes, smiling over at me as though she had been waiting for me to arrive.

My mouth dropped open, knowing that it must have been the portrait Lennox had been searching for. Mary's portrait. The one John had hidden.

"Ah. I thought you might find that."

Kneller's voice didn't startle me. I didn't even turn around. My eyes were fixed on the woman who, had she not been smiling so sweetly and happily, might have been me. Kneller's hand found my arm and he wrapped his fingers around it, though I had no plans to run; I was too busy finishing putting everything together. That was why John had been outside that night: to give the portrait to Kneller to hide it from Lennox. I imagined him carrying it outside, struggling to walk with it through the unshoveled snow, and then to find the ferryman waiting patiently for him, completely unaware that the other man was readying to attack him while his hands were occupied and his mind was fixated on the brother-in-law who had just shown up at the door hours before ...

"So you've figured it out," Kneller said calmly.

I shook my head.

"What? No –"

"It's all right, Alexandra. I thought you might. You're a very smart girl."

I continued shaking my head. I didn't know what else to do. But there wasn't anything else to do, I realized. He had been my last hope of getting away from the island,

and there was nothing left but a sinking dread within me now.

"Don't worry: I'm not going to kill you," he chortled. The sound did nothing to appease me. "So, the letter opener gave me away? And here I thought it would throw everyone off."

"It did at first. But ... you said you helped Mrs. Marlowe with the mail, and Amalia said that John opened the letters you'd written to Mrs. Langston."

His eyebrows raised.

"You have quite a memory."

"I know." I paused, wanting to stop but unable to do so. "And you knew Lennox was outside that night, but you couldn't admit it without admitting you were out there, too. Killing John."

Kneller smiled.

"That was the hardest part," he mused. "Seeing him walking out to the graveyard after I'd done it, thinking that they'd find out he was out there and blame him immediately, then hearing you say you'd locked him in."

"I did lock him in. He just had another key."

"I told you he was tricky."

"But he's innocent," I said.

"No, no, Alexandra: none of them are. That's why I'm glad it went this way. I only wish I'd been there to watch them unravel and blame one another. I'm sure you didn't appreciate it."

"How'd you do it?"

"What do you mean?"

"He didn't die from the stab wound, so how'd you do it? Poison?"

Kneller made a soft sound. I couldn't tell if it was of awe or annoyance.

"You realized that, too?" he asked. "I'm impressed."

"I didn't. Lennox was the one ... he said the letter

opener wasn't long enough to reach his heart, and there wasn't enough blood."

"John didn't have a heart," Kneller replied. "That's why I strangled him."

"So the letter opener was just for effect?"

"It was for a lot of reasons, but mostly because they'd have known it wasn't any of the women if he'd been strangled. Of course, they might have pinned it on Isidore, but I couldn't take the chance. Maybe if I had pushed John out a window they would've suspected him more."

A jab of pain hit me squarely in the back like a bullet piercing the flesh. I looked back at Mary's portrait. She was so life-like that she nearly seemed to be moving, and her smile tugged at the corners of her lips as though she knew all the answers already and was simply waiting for the rest of us to catch up. I wished that I could ask her what had happened to her. More than that, I wished that she would answer me.

"I'm sorry about Mrs. Langston," I said, my eyes still on Mary.

"I'm sorry about *Mrs. Langston*, too."

I wondered what he had expected to come out of all of this: that Rachel would be happy he had killed her brother? That the two of them would finally be together regardless of her husband? Or was the outcome not important to him – did he know it would be dreadful no matter what he did or didn't do – so he had chosen to act solely for the purpose of revenge and let everything else fall however it so chose?

And despite my fear and dread, I found that I didn't blame him for what he had done. A part of me wondered what might have happened had John lived, but the sickening recollection of his hot breath in my ear and his low, menacing voice gave me no desire to dwell on it.

"I have known the eyes already, known them all –

the eyes that fix you in a formulated phrase," I said, staring into Mary's painted eyes as the poem finally, fully made sense to me. *"And when I am formulated, sprawling on a pin, when I am pinned and wriggling on the wall, then how should I begin to spit out all the butt-ends of my days and ways? And how should I presume?"*

Kneller was silent. I turned to face him.

"It's a nice poem," I said quietly.

"I hope you're not just saying that because you're still afraid I'll kill you," he replied.

"No, I think I understand it now." Because that was what I had been longing for out of life, I realized – to find someone who would fix their eyes on me, and not in a formulated phrase – not in the judgmental, condemnatory stare that I felt trapped in – just *fix me,* before it was too late.

He reached up and put a hand on the side of my face, gazing at me earnestly. I could see myself reflected in his eyes, and it finally occurred to me who he reminded me of: myself. And I *was* him, in some shape or form, cold and bitter and hateful of all the ways that life had gone wrong, yet still enamored with it even so, and steadily waiting for something that would make it all better. And as it dawned on me, fright came with it, because nothing had made it better for him, and nothing would make it better for me if I remained as isolated and trapped as he had made himself.

"I have to go back," I said. "I have to get Lennox."

He dropped his hand down. It curled around my upper arm.

"I can't let you do that, Alexandra."

"You know he didn't do it –"

"What about what happened to Mary?"

"He didn't kill her!"

"She was pushed out of that window – only a fool would believe otherwise."

"Then someone else did it! He was with Mrs. Marlowe. Why would she lie for him?" I gave him a pleading look, willing him to let go of his hatred for the other man. "The family was all at the house when she died, weren't they? So what makes you think it couldn't have been one of them?"

"None of them would have killed Mary."

"You're giving them an awful lot of credit! Bernadette killed her husband, didn't she? Marjorie killed her children? John pushed Mr. Langston off a cliff? What makes you think it wasn't one of them?"

He shifted his jaw.

"Maybe it was. I don't really care anymore – but I do care about you." He looked at me sternly. "If you go back there, they'll kill you."

"I have to try –"

"Then be practical about it. If you want to save him, then I won't stop you – but I will implore you to do it in a better way. You can get off the island and go for help."

"No, I can't. There's no way off –"

"Yes, there is. The ferry's on the north end of the island – you have to go through the woods to get at it."

"What?"

"You thought I'd actually set the ferry loose? I knew I'd need a way to escape once they figured out it was me." He gave me a sorrowful smile. "I'll explain how to operate it. It's not so difficult."

"But ..." I began, but I didn't know what else there was to say. He was right: if I went back to the house, then they would surely kill me. If I escaped and alerted the police, then perhaps there was still a chance for Lennox. "Thank you, Mr. Kneller."

"Don't thank me yet: you might crash on your way. Now let's get you some real clothes so you don't freeze to death on the way."

"Couldn't you just bring me?"

"Oh no," he said. "There's no point in escaping now."

Not without Rachel, I knew he meant.

He moved to circle around me, but I stopped him.

"Mr. Kneller – how does it end? The poem?"

He chuckled, but the smile on his lips didn't reach his eyes.

"I have heard the mermaids singing, each to each: I do not think that they will sing to me," he quoted. *"I have seen them riding seaward on the waves, combing the white hair of the waves blown back when the wind blows the water white and black. We have lingered in the chambers of the sea by sea-girls wreathed with seaweed red and brown – till human voices wake us, and we drown."*

CHAPTER EIGHTEEN

I pulled on a pair of his pants and socks, my limbs still aching, then donned his heavy jacket and tried not to think of Rachel wrapped in my own coat in the Augustus Suite even though she didn't need it anymore. Kneller wandered away downstairs as I dressed. I found him in the kitchen writing on a piece of paper. He slid it into the book of T.S. Eliot poems open on the table, then showed me out the back door.

I followed him out into the snow. He was just an outline in front of me, some strange being that had lost its true form and was wandering in search of it. We weaved in and out of the trees, the white snow leading us through the darkness, until at last we came to the rocky shore where the ferry was tucked away. It was already facing outward toward the ocean, bobbing up and down on the waves in a beckoning way as though anxious to leave. Kneller hopped in and started it up. I scrambled in after him and ducked beneath the small shelter with him.

"Alright, here's what you do," he called to me over the roar of the engine, showing me the wheel, lever and buttons. I nodded as he talked me through it, taking in his directions carefully and watching to see which switches he flicked, but I could barely think. My mind was on Lennox and it wouldn't leave me alone. "Do you understand?"

I nodded again, but my throat was too tight to speak. Kneller hopped back down to the rocks and untied the rope holding the ferry in place. My hands shook as I took the wheel; it vibrated beneath my palms and shook my arms.

I pushed the lever forward and the ferry shot across the black water, propelling me away from the island. The sky was as dark as ever, starless and cold, and it felt as though

I was descending down a leaden tunnel. When I had gone a ways out, I turned the wheel to curve around the island, looking back at where I had left Kneller. His form was just a sliver on the shore, barely visible against the stark white snow, and then, slowly, it began to disappear into the inky water.

He was wandering out into the ocean.

I tugged the wheel sharply, sending me slamming into the side of the boat. I righted myself and tried again to turn the ferry back to the shore, but the engine gave a horrible sound: it had stalled. I twisted the key in the ignition, desperately trying to restart it, but the ferry only cried out in protest and stayed in place, still except for the way it rocked against the waves. My neck cracked as I turned to look at where Kneller stood in the water. What was he doing? Trying to get to me? He must have changed his mind: he wanted to go back to the mainland, too, rather than stay trapped with the Marlowes any longer –

But as I watched him, still trying to restart the engine and reach his half-gone form before it was too late, he waved at me. Not a wave of greeting or beckoning, but a wave that told me to go. He didn't want to be saved. He wanted to die.

And as I turned the key once more and the engine whirred to start up again, he walked straight into the black water, and the ocean welcomed him as though doors had opened between the waves to usher him inside, then shut tightly closed again to prevent me from following him. And he was gone. Gone with Rachel, maybe. Gone with Death, who held his coat and snickered. Or just gone. And as I realized it, watching the spot where he no longer stood and knowing that he wouldn't reemerge, my insides clenched and my breathing hitched. *We have lingered in the chambers of the sea by sea-girls wreathed with seaweed red and brown, till human voices wake us, and we drown.* The dream of what he had hoped his life might be decades ago with Rachel had vanished, and with it went all desire to live the solitary existence that he had grown accustomed to but had never wanted to. And as I considered it, unexpected tears came to my eyes: for him, for Rachel – for Lennox – all of whom whose lives had been so horribly ruined by the man who had tricked me, too, into coming to the island to be a part of his twisted game.

"No," I said aloud, my voice barely audible even to my own ears beneath the howl of the wind, though it hardly mattered. "No."

Because I wasn't going to leave – not like this. Not without Lennox. If he was still alive, then he might not be for much longer.

I sped around to the other side of the island, barely able to slow down enough before reaching the dock. The side of the ferry bumped up against it and threw me forward over the wheel, then jolted me backwards onto the floor. I switched off the engine and hastily tied the line to the dock, then half-ran, half-limped up the path toward the house, wildly trying to form a plan in my head. I just had to get to him, I told myself as my feet plunged in and out of the snow. I just had to see if he was alive, and then I would think of what to do next.

I clambered up the front steps and went through the door, wishing with everything within me that the household had gone to sleep. The silent Foyer greeted me momentarily, but muffled voices came from above. I rushed towards the stairs, running up them to the second floor landing, but –

My feet caught on something slippery and I nearly pitched backwards. I grasped the banister to keep upright, and as I straightened, the voices of the Marlowe women floated over to me: they must have been gathered in the Baxter Room. I started forward again, but –

"Mr. Langston?"

I couldn't stop myself from speaking, for he was standing fully-clothed but soaking wet in the hallway outside the Mabel, Baxter, and Lillet Rooms. His pale, milky eyes moved over to me and he raised a shaking hand, unbending one finger as he moved it arduously up to his mouth; the rest of his fingers were closed over something gold. I halted, not understanding until he pressed the finger to his lips. He was telling me to stay silent.

I looked down at where my feet had slipped over the liquid on the floor, its putrid smell filling my nostrils, then spotted the empty container next to him. I had seen it before in the Smoking Room: it was the container of butane.

"Mr. Langston – don't!"

The voices from behind the Baxter Room door ceased, and in the several seconds that ticked by in complete silence, I knew I ought to run, but I couldn't move. Not when he was about to –

"She's not dead?" Amalia screamed from somewhere behind me. "Marjorie – get the gun –!"

Thudding footsteps came next, and I wheeled around – nearly slipping again – as Marjorie came out the door to join Amalia. Her eyes were wild but glassy and she struggled to pull the gun up to her shoulder. She was completely drunk.

"Raah! Rahh!" James shouted at me, flailing his arms at me to go back downstairs, but instead I leaped forward toward the staircase that would bring me upstairs.

BANG!

The bullet struck somewhere behind me. The glass of the wall lamp shattered and flew to the floor.

"Shoot her, Marjorie! Shoot!" Amalia screeched, and my wet boots slipped on the steps and I went crashing down to my knees. I flung my arms out to grab for the landing, yanking myself upwards, but Marjorie's footsteps came running down the hall toward me. She would have me cornered whether I made it upstairs or not, and even if I somehow got to Lennox, there would be no way to get him out ...

Ching.

The sound seemed to hang in the air for hours as though time had stopped. And I recognized it from hearing the distinct chime before: the high-pitched ring of gold on gold. It was the sound of Marjorie's lighter, the one that she had accused me and Lennox of stealing, the one that, as I turned around in horror, I could momentarily see in James' hand as –

The tiny flame emerged into the still air, gentle at first, then flying out to grasp at the butane covering his clothing, then down to the floor where he had poured it over the wood. It *whooshed* as it spread, a terrible sound that grew worse by the nightmarish scream he gave as it engulfed him, and then the Marlowe women's screams joined in –

"Get out! Get out!" Marjorie screamed. "Birdie! Edie! Cassie! Get out!"

Their thundering footsteps took them down and around the hallway to the other staircase, and I scrambled up to the third floor landing and yanked off my butane-soaked boots, flinging them down the stairs away from me. I ran down the servants' corridor hallway and towards the maid's room, not stopping to think of what had just happened, not stopping to think of what I was doing, and not stopping to consider that Lennox might already be gone.

"Where's Cassie?" Edie's voice came from below. "Marjorie – wait! Where's Cassie? Where's Cassie?"

I sped to the bedroom door and grappled with the handle to twist it open, then ran across the floor and slammed into the nursery door. It hit something and bounced back at me. It was the cot I had tucked beneath the knob, preventing it from opening.

I pounded my hands against the wood.

"Lennox!" I shouted. "Lennox! Move the cot!"

My hands throbbed in pain but I kept pounding, screaming through the wood for him to open the door for me. My words were unintelligible, marred by cries of anguish, and I threw my whole body against the door as the truth finally set in: I was too late.

Then –

Scraping came from inside the room. I slid down to the floor, my ear pressed to the door to hear if the sounds were real and not in my imagination, and then the barrier behind it gave way and the door opened just a few inches more.

I scrambled inside, my eyes searching for him through the darkness. And there he was, laying on the floor, one arm clutching the cot that he had pulled away and the other holding his blood-soaked leg.

"Lennox!"

I shoved the cot out of the way, then grabbed him and dragged him to his feet. He was far heavier than I had expected. He slumped over my shoulder as I tried to get him to stand.

"Mary," he murmured into my shoulder.

"No, it's me. Alexandra."

"Mary," he said again, even softer. "Mary, I'm so sorry."

I pulled his arm over my shoulder. His eyes were unfocused: I wasn't even certain he would notice that the house was burning down. I heaved him up further, looking between the window and the door as I debated what to do. He couldn't climb down the yew in his state, and I wouldn't risk letting him fall.

"Mary."

The name was digging itself into my mind, bringing

up thoughts I didn't have time to dwell on. *She was pushed out of that window* – Kneller's voice said in my ear. *Only a fool would believe otherwise.*

"Come on," I said, pulling him to the door. "We've got to get out of here."

"Mary," he said again as we half-walked, half-stumbled from the room. Edie's screams were still audible below, haunted and ghostly through the old wood.

"You can't die! Please! Please!"

Something in her frantic voice jogged my memory, and I though tried to push the thought away, knowing that I didn't have time for it, when Lennox said the name once more and Edie gave another scream, the voices melded together and my mind took over.

Three murders in one family ... Four if you count Mary, Bernadette had stated. To which Edie had replied in a panic –

No one's counting Mary.

We reached the stairwell and he slumped up against the wall.

I can't watch someone else die in here! Edie's voice screeched in my head. But she had only found Mary on the ground, hadn't she? Because if she had watched her die in the room, then that would have meant ...

"Sit down –" I told Lennox. "I can pull you down –"

He was barely responsive. His knees bent and he sank down to the topmost step. I moved in front of him and grasped him by the ankles, pulling him with a *thump thump thump* down the stairs.

It had been Edie who found Mary's body: Edie who had apparently never been the same again after she had died. Edie who had taken the Christening gown belonging to Lennox's dead son from the nursery. And it must have been Edie, then, who had stabbed the lifelike doll in her room with the piece of stained glass, when the only stained glass window in the house had been the one that Mary and the baby had fallen through ... I shook my head to clear it. I wasn't thinking properly. For how could the fearful, faint-hearted woman who jumped at the mention of ghosts have killed her sister?

No one knows how long she'd been laying there when Edie found her.

We reached the landing and I heaved Lennox back up. The staircase closest to us was blocked by fire. I pulled him toward the one on the far side of the hall. Flames followed us, grabbing at everything in sight as they continued to eat the house alive.

"Sit down," I ordered Lennox again, but his unfocused eyes had muddled beneath a frown as he stared into my face.

"You're not here," he murmured. "You're not ... you're a ghost."

I'm telling you that it was a ghost! No wonder Edie had an obsession with ghosts that she was certain were haunting her. They *were* haunting her. *I* was haunting her. The way she had spoken of seeing Mary in her mother's room, not knowing that it had been me standing there after Mrs. Tilly had sent me to the Augustus Suite to find her, and the way she had fled upon seeing me in her room when I had taken my hair down ... Bill's words rang in my ears next: *You talk in your sleep! You beg for forgiveness!* But he had gotten it wrong. She wasn't begging for forgiveness for her children's deaths: she was begging for her sister and nephew's.

And then, through the thick smoke, came Edie's voice again – so frightened and desperate that it sounded as though it was one of my memories.

"Cassie – you've got to come out!"

I turned my head toward it. Why hadn't she left?

"No!" Cassandra's voice returned, and it was no longer the child-like one she had so often used, but the harsh, angry tone she had adopted to impersonate her mother. "They're trying to drive me out! They want my house!"

"Cassie – please! You'll die!"

"I haven't left this house in sixteen years and they won't make me do it now!"

It felt as though my skin was melting off of my face, and yet I couldn't move.

Leave her, I said to myself. *Let her die like she let her sister die.*

But if I did that, then no one would know what she had done. I yanked Lennox back up and hobbled blindly through the smoke toward her. She had collapsed outside the door of the Augustus Suite.

"Get out of here!" I shouted at her. "Come on! The stairs will be blocked any second!"

She was shaking all over, sobbing into her hands. There was no way to grab her while holding him.

"Mary," Lennox murmured again into my hair, and the realization of how to get them both out trickled over my skin.

"Edie!" I said, changing my voice to a softer, higher tone that I hoped matched the one of the woman in the portrait I had just seen at Kneller's. "Edie, it's me! It's Mary!"

Her head jerked up and she wheeled around to face me, her eyes widening.

"N-no – no, it can't be –"

"You have to leave the house, Edie," I said. "You have to leave and tell everyone what you've done!"

"No – no, you're not –"

Her eyes had narrowed, trying to see me through the smoke, and the disbelief in them was too strong. I searched my memory, trying to find something that would make her believe it was her sister rather than me.

"You Made Me Love You," John's voice spoke in my head, referring to the song that had played on the radio the first night that Lennox had come to the house. *"Mary loved singing this."*

I opened my mouth, letting out a cough as smoke poured down my throat, then forced myself to remember how the song went.

"You made me love you: I didn't wanna do it, I didn't wanna do it," I croaked out, the lack of air strangling my voice into a haunting sound. I had no idea what Mary's voice sounded like other than Marjorie's mention that her singing had been off-key, and all I could do was hope that Edie was convinced. *"You made me want you, and all the time you knew it, I guess you always knew it –"*

"No," Edie said. "No, no, no –"

"You made me happy sometimes, you made me glad," I went on, and as I sang, Lennox's grip on me tightened as though he was being shaken from his stupor. *"But there were times, Dear, you made me feel so bad ..."*

"No! Mary, no!"

Lennox pushed against me to straighten up.

"You have to tell everyone what you did to me, Edie," I said. "It's the only way –"

"No," she pleaded, scrambling to retreat further into the master bedroom. "No – please – I didn't mean to –"

The door she was leaning against opened and she stumbled into the room to get away from me.

"It's the only way I can stop haunting you, Edie," I said, following her inside. The open windows dispersed some of the smoke in the air. "Just come out of the house and we can tell them."

"No – no, Mary – I didn't mean to! Please! I didn't mean to!"

"But you did, and now you have to admit it to everyone I left behind. Admit it to my siblings – admit it to my husband!"

"But it wasn't my fault!" Edie cried, tears running down her face and dragging the black soot down her cheeks. "The window – the baby – you weren't supposed to fall! You weren't supposed to fall!"

As I took another step toward her, she took another back, unable to be any closer to me.

"Please! Please!" she said again, and her voice was so strangled that it was barely recognizable. "Mary, *please!*"

"Tell Isidore why you did it," I said, my heart pounding as Lennox's fingers clenched my arm. "Tell him why you killed me and Oliver."

"I didn't mean to! You know I didn't mean to! But you wouldn't let me hold the baby, and you knew I just wanted to hold him, but you acted like I was a monster! Like it was my fault that my children died! I was a good mother! I was a good, *good* mother! I just wanted to hold him! I just wanted to hold him –!"

"*You* did it?" came a voice, and I whirled around. Cassandra was on Mrs. Marlowe's bed. She was still dressed in the funeral gown and adorned with the heavy, gaudy jewelry that didn't belong to her, and yet there was no longer any sign of the dead woman. The face that I had seen beneath the veil only hours before had changed once again: it was bloodied and swollen, and one side of the mouth had been pulled down into a permanent frown. "You killed my baby? My Mary?"

Her chest rose and she stood up, looking more ghostly now in the smoke than she had even with her veil on. Edie gave a start.

"No – Mother – I didn't mean to! I didn't mean to!"

Cassandra moved toward her, and her gruesome face

was marred further by the look of sheer wrath that pulled at every crevice in her skin.

"You killed my baby!"

She leaped toward her, but only I seemed to realize her mistake. Edie jumped back from her to flatten herself against the wall, only it wasn't the wall at all but the open window –

Cassandra's form pounced on top of her sister's, causing Edie's lower back to hit the windowsill. Together they flopped backwards over it. Edie's hands flew up to grab the window frame, but before the fingers could reach them her feet were jolted from the floor, and with Cassandra on top of her there was too much weight pulling her down –

"No!" I shouted, and at the same time, a man's voice hollered the same thing.

They disappeared through the emptiness. There was no sound that followed over the crackling of flames.

I grabbed Lennox and turned to hurry from the room, but was met with the sight of Bill in the doorway. He must have come back to get Edie when she hadn't come outside. His face was startled and pale, and he was staring at the spot where she had vanished through the window in horror. I opened my mouth to try to explain what had happened, but before I could, he turned and fled down the stairs.

I heaved Lennox further onto my shoulder and went after him. They would be fine, I thought: they had only fallen from the second floor, and the thick snow would break their fall. And they had to be alright, because Edie had to admit to her family what she had just admitted to me.

We reached the stairs and I forced Lennox back down to a sitting position, then grabbed his feet and pulled him downstairs.

We reached the Foyer and I pulled him along the hallways and through the rooms to the servants' door. The frigid air slapped me as I dragged him through the snow and around the back of the house. Bill's outline was visible ahead of us, still and illuminated by the flames that leaped down above us. I halted before I reached him.

Cassandra and Edie hadn't fallen in the snow, but rather onto the back patio that Bernadette had insisted Kneller shovel down to the bare stones. Edie's crumpled body laid atop it, and there was no mistaking the dark red stain that seeped out from her colorless hair to create a halo of blood around her head. Cassandra was splayed over her, her arms outstretched but unmoving, and her already damaged face was now broken beyond repair. The entirety of it had been smashed inward, and her head sat at an odd angle on her neck.

"No," I said. "No!"

Bill dropped to his knees. He rocked slowly back and forth in front of the terrible scene, his breathing heavy and erratic.

"Mr. Burton –" I began, "– I – I'm so sorry."

He didn't answer. For a moment I stared at him, wondering if I should try again to explain what had transpired, but then voices from around the corner sounded and I grabbed Lennox to pull him down the path.

"Frank! Where's Frank?" Marjorie's voice said from up ahead. "He needs to put this out!"

"He's – not – answering – the door –" came Bernadette's voice, her figure just a huge blob of an outline as she waddled back down the path from the guesthouse.

"What do you mean 'not answering?'" Marjorie screamed. "He's not paid to not answer during emergencies!"

"Well, he's not answering!" Bernadette repeated.

I led Lennox away from them to go around the other side of the house. The darkness could only cover us so much, though: we would have to go straight past the

Marlowes to get to the dock, and the struggle of supporting his weight and walking in bare feet would make it nearly impossible.

"Come on," I huffed, speaking more to myself than Lennox now. "Come on – we can make it –"

I pulled him off the path to go around the front clearing, trying to avoid the family. They were screaming and waving their arms, and for a moment I felt a twinge of hope that they would be too distracted to notice us, but –

I slammed into something hard, my balance thrown off from the sudden stop and Lennox's weight. We fell sideways to the ground, sinking into the deep snow. I scrambled up again, not understanding what had hit us, when –

"You."

Mrs. Tilly glared at us, her face illuminated from the blaze of the house. She snarled as she took in the sight of us, her cheeks reddening in anger.

"No – please –" I started. "Please don't –"

"Mrs. Pickering!" she exclaimed. "Mrs. Carlton! They're here! They got out!"

I raised my hand and struck her across the face, but not fast enough to halt her words. The Marlowes' voices halted, and I knew there was no way to get away now, but I dragged Lennox forward even so, desperate to make it to the dock with him.

"They're here! They're over here!" Mrs. Tilly repeated, taking off toward the Marlowe women to alert them, and I dragged Lennox in the opposite direction even though I knew there was no chance of escaping now. His injured leg wobbled uselessly beneath him as we hobbled through the snow.

"Get them!" came Marjorie's voice. "Grab them!"

"Come on, Dr. Lennox –" I panted. "Come on – you've got to move faster –"

"There!" shouted Amalia. "They're right there –!"

"Please," I begged him, though I knew that he couldn't possibly do what I was asking. "Please – we've got to run –!"

Footsteps were upon us: steps that crashed into the snow and flung it from side to side as they neared us, and my feet burned with cold and pain, and my legs weakened from the weight of trying to heave Lennox any further, and I felt myself falling downwards toward the ground, accepting the defeat that my mind couldn't –

"Here!"

Someone reached us and grabbed onto Lennox, pulling him from my grip just as I hit the ground. I blindly stared up into the darkness at the form of his captor, the shape illuminated by the dancing flames in the distance, and I cried out even though I knew it would do nothing to stop them from taking him away from me. I had failed. I hadn't been able to save him.

"Come on!" the voice said to me. "Get up!"

And before I knew what was happening, Bill had reached down and yanked me by the arm to bring me back to my feet. He put one of Lennox's arms over his shoulder. I slid beneath the doctor's other arm to help him.

"Go to the dock!" I told him. "The ferry's there!"

We hurried off toward the cluster of trees. The house was spitting and crackling so loudly that the ocean barely made any sounds above it. My legs were soaked and Bill's breathing was labored, but finally, finally, I saw the ferry bobbing up and down ahead waiting for us.

We pushed Lennox inside and undid the line, then jumped in after him. My hands were shaking so much that I could barely start the ferry up.

"Here – steer!"

I shoved Bill over to the wheel and then dropped to my knees beside Lennox. He had curled up on the floor, his murmuring unheard beneath the howling of the wind. I pulled off Kneller's coat and laid it on top of him as Bill yanked the wheel to turn us away from the shore.

"Wait! Wait!" came Amalia's screams as she reached the dock. "You can't leave us here! You can't –!"

But as the ferry sped away from the island, her screams were drowned by the roaring engine. The Marlowe house was nothing but a huge bonfire in the distance, dancing beneath the sunless sky and reaching out to try and touch the nearby pine trees. It gave a cry as it burst, exploding from within as though its heart had been flung from its chest, then writhed in its place as it burned like the distress signal from a red flare. And as I imagined the wood burning and the porcelain shattering and the silverware blackening, I breathed a sigh of relief.

"Alexandra," Lennox murmured, pulling my eyes away from the disappearing island.

"It's alright, Dr. Lennox," I told him, leaning down so that he could hear me. "You're going to be alright."

"Alexandra."

"It's alright: don't try to talk. We're going to get you help."

"Alexandra," he said again, and he reached up and grasped my hand. The blood covering his fingers rubbed off onto mine, and his pain-stricken face stared at me with such reverence that, had he not said my name three times, I might have thought he still believed I was Mary. "Thank you."

I gave his hand a squeeze in return. He visibly relaxed, his face managing a smile, and leaned his head back against the floor with one hand still clutching mine. And I knew that, when we reached the shore and Bill ran to get someone who could help get him to safety, I would be sorry to let him go.

The car pulled up to the front of my building shortly after nightfall. I had just come outside to light a cigarette since my aunt refused to let me smoke in the apartment, and barely paid it any mind other than to note that it was far too fancy a car for the area. I stepped back to lean against the weathered stone wall, hoping to avoid the path of the melting snow dripping from the roof above, when the car window opened and someone called over to me.

I paused midway through a drag, not quite able to hear the voice over the sound of rain hitting the slick pavement, and squinted over at the car. The window on the backseat had been rolled down to reveal an old woman in a blue coat and hat. Her outfit matched her Bentley perfectly.

"Alexandra Durant?" she called.

"Yes?"

I took a few steps closer to her, my cigarette still clutched between my fingers. The damp air moistened my skin in a mimicry of sweat, though nothing about her sweet tone made me uneasy. Still, I reasoned, people didn't often come around to my place of residence calling my name unless they were police officers with inquiries about John Marlowe's ongoing murder investigation – which, despite Kneller's written confession, wouldn't seem to leave me alone.

"My name is Adelaide Dabney," the woman said. "I've been looking for you."

"Why?"

She smiled, revealing short square teeth that had yellowed with age behind her red lipstick.

"Would you care to take a ride with me?"

"No."

Mrs. Dabney faltered a bit at my response. The cold weather was wearing on my demeanor the way it so often did, though, and I couldn't be bothered if she found me rude. She left my view as she leaned forward to speak to her driver, but a moment later she popped back into place and the car engine turned off, sending the street back to its peaceful quietness.

"I do hate to bother you," she said, "but it's very important that I speak with you. It will only take a few minutes."

I took another drag from my cigarette and shrugged.

"You see," Mrs. Dabney went on a bit more hurriedly, perhaps noting my indifference, "I've heard about you, through various friends, and I have an offer for you."

"And which friends are these?"

"Pardon?"

"Which friends are these?" I repeated, "since I seriously doubt you and I have any common acquaintances."

Mrs. Dabney gave a little chuckle, possibly to hide her uneasiness with my blunt tone. She leaned further out the window.

"David Richardson, for one. William Burton. Isidore Lennox."

My hand twitched, sending an ember from the tip of my cigarette flying down to the ground. I didn't care how big her social circle was: the idea that my old thesis adviser, Bill, and Lennox all just happened to bump into her and tell her about me was far too coincidental. She had undoubtedly sought them out to question them, and the thought made me uncomfortable.

"And what did they tell you about me?" I asked casually.

"Oh, lots of things. It seems you have *quite* the talent for remembering things."

"I do. What's it to you?"

Mrs. Dabney chuckled again. It was far too reminiscent of the way Lennox always smiled at my bluntness, and I couldn't help but wonder if he had told her the details of my personality along with whatever other information she had inquired about – though I couldn't bring myself to ask.

"I happen to be in need of someone who can remember things when I cannot," Mrs. Dabney said. "I have a large social circle, and a woman of my age finds it harder and harder to recall the details of what her friends are doing, much less her friends' children and those children's spouses, and on and on. I'd like to hire you to remember for me."

The hint of intrigue I had been entertaining withered away. She wanted an assistant: nothing more and nothing less. I wasn't sure what I had been expecting, but now that I heard what she was after, it occurred to me that upon seeing her fancy car pulled up to the front of my building, I had been hoping for something more. A thrill – an adventure. For as much as I hated to admit it, I missed the excitement I had felt when I was on Exeter Island. I missed the danger and the mystery that had pulled me out of the humdrum my life had become after years of obsessing over a degree that would never be finished, and I missed the way my memory had been used for something greater than just the mere repetition that proved it wasn't slipping away. And I missed Lennox, too, and I hated that I had thought the old woman might offer me an excuse to see him again that wouldn't require me to admit as much.

"It sounds like you're in need of a secretary," I said tiredly, dropping my cigarette and taking out another with the intention of returning to the solitary state she had interrupted. "I'm sure there are plenty of girls with the appropriate degree who would be happy to work for you. So thank you – but no thank you."

"Wait –"

She fumbled with the handle to open the car door, and her driver jumped out to get it for her.

"No, no – that's fine, Damien," she said, waving him back to his seat. "I'm quite capable –"

She didn't look very capable, but she managed to slowly make her way out of the car and up onto the sidewalk where I stood, unsteady as she was.

"You misunderstand me, Miss Durant," she said as she neared me. "I don't want someone standing next to me with a pen and paper whilst I'm trying to make small talk. I need someone who can remember things without prompting, who can whisper in my ear to tell me who's walking toward us and give me a summary of who they are. I need someone subtle. Someone like *you*."

"I'm not sure anyone described me very well if they told you I was 'subtle,'" I said flatly.

"And did they describe you incorrectly when they said you're sharp, clever and resilient, as well?" she challenged. "Make no mistake, Miss Durant, they had their fair share of complaints. David said that you were unreasonably stubborn and always looking for faults when you ought to have been looking for a husband, but he didn't deny you've got a talent."

I held the smoke in my mouth without fully inhaling it as I thought.

"What did Dr. Lennox say?"

Mrs. Dabney smiled, once again revealing her short little teeth.

"Oh, he had lots to say about you – especially when he was pumped full of morphine," she said. "You don't need an old woman to tell you any of it, though."

"Don't I?"

"Pardon?"

"I don't know who else is going to tell me, is all."

I crossed my arms, a mixture of embarrassment and annoyance pounding at my chest. Lennox had asked me to call him, but I hadn't been able to – though his phone number played in my memory late at night when the loneliness sneaked in with the dark. He had offered me lots of things when I had last seen him: to talk to the university, to help me find a spot at another, to get me a job in New York, to pay my rent – but I didn't want any of those things from him, and the things I did want from him I was too uncertain of attaining. And I couldn't deny that the events on Exeter Island had changed my heart, but I also couldn't deny that it didn't seem to matter since my situation – my life – hadn't been changed with it.

"I've known Isidore for many years," Mrs. Dabney said, breaking into my thoughts. "I never knew him at his best, but I knew him at his worst. You saved his life, you know – and I don't mean by getting him out of that burning house. He was haunted for years over the death of his family. He's not haunted anymore."

"Did he say that, or is that your interpretation?"

"He said it, though you'll forgive me if it's not his exact wording. If I could remember it verbatim I wouldn't be here hiring you."

"Well, I don't need to be hired. I have a job already."

"Your job as a waitress at the little diner down the street, you mean?" Mrs. Dabney countered coyly. "I think we both know that you can do a little better than that."

I narrowed my eyes.

"I'm a thirty-year-old woman with a Master's Degree in psychology and no husband, Mrs. Dabney," I replied, "so I think you and I both know that I really *can't* do much better than that." I dropped my cigarette and stomped it out next to the first one. "Now, if you don't mind, I need to get back inside before my mother gets worried."

"Oh, Miss Durant – just one minute more. I've come a long way to see you –"

"Then you wasted your time."

"Not yet, I haven't. I read about you in the papers after John Marlowe died, you know, and I spoke at length to the police about you. They said you solved not one, but *two* murders single-handedly."

"That's interesting, considering that they didn't *believe* me when I told them about the second murder," I said, trying not to sound too bitter as the memory of recounting Edie's admission to the police floated back to me.

"Oh, they believe you," Mrs. Dabney said with another chuckle. "They won't *do* anything about it, but they believe you."

I threw her a skeptical look.

"I'm not sure what this has to do with anything," I said.

"Then please let me explain. In a few weeks' time, I'll be embarking on the RMS Queen Mary and sailing to England with some family members and close friends, and it's imperative that I have you with me. I would pay your way, of course, as well as wages for your time."

"I'm just not interested," I said. "Good night, Mrs. Dabney."

I made to move away but was stopped by her hand on my arm. She was a head shorter than me and her fingers were bent with arthritis, so the firmness of her grip took me off guard.

"But I would make it worth your while. You could name your price."

"Sorry, I've learned my lesson about taking large sums of money from people I hardly know," I said. "So thank you, but no thank you."

"But Miss Durant, you really don't understand: I *need* you to accompany me."

"And I'm sure you can find someone else," I said, prying her fingers from my arm. "There are plenty of people with good memories who can help you remember what's going on in your social circle."

"But that's not all I need," Mrs. Dabney said, shuffling sideways so that she was in front of me again. "And that's why I need you – that's why I've come all this way – and I really can't accept a no."

She leaned in close to me, filling my nostrils with the scent of strong peppermint oil and bergamot, and her milky eyes widened in a near-comical way.

"You see," she whispered, and she gave another little chuckle as though realizing she probably ought to have just told me at the beginning of the conversation, "I need you to come so that you can find out who's going to murder me."

Laura Giebfried is the author of six novels. As a native Mainer, her stories are often set in New England. Giebfried has a degree in Psychology, New Media, and two certificates in screenwriting. As of 2020, she is working on her Master's Degree in Forensic Psychology.
This is the first novel that she has co-authored with her husband, Stan Wells.

Stanley R. Wells is a former actor who guest starred on several television series including *M*A*S*H, Bret Maverick, Palmerstown, USA,* and co-starred in the Emmy winning television production of *The Miracle Worker.* In the late nineties he opened The Empty Stage Theater in Los Angeles where he wrote and directed the critically acclaimed play *Three* and directed the improv groups The Transformers and The Waterbrains, who are still performing regularly in LA more than twenty years later. Wells still teaches and directs improv in Bangor, Maine, where he currently lives with his wife, Laura Giebfried, though now he devotes most of his time to writing novels and screenplays.

Made in the USA
Columbia, SC
22 April 2020